# MISS
# PEGGY LEE

# MISS
# PEGGY

# LEE An Autobiography

DONALD I. FINE, INC. NEW YORK

Library of Congress Cataloging-in-Publication Data
Lee, Peggy, 1920-
  Miss Peggy Lee.

  1. Lee, Peggy, 1920-    .  2. Singers—United
States—Biography.   I. Title.
ML420.L294A3 1988 784.5'0092'4 [B] 88-45420
ISBN 1-55611-112-6

Manufactured in the United States of America
10 9 8 7 6 5 4 3 2 1

Designed by Irving Perkins Associates

Grateful acknowledgment is extended to Jerry Leiber and Mike Stoller
for the right to reprint the lyrics from "Is That All There Is" on page
1. Copyright © 1966, 1969 Jerry Leiber Music & Mike Stoller Music.
All rights administered by WB Music Corp. All rights reserved. Used
by permission.

Grateful acknowledgment is extended to Johnny Mandel for the right
to reprint "The Shining Sea" on page 252. Lyrics by Peggy Lee, music
by Johnny Mandel. All rights reserved. Used by permission.

Every effort has been made to trace ownership of all copyrighted
material in the pictorial galleries. In the event of any questions arising
as to the use of any material, the author and publisher, while
expressing regret for any inadvertent error, will make the necessary
corrections in future printings.

Dedicated to my daughter, Nicki Lee Foster,
and my grandchildren, David, Holly, and Michael

With love,
Mama Peggy

To my editor and publisher
Donald I. Fine with my
deep gratitude.

# Prologue

"Is that all there is?
Is that all there is?
If that's all there is, my friend,
Then let's keep dancing,
Let's break out the booze and have a ball,
If that's all there is . . ."

I picked up the needle from the demo record on the turntable and said to Snooky Young, "Isn't that wonderful?"

"That's a weird song," he said. "You going to *sing* that?"

"Yes, I think so. I can't get it off my mind."

"Well, you do all those kind of arty songs and people seem to love them . . ."

I thought of "Don't Smoke in Bed" and a few others and remembered how I often had to fight to get to do things I believed in, but little did I know at the time what a battle I'd have with "Is That All There Is?" Before this, its authors, Jerry Leiber and Mike Stoller, had written "I'm a Woman,"

1

truly my cup of tea, and, of course, their huge success with Elvis Presley's record of "You Ain't Nothing But a Hound Dog" (although I still think "I'm a Woman" was more colorful, filled as it was with word-pictures, and it *did* swing).

When I came to record "Is That All There Is?" there was resistance everywhere. They said it was too far out, they said it was too long, they said and they said . . . So I went to Glenn Wallichs with a demo record (something I hadn't done before), and Glenn seemed embarrassed. "Peggy, you don't have to play a demo, you helped *build* this Capitol Tower. You just record anything you want."

Delighted to hear it, Jerry and Mike and I set about doing just that. Earlier, Johnny Mandel had brought me one of Randy Newman's very first albums, telling me, "You'll love *this* fellow," which I did, and I asked him to write the arrangement. It turned out to be perfect for his style.

So now the record was made, our faith in it ran high—I couldn't believe my ears when Capitol Records said they were turning thumbs down on it.

Is that all there is?

No, because, fortunately, there was a television show they wanted me to do, which I wasn't too keen about. Well, you know what I did. I said, "Yes, if you'll release this record, I'll do the show," and they agreed.

Hallelujah. It became a hit, went "across the board," but that's not all there is to it. It dramatized for me what my life had been and would continue to be, a struggle, sometimes for things more serious than a song, but the lesson was there—stick to your guns, believe, and more than you ever imagined can happen!

# Book One
# BIG BAND

# One

BENNY GOODMAN listened intently as I sang late that night in 1941 in the Buttery, a chic little room in the Ambassador West Hotel in Chicago. I was blonde and twenty-one and swathed in one of Mlle. Oppenheimer's opulent gowns, and I was singing "These Foolish Things." Not so long ago I had been pounding the pavement in Hollywood in worn-out shoes. But in Chicago word was getting around about the new singer, and the great bandleader Glenn Miller had been in the week before and told me how much he liked me.

Jazz pianist Mel Powell was playing with Benny Goodman's band at the College Inn in Chicago, and he accompanied Benny and Lady Duckworth when they arrived that night at the Buttery. Lady Duckworth, the granddaughter of Commodore Vanderbilt, was married to an English lord, but it seemed she and Benny had fallen in love. At the time Benny was the most popular musician in the world, and Helen Forrest, his girl singer, was about to leave his band.

They all settled down at a table and ordered steak. Mel

5

Powell would later tell me that when I came on stage and started singing, Benny mumbled, "I guess we've got to get somebody for Helen." Mel thinks he decided to hire me on the spot.

It certainly didn't look that way to me. The musicians I was working with, "The Four of Us," were excited that he was in the audience, but from where I stood it looked like he was just staring at me and chewing his tongue. I would learn that was just preoccupation, but at the time I was sure he didn't like me.

Helen Forrest, who was probably the most popular vocalist of the day, was moving to Artie Shaw's band. Maybe it was over money, but the world of popular music was a small one in those days, and it wasn't unusual for big band vocalists to move around from band to band, sometimes returning to the same one in a few months' time. Some of the top big band soloists in the '40's included Doris Day, Frank Sinatra and Dick Haymes. Dick replaced Frank in Harry James' band when Frank went on to Tommy Dorsey, just as Helen was now going from Benny to Artie Shaw. Helen's leaving meant that Benny's floor show at the College Inn was going to be without its star band vocalist. Lesser bands, like Claude Thornhill's, always needed an established star-singer to help draw crowds, but Benny Goodman was so successful on his own that he could go for what he wanted, and never mind "name-power," including a fresh, unknown girl from the prairies of North Dakota like me.

Actually, I didn't intend to be a jazz singer, but jazzmen say that's what I am. Louis Armstrong said I always knew how to swing. He wrote it on a photograph he gave me. I'm proud of that. I seem to just understand about swinging—I always did. I remember the first day in school when we were clapping

6

our hands, and I could do it, and there were only a couple of us in the class who could. Who knows why?

Whatever the reason, the morning after Benny Goodman saw me at the Buttery, my roommate Jane Feather told me Benny Goodman called. I refused to believe her.

The rest of our conversation went like this. I remember it well—how could I forget it?

"You *have* to believe me," Jane said. "It was Benny Goodman's voice. He wants you to call him about working for him."

"Oh, I can't believe that. He was in the Buttery, and I saw the look on his face. He couldn't have liked me—"

"Well, I'm telling you. He called and you should return the call. Don't be silly, what can you lose—even if it's a joke."

"You're right. I'll call him, but what do I say?"

"Just tell him you're returning his call. I'm sure it was Benny Goodman."

"Okay, you're right, what can I lose?"

I dialed his number. "Hello. This is Peggy Lee. Is Mr. Goodman there?"

"This is Mr. Goodman."

"Oh—did you call me?"

"Yes, I did. I want to know if you'd like to join my band?" I wasn't even to have a rehearsal with Benny. All he said was, "Come to work and wear something pretty." After I hung up, I looked at Jane in shock.

"I swear to you," she said, "it's Benny Goodman."

"No," I insisted, "somebody's just playing a joke." After all, he was one of my fantasy figures—I spent money I didn't have on "Don't Be That Way" in the jukebox on Balboa.

I arrived at work at a nice dress, as requested, and there was, indeed, no rehearsal. Mel Powell was there, and, God bless him, he was such a help to me. Someone told me the songs I would be singing, and, luckily, I knew them all. Mel would give me four bars and I would count and listen hard for where I was supposed to come in—jumping in at the last moment and hoping for the best.

Mel picks up the story, and I'm grateful to him for it . . .

"Peggy must have been a nervous wreck. Her first assignment was to make a recording. Columbia Records, to whom Benny was contracted, always came out to wherever the band was playing. So they arrived in Chicago to record. There Peg was, making a recording with Benny Goodman just a day or two after she joined the band.

"She met CBS producer John Hammond in the control room, and he handed her the sheet music for 'Elmer's Tune.' This was a pretty tough rap for a kid. There was no taping in those days. You just made records. If you blew something, you started from the beginning. You didn't say, 'Well, let's take it from measure 39 and splice it.' She was so nervous. The sheet music John handed her made such a racket, and they didn't have high-tech ways of beating that, so, unfortunately, it sounded like a forest fire that was going over the brass, over the saxophones.

"Peggy had probably been up all night learning this thing, and then she came in, and the arrangement was disorienting because 'Elmer's Tune' was very clever, very fancy, full of stuff.

"I led her into an adjacent studio and we sat down and ran through a couple of things that were in the arrangement, especially the cues for her, and it was sort of like bop-bop-ba-tump-de-tump. I was constantly cueing her about where she came in, and told her that during the recording of the arrangement I could always improvise something.

"I also told her, 'You're going to have your first tone, Benny won't know, nobody will know. I'm just gonna pop that in there in the midst of what seems to be just a ramble over the band while the band's playing. You catch it from that;

8

that'll be *cue, count four, and go.'* Well, I think she's never forgotten it." (He's so right about *that.*)


I started singing with the Goodman band in the middle of their College Inn engagement in Chicago. With no rehearsal, I was so nervous I thought the spotlight was alive. I would sit there until Mel cued me, then I would start counting and come in wherever Eddie Sauter's modulation had taken us. I don't think it ever occurred to Benny that singers, who have to memorize everything, *need* a rehearsal. Well, he did have us rehearse on regular rehearsal days, but this was something quite different. I just happened to know the songs because I'd been a fan. I mean, you can't walk up to the microphone with a sheet of paper in your hand. The musicians have theirs, but the singer has nothing but what she or he is hearing or has memorized.

That first night with Benny I remember singing "My Old Flame." The critics were cruel. They captioned a photo of me in Downbeat magazine, "Sweet Sixteen and will never be missed." I had a cold, and I was singing in Helen Forrest's key. I went to Benny and said, "I'd like to quit, please."

He just looked at me. "I won't let you."

So I stayed with Benny, though it did mean taking a decrease in salary, and there were no more lavish gowns from Mlle. Oppenheimer. But there were real career advantages— for Benny too. Why? Because I had in my possession a wind-up phonograph and a recording by Lil Green called "Why Don't You Do Right?" Benny paid me $10 for recording "Why Don't You Do Right?" and no royalties. My weekly salary was $75, out of which I had to pay for my own room and board. "Why Don't You Do Right?" became the biggest selling record in America when we released it a couple of years later. And it stayed there for a long time and still sells.

After the College Inn, we did some one-nighters. Mel

Powell was a lot of fun, I liked him a lot and I still do. On the road with Benny, Mel and I would ride together in the bus and sing—he'd do the brass parts sometimes and I'd sing the reeds, or vice-versa, to things like "Down South Camp Meetin' " and "Stealin' Apples." I knew the parts from listening on the stand every night.

When Mel Powell and I sang, the miles would fly by. We went on to Toronto for some kind of exposition. They would just tell me when the bus was leaving, and I would pack my laundry—damp or dry—and hope I wouldn't catch cold because of my wet hair—we didn't have portable hair driers then; at least, I didn't. And they didn't have plastic baggies either, so handy for damp laundry.

Never mind, who cared? We were on our way to New York. To the Big Apple!

When I arrived in New York, in 1941, the bellman brought my luggage and led me to the door of my first Manhattan residence, pulled up a shade, and slid up the window to let in some air. It wasn't the Waldorf, but like Morty Palitz, one of the Columbia Record execs, had said, the Victoria Hotel was a nice respectable place for a young woman, the rent wasn't too bad, and it wasn't the Forrest, where all the musicians stayed. By which he meant the Forrest wasn't quite respectable and a girl could get in trouble.

I hurried to the window and looked out and saw, way down below, the cabs and cars moving along like bugs in a line. The Black Building in Fargo, N.D., was eight stories high, and until now that was as high as I'd ever been, except for the Curtis Robin biwing plane Ole Olson had flown me in over the green patches of Dakota farmland. I had wanted to be up high so badly I had even danced the Charleston for him—right there in the field. And, just as I had looked in awe over the side of the little plane, I now looked out the window of the Victoria and gasped at the sights below and

beyond . . . The Roseland Ballroom sign blinking at me—
ROSELAND, ROSELAND, ROSELAND. And I felt a tickle
in the pit of my stomach and backed away from the window
for a minute, but then I was right back again, looking, looking . . .

After the first few hectic weeks of being with Benny,
singing in the College Inn, going on one-nighters in all kinds
of weather, even to Canada, now we were going to slow down
a little in the big town and play the New Yorker Hotel. In
1941 the New Yorker was really a luxurious hotel, or at least
so it seemed to me. It certainly was a busy place, people
whipping and whirling around through the revolving doors.

Then the magic of walking into the Terrace Room when
the sparkling Ice Show was finished and sitting on the same
stage with Benny Goodman, and now when they played
"Don't Be That Way," it came out of the band live—not the
jukebox.

It was great to be on the same bandstand with those
brilliant musicians behind me—Mel Powell, Jimmy Maxwell,
Big Sid Catlett, Cootie Williams, Billy Butterfield, Cutty Cutshall, Miff Mole, Hymie Schertzer, not to mention the show
in front of me, all the beautiful people dancing by. The room
was full of stars . . . Franchot Tone danced by with Joan
Crawford. Alfred Lunt and Lynn Fontanne chatted at their
table with Katharine Cornell. Gary Cooper was joking with
Mayor Fiorello LaGuardia, and Cole Porter.

Every night the room was charged with electricity for me,
although some would have said the cold Scandinavian never
felt any of that. Later they called me "cool," which suited me
fine. I was to learn there was a rule about the musicians not
fraternizing with the girl singer, but we all became friends in
spite of it. Soon Benny was taking me to 52nd Street to catch
some of the other acts in town, and one night we went to hear
Fats Waller and sat through set after set. When Fats came

over to our table, it was the first time I ever asked anyone for his autograph. Fats took out an ace of spades and signed it for me.

There was also a writer named George Simon who was around a lot when I sang with Benny. He was one of the "Simon & Schuster" Simons—Carly Simon's uncle. We started dating, but then I met Peter Dean, whom I absolutely adored. A singer and an ad man—and what a charmer. They even called him "Snake Hips" because of a dance he did when he sang.

One night at the New Yorker, I was singing "That Did It, Marie" when Count Basie danced by the stage. He winked up at me and said, "Are you sure you don't have a little spade in you, Peggy?" I also met Louis and Lucille Armstrong at this time, and it was love at first sight. Duke Ellington came to hear me, and later nicknamed me "The Queen." And that stuck until years later, when the disc jockey William B. Williams christened me "The Elegant One."

Thanks, fellows.


One evening a handsome RAF pilot, we'll call him Sean, limped into the Terrace Room and was seated at a table right next to the bandstand. I couldn't help but look at him and wonder, among other things, why he was limping. When we finished our set, I walked by his table and said hello . . . we were encouraged to do that. He asked me to sit down, then told me he was a fan of Benny's and that he was enjoying my singing.

I noticed he kept requesting sad songs, one of which was Cole Porter's "Begin the Beguine," apparently his favorite. I was uneasy, not quite sure why, but he had such a . . . tentative air about him. If I tried a joke, he would only smile, as though to thank me for trying. Finally he told me about joining the

RAF, that he was from Illinois but had volunteered to help England. We weren't even in the war yet.

Well, we spent the whole evening together, between sets, that is, and when we were finished and were about to say goodnight, I felt myself trying to arrange another time with him . . . like the next day, a Saturday lunch when we did our matinee after the Ice Show. He agreed.

When I was all of a minute or two late for our date, he called my room. "Where are you? Aren't you coming down?" I told him quickly I'd be right there, that I was sorry.

He had brought me a bracelet from the hotel gift shop, but I felt reluctant about accepting it until he said, "Please, you've been so good to me, it's just a thank you." Of course I took it then, though I wasn't sure what he meant about me being so good to him.

After our lunch I went back to the bandstand and we played "Begin the Beguine" again. When the luncheon set was over, I asked him to come upstairs. Once there, he began to open up to me, to reveal his deep feelings—especially about how he thought he would never get over having killed people. He said he couldn't go back into the service because of his injury, but didn't really want to, plagued as he was with the memory of the bombs he had dropped on people—innocent people. Was he a coward?

"No," I told him. "Of course, you're not. You've just been through something pretty terrible and—"

"But what do I do with my life now?" he said. "I'm a coward and a . . ." He nodded toward his injured leg.

"Maybe you could be a . . . forget it," I said quickly. I was going to say commercial pilot, which would really have sounded dumb.

He gave that wistful smile as if to say, "You just don't

understand." I thought I did, but, as it turned out, I didn't. Not then, at least.

We made a date, finally, to have dinner and meet in the Terrace Room when suddenly he said, "I want you to have these," and he took off his wings and gave them to me. I was taken aback. "You're not supposed to give these . . . You're not supposed to take these off unless—"

I cut myself short, and he gave them to me, along with that odd sad smile, and I said, "I'll keep them for you . . ."

This time I rushed so I wouldn't be late for dinner, but he was already there. He seemed distant. We didn't order dinner; we just talked idly about Benny and the band, and suddenly I realized it was time to go back to work. I excused myself to go to the powder room and smiled at him. "Be right back," I said as I left.

I came out of the powder room a few minutes later, and knew right away there was something in the air. One of the girls who worked at the hotel said, "Isn't it terrible about that young pilot?"

Well, I *knew*. I ran out of the Terrace Room. The phone was ringing in my room. It was Benny, and he said, "Don't talk to anyone. That pilot you've been talking to just shot himself through the head."

Shock. Benny saying, "Come down and go to work. It will do you good—"

"Oh, Benny, I can't."

"Come down right away."

I did. Somehow. Alec Wilder and Freddy Goodman fed me cognac, and I sang in some strange manner I didn't recognize.

The next day the pilot's brother came to New York to make arrangements. He said he had been talking to him on the phone when he shot himself, and, although he was in

shock too, he made me feel a lot better when he talked to me
. . . "You mustn't blame yourself for anything. I'm just glad
you made his last hours as pleasant as you did."

I gave the wings and his identification tag to his brother
to give to his mother and dad. There was nothing else left to
do but say a prayer for him. That man had touched my heart.

But life went on. After the first New Yorker engagement, the
band went out for a string of one-nighters, Mel Powell and
I again singing brass and reed parts on the bus, this time to
"Clarinet a la King." Mel . . . what a mind! . . . was writing
such instrumentals as "Mission to Moscow" and "The Earl."

One night Benny was playing "The World Is Waiting for
the Sunrise," and the ballroom was jammed. A girl right next
to the bandstand, looking up at Benny dreamily, suddenly
fainted away. Benny kept playing with his eyes shut, and I
honestly doubt he noticed. Somehow we managed to get
someone to carry the girl out into the air.

That night Benny and I took the plane to our next stop,
a *bumpy* prop flight. Everyone on the plane (except Benny and
I) was sick to their stomachs. Lots of those bags passed
around. At one point Benny leaned over to me and said, "You
okay, kid?" and I, tightlipped, nodded that I was. What a liar!

When we finally landed, there was a limo waiting, but
neither Benny nor I knew where we were going. Fortunately,
the driver remembered seeing an advertisement about where
we were playing. Benny was always a bit preoccupied, but
there was something lovable about him, a little like the ab-
sentminded professor. Mel Powell's wife once said, "The
question with Benny is whether the plug is *in* or *out*." Sometimes he would come racing out of a building with his hat on
sideways. There are hundreds of stories about Benny and his
preoccupation with his own thoughts. I remember once he
went into a burger place and ordered a hot dog. The waitress

said, "We don't have any hot dogs." He told her, "But I'm Benny Goodman." She said, "We *still* don't have any hot dogs." Benny had a problem with that.

In between these one-nighters, Janie Feather and I found an apartment in Greenwich Village on 12th Street. It had not one but *two* fireplaces, and we just flipped. We immediately set about to keep house; my big contribution was to buy a peck of potatoes, which she found very amusing, *and* I also bought a bag of flour, some yeast and other ingredients for making bread. We had an absolutely wonderful time buying pillows for our couches, towels for our bathrooms, which we cleaned and shined.

Homemakers at last. Sort of.


About this time I was falling a little in love with a Flying Tiger from General Chennault's American Volunteer Group. During the war it was easy to do that because you were afraid to let them go, afraid you'd never see them again.

When we first met, Frank was stationed in Washington, D.C. I would manage to get down to see him on my day off, and he would come to New York whenever he could. It seemed as though we were always meeting in a crowded station and always planning our wedding. One of those times, I had set the bread and put it in the warm closet to rise. I stayed in Washington a little longer than expected, and I got a frantic call from Janie asking me what she should do with the bread-dough that was spreading all over the closet! I caught the next train.

We were playing a theatre in Bridgeport, Connecticut, and I was to meet Frank (my fiance, by now) in New York the next day. We even had the rings, the license and all. Frank managed to get a call to me during our half hour to tell me he couldn't meet me in New York the next day—they were flying out on a secret mission. I was shocked and, I thought, brokenhearted.

I stood there, staring straight ahead, and Joe Rushton, our bass saxophonist, couldn't possibly help noticing my pale, rigid face. Without a word, he handed me a bottle of gin. I tried to tell him I didn't drink, but he poured a glass of gin anyway. "Here, this will stiffen you up. You have to go out there and *sing* now."

I drank all of it.

At the time I had no idea I was allergic to gin, but I soon found out. Benny was playing "Skylark" beautifully, and I came staggering out to the microphone . . . "Skylark . . . have you anything . . ." and then nothing would come out. I stared at the audience. The audience stared at me. They laughed. I tried to back up from the microphone, barely able to move. By now they were laughing and I was thinking, how cruel . . . but of course they don't know about Frank . . .

Meanwhile Benny, trying to figure out what was the matter with me, just stood with his clarinet at his side, his clarinet with the reed toward me at about mid-thigh, his *good* reed pointing toward me. An invitation to disaster . . . During those days Benny had a stream of dignified gentlemen who would visit him with briefcases of reeds and he would run a scale on one after another of them. Most of the reeds didn't suit him, so he would promptly flip them into the waste basket. Well, I crashed into and broke the one good reed it had taken him so long to find. Smashed it. He put the clarinet to his mouth and tried to play, but, thanks to the ruined reed, it came out in squawks and squeaks. I ran off the stage and hid in the dressing room, sure Benny would fire me, but he didn't.

So the reed was gone, and so was my flyer. During the following months, I sent candy and cigarettes and socks and wrote letters but received only one *piece* of a letter: "Darling,

I'm going to take a chance and tell you more than I should—" The letter was cut off at that point by the censors. I never heard from my flyer again.


We were sitting in a cafe in Passaic, New Jersey, on Sunday, December 7. Well, you all know what we heard from President Roosevelt. *"We are at war."* A shudder went through everyone, and it was *really* hard to go back to the theater and carry on as though everything were normal.

But, like they say, the show must go on.

We did begin doing bond show after bond show—mostly in Times Square between regular shows, and things became more and more hectic . . . We were playing in Prospect Park in Brooklyn, surrounded by metal bars because the crowds would push up and practically impale themselves. Benny and I had a huge hit record at the time, "Somebody Else Is Taking My Place," and the crowd sort of went wild when I sang it. It, of course, was right in the mood of the war, and people could especially identify with its theme. They loved hearing Benny do "Clarinet a la King" and became even more demonstrative when we performed such as "The Way You Look Tonight," "Don't Get Around Much Anymore" and "Where or When." After one show, my gown was ripped off, as Dick Haymes, the male vocalist, and I ran to escape in the subway. A Navy pilot helped us get away. I'm convinced we never would have made it without him.

That same night, I came stumbling home, wondering what was next, opened the door to the apartment—and a wave of heat and smoke hit me like a blast from a furnace. It turned out to be that the smoke from the fireplaces had mixed with the hot, humid air.

A Coke, I thought. I'll get a Coke . . . So out to the kitchen, and I felt something drip on my head—there was a big bulge around the light cord and bulb, an obvious leak. At least my brother Milford had taught me enough about electricity to know that water would conduct it. Rooted in place, I looked down at the floor, to see armies of ants crawling in, or out, of the cupboard. I confess, I started to whimper like a frightened baby and decided I'd better get out and tell the neighbors upstairs. So I opened the back door to go up the steps and . . . found the steps loaded with our Coca-Cola bottles. I pushed back a narrow place on each step so I could move up and outside to call for help, but I *missed* and came sliding down the steps with ants and broken glass all over me.

Fortunately, about this time Janie came home with a friend and rescued me. I must have been a fright, sniffling and scratching, not exactly the girl who had been singing on the stage only an hour ago with fans applauding and asking for autographs.

Like the song says, "If they could see me now . . ."


In 1941 the bobby soxers were storming the Paramount Theatre in Times Square. I was there with Benny Goodman. Frank Sinatra was the "Extra Added Attraction," and he certainly was!

Just before I'd joined Benny's band, Frank had been with Tommy Dorsey, and they'd had a big hit with the Pied Pipers called "This Love of Mine." Day after day I'd gone to a particular neighborhood juke-joint in Chicago because this place had "This Love of Mine" on its juke box. I would dreamily sip my frosted Coke while endlessly playing Frank's hit, using up all my nickels.

And now, in 1941, I was to sing at the Paramount Theatre in New York at the same time Frank Sinatra was appearing. We used to lean out the windows of the dressing room to see the crowds of swooners, like swarms of bees down there in the street, just waiting for the sight of Frankie.

It must have been unimaginably exciting for him . . . his

days filled with interviews and autographs and all the things that go with the fireworks of sudden fame, to say nothing of all the performances that could be crowded between newsreels. Everything that led up to Frank's performance seemed not quite so important. Benny played as great as ever, I sang my songs and got some attention, but it was electric when Frank came out on stage.

One day I had the flu and became violently ill. I tried to make every show, but finally I just couldn't. That's when Frank discovered I was really having a bad time in my dressing room, and, from that time until I was well, he was my special nurse. First he brought me blankets to stop the shivering. Then, when it was possible, a little tea; later a piece of toast. Meantime, he was out there singing from six to eight shows a day in that huge theatre with the cheering crowds— "All or Nothing at All," "I'll Never Smile Again" . . .

Through the years there were many other kindnesses that Frank showed me. I won't forget those, but I'll especially never forget what he did for me in the middle of his first great triumph.

You see, he could have been too busy, but he wasn't.


Mel Powell tells this story about me (and it's absolutely true):

"We were doing one-nighters all over the country. The band was very successful, and we chartered trains to travel around. My roommate was a fellow named George Berg. We became good friends and shared a compartment on the train. A lot of guys in the band were, if not utterly crazed, at least moderately loony. But we were peace-loving guys and attempted to stay somewhat by ourselves.

"We were in Pittsburgh—next stop St. Louis. We had finished the date early. It was about eleven o'clock, and we had the luxury of a little time, because we weren't due to leave until 2:00 A.M.

"George, who'd been on the road a thousand years and claimed to know the best eateries, proposed that we go to a special ribs place, pick up a couple of portions, go down to the train-yard and get aboard our cars early. They probably wouldn't even be attached yet. Nobody would be there; we'd just sit quietly. It would be a pleasure.

"Now, George used to be a big fan of marijuana. He never drank, just marijuana, very pure. I didn't care for grass. For me a couple of quick shots of Scotch would do the trick nicely, and so I thought, terrific. After a hard night's work, we'll go out there, I'll have my Scotch, he'll have his 'gages' (as he used to call it) and get rested, nobody to bother us. If the other guys wanted to get loaded, let them.

"We got out to the railroad yard, only to discover it absolutely deserted. After stumbling around in the dark, we somehow located one of the two coaches with 'Benny Goodman' painted on the side.

"We found the little drawing room we were to share, got undressed and into pajamas and took out the ribs. George began to smoke; I had a couple of drinks. We were just congratulating ourselves on our farsightedness, revelling in our aloneness, happy, in a desolate railroad yard somewhere in St. Louis, when suddenly there was a knock at the door. Shaken, I went to the door, opened it, and there was Peg—terror stricken—panicked—in tears. Now I was really unnerved.

" 'What's the matter, Peg?'

"She could hardly speak.

" 'I came out early, wanted to be alone, so I came out early . . .'

" 'Yes,' I said.

" 'I went to my room . . . and there's a dead body.'

"It was the dead of night, she was near-hysterical, the band wasn't due for an hour and a half. 'Wait, I'll get my slippers,' I said.

"She put her hand in mine. We walked down the little corridor to her place, and I sort of peeked in, already beginning to get weak-kneed, knowing right then that I was not a dead-body man, and I saw a head—covered with blood. So it was not just a question of a dead body. There'd been bad business here. I looked around but I didn't see the body.

" 'It's in my closet. Mel, I didn't even notice the head.'

" 'Are you kidding?' I said. It was on the floor. Yet it seems she'd actually missed it, had gone to hang up her coat, opened the door of her closet . . .

" 'Look, Babes, I think what we've got to do is jog down to the station, it's about a quarter of a mile, and talk to someone, tell the police or something.'

" 'Well, gee, I wish you could get it out of here for me,' she said.

" 'Peg, I don't want to get near a thing like this,' I said, beginning to back out the door—just as a couple of guys, obviously feeling the other side of marvelous, arrived. Freddy Goodman, Benny's brother, who was road manager for the band, and Lou McGarrity, a trombone player.

" 'What's the matter?' Freddy said, and before anyone could say anything, he saw. 'What the hell's going on here?'

" 'There's a *body* in the closet!' Peggy yelled.

"They were right behind me, the corridor was small, and suddenly they'd shoved me back into the room, and, the first thing I knew, we're all right in front of the closet—Freddy on my right, McGarrity on my left, Peggy in back of us.

" 'Wait!' I began, but Freddy was already opening the door. I'm three inches from the cadaver, and I don't want to look, so I turn my head away just as it begins to fall on me. I feel this tremendous body weight, this dead weight, and I'm pushing against it in absolute revulsion, and I hear Peggy yell, 'Mel, watch out, it's falling!'

"I tried to back off, but it's too heavy, and I go down with it on top of me, and, oh God, I'm trapped on the floor, and

22

I'm about to have a coronary, when I hear laughter—from the *cadaver*. And at last I look, and it's Sid Weiss, the bass player. He's wild, shaking, and catsup from his face is dripping on mine.

"*Peggy* had set it up. She'd staged the whole damned thing, and now she was screaming, and Sid Weiss was picking me up, or what was left of me, from the floor, too stunned to think, and yet wondering even then at the labyrinthine plans the woman had gone to.

"Still, even as I tell the story, the image that most clearly remains with me is this—a pair of slippers aligned perfectly outside Peg's door in the corridor—George Berg's slippers. My friend, in a marijuana haze, had obviously seen what he supposed was a headless thing begin to drop out from Peg's closet, and had jumped clean out of his slippers."

Scared out of his slippers, you might say. Well, a little comic relief goes a long way. And, besides, there was method in my madness. It seemed every time an accident happened I somehow was on the scene. I would come to work and say, "Guess what happened to me today," and the fellows would look at each other as if to say, "Sure, we know." So that's how and why I happened to plan this little ghoulish joke. Sid Weiss was the right size to fit into the closet, so I just talked him into it. Anyway, they didn't tease me after that.


If my life had taken a near-180-degree turn the day I met Benny Goodman, it was now about to take another. It began the day Benny hired a new guitarist named David Barbour. When we fell in love, Benny did not like it at all. This despite the fact that he had now married Alice, the former Lady Duckworth, who sent me a charm bracelet from Tiffany's with a card saying, "I'm glad I don't have you for competition."

She didn't. I was head-over-heels in love with dark-haired, handsome David. Both of us sensed Benny was probably going to fire him if we kept seeing each other, but we couldn't help ourselves. Nothing, not the hit records, not the cheering fans, not the new stardom I'd achieved, nothing was as important to me as David and what *we* had together. I knew that I would give up everything for him if necessary.

Though love and romance and marriage and motherhood lay ahead, I think I knew even then that it was going to be a rough, rough ride. But one I had been well-prepared for, beginning with my childhood and early years that I had somehow managed to survive growing up in North Dakota.

One night at the Copacabana in New York, I jumped out of the limo and ran for the elevator because I was without makeup and I was late. All you could see was a big pair of dark glasses with a hat pulled down and a coat pulled up.

I was pressing myself against the wall and ringing for the elevator because I felt a lady running up behind me. She came up almost nose-to-nose and said, "Are you Peggy Lee?"

And I said, "No . . . not yet."

I was born Norma Deloris Egstrom on May 27, 1920, in Jamestown, North Dakota, and I'm still growing up.

# Two

ON MY father's side, let's start with John Erickson, who was born on a farm near Stockholm, Sweden. I had always been told that Norwegians and Swedes didn't get along together; however, John met and married Bertha G. Olson in Arndal, Norway. I had also been told I was three-quarters Norwegian and one-quarter Swedish, but let's just say I am Scandinavian.

John left for the United States. Crossing the ocean, he was shipwrecked, and John and five other sailors made a raft, and for thirty days they floated on the ocean. Four of them died. A ship picked up the remaining two men, and they were eventually taken to Bellevue Hospital in New York. John would have a six-month loss of memory, and after his release he refused to sail again. I should think not!

He did, though, finally remember Bertha and wrote to her in the old country, where her parents thought he had deserted her. He had no idea until then that he had a son, Eric Emil Erickson. It took seven years before John had enough money to bring the family over to New York, and Bertha's sister accompanied her and the boy Eric to the United States.

The second son, Ole, was born in New York. He was my daddy, Marvin Olaf Egstrom, and he had three brothers, Eric Emil, Edward and Julius. Later, when they all got their citizenship, Marvin kept one family name, Egstrom, while the others all remained Erickson after John.

On my mother's side, Oleana Johannsdatter was born in Toten, Norway, on September 14, 1879. She married A. L. Anderson in Redwing, Minnesota, and became quite a famous milliner. She made grand hats of ostrich plumes and velvet with fine tulle and malines. (She left a huge box of ostrich plumes dyed all different colors and beautiful velvets and veiling.) People would drive hundreds of miles by horse and buggy to buy Grandmother's hats, which sold for fifty dollars and up. According to the 1897 Sears and Roebuck catalogue, less fashionable hats sold for two and three dollars. Untrimmed, they sold for as little as fifty cents.

Grandmother must have been one of the first liberated women. When she died in 1922, the headline in the Volga papers read: "Business Woman Passes Away."

(My sister Della made a gown for me from a bolt of Grandmother's malines. It was so fragile and beautiful, and she sewed it all by hand. Years later, when I began my career as a professional singer I was playing a little place in Grand Forks called the Belmont Cafe, I wore this same gown, and, when the spotlight hit it, the malines disintegrated and fell in pieces, and I was left standing in my slip.)

Oleana and A. L. Anderson had two daughters: Josephine Mathilde and Selma Emele, Selma born February 13, 1885. Selma Anderson and Marvin Egstrom met and fell in love and eloped in Volga, South Dakota, when she was sixteen years old. Her mother, Oleana Anderson, was such a strict disciplinarian that Selma was afraid to tell her she had eloped. "Either you tell her or I will," Marvin said.

When Grandmother Anderson heard the news, she was

shocked for a moment but then said, "Well, if you're old enough to get married, you're old enough to run your home properly." So she put Mama in a finishing school, and I'm glad she did. Looking back on these family histories, I have gotten to be rather fond of Oleana and suspect that even my own home is run more properly because of the example set by my mother.

Selma Emele Anderson and Marvin Olaf Egstrom had seven children: Milford, Della, Leonard, Marianne, Clair, Norma (me) and Jean; Gloria was stillborn.

Selma loved her father. He had lived with the Indians and, thanks to them, had learned how to filter water through charcoal. He went on to invent the first charcoal filter, which, as they say, bore his name—the Anderson Charcoal Water Filter. (Later his son Leonard would persuade him to sign over the patents for the water filter. It's my understanding that he drank the profits away.)

Grandfather Anderson was fascinated by the notion of perpetual motion and kept pursuing it until he went blind, after which my mother brought him to live at our house. He absolutely fascinated me with his stories of the Indians and other people he knew, like Wild Bill Hickok and Calamity Jane. When my mother became ill, he had to be sent to a home—a double loss for a little blonde girl named Norma . . .

With Spotty, her small black dog, she was watching her Mama in a hospital bed, but the bed was in the parlor. There was a nurse walking quietly out the door in soft white shoes. She saw her mother struggle to get out of bed and try to drink the water out of the flower vases. Some of it spilled on the floor. Poor Mama, she was *so* thirsty. They took her flowers away.

The scene changed and the bed was gone. Instead, there was a coffin, and in it lay her Mama, sleeping so peacefully, looking so tiny and beautiful.

27

People stood around with sad faces, and the ladies were all wearing hats. The little towhead broke the booming silence, "Can I see my Mama?"

Wordlessly, they placed a straight chair by the coffin and lifted me up. A Scandinavian lady standing in the group behind me whispered loudly, *"Ven* are dey going to make coffee?"

Then they closed the lid and gently carried her out the door.

"Where did they take Mama?"

"To heaven with God."

"Where's God?"

"Up there."

Now the days all ran together. I was a strange child. I had been alone a lot while Mama was in a coma for all of those months. The quiet came naturally, and my dog and I watched everyone go about their business with wide eyes inquiring. I became curious about nature things. Leaves, flowers, little rocks—sometimes I'd turn them over to see what was growing underneath. Strange to remember one little rock after all those years.

It all had something to do with Mama. Someone said they had put her in the ground, and someone else said she was "up there." So I'd lie on my back and look up at those big white thunderclouds we used to have in North Dakota, and I was sure that one day Mama would peek out from behind those clouds.

Somehow that felt so good, just thinking she was near, but when the wind blew the clouds away, I was left with the same old question—where did they take Mama?

Well, maybe one day I'd know.


The first time I saw Min, the lady who was to be my stepmother, she was dangling a ball of candy on a rubber string.

She had a gold tooth. She was smiling, but I could tell she wasn't smiling at all. It was as if I knew what was going to happen. Children are like that.

Florid face, bulging thyroid eyes, long black hair to her waist pulled back in a bun—heavy breathing—German descent—wore cotton dresses from Sears, Roebuck or Montgomery Ward. (During the depression they used to call their catalogues "wish books," for obvious reasons.) Read *True Romances, True Story* and similar magazines. Ate chocolates—lots of chocolate-covered cherries and Whitman Samplers. Drove the Model-A Ford like it was a Ferrari.

Obese—strong as a horse, she beat everyone into a fright. Even the men were afraid of her. She would trick people into a corner and attack the most sensitive spots. When others who didn't know her were around, she would talk in a sickeningly sweet way.

I stood there in front of her with my hands behind my back, wanting very much to have one of those jawbreakers, which were covered with little specks of candy. I think it took about a week to eat each one.

"Look what I bought for you," she puffed. I finally gave in and reached for one.

Somehow I knew then that they were soon to be married. It was a year after my Mama's death. She had been my sister Della's nurse when little Paul was born. Mother had died in August, and now it was December 27th.

There was a December blizzard, so Daddy built a roaring fire. We had gone to bed. I was sitting on the bed in my Daddy's room—when Milford came running in.

"Dad, the house is on fire!"

"Naaaw, you go to bed."

"No! Put your hand on the floor, you'll see!"

Daddy swung his feet over the side of the bed and quickly discovered why Milford was standing on one foot and then another. He put his hand on the floor and confirmed it. During the next few minutes he was acting in shock as I watched him putting on one layer of clothing after another. Poor Daddy, I think the things that had been happening, one after another, were just too much for him.

Milford was running around rousing Leonard and Clair and Marianne, you could hear the brothers shouting . . .

Clair said, "Leonard, where are my pants?" And Leonard: "To hell with your pants, I've lost my sock." Poor bewildered Marianne took off her nightie and made a half-hearted try to put on her clothes, but mostly she just sat there until she was ordered out of the room, carrying her clothes under her arm.

We all went outside into the cold, whistling blizzard; Marianne in a nightie, and I guess that's what I was wearing too.

They moved my sister Della out of the house with the newborn baby, bed and all, right into the thirty-five degrees below zero and the pelting snow.

My sister Marianne and I watched like it was a ping-pong game while the firemen ran in and out of the house, throwing furniture on the lawn and soaking it with water (thereby, by the way, invalidating the insurance).

I kept asking about my neighbor playmate: "Where's Jeanie Finkbinder?" But either they didn't hear me or weren't much interested in my questions. The flames were crackling and the smoke blended with the whistling snow. I suppose the fire was keeping us warm, otherwise we surely would have frozen.

We stayed overnight at the Finkbinders' house, but all we could smell was smoke, and the next day we were sent to the Lipperts' house. They were Min's ex-in-laws. Her husband had blown his head off by sticking it into a big gasoline tank and lighting a match. I wondered if he did it on purpose.

Sometimes we would stay with the Schaumbergs, who were Min's parents. They had a nice house and they were good to me. Grandpa Schaumberg would sit in a big oak rocking chair by a Boston fern puffing on his meerschaum pipe, and somewhere nearby was a giant clock that tolled the hour as it ticked loudly while he read his newspaper that had been sent to him from Germany.

Sometimes I would watch him peel potatoes the thinnest way I ever saw a potato peeled. He would peel the whole potato without breaking the skin, and it would come out the other end of his paring knife like a spiral. I remember he always brought green bananas from some refrigerated freight car. I don't remember ever eating a ripe one. It didn't matter, though, because I knew Grandpa Schaumberg liked me.

Every afternoon they would tell me to go into the parlor and take a nap—which is one way to get rid of a little kid, I knew that even then. Well, I would go in there and, wonder of wonders, there was a player piano that I would pump as hard as I could, down on my hands and knees. Sometimes they would make me stop and I would lie there and count the buttons on the leather couch.

I would get lonesome for Daddy and would go out and sit by the iron picket fence—waiting and waiting for Daddy to come. He very seldom did. But I still remember one day sitting there plucking grass and trying to make it whistle, as I had seen some bigger kids do. I put the blade between my fingers and blew on it—once in a while I would actually get a little whistle. All of a sudden I saw some pointed yellow shoes and I looked all the way up from the pointed toes, up to the knees, up the clothes, and it was Daddy smiling down at me. When I finished squealing with delight, he told me he had come to take me to dinner at a cafe, where we would have hot roast beef sandwiches with gravy all over.

It's funny, I don't remember any other time my Daddy took me to dinner. But that was certainly a great hot roast beef sandwich . . .

\*  \*  \*

Summertime in North Dakota could be wonderful. Especially if you were anywhere near the James River and you went on a picnic where the trees hugged the river banks and the river broke up the flatness of the land.

I remember the park where my brother Clair and I were sent out with gallon syrup pails to pick gooseberries. I would fill up my pail (I would pick like mad because afterward we would be allowed to go swimming), and Clair would talk me into trading buckets. He would say, "Here, Hootchie, I'll trade you buckets," and I would do it. When I would go to the Lipperts' and pour out his bucket, and find out he had stuffed the bottom with grass and leaves, I was so embarrassed because it looked like *I* was trying to cheat. (As much as he loved me, Clair loved to outsmart me.) The Lipperts would send me back to pick more gooseberries, and brother Clair would go swimming. (It took me a long time to get even in the practical joke department, as you've already heard.)

When it was watermelon weather, we children ate watermelon and marched around the block with the rinds on a long stick. It seemed like the thing to do. We also played king of the hill, hopscotch, and I was always careful not to "step on a crack, you'll break your mother's back." I don't know why stepping on a crack bothered me so much when I knew my mother was gone, but they had said she was "up there," and I suppose I just wanted to know she was all right.

When there were thunderstorms at night, I was petrified. They told me if you were near feathers you would not get struck by lightning, so I walked around with a pillow all night long, feeling fairly safe.

We were always moving, and now were living up on 215 Milwaukee Street East, where there were few of the comforts of home. Nights went by when Daddy didn't come home until very late. I was afraid, not knowing where he had gone, but sometimes I would finally fall asleep with my head on my arms on the dining room table.

Sometimes he would sing me an Irish lullaby, using a broad Irish accent. It was supposed to be funny, but I thought it was sad. He would explain that he just wanted to make me laugh about McGinty, who went to the opera show and nearly went berserk when he saw the hootchie-kootchie dancers and tried to join them on the stage. They did everything to that poor man, including sticking his head in a pail of ice and turning the hose on him. That was more than I could bear, and, when I cried, Daddy would say, "It's just a song, honey." But I knew better.

Once in a while I would have a toothache, but as soon as Daddy put his warm hand on my cheek it would disappear, and I'd go to sleep so fast you wouldn't believe it.

Sometimes I followed Daddy to work, and he had such long legs that I couldn't keep up with him. If he noticed, he would stick his first finger out, and I would grab it, and he would take me to the depot with him, me trotting as fast as I could to keep up with his giant steps. He would put me on a big stool, give me some paper and rubber stamps and I would stamp away very nicely until he could find a way to get me home.

(There was also a little boy who told me where some jellybeans were kept in the warehouse, and we would sneak in and take handfuls of jellybeans and tiptoe out in back and eat to our hearts' content.)

One day Daddy didn't see me running behind him. He must have been in a hurry, and suddenly he turned a corner and he was gone. I sat down on the sidewalk and began crying. A lady gave me some toys to play with. "Don't worry, your daddy will be here to pick you up." I remember how puzzled I was to know how Daddy knew where I was. I guess

I decided daddies just knew everything. It was by a telephone, of course, but I had never heard of a telephone.

The day after Daddy and Min married, he hadn't been out the door five minutes before she laid down all the ground rules.

I had done the unforgivable. In a strange house, terribly lonesome for my Mama and missing my Daddy, I wandered into their nuptial chamber crying, "Mama, Mama."

Well, I guess you know the battle lines were drawn for the next eleven years. She didn't even need an excuse. "Norma, you go out there and cut yourself a willow switch, and don't try to cut a little one, because if it breaks you'll have to cut another one!"

Her florid face would flash in front of me as the switch kept cutting into my skin. After she had vented her anger, she would make a little speech about my not bothering my father, and that if I told him, there would be "more where *that* came from."

All of the kindness was gone. Where were the tender smiles and happy laughter with rustling taffeta and crystal sounds and the feeling of fresh linens and the smell of flowers? It seemed like yesterday Mama was still there making lovely delicate things for us—baking delicious cakes and cookies, singing and laughing, playing games with us, playing her prize possession, a Circassian walnut piano. And then she was gone, and there was this ominous heaviness and anxiety everywhere.

Although I was only five years old, my work had just begun. Min would have me stand on a box to wash dishes. If the water was not hot enough, she would pour boiling water over my hands. I began to be terrified of what each new day would bring. What was life all about? Did this happen to everybody? Was I any different?

I'd wonder—why was my Daddy my Daddy. I loved him,

34

and I am glad he was my Daddy, but why couldn't I have belonged to the Zellers down the street? I once heard them talking about adopting me, but my Daddy wouldn't have liked that. I was his favorite, I guess, because I was the youngest.

One very hot day we had a rip-roaring North Dakota thunderstorm. It cooled the air and everything seemed so beautifully fresh and clean, smelled marvelous, and I went out to join the other children in the neighborhood wading in the puddles. But I slipped and fell in the mud puddles, and within minutes Marianne and I were being soundly whipped. For her grand finale, Min broke the skin on our backs. We ran upstairs and listened through the register. Min and Daddy were talking about "the books" again. A mystery . . .

I often wondered why Daddy and Min got married. Was it because of what Marianne and I heard through the furnace register about Daddy being asked by Mr. Stebbins to "fix up the books a little for the good of the railroad"? It was something about the "per diem" reports. Was Daddy drinking and he told her, and then she might tell on him?

Anyway, I didn't want to imagine him loving her after Mama.

I went to the first grade, my only real bright spot. I loved school *and* our teacher Ella Fetcher, even though she had to scold me in front of the class when I put my first "100" paper in my mouth while pretending to be looking for something in my desk. "You can put your paper away now, Norma. Everyone has seen your 100 mark." I blushed red as a beet.

Miss Fletcher would draw a birthday cake on the blackboard for whoever's birthday it was. She would say, "What kind of frosting do you want?" and then she would draw all kinds of colored roses and flowers and put the candles on it.

"Blow out the candles and make a wish," she would say, and you would pucker up to blow. While you did that, she would take the eraser and wipe the yellow drips from the candles off the cake, and, of course, you would always get your wish, because you always blew out all the candles.

I should have wished not to move to Nortonville! Jamestown had been exciting with the big railroad stations for the Great Northern, the Northern Pacific and Sioux Line and, of course, the Midland Continental Railroad that was one hundred miles long and held them all together. When the line first went in, the original train engineer was British. Every time they ran out of track, they'd stop and make a town, and they all ended up with English names likes Jamestown, Wimbledon and Edgeley. It always sounded so grand to me when the conductor would announce that the Midland Continental would be stopping at Jamestown, Wimbledon and Edgeley.

You see, it was a very important railroad because it was the only way the miles and miles of flat prairie could be connected and carry all those freight cars, refrigerated cars and flat cars so they could get to all those far off places. (One time the refrigerator car broke down and we had oranges forever! When you lived on the prairie in those years, an orange was a magical, exotic fruit—you could even eat the skin and smell the scent of the oil in the orange peel.)

Mr. Simmons, the engineer, would lean his elbow out the window and pull the big old whistle. I used to wonder why he leaned out the window, because I was sure the train would have stayed on the track anyway, but what did I know? One day Mr. Kellogg, the conductor, told Mr. Simmons to let me blow the whistle, and I don't think I'll ever again feel the surge of power I felt when that big blast came out. I jutted out my chin just the way Mr. Simmons did. He laughed so hard and tried to put his striped cap on my head, but it fell down over my nose, which made him and Mr. Kellogg laugh even more.

But now, all that was over and we were moving from Jamestown to Nortonville, to the most dreadful part of my life.

The railroad demoted Daddy to the little station in Nortonville, which, I think, just about broke his heart. I heard they didn't approve of the marriage. Neither did I.

It was the midst of the Depression. Nortonville was a tiny town surrounded by farms, with about one hundred and twenty-five people wandering around trying to survive and make some sense out of life, usually failing, or so it seemed.

Daddy looked very sad and began to drink more . . . as late as two in the morning I'd find him down at the depot singing and talking to the railroad tracks with a Ralph somebody.

Marianne, Clair and I didn't find much happiness. I remember helping Marianne gather her clothes and hiding them out behind the barn so she could run away to live with our older sister Della and her husband and little Paul. I was beaten but I refused to tell where she had gone; this beating left me so bruised and bleeding it was hard to cover it up. Marianne and I had survived a number of beatings together, and a closeness had developed between us that would never be broken.

My brother Clair would try to make me laugh but mostly the joke was on me, because he was always talking me into milking the cows and then he would "help with the dishes," but he had always disappeared when it was time for his end of the bargain.

As for Min, now she had opened up her whole bag of tricks . . . hit me over the head with a cast-iron skillet, beat me with a heavy leather razor strap with a metal end, which made a scar on one side of my face that even now tries to show up in a photograph.

It didn't matter to her what her tool of torture was; she would use anything that was handy—2 by 4's, for example—and she loved to drag me around by the hair. I was always covered with gouges from her nails digging into my arms or wherever she happened to light.

Mental cruelties were another story. She was constantly saying my head was too small for my body and my hands were too big. I was just all *wrong.* She would also say, "You'll come home with a big belly," but I had no idea what she meant.

My teacher, Mr. Earl Clark, used to try to help by ringing the school bell longer when he saw me running down the road. He would ring it until I reached the safety of the school-yard so I wouldn't get a tardy mark and be punished for being late. He really was kind to me, and I have always been grateful.

Later I helped Clair get away. He tried to get me to come along but I couldn't leave Daddy with *her.* I had to stay there.

By the age of seven I was keeping house. By ten, I was baking large batches of homemade bread, milking cows, churning butter, cooking and cleaning. The next year I had my first job, outside taking care of a newborn baby and the mother, plus the farm animals, cooking, cleaning, milking cows, washing clothes with water I carried from the creek. (This family was so poor they didn't even have a well.) The whole area was so primitive there was no electricity, no indoor plumbing. Inside, there were kerosene lamps, Benjamin Franklin stoves, wood-burning ranges and no music, unless I sang. I was paid two dollars a week, no days off.

I guess everybody has to be someplace.

When I would bring the cows in for milking, the bull was to be kept separate and stay behind in the pasture. That's what he was supposed to do. Well, I watched him out of the corner of my eye while I brought the cows out, and *he* was watching *me*. I was fumbling with the makeshift closing of barbed wire that had a harness evener on one side that was to be slipped through some harness rings attached loosely to a fence post. The barbed wire was a little taut, especially if you were as scared as I was, with the bull steadily approaching—eye to eye now. With one last desperate tug to slip the harness through the rings, it suddenly acted like a big slingshot and hit me right in the eye. I went out like a light.

When I came to, I heard some very heavy breathing. I cautiously opened my eyes to see two large nostrils sniffing at me. Nose-to-nose, we were.

After I realized he wasn't going to *eat* me, I wasn't afraid of him anymore, and he lost interest in me. I *was* glad to go home in the fall, however, even if Min was there.

Shortly after the bull, I met Everold Jordan, known to me as Ebbie, who was to be my best friend. Whenever he could, Ebbie would come and help me with the heavy chores, and, in turn, I would help him shock grain, pitch hay or whatever was to be done at the Jordan home. He knew about Min but we didn't talk about it.

After we did our chores, we drank Rawleigh's Mouthwash together, thinking we were terribly sophisticated, as we stanchioned the cows in the warm barn and took turns telling each other our joke, the only one we knew: about the man who got his nose cut off and his toe cut off—they put his nose back on where his toe should be, and his toe back on where his nose should be. And after that, every time he had to blow his nose, he'd have to take off his shoe.

Then we'd laugh and laugh. I still do when I think of it. Well, I told you I was still growing up.

39

MISS PEGGY LEE

* * *

When I saw the smoke coming out of the chimney at the town hall, I knew it meant something special was happening there. Anything would have been special in our little town of Nortonville, but this was really something special, and I ran down to see what it was.

It turned out to be a double-feature. Two movies! Ginger Rogers in THE THIRTEENTH CHAIR and Al Jolson in THE JAZZ SINGER. Oh, I could hardly breathe. A real movie. A traveling show. (Little did I know that one day I would sing duets with Al Jolson on his radio program and co-star with Danny Thomas in THE JAZZ SINGER.)

The town hall wasn't even a theatre, it was just a hall where they held *everything*. Basketball games, box socials, dances where Clyde Moller and his family would play. One of the Mollers chorded on the piano while Clyde played the valve trombone. They would play "You Are My Lucky Star," and the dancers would stand there and pump their arms up and down before they took that first step. You could almost guess how good they'd be by how long they pumped. It was even exciting to go outside and hear the music coming through the walls. A few of the men had half pints of home brew and tipped their heads back and guzzled. Mysterious and sophisticated, well, I mean, how often could you hear music coming out of the walls or hear them making those sounds men make when they take a big swig and blow the fumes out of their mouth?

I was so excited I can only remember part of the movies—Ginger Rogers must have been a child then, and she looked so beautiful. Al Jolson was singing "Sonny Boy" in blackface, and, of course, I was crying my eyes out. Hard to believe then that down the road a bit I would have the honor of meeting Miss Ginger Rogers and that she would be visiting me in my dressing room.

\*   \*   \*

There were no street names or numbers on the houses in Nortonville. You would just refer to the name of the family who lived there—the Conitz house or the Hollingsworth place—but you would go up the "sandy road" from "downtown" or the depot to the Egstrom house.

One day I was going down the sandy road with two dozen eggs to trade in for sugar, singing at the top of my lungs. But the sand was pulling at my ankles and it knocked me over—on top of the eggs. I sat there for a long while and tried to figure out how I would tell Min . . . "Uh, I was walking down the, uh." No, that wouldn't do. "A big wind came up when I was walking down the, uh." No, that was a lie, and she'd never believe it. "Well, the bag slipped out of—" How could it do that? I was hanging onto it for dear life!

I guessed I'd just have to blurt it out and take my lumps. Which I did.


It was 1929 now, the stock market had crashed and we began to see men crawling down the sides of the trains and rolling out from the rods under the cars. The trainmen just ignored them; they knew who they were.

The stockyards, down a ways from the depot at Nortonville, became the hobos' hotel. The railroad ties and heavy boards used for construction were a weathered gray, not very inviting, but down there, semi-protected from the elements, were the hobos who rode the rails during those Depression years. When the train stopped, the "bo's" would hop off and find a little place to make a campfire. Sometimes they could steal an egg or two from a chicken or take the whole chicken, for that matter.

There was one traveler that really shook me up. He was wearing burlap wrapped around his feet for shoes. Poor man!

41

And he really needed to see a dentist. I can't ever forget that egg that slid over his broken teeth.

I felt for these fellows, told them where we lived up the road so they could come and get a free meal. They did. They came up and asked for work, like chopping wood or hauling in coal. Oh my Lord, I felt sorry for these men. They came from all walks of life and had just been mauled nearly to death by the Depression. They could barely manage a smile, but they surely let me know they appreciated the trust from this strange little girl.

Somehow, my Daddy found out about my breadline and he nearly went berserk. It was one of the few times he scolded me, because, naturally, he was afraid of what they might do. But they didn't do anything bad. Just the opposite . . . they chopped the wood I would have had to chop and all sorts of other things. I appreciated it, and they would say, "Thank you, ma'am, God bless you," as they went on their way.

Probably wouldn't be that way nowadays with drugs and all, but what those poor souls needed most was a friend. Even me.


This was one of the times Min went to Jamestown, which meant she'd be gone all day and maybe even part of the night. My sister Della had sent me an embroidered silk cloche hat— pale, peachy pink . . . I never was allowed to wear anything given to me; it was always kept for something "good," but there never *was* anything good. Well, with Min off to Jamestown, I dared to go over to Ebbie Jordan's house. We went out in the barn to play hide and seek. I crawled up the manger post and got up as far as I could over the stall, where canvas binders were stored, tied up like tarpaulin. Terrific! I could get on top of that and watch Ebbie go crazy looking for me. I had barely got out there, when the whole thing gave way and dropped me. I lost my hat (never bothered to look for it), got scraped all over my forehead, and quickly brushed my bangs to hide the scrapes. Ebbie looked at me and sang out, "One-two-three for Norma!"

Until my forehead healed, I lived in fear that Min would say, "What happened to your hat? What happened to your forehead?" In defense, it became my habit, whenever the slightest breeze would blow, to slap my forehead to make sure my bangs were plastered down. Luckily, Min never found out.

It was 1930 now and I was ten.

I had been up all night with waves of nausea and retching, then fell into some sort of delirum. I remember seeing my brother Clair standing at the end of my bed . . . "What's the matter, Hootchie?" he was saying, and I couldn't even answer him. I had ripped my nightie while I was writhing about. I guess I was trying to get out of the pain. He had come back from looking for Min, who was showing her "nice" side to the Ladies' Aid Society. Somehow he had managed to get her out of there and back to me. I'm quite sure she hoped I would not pull through. A midwife like Min should have known the symptoms, should have known I had appendicitis (and by that time it had burst and peritonitis had developed). Remember, in those days we had no antibiotics.

They had all left early that morning, but Clair hadn't gone to school and had brought her back. He was frightened enough to fight her. Somewhere he had picked up a double-barreled shotgun, and the next thing I remember was Clair telling her with cold anger she had better get me to a doctor.

"How am I going to do that? There's no doctor around here—"

"Yes there is. In Edgeley. Get moving. You're not going

to let her lay there and die. You move or I'll shoot you."

He pulled one trigger and then the other. Thank God, both barrels were empty.

Dimly it comes back that they put me in the car and drove me eighteen miles on a rough gravel road to Edgeley and Dr. Green, a drive that in those days took about four hours. I really don't remember much about that ride.

The "hospital" was over a small bank—three or four rooms and the operating room. The whole place, I remember, smelled of ether. There were some fairly primitive surgical tools in glass cabinets, and the operating table was black leather. There was also one nurse, but she was a patient too, and there was another doctor besides Dr. Green in another room. I heard him moaning. Someone said he was "taking a cure."

They laid me down on the black table and put me to sleep with ether. As I was going to sleep, I could hear flapping sounds in my head. They seemed to come first from one end of the room and then the other. That was my first encounter with ether, and I didn't like it at all.

When I came to, I wanted water so badly . . . but I couldn't find any, and there was no nurse to bring it to me, so I got up and looked for it—and *that* saved my life. The walking was good for me, although, of course, I didn't know it at the time, and in my condition walking was very painful.

Each day I would walk to the window and stare at an enormous tumor they had removed from some woman. They had placed it in a pan and put it out on the roof of the annex building. It started out as large as a small watermelon, and the last time I saw it, it was like a small cantaloupe. I guessed they'd forgotten where they put it.

Then, finally, came the day to go home. Though still bandaged, I took the train—Edgeley was at one end of the Midland Continental Railroad.

I guess I hoped someone would be glad to see me, but

44

there she was—frightening as ever—Min. I had been gone ten days, but the only thing Min had missed was my work. She made up for it fast, told me to scrub the floor. I was so weak I could barely carry the bucket and scrub brush, and was so dizzy I could hardly see the floor. But I was afraid not to try. I honestly think she was frustrated that I had survived. I thought so then, I think so now.

My abdomen was fairly heavily bandaged and had drain tubes for the peritonitis. But that didn't stop her. Suddenly she was kicking me in the stomach, and she just kept kicking until she broke open the incision. I retreated behind the wood-burning range, and, when it seemed safe for me to come out from behind it, I found some bandages and tape and did my best to put myself back together.

When I saw Dr. Green the next time, he was horrified. I didn't tell him who did it, but he said he knew. He patched me together and sent me home. There wasn't, he said, anything else to do.

But this was a little more than I could stand, and I told Daddy. He tried to protect me, and she beat *him.* It was blizzarding again. I grabbed my overshoes but only got one on—the other was on the porch—and I was running. Daddy was coming right after me, telling me to run. Min was after him with a poker. We got away from her, and Daddy grabbed my hand and took me to our neighbors, the Bucholtzes. They were as terrified of her as everyone else and stuck knives in the door jamb so she couldn't get in. Later they told me she had a butcher knife in her overcoat pocket, they thought they saw the handle . . .

After two or three days, Min went to the depot and begged Daddy to bring me back. Of course, she wanted me back, there was housework to be done. I guess she convinced Daddy that she would never touch me again. Anyway, he came and got me and I was *very* reluctant to go with him, as you might imagine. I didn't believe her, and I was right. Only

45

a day went by and she was at it again. It got so that if someone just walked by me I would flinch . . . During those years she had me butchering the animals I thought of as pets—the same chickens I had scooped up in my arms and brought inside when they were standing in the rain, drowning. I always felt she was trying to kill me, and I would run around to the side of the house and sit and hug my little dog. I think the love that came from that little dog may have helped me go on.

. . . And I remembered Mama. One day when I was sitting in the attic looking at pictures of her, Min found me and the photos of our whole family. She burned them all, but she couldn't burn my memories. Not then. Not now.


Nortonville was full of characters.

There was a man named Fred Bitz, thin and wiry, a small man with black eyes and a face all drawn up toward the center. I used to see him every few days when he would come in to the depot with his cream can—we would weigh it and pay him his cream-check and he'd be on his way, to get himself a drink, I guess. He was a quiet man, didn't seem to take up much space.

One day he came in, got his check and then we didn't see him again. Not until one day when I was out in the bean field in the August sun that got to be around 105° or 110° at that time of the year. You could see the heat waves rising from the ground.

Hopping down the row, I raised my head to wipe the perspiration from my forehead and happened to look over to the left and slightly in the distance. Something shimmered through the ragweed at the edge of the field.

Ebbie Jordan was with me helping pick the beans. "What's that green thing in there?" I asked him.

"I don't know," he said. "Looks like a car. Let's go see."

As we approached, Ebbie said, "Looks like Fred Bitz' car. What's it doing there?"

"I sure don't know. Yes—it *is* his car. Model-A Ford. What's that smell?"

"Oh, my God. Who's in that car?"

We looked in, and there was Fred. We figured he'd been there since that last cream-check. Blue flies were buzzing and maggots were crawling all over.

We ran! There wasn't any law to call, so we just told anybody we came to and brought them back.

It seemed he'd rigged up the exhaust pipe to the front seat. Or did he? No one ever knew for sure. The very last people to see him were the folks at his moonshine-selling brother-in-law's house.

After they buried him, some folks wanted to dig him up again for an autopsy, but his brother-in-law didn't want that. No one ever really knew what happened, but they certainly wondered. I still do.


And then there was Hoover—a little six-year-old boy, who seemed to be going on three. Hoover was fascinated by one particular duck that sat in our only pond. Most any time you could find him down there with a bucket trying to drain the pond.

If you asked him, "What are you doing, Hoover?" he would answer, "I'm going to get that duck."

In a way it made sense.


And I had my ambitions.

The ad said, "If you sell two dozen cans of Cloverleaf Salve, we'll give you coupons toward a diamond watch," and then, of course, there were a lot of lesser prizes. Right then

I said, "That diamond watch! I'll get that diamond watch!" Let Hoover have his duck. So I wrote in for the first two dozen cans of Cloverleaf Salve, which had all kinds of good things like carbolic acid and vaseline and I don't know what all. The excitement of that salve arriving! I *never* got a package before. Couldn't even imagine how it could find its way to me.

Anyway, I sold salve "till the cows came home," as they used to say, and every time I sold two dozen cans I was sure I'd get the watch, but I didn't. They would just say, "Now you've almost sold enough salve to"—yes, you've guessed it—"to get the diamond watch, or more Cloverleaf Salve."

But I kept at it . . . There was some horseradish growing near the artesian well. I nearly broke my back digging it up, then ground it in the meat grinder, the tears rolling down my cheeks, added a little vinegar and sold it for ten cents a quart.

I should have had a manager.

Even with Ebbie I wasn't too successful at business ventures, one of which I'm a little ashamed. We made radish sandwiches and seasoned them with a little chicken manure for our imaginary restaurant customer—Hoover. Hoover never knew why we snickered, and he thought they were delicious.

Ebbie and I used to ride around on an old plow-horse named Beans. There was plenty of room for both of us, but one day a little boy—I think his name was Robbie McClelland—asked Ebbie if he could ride with him that day. Ebbie said, "No, not today, Robbie." He smiled back at us, gently slapped old Beans with the bridle rein and rode off. The horse stepped into a gopher hole, pitched forward, throwing Ebbie off, and then fell on him.

Ebbie's shocked family mourned him deeply. I did too. I loved Ebbie very much. We had been through so much together. Though, like I said, we'd never discussed Min, he showed a sympathetic awareness of my predicament. He just tried to help me and make me laugh.

*   *   *

Springtime was my favorite, still is. After cold weather the snow would melt and crocuses would bud and bloom, and pussywillows would stand so straight with those soft little buds all up and down. One day in May when I was about nine, I went down to Bone Hill Creek; no one around, not a soul. The creek was swollen with spring water, and the C.C.C., the Civilian Conservation Corps, had built a dam to hold it all there. I didn't see any reason why I couldn't swim the way other people did. Everyone could swim, couldn't they, if they just tried? So I stripped down to my panties and started to wade into the creek. It had a mud bottom that didn't feel as good as it sounds. As I walked out into the deeper water, it began to sway my body around and I began to lose my balance. Now I was getting frightened, trying to walk on my toes, and there wasn't anything to walk on.

For a second I dared to look over my shoulder, and suddenly the shore was a lot farther than I thought. Somehow, with all my wiggling, I had left the shore behind, and, even though the creek wasn't terribly wide, I was too far out—too near the middle, and where was the bottom? The water came up to my mouth and I had to swallow some. Then, panicky as I was, I started to dog paddle, and thank the Lord, I somehow managed to get to the other side and went down the side of the creek to a narrow spot where there were rocks, so I could go back and get my clothes. I decided to try a swimming lesson another day with someone there.

I told you I was a survivor. Also lucky.


Way out behind the little town of Nortonville, there were the mounds. I'd found them while I was looking for arrowheads and tomahawks. It was strange and quiet there. Someone told me they were Indian graves, and from that day on I knew I was on sacred ground and tried to behave that way.

A deep feeling of sadness would come over me when I sat there on the ground, and I wondered if those arrowheads had been part of the battle that killed the Indians who were buried there. A child's imagination was at work, and I could see them in their headdresses quietly walking around in a circle. After I was scared enough, I'd run home. Somehow I felt I knew those Indians.

Maybe it was partly my grandfather's doing . . . Those stories he would tell me about the Indians, and those hand-beaded gloves they had given him that he'd show me. When it was cold and my hands felt like icicles, I would run in and crawl up in his lap and he would take my hands and hold them in his big hands while he blew on them until they felt warm and comfortable.

He was wonderful. I think I loved him.


When I was about eight or nine, we moved from the house up the sandy road to upstairs over the depot. I don't know why, maybe it was the Depression. Times were really tough. I remember expressions like "Easy on the butter, kids, it's fifty cents a pound," but we had our own butter from our cows, old Billy and Sally.


This particular Sunday morning, I had awakened very early, milked the cows, separated the milk, washed the separator, put a pot roast in the oven and gone to church. I always liked to go to church early so I could play the piano, probably the only one in town. I'd play "Out of the ivory palaces, into a world of woe . . ." until someone came in and I'd stop. Incidentally, everyone in Nortonville used this church. Had to, it was the only one.

Services were over, and we all came out of the church and started to walk across the field to the depot. I looked up and saw smoke billowing out of the windows! I ran as fast as I could across that field and around the side of the depot to where the door to our living space was.

And there was Min, who had slipped on some ice by the pump and couldn't get up. Her leg was broken, you could see the bone sticking out, and of course she was in a lot of pain. It was a good thing for her that she had slipped and spilled the water—otherwise she would have been up the stairs trying to put the fire out when the gasoline stove exploded. There wasn't anything I could do but run for help, which I did.

I must say, we were not exactly sad that she had to go to the hospital for about eight weeks, and people sent things from all over the state, including a pair of lady's shoes with high heels and pointed toes that I wore with rubber bands to hold them on. When Min came home from the hospital, she cut off the heels and made me wear them to school. They turned up at the toes and, of course, the other kids laughed.

Many years later I ran into a fellow named Kermit Clemons, who didn't know about Min's cruelty. I think Kermit's mother probably only knew Min at the Ladies' Aid Society. Actually, I never did dare tell anyone except Ebbie and one other friend about what Min did, but she told her mother and I got another beating for telling.


About this time I found another dog, and, oh, what a loving dog he was. Rex, I named him, because, even though he was a mixed breed, he was a king to me. He was kind of silver-gray, and his eyes were amber and full of adoration, adoration for me but not for the pack of hounds who were his mortal enemies. One day they got to him and ripped him from one end to the other. Somehow he managed to drag himself home, and when I saw him, I cried so hard I could hardly see.

I did manage to carry him upstairs, though, and make a bed for him, then cleaned his wounds and tried to get him to drink some water. The poor thing couldn't even raise his head, but he feebly wagged his tail to let me know he appreciated me.

He died right after that, and I carried him down by the railroad bridge. I thought he would be protected there under the bridge. I covered him with an old khaki army blanket and put stones around him so the wind wouldn't whip the blanket away.

Many times during that winter I went to visit him, and in the spring, when the ground thawed, I buried him.

Long live the King. Life went on.

One freezing morning when the cows had been milked, there was still laundry to be done, scrubbing the shirt collars and cuffs with Fels Naptha Soap until my knuckles were bleeding, then putting them into the hand-operated washing machine. I thought that everyone lived this way, in the gray chill of some impending violence. And some violence not so impending, including Min's, and being taught to butcher animals and pull out their innards, animals that had been my pets only yesterday.

One particular morning the frozen suits of underwear filled the lines like stiffs. My stepmother and stepbrother had driven into Jamestown. I walked quite calmly to the medicine chest, took out a bottle of Lysol, with a skull and crossbones on it, poured it into a glass, and had just put it to my lips when my stepbrother came in. He'd forgotten something, and it startled me enough to pour the stuff into the sink. He went back to the car, never knowing what I was attempting to do.

You may well ask, "Where was your Daddy?" Well, he was probably out trying to drown his sorrows, and, besides,

I tried to hide everything from him. He was troubled enough on his own.

I had a stray thought then: I'll leave when I find out where these railroad tracks lead.

In 1934 we moved to Wimbledon, a slightly larger town than Nortonville, and Min was left behind most of the time in Millarton, where she'd been transferred by the railroad. Daddy took advantage of that, and I was left to run the station, while he drank way too much. The Midland Continental Railroad was founded and funded by a widow who intended it to run from the Canadian border to Florida, but ran out of money after one hundred miles. It not only had a great steam engine but also a truck and a Model-A Ford on railroad wheels. When there wasn't enough freight, they would use the truck or the Model-A Ford (which they called Snowbird) to deliver the mail or to take the cream cans in to the dairy.

The train would stop wherever people were waiting along the track, often using the railroad to take them to the nearest doctor or to pick up some mail or baggage. Most had no other way of reaching their destinations. There were very few passengers actually riding on the train. I remember back in Nortonville I would sometimes play restaurant on the passenger coach—setting the old straw chairs facing one another, while leaving one flat in the middle for a table, then serve the imaginary people with cups of water, yelling orders while I ran up and down the aisle.

One day I hung a roll of toilet paper off the end of the caboose, and, as the train rolled, it unravelled. I always did like flags. Kellogg and Simpson knew how things were for me so they didn't mind, and besides, who was going to see?

(I had a fierce pride in that railroad, and when I got a little older, if I ever heard someone make a derogatory remark about it, I would take advantage of my position as editor of the high school paper in Wimbledon and write a scathing editorial.)

The track ended in Wimbledon. If you wanted to go to Jamestown or Nortonville or Edgeley or some other smaller place, you could, but this was as far as the Midland Continental went at this end, which I guess was why, even in my mind's eye, I couldn't see any further. (I still wonder where those cars went.)

Across the street was the depot for the Milwaukee, where we would always exchange waybills, and I was proud to have only seventeen mistakes on the first per-diem reports. There were aluminum seals with a little ball on the end and numbers embossed on the metal, and you were supposed to keep track of those numbers.

I can still see my Daddy walking from our depot to theirs, waybills in hand, hat cocked at a just-so jaunty angle. Amazing, now that I think of it, no matter where Daddy went, he wore a three-piece suit—with a vest, that is—and neatly shined shoes and clean shirts and, now and then, a hat. It strikes me as being a bit sad that he would get all dressed up for a tiny town like that. Perhaps in his own mind he was still Superintendent of Transportation or at least Station Agent . . . Why should I have been embarrassed if he'd have a little too much to drink and do an Irish jig in the post office? He wasn't even Irish, but you'd sure think so with his singing and dancing.

It's okay, Daddy. Sing me an Irish song.


When the train came in, I'd be so glad to see Kellogg. I didn't always see Simpson, but Kellogg used to let me take some hard coal from the train so it would make it easier to start the fires in the depot—especially in the winter, when we had mostly lignite. I never could figure out why they called it hard coal. Lignite was soft, and anthracite was hard, but they called anthracite soft, probably still do. It was the lignite that used to keep the home fires burning, though.

During the winter in the depot in Wimbledon, I'd have to lug in approximately a ton of lignite to bank four different stoves throughout the night. You'd have to stoke the stoves and then lug another shovelful alongside, so that sometime during the day, or usually night, you could replenish the fire. What a job. I learned to lift with my thighs, and learned about leverage, which comes in handy once in a while.

When it was time to melt snow for bathing and washing, I'd put a copper boiler about three feet long, a foot-and-a-half wide and about two-and-a-half or three feet deep up on the range and fill it with snow to melt into soft water. I'd make it a game to go out with a shovel or spade and, when the snow was just hard enough, cut a big square to carry into the boiler. The game, or the trick, was to see how big a square of snow you could carry into the kitchen without it breaking all over the floor. Even if it broke, though, it wasn't too bad because you could sweep it around and out the door with a push broom and have a nice clean floor. The real trick was to get the boiler full of water down off the stove. That was usually accomplished by smiling slyly at some unsuspecting man that came by.

The part I liked best was that Daddy was around, even though he was drinking. At least he was fun.


I found the telephone fascinating. There was one on the wall with a handle to grind, but the one that stood on the desk had a carbon cone for a speaker, and you could hear the conversation all along the line on this "company" phone. When we'd have those big snowstorms (at least one a year), the train would get stuck and sometimes even snowed under. One of the trainmen could crawl out and hook the telephone wire on the train to the regular telephone line. You could hear *everybody* talking out there . . .

"Well, we're snowed under all right. When do you think those snowplows can get out here?" . . . "Oh, I don't know, depends on how much they have to plow through." . . . "Okay then, but bring us some food, we'll probably be here a while." . . . "How about some Baby Ruth bars and some Snickers?" . . . "Yeah, we could use some of those too . . ."

Well, I used to listen and picture all this going on, and somehow it sounded so cozy—cozy, my eye, I'm sure they would have said.

Usually there was one train a day, unless they sent out a "special." Those other lines—the Milwaukee, the Northern Pacific, the Sioux Line, the Great Northern, the Santa Fe—all kept us busy transferring from one line to another.

Even at fourteen I don't think I did too badly at running the depot. One time, though, I made a big mistake. There were two junkmen who were always competing to see who could get the most scrap iron out of there, and they had to book the loading platform in advance. Well, not realizing how long it would take them, or even that it was important to them, I reserved the loading platform to both of them at the same time. If I hadn't been so young, I don't know what they would have done to me. I guess Daddy was a little under the weather so I had said I could handle it.

I used to hear remarks from people: "They'll be sending that back in bullets" and "that will all be coming back to us." It sounded important, and it was, but I didn't understand. This was 1934. It took only seven years—to December 7, 1941—for this scrap to become the stuff of war.

Momma and Daddy.

Jean Bernice Egstrom, my sister.

Selma Anderson and brother Leonard.

Della, Marianne,
Norma (Peggy), and Jeannie.

My beloved sister, Marianne.

Daddy's last picture just before he died.

The Black Building,
WDAY. I thought this was
as tall as the
Empire State Building!

Ken Kennedy, program
director at WDAY. He's the
one who named me Peggy Lee.

**Sev Olson and his orchestra from Minneapolis. Sev was my first serious romance.**

Miss Peggy Lee and the big brass at WDAY.

"Miss Peggy Lee" as I was officially known...

**Governor William Guy of North Dakota with my portrait
at the state capitol.**

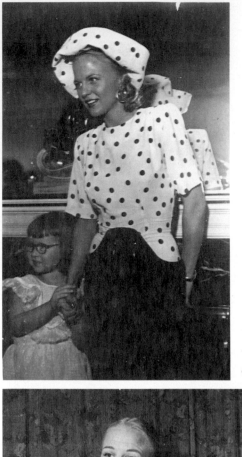

Peggy and Nicki.

With Mel Torme, having fun on a television show.

(Photo credit: Gene Lester)

Johnny Mercer, Peggy Lee, and Glen Wallich. I'd just won
the 1946 Down Beat Award.

(Photo credit: Gene Howard)

Composing music with Dave Barbour.

Peggy, Nicki, and Dave Barbour.

The Paramount Theatre in New York City where Dave
and I were performing.

Peggy and Woody Herman doing a radio show.

Peggy, Jimmy Durante and Arthur Treacher in the Santa Claus Parade, 1947.

(Photo credit: Gene Howard)

The recording session for "Mañana" with Dave Barbour and
Carmen Miranda's rhythm section. They marched out of the
studio playing "Mañana".

Louis Armstrong,
Frank Sinatra, Peggy Lee
and Bing Crosby.

Mary Livingston,
Peggy Lee, Jack Benny,
and Skitch Henderson.

# Three

HOW COULD it be so hard to get away from nothing? I was looking out the window, looking at the flatness, while absent-mindedly washing a plate and wondering what the future held for me.

"Yes, I *am* going to be a singer. I *know* it."

I stood there feeling as if a nice friend had just come over and whispered this fact in my ear. For me that's what it was— just a matter of fact. Also a comforting thought. No matter what happened afterward, I would remember that moment.

I had always sung. I sang before I could talk. They told me that when I was in the crib I sang. When other children would be playing games, I always wanted to be around music; if there was a piano or Victrola around, I was playing it. Although I was alone a lot, I was never really alone, because there was always music.

I would go around singing, "I Never Had a Chance"—a song of unrequited love that I had yet to experience, but it was fun to pretend. I learned "Moonglow" and "In My Solitude" and other songs . . . what a glorious feeling to put myself in those moods, whatever they were, and feel I was going to convince someone it had really happened to me.

One summer a few years earlier, when I was eight, I went to Spiritwood Lake—travel, it seemed, would broaden me. I saw a drunk passed out in the hot summer sun, flies crawling around on him, and immediately thought of Fred Bitz. Except this one was breathing. There was another little girl there, and we were both looking at the drunk, and out of the blue, needing to say something but not show my fear, I announced, "I'm going to be in show business someday." She said, "Oh yeah? What are you going to do?" I said, "Sing, like this," and promptly broke into a chorus of "Here comes the showboat, here comes the showboat, shuff, shuff, shuff, shufflin' along . . ."

I didn't even *know* that girl, and she believed me, and now I believed it, too. It was nice daydreaming about that day, and the whole trip to Spiritwood Lake. After all, it was the only vacation I'd ever had.

I would get up before dawn and take the fishing pail, the bait and the pole and get in the rowboat and row out, the oars kalunking along, and catch perch and pike and a few shiners too, but you threw those back.

In the kitchen at the pavilion, I cleaned the fish and helped clean up the kitchen, peeled potatoes or whatever they wanted. Rudy Vallee was singing on the radio, and I sang along with him.

Well, they said I was so good they were going to hire me for eight dollars a week the next summer. You bet I'd take the job. But the next summer they didn't call me for the job, after I had spent all the money I would have earned in my mind, picking out school clothes and presents for anyone I could think of out of the catalogues. I learned that one about not counting your chickens before they're hatched. It still was the best summer I ever had, though.

There was a legend of Spiritwood Lake—that, whenever there was thunder and lightning, two logs would come up out of the middle of the lake and bob around together, representing the Indian girl and her lover who had drowned out there because their folks wouldn't let them get married. I *saw* the logs . . . I guess the legend was why they called it Spiritwood Lake.

When I went back to Nortonville, I learned another lesson, the hard way. At Spiritwood I'd learned to swim very well; swam a mile behind a boat and dove off the high tower; actually twice, because the man said he'd give me a whole quarter if I'd dive off the high tower, so I did, but he said he didn't see me and made me do it again. Of course, he saw me. How could he miss me with the belly-whopper splash I made both times. But I believed him at the time.

Anyway, when we went back to Nortonville, I was going to show off again, so when we drove down to that Civilian Corps dam, I just ran out on that board to spring up and do a lovely swan dive—only the water had drained way down, and I went head-first into the mud, feet sticking up. The water had been ten feet deep and now it was only up to my knees. So I got it again—don't count your chickens, *and* don't show off. Not bad lessons for life—especially for a singer's life.

Ivar Knapp was either the superintendent or the principal of the school, I don't remember which, but he was the authority figure and also a very nice fellow. Still, I wanted to sing so badly I found it difficult to believe he actually would give me permission—but he did. We made a deal that if I would get my homework in ahead of time I could go to Valley City and sing with Doc Haines and his orchestra. I'd met Doc when he'd once played Wimbledon. It seemed everyone in Wim-

59

bledon always knew I was going to go *someplace,* and someone pointed me out to Doc and said, "That's our little Hollywood girl, you ought to use her." Doc was dark and handsome, and I even liked his glasses. He was also a college student, which made him seem really glamorous and sophisticated. Well, with the prospect of singing with Doc's orchestra in view, you can bet I applied myself at school, which included working for the National Youth Association (like the WPA) to the tune of $12 a month for washing blackboards and halls.

Mr. Knapp kept his word, I kept mine, and so off I went, hitchhiking to Valley City to sing with Doc Haines. Valley City wasn't very far from Wimbledon, and I promptly got a ride on a bread truck.

When the big day came, I sang with Doc Haines on a program on KOVC. How did I get so lucky? *I* soon had a sponsored radio program on KOVC! My sponsor was a restaurant, a college hangout, and they paid me five dollars, plus all I could eat. But I was so self-conscious, like trying to act really sophisticated when I twisted the spoon around in a butterscotch ice-cream sundae. It took me years before I'd order another one of *those* again. (Years later Art Carney told me that he had the same trouble with butterscotch. Loved it but just couldn't handle it.)

I usually sang with a megaphone, just like Rudy Vallee. There was this time when we started out in a blizzard, had our trailer loaded with all the instruments and a newly painted sign shaped like a rainbow on the side that read "DOC HAINES AND HIS ORCHESTRA." We were riding along, so proud of that sign, when all of a sudden the trailer started swaying in the snow and pulling the Overland Buick back and forth with it. The Buick was heavy enough to hold with the tire chains, but the trailer slid and flipped over in the ditch. All our laughing stopped right then.

The fellows piled out and gathered the instruments that had spilled into the ditch and snow when the door to the trailer flew open. The other car with us had to go back in to Valley City and borrow Mrs. Norgaard's clothesline to tie the big bass on top of the Buick, then we all piled in again and were on our way.

By now the storm had picked up and it was hard to see where we were going. At one point we stopped in a hurry when we heard a train whistle over the wind and the sound of the rolling cars. It was a good thing we did. There was a long freight train, and we couldn't see it . . . We would have plowed right into it. The engineer must have known that road was there and blew the whistle just in case.

Well, we finally arrived, and there were all of three couples standing there waiting to dance. Never mind. An audience of one was still an audience. I sang "Moonglow" into my megaphone, and they could even hear a little bit of it, if they danced near enough.

Doc gave me fifty cents for the night, but I knew he was hungry, so I bought us both a bowl of chili with crackers.

I think I had a crush on Doc. He used to call me his "little blues singer."


Wimbledon in that year of 1934 seemed like it was full of cobwebs. The railroad station was old, the hotel across the street was old and mostly deserted; a family lived there—a mother and father and a girl named Helen, who was my playmate—but there were almost never any customers or guests. Except once.

It was hot. I remember Helen and I had a big galvanized washtub down in the basement, and we sat in that tub for hours or at least until the sun went down. I can still see that hotel. The lobby had a great wide picture window in front so you could see who was inside. There were a couple of rocking chairs and a big brass spittoon between them. I used to think I saw an old man sitting there rocking, but now I'm not sure.

He must have died. Anyway, he wasn't there anymore when Helen's folks left on their trip and got my father's permission for me to stay overnight with her.

There was a check-in desk and a big book to register names and a bell to tap for a bellboy, except there weren't any bellboys. Behind the front desk there were boxes for the keys and the mail, in case there ever was any. There was even a dining room, and on the second floor were rooms, but only two beds had mattresses.

When we heard the bell ring at the desk downstairs, we nearly jumped out of our skins. We ran down, and, believe it or not, there were two men asking for rooms.

Well, we really played our parts, welcomed them like royal guests. Of course, we had to explain that we just had the one room available. They didn't mind, they said. They were so tired they'd take anything. They seemed a little reluctant to sign the register, but I figured they thought, what the hey, we might as well humor the little brats.

We asked if they would like something to eat, and yes, they said, they would. Again we had to apologize, that we only had egg sandwiches, but you can't go too far wrong with those, and we were soon serving them in the dining room. This was great, we never expected to have so much fun.

After they finished eating, they were anxious to get some rest because they said they really had to get going in the morning. So we ushered them to their rooms, wished them a good rest, and tried to calm ourselves down as we washed the dishes and put everything in order.

Helen said no one *ever* stayed there. Maybe business was catching on? Maybe we'd have more people? But what would we feed them? I could go across the street to the depot and get a little something for their breakfast . . . We babbled on until we wore ourselves out and went to bed from sheer exhaustion.

Thank God, when we woke up they were gone. They

hadn't paid, which was hardly a surprise when we found out they were two fugitives wanted for murder!

They had picked the perfect place to hide.

And up on Main Street there was a candy store, a cafe, a general store, a post office and a milliner's shop.

It was so eerie, that shop. There was a small bay window with a couple of hats—dusty hats—sitting in it. No lock on the door. They were all gone now. I'll never forget how Helen and I tiptoed in that first time. All the furniture was still there, and the wind blew old letters and papers back and forth across the room. We went into the kitchen, where all the pots and pans were still on the stove with old dried-up food in them.

And then we learned the whole family had died of diphtheria, except the widow, and she had just high-tailed it out of there. From wherever she had gone to, she always paid all the taxes due so no one could touch the building, even though everyone said it was an eyesore.

Any time you wanted to feel spooky, you could just go in there.

Another big attraction was the wonderful souvenir that Harry Hanson had brought hack from Hollywood, where he used to be a "prop" man.

Everyone would go and see it and marvel over the fragile beauty of it, me included.

He said it was Janet Gaynor's brassiere!

It was really a lovely bra. I enjoyed the fantasy of it, too.

Before going back to school, I worked one summer on a farm at harvest time for the threshing crew of Mr. and Mrs. Ferd Flohr.

I never got over how that woman worked, and I should

know, because we worked side by side. Besides the regular chore of getting the cows in and milking them (they wouldn't stand for my fingernails now), I'd cook for a whole crew of men. In the early morning darkness, I'd locate the cows, thanks to their mooing. They would be heading in toward the barn with their udders heavy with milk. I'd have to get them in the barn, milk them and separate the cream from the milk in the big McCormick-Deering separator, then run into the house with the fresh cream and milk and pop the biscuits into the oven, get the oatmeal ready, fry up some bacon and eggs; maybe give them a little fresh rhubarb sauce or some honey for the biscuits. And coffee and Postum.

After breakfast there was canning to be done. Fresh fruit, like peaches and pears, and sometimes tomatoes, to be put up in Mason jars, place them carefully in the big copper boiler (as if we needed any more heat). While they were cooking away, it was time to clean the house, scrub the kitchen— sometimes wash clothes, but, glory be, Mrs. Flohr had a Maytag washer that would putt-putt all those clothes clean.

One noontime I had cooked a huge pot of stewed chicken and dumplings for dinner and was taking it down to the cellar to cool until dinnertime. It was dark going down there and I couldn't see over the pot. Naturally, I slipped and fell all the way down, the chicken and dumplings going everywhere. I landed in the coal bin—a drumstick here, a wing there and gravy all over me, including my hair.

I picked myself up and hobbled up the steps. Mrs. Flohr and the men were laughing so hard you could say they might have split their sides.


Mrs. Flohr was really so nice, not anything like Min, but I felt sad she never seemed to do anything but work. I didn't do anything else either, but I was used to it. And I was younger.

You know, Mrs. Flohr treasured green grass so much that

you had to walk a different way every time you went to any of those buildings outside, so you wouldn't make a path.

When I heard she had died of cancer, I cried, not so much because she died, but because she hardly ever had any fun. Just hard work all the time.

I was luckier, I had some time off. Like when I was allowed to go to a pavilion for an amateur contest. I sang "The Glory of Love" and "Twilight on the Trail" and won five dollars. I was so proud—but it was just enough to pay for gasoline and beer for my brother. Never mind . . . I had won. I *sang* and they *liked* it. It all still echoes down the years: "You've got to give a little, take a little, and let your poor heart break a little. That's the story of—that's the glory of—love."

I won a special prize for interpretation. People understood that I understood the words. Because it touched my heart, it touched their hearts. Either I understood it or I wouldn't sing it.


Back to school, which was always fun for me. I was pretty good at it, except in a few things like Home Economics. I chose the most difficult thing to sew out of the most difficult fabric—a silk pongée brassiere. Not because I wanted to show off but because I wanted a silk brassiere. As I would in later newlywed years, I wanted a sheer black negligee, and, using no pattern, I wound up with a dozen sheer black potholders. Reading directions is very important, yes, indeed. My brassiere was held up to the class to show what *not* to do.

Mostly I got along fine with my classmates and teachers. I always remember a poem written, I think, by my classmate George Brenner, who's at least a physicist by now: "He who sitteth upon a pin/may not see the point, but/he will get it in the end."

For years I thought that the wittiest saying, but it's like the Katzenjammer Kids. For years I never liked them at all, but I would read them religiously every Sunday, until one day I revolted. I put the paper down and declared, "I don't have to read them any more." That was that, and I didn't. I had begun to free my own mind, which is the way it goes . . . some of us just go along believing what we read in the papers, in a book or a magazine until that marvelous day people stop intimidating us—or should I say we refuse to let them intimidate us?—and we think and do things on our own.

The teen years went by so fast . . . I had ping-pong photos taken in a little booth like everybody else and hoped some unknown lover would want one. They were terrible—the ping-pongs, that is. I don't remember any lovers—just friends, like the Joos brothers. One of the Joos brothers used to ride by the depot on a horse and the other went to Valley City College. The college boy played the trumpet and had the most beautiful eyelashes I ever had seen.

When I was singing at KOVC in Valley City, suddenly all the fellows I saw were particularly good looking, starting with Doc Haines, but I wouldn't let them know it, not on your life. They would look in the studio windows, and I felt like Clara Bow. You know, the "It" girl.

Then, the summer when I was washing dishes in a Jamestown restaurant, I met Red Homuth. He was easily the best looking thing I'd seen, *and* he was an older man—well, he was the captain of the football team. Red curly hair, blue eyes, freckles and a great smile.

He liked me, I liked him. One night when I was very anxious to see my Dad in Wimbledon, Red offered to drive me to see him.

We arrived in Wimbledon going at a pretty good clip in his mother's car. The world was getting better all the time

66

. . . I rarely saw Min now, which was the best thing that could happen. Plus, here I was, going someplace with my *boyfriend.*

Daddy was so glad to see me and seemed to like Red . . . I think he realized it wasn't serious. When it began getting dark, Red, who had to get up early for his job driving the truck for the Nash Coffee Company, started sending out hints about getting on.

As we started back to Jamestown, I said to him, "Let me drive. I *did* learn, you know, and you can get some sleep."

Red hedged a bit, then said, "Well, I don't know about that, this is my mother's car, are you sure you can handle it?"

"Sure," said I. "It's nearly straight all the way and probably no cars."

"Okay, Norma, you're on," he said as he stopped the car, slipped over to the side, reached over me and opened the door.

I jumped out and ran around the car with the gravel crunching around my shoes. It got dark in a hurry out there. As far as you could see, there wasn't a light or a thing in sight. Dark, dark, flat prairie.

After an embarrassing, jerky start, we got underway and, as soon as he felt more or less safe that I could drive, he leaned his handsome red curly head back on the seat and went to sleep.

I don't know how familiar you might be with livestock signs in the country: from out of nowhere, not necessarily at a crossroad, in fact probably not, a sign will suddenly appear with the message . . . "Warning. Livestock Crossing. Cattle Crossing. Watch for Horses."

In the pitch dark, what did that mean? Before I had time to wonder any more, a herd of horses came out of the ditch right in front of us. I think I saw eyes glowing, but I'm *sure* I've never heard such a clatter and bang and crash. One went right over the top, a couple crashed into the front and off the sides of the car, hooves banging. The fenders wound up somewhere behind the car. The headlights of course were now out, had gone flying off, and the awful crunch we heard was the engine being shoved up *between* us in the front seat. Gradually, other things dropped off the car. Followed by an unearthly silence.

Finally I said, "Well . . . I guess I'd better squeeze out of here and see what I did."

Red gave a big sigh. "Don't bother. I don't have to get out to know what you've done."

It was hard to believe that neither of us was hurt, but somehow our budding romance wilted right there as we waited for a car to come by. One horse was killed, the one that went right over the top.

I didn't see Red for a long time after that, but school went on. Halls were scrubbed, blackboards were washed, I kept the depot clean, helped Daddy and hitchhiked to Valley City to sing with Doc and at KOVC. Doc was so nice and my crush on him was just as strong as ever. I also had the co-lead with Carl Erickson in the high school play. We thought we were wonderful, but I'm not so sure anymore. Actually, I'm sure Dorothy Trangsrudd was best of all, but who wanted to admit it at the time?

After graduation I couldn't *wait* to get out in the world. I kissed Daddy, took my meager belongings and left for Jamestown again and my first very own residence.

It was the corner of a basement with a bed and an orange crate, but it was clean and safe. The only problem was knowing when to get up for my new job as relief girl in the Gladstone Hotel Coffee Shop. In the darkness of the basement, I could have slept my life away until the people who owned the house gave me an alarm clock.

The excitement at the hotel . . . the heat and bustle of the kitchen, the flour rolls that would come sliding out of the hot ovens, the big chef Tony barking orders, the waitresses smoking cigarettes on their "breaks." When the waitresses went back on duty, they all left their cigarettes in a heavy plate, and the stale smoke would continue to curl up into the empty air. Meanwhile, I ran in and out of the kitchen acting like I was a real waitress.

Which was how I met Bill Sawyer. He had been with the Cleveland Indians for a while, but now they'd farmed him out to the Fargo-Moorehead Twins. Bill was the first big brother in the outside world I ever had. He was the opposite of a wolf. Not only a nice guy but a smart one. He eventually became a professor at Western Reserve University and gave me all sorts of good advice.

He heard me on radio station KRMC in Jamestown, which just happened to be in the Gladstone Hotel. When the team would come in for coffee, they would tease me, and I guess Bill felt sorry for me. Anyway, he came over to the counter and asked if it would be all right if he wrote me a letter. It was the first time anybody had ever asked me that. Fact was, I had never had any requests for my permission for anything in my life. I thought it was very nice of him, and the letters turned out to be full of platonic advice—what books to read, be careful about going out with strange men . . . Like an older brother.

He even arranged an audition for me at WDAY, *the* station in Fargo, and then drove me there—nearly a hundred miles (a long trip at that time). Well, here I was going with at least a comparative stranger and I was nervous. After all, we were going to have to stay overnight, but as it turned out we stayed in separate rooms at the hotel.

He took me to the radio station, and suddenly we were out in the waiting room. Through the glass door I could see the head man, Ken Kennedy, a tall man with reddish hair and blue eyes, with a dimple in his chin.

Bill literally had to shove me toward the door. I was just standing there, rigid. "Come on, Norma," he said. "You've come all this way, you're going *in* there. *Now.*"

69

And somehow I did. After all, here was my big chance. Ken Kennedy brought in a pianist, I sang "These Foolish Things" for him, and he put me on the air that afternoon.

"You have to change your name," he said. "Norma Egstrom . . . it doesn't sound right. Ladies and gentlemen, Miss Norma Egstrom? No, won't do at all. Let me see. You look like a Peggy. Peggy Lynn. No—Peggy Lee. That's *it!* Ladies and gentlemen, Miss Peggy Lee." I was dizzy with excitement. I sang, and they *liked* it, and I had a new name . . . too much . . .

So back to Jamestown and a brief, sweet-sad farewell to all my new friends, including the gruff old chef who held me on his lap. "Yah . . . I knew our girl vud make it big. You don't forget and you stay like you are, so schweet und nize."

When I arrived in Fargo, I thought it was the biggest city in the world. The main street, of course, was called Broadway, and I promptly walked up and down to the end of the street (which, naturally, was called Lower Broadway).

Finally I saw a sign, "Hotel—Vacancy—$2 and Up." Which really was more than I could afford, but I decided it was worth trying for a few days. I walked up a flight of steps to the desk in the lobby, where the clerk was not smiling.

"May I please have a room?"

"No vacancy."

"But your sign said—"

"*I* said no vacancy."

Later I would learn it was what was quaintly referred to as a house of ill repute.

That wasn't the career I had in mind.

Then I heard of a girls' rooming house at 606 Fourth Street, North. The price was right, so I moved in and promptly made friends with the other girls. Life at 606 was so different from anything I'd ever known. Most of all, it was exciting, being on my own. My roommate's name was Pinky. She was funny and fun, but also responsible for my oversleeping for one of my three or four jobs. Pinky had left a note saying, "When you hear the alarm clock out in the hall, it will be time to get up." Out in the hall? I never figured that one out.

My schedule went something like this: around five A.M. I would return home from Regan's Bakery, where I worked from four P.M. to four A.M. for thirty-five cents an hour. Slicing and wrapping bread became a game to me. I'd do it all in rhythm and run for the cold shower to wake me up when I got tired. Once I got caught in the conveyer belt; it ripped my uniform right off and tried to wrap it. I would sleep until nine A.M., then into the shower, dress and rush to WDAY to rehearse and perform on the Noonday Variety Show for one dollar and fifty cents a show. When I was lucky, Ken would arrange for me to earn another fifty cents a line reading commercials for the big controversy over open-toed versus closed-toed shoes.

And there was a short stint in a Greek restaurant as a waitress . . . I always seemed to "flunk" waitress . . . and I wrote commercials for a local jeweler about love and blue-white diamonds. I also played the role of "Freckled Face Gertie" on the Hayloft Jamboree with Mary Lou, Jeanne Alm, Ken Kennedy and Howard Nelson, and occasionally sang with Lem Hawkins and the Georgie Porgie Breakfast Food Boys. Lem wanted to me to sing "Sweet Violets," but I drew the line there . . . During my spare time (ha!) I did some filing at WDAY, which was how I found out about the good composers and lyricists—Jerome Kern, Otto Harbach, Cole Porter, Rodgers and Hart, Gershwin, Johnny Mercer, Harold Arlen. The giants, and pure gold to a girl just discovering them.

*   *   *

One day out of the blue I received a letter from Gladys Rasmussen telling me how beautiful California was. I was making conversation with my landladies at the time . . . "I might go to California," I said with heavy nonchalance. It sounded important, at least to me, and I very seldom had anything important to say. They said, "Really? When?" I said, "Oh, I don't know, I have to . . ." and then it frightened me because I didn't *really* know whether or not I was going to California. I said I had to get my father's permission for anything, but I somehow felt he would say no because California was like going to the moon, or at least to Australia.

He surprised me, though, and not only gave his permission and blessing but also gave me a railroad pass. My landladies and all the girls at the rooming house gave me a farewell party, and then, of course, I *had* to leave, and I sent a telegram to Gladys telling her when I would arrive. Scared to death.


No sooner had the conductor called out "all aboard" than a man, your typical lecher, found a way to sit next to me, then proceeded to give me little touches and pats. I was the proverbial babe in the woods, only seventeen, and this was my first big trip. I just didn't know how to handle the situation.

Lucky for me there was this woman wearing an electric blue dress, and I'll never forget her. She was fairly large and in her electric blue dress she was a presence that lit up the whole car. She noticed the hanky-panky going on and came right over to me. "I'll sit by you," she said.

I was in the middle like a sandwich, squeezed in between the lech and the lady. She kept poking me with her elbow, the kind of pokes people give you when they want you to notice something, but they always poke a little harder than they need to. After a while I wasn't sure which I disliked more—the pats or the pokes.

This situation went on until we got to Salt Lake City, where we all got off; there was to be a six-hour layover. The lady turned out to be my lifesaver. She took me to the home of some Mormons, who let me have a nice soak in the bathtub, gave me a lovely meal and took me sightseeing. I saw the Mormon Tabernacle and heard the pipe organ; I was enthralled. When I left, they said, "Now, dear, if you have any trouble getting work or anything in California, you just come back here to us, and we'll take care of you." I've never forgotten them. When we got back on the train, the man had some gold nuggets he kept showing me. Fool's gold, no doubt . . .

Finally, after God knows how many days, we arrived in California, and there on the platform was Gladys Rasmussen with a small welcoming party. The first sight they showed me was Hollywood Boulevard, which at that time was beautifully clean, polished as someone's marble living room. (I have a star there somewhere now.) Then they took me to have a cheeseburger . . . I had never heard of one! All of this was leading up to seeing the Pacific Ocean for the first time, the "Milkman's Matinee" playing on the radio while we drove. I can tell you I've never had a better cheeseburger, the ocean has never looked so big, and the Hollywood streets have surely never looked so clean.

Having sold my graduation watch to my landladies in Fargo for thirty dollars, by the time I arrived in California, I had only eighteen dollars left. My friend Gladys Rasmussen had even less. There had been a serious flood in Los Angeles, and the restaurant where she worked as a cashier, the Circus Cafe, had been flooded, so she was out of work and broke.

I moved into Gladys' rooming house without the landlord's permission, and we would sneak out of there at seven in the morning so we wouldn't be caught . . . she was behind

73

on the rent. Obviously, we had to do some creative thinking until we could pay. We broke the money down so we could each have twenty-five cents a day for the "big little rib steak" at the Cunningham Diner, plus twenty cents apiece each day for streetcar fare. All this would enable us to get to the employment offices in downtown Los Angeles, where we would sit for hours and watch the stream of people going in and out—most of them with jobs.

I looked much younger than my age and didn't seem to qualify for anything they had to offer, or so *they* thought. When our funds hit an all time low, we had one depleted jar of Laura Scudders peanut butter and one loaf of bread between us, I suddenly lost my shyness, walked up to the desk and said, "I can do any job you have here." The lady said there was one left, but it was in Balboa. Could I get there? "Yes, I could." I could also go to the moon. Gladys had to stay in Hollywood to guard our room and clothes, and I hitchhiked to Balboa.

The job turned out to be short-order cook and waitress, but only during the time the students were in Balboa for Easter break. When I arrived at Harry's Cafe, he said, "Have you had any experience?" I decided to be totally honest. "No, but I learn fast." (Later he told me he decided to give me the job because I was honest.) He also found a place for me, at a Mr. Anderson's, who had rows of little yellow cabins—kind of enlarged cabanas.

Much too soon the Easter break was over, and since I had been making all of nine dollars a week, there wasn't much left. I discovered many other teenagers were in the same position but didn't have as much experience with survival as I did, and which I put to good use making a run every day to get fish, mostly barracuda from the fishing boats, as well as day-old bread from a bakery, oranges that a nice man let me pick from his trees, and day-old milk from a dairy.

I started this life story talking about overcoming adver-

74

sity because from the tenderest age it was, and remains, a central theme in my life. From getting a song recorded against prevailing wisdom to a literal fight for survival as a pre-teen and teenager has a connecting link. Adversity also links up people. We had a grand ambition to pool our resources, buy an old shell of a boat and go out and find abalone and make those ornaments and pins that said "Mother Dear" and other smart sayings. We didn't get the boat, let alone the abalone, and I'm just as glad because, frankly, I never did like those pins that said "Mother Dear." Who's supposed to wear them?

Mr. Anderson came to the rescue again. He also owned the FunZone and helped me get work there as a barker at a dollar a day, if it didn't rain, which it did a lot. A shy kid barker was what I was, and people seemed to get a kick out of that; I even developed a regular clientele.

The balloon stand had me saying, "Three for a dime; you break one, you win." The "Hit the Wino with the Baseball" was almost my downfall because I felt so sorry for that man. In carnival language he was known as a "geek," a man who has gone way beyond caring any more and probably doesn't know where or even what he is. People would throw the baseball, which would trigger the mechanism to dump him in the water, then the poor old soul would crawl out and get back on his perch. I never even knew his name, and he didn't care.

There was also an old lion tamer who must have done very well because he owned the Ferris wheel and merry-go-round. Everyone had long since stopped caring about his scars, but I was new and fascinated by them. It paid off, because every time I would let him show me his scars and tell me how he got them he would let me ride on the merry-go-round or Ferris wheel for free. The scars were his identity, and he appreciated somebody's caring.

Sometimes, when I was off work, I would be a shill for

the "Hit the Ducks on the Treadmill" stand. I was pretty good with a slingshot, so I could gather a crowd. They didn't pay me any money but did give me a BIG plaster cat that I was very proud of, even though I wasn't exactly sure what to do with it. Never mind, it was my first trophy.

Two guitarists, nephews of one of the concessionaires, told me they couldn't figure out what I was doing there, I sure didn't look or sound like a barker. They would come to my stand and talk to me about how I got the job, where I was from, where I had worked. When I told them I had been a singer at the radio station, they told me to meet them out on the pier and they would bring their guitars so I could sing. I was thrilled. I hadn't sung for quite a while.

I was pretty sure they thought I would sing some cowboy song like "Bury Me Not on the Lone Prairie" or some such, but when I met them on the pier and they asked what did I want to sing, I said " 'The Man I Love' in A-flat." They seemed absolutely bowled over that I knew the key. In Jamestown and Fargo I had learned my range from the accompanists, and when I started to sing, they said, "Well, you shouldn't be here," and they talked me into hitchhiking back to Hollywood and auditioning at the Jade.


A not so funny thing happened on my way to the Jade. My shoe was coming loose, as it had been all the way up Hollywood Boulevard. I wore a beige pantsuit made of hopsacking that originally had a large, colorful silk sash. The tops of my beach shoes had worn and pulled away from the cork soles, and there was no money for new ones. I had cut a piece from the sash and sewed it, firmly I thought, to the cork sole. It did last until I started walking toward Highland Avenue, then suddenly one shoe started flapping and the other looked as though it would go any minute and I'd be back to barefoot.

Fortunately, I had tucked a large safety pin in my bag. I

76

raised one foot up on the mailbox and just barely succeeded in pinning the top to the bottom. It only lasted for a couple of blocks, but by then I was there. At the Jade. My Mecca.

Barefoot, I went in and auditioned for Chuck Barclay, the master of ceremonies, who, thank God, hired me. I literally had spent my last dime on a Coca-Cola.

In 1937 the Great Depression was still very much on. Outside and up the boulevard, you could buy a hot dog a mile long for ten cents—actually, it was a foot long but, even so, that was a lot of hot dog for ten cents, and, with the sauerkraut, you could call it a meal, which I did.

Inside the Jade Room, the darkness and the Oriental decor, the smell of the gardenias and Chinese food, the waitresses in their satin coats and satin pants moving silently about on the thick carpet, carrying cooling drinks, egg rolls and butterfly shrimp, created an air of mystery . . . especially for a seventeen-year-old girl from North Dakota.

There was an enormous carved dragon that formed the bar, where you might see a movie star, a G-man or someone looking for a tourist he could "roll." I was to learn that expression meant to relieve someone of their bankroll, or at least I thought that was what it meant. You don't soon forget seeing a confused, stumbling man weaving out the door into the night, wondering where his money had gone.

The Jade also had a good reputation for hiring out-of-work entertainers for very little money. People like Hal March, of *$64,000 Question* fame, who was there for a little while. Louis DeProng, long-time choreographer and dance director at 20th Century-Fox, the Brown Sisters of the original "Marie" fame (before Jack Leonard made it so famous with Tommy Dorsey), Lillian Randolph from "The Great Gildersleeve" show, Phil Moore, who later became well-known as a vocal coach and a bass player, and who had kind brown eyes and said "swell" a lot, and, of course, Peggy Lee, star of stage, screen and radio . . . Oh yes—and Jabuti—who

77

had magnificent long red hair, which she used to great advantage as she bumped and ground her near-perfect body over a slide trombone while she played "Wang Wang Blues" and thereby covered an enormous nose and somewhat prominent teeth. Between shows she read big thick books. An intellectual, I figured. Good folks, all of them. I remember, for example, how Louis DaProng would take pity on me and dance an extra set so I could sit one out when the hour got very late and eat some Chinese food before the long walk home.

Larry Potter, owner of the Jade, smiled more than most people who have the troubles of a club owner. I could only guess he was in his forties. I was sure, though, that he adored his pretty blonde wife, Sue, and it certainly seemed the feeling was mutual. He thought it was charming, or so he said, the way I clenched my fists and left my thumbs stuck up in the air when I sang. Obviously, though, something had to be done about my wardrobe, so Larry took me to the May Company basement to buy a gown, a nice simple one.

And there was Mary Norman, a regular singer at the Jade, who not only gave me a magnificent gown but taught me how to apply makeup and even helped me select my songs. I've always felt bad that suddenly Mary wasn't there, and I was. I'm not sure there was any competition, but you can see how I'd feel that I'd taken her place without even trying. Her red pleated gown was left behind, and I can only hope Mary went on to something better. She deserved it.

Irene was my guardian. She watched me very closely if she saw me sitting with someone while she waited tables. If they offered me a drink, Irene gave me orange juice.

Chuck Barclay, the master of ceremonies who hired me, was tall and terribly handsome, *and* the greatest big brother anyone could have. Well, second greatest.

One evening Larry Potter, the owner, was sitting with a gentleman I had never seen before—at least, he wasn't a regular customer. He requested that I sit with them and then offered to drive me home. I still can't believe this myself, I was so naïve, but to me it seemed only a kind gesture. Also, the fact that he was sitting with Mr. Potter seemed a sort of guarantee. Whatever, I was lulled into thinking it would be all right.

Until, that is, after I was tucked securely in the car and he started driving in the wrong direction. Even I could tell that.

"This is not the right direction . . ."

"Oh, I just wanted to get something to eat."

"I'm not a bit hungry. Would you mind just dropping me at home first?"

"Come along, I don't want to eat alone."

Instinct told me that he was not taking me home. It had to be an instinct, I didn't seem to have much intelligence going for me. I started to pray.

Somewhere in downtown Los Angeles, he stopped in front of a shabby-looking club. He knocked and actually looked through a peephole. Inside there were several people sitting in a booth, and they all seemed to know this man who had brought me. (I can't remember his name. Let's call him Sam Banks.)

Everyone was drinking, especially Sam. I found myself in the back of a booth, sandwiched between two men. The women were gathered around Sam. The man on my left tried to make a little conversation, but I was too frightened to talk and too busy praying. He seemed to understand. We both watched Sam getting drunker by the minute, which this man seemed to think was a little unusual. Suddenly he whispered to me, "I'm going to get you out of here. Follow me, stick close."

We scooted out of the booth, and Sam suddenly loomed up in front of my friend. There was a terrible fight, and, fortunately for me, my new friend won. The next minute we were rushing out of the club and running for his car.

When we were safely out of the area and he was breathing a little more easily, he said, "Look, you don't know what you just got away from, but I'm going to tell you. I don't know why I should do this, but you remind me of my little sister. *You,* young lady, were headed for white slavery, and nobody would have heard from you again. Nobody."

I started to cry, he patted my shoulder and said he was now going to take me home. "By the way, what's the address?" I mumbled the address on Gower. "Promise me you'll never get yourself in a mess like this again. Okay? I mean you're really lucky. You kids running around here trying to be a star . . . *promise* me?"

"I promise, I don't want to be a star," I said obediently. And at that moment I guess I meant it.

Chuck Barclay was shocked to hear what had happened, and he and Bob the bartender, Paul the bar boy, Irene my guardian, Chuck and Carol, Larry and Sue all doubled their security.

Still, there was one man who came in night after night, and I could tell he was watching me, that he seemed to like me, but I was too frightened from the other experience to respond. Then there came a night when *he* asked if he could drive me home. *No.* I wouldn't take that chance again.

"Why not," he said. "I'm really pretty harmless."

"Well, I don't really know you—"

"If I get Chuck Barclay to chaperone us, will you let me drive you home?"

I said I guessed that would be all right, and it was.

In fact, we would become good friends. When I saw him again during World War Two, he was wearing a sailor suit, and shortly thereafter he went to sea. Years later, in the late forties, I was sitting in the assembly at Westlake School for Girls and heard a friendly voice next to me saying, "Peggy, I *wondered* when I'd see you again. It seems my daughter is in your daughter Nicki's class."

80

Good lord, what goes around does, indeed, come around. No romance would bud, but I did ask him why he had seemed so mysterious those many years ago. He said, "I was a G-man."

Still mysterious, I thought, and we left it at that.


I used to go from our new rooming house on Gower to the clinic on the corner of Gower and Hollywood Boulevard, where they kept telling me how bad my throat was. It seems they were right, because one night I fainted and had to be taken to the Hollywood Presbyterian Hospital in a squad car. The doctor thought I should go home. "You should have surgery, and you need to be near your family."

He probably had a good idea, though I was reluctant to admit it. Among other things, two dollars a night didn't exactly add up to luxurious living. My walk back-and-forth from Gower to Highland, which gave me a three-mile stretch each night, wasn't too good for me. There was a community kitchen in the rooming house, and sometimes one of the other hungry tenants would share a little of our food . . . All of which added up to poor nutrition, and the "after-hours" was not good for my fragile condition.

Still, I resisted until the day I almost lost it in the waves. Normally a very good swimmer, I got caught in a riptide. I was wearing one of those big housecoats and playing with the waves. Gladys and I would run out with them and run back in again. This time she was ahead of me and had already run back when the riptide—one of those really dangerous waves—came and filled my housecoat with sand and swept me way out. I never would have believed it would take me out so far, and I almost drowned.

After that brush with death, I finally wrote to my sisters. I had not told them where I was because I wanted to wait until I was more successful. But I finally realized how close that white-slavery experience and this near-drowning came to making me a statistic, and for my family a "missing person." Almost immediately, Sweeney, my first boyfriend at home, came right out and got me . . . I guess he was in touch with my sisters. Sweeney, the *college* student, should have been a welcome sight with his dark-brown wavy hair, dazzling blue-gray eyes and gorgeous perfect teeth that actually sparkled when he smiled. (Sweeney also worked in the local movie house, first as an usher and then as the manager.) Yes, Sweeney should have been treated like a godsend, but all the way back to North Dakota, to Hillsboro, I hardly spoke to Sweeney. Sure, my throat hurt, but I guess my pride hurt even more.

Dr. Cuthbert, a tall, thin, aristocratic-looking Englishman, the man who would operate on my throat, was like a godfather to our family.

My sister Marianne, ill with undulant fever, had bravely been trying to take care of our sister Della, who was now divorced, and Tyke, as we called Della's little son Paul. Also our brother Clair and the nicest "stray" I ever met, Ossie Hovde, plus a mixed-breed dog named Piggie, presumably after the one who went to market.

Now I was to find them in a tiny house in Hillsboro, N.D. I couldn't bear to see them struggling along this way, even though I wasn't in very good shape myself, but in my daydreams . . . I specialized in daydreams . . . I would drive up in a big car loaded with gifts for everyone . . . "For me?" they would say. "Yes, and there's *lots* more," I would say. (It would take years to turn those dreams to reality, but it did happen.)

Since Nortonville, I hadn't seen them for a long time except for a couple of very short visits. Every meal was an adventure—what was it going to be and how were we going to get it—but we loved each other, and that made up for a lot, including a meager diet.

My memory . . . my impression . . . about Hillsboro was that it was a small town that looked all gray to me. Outstanding to me were Doctor Cuthbert's office, and the way people who saw each other quite often would dress up for each other in clean overalls for a Saturday night when they came in to get grocery staples and maybe a beer. The Scandinavians would greet each other with great good humor . . . "Oh, are yo-o-o-o in town today to-o-o-o?" with a pronounced accent.

Also memorable was a forty-year-old lady named Frances, who skipped up and down her backyard saying, "I'll bet you can't do this when you're forty!" (Well, Frances, I vowed to show you, and, when I was forty, I was flying and dancing all over the world just for starters. Our whole attitude about age changes as the years go by, doesn't it? I never even think of it unless I'm forced to, which I'm convinced is a secret of longevity. It's just *now* all the time.)

While I was pondering the challenge of Frances, Dr. Cuthbert was filling me with something to coagulate my blood in preparation for the throat surgery. My blood was too thin from malnutrition in California, and I was now finally having a tonsillectomy. What followed was a black comedy. The first surgery, performed in the doctor's office, was not a success, and after bringing me home (there was no hospital), he rushed back on an emergency basis and tried holding clamps in my throat, leaning over the bed, while the dog Piggie was chewing on his leg, trying to protect me.

He had to give it up and prop me up in the back seat of his car, with a large pan in my lap, my sister Della bug-eyed and pale with fright. He drove as fast as he could from Hillsboro to Grand Forks to the Deaconess Hospital. Fortunately, he had called in advance and they were prepared for surgery to stop the hemorrhaging. While I was given transfusions,

Della kept saying, "You look like you're made of wax." I tried to assure her it wasn't so.

While recuperating, like most people, I did a lot of thinking about my family and life in general. It was one of those bitter cold times in Grand Forks, and, as I looked out the window at the frozen chunks of slush sprinkled with fresh snow, I watched a sparrow hop around chirping happily as he pecked away at some horse manure. I remember thinking, "If that little sparrow can make it, I can make it too." I started to get well after that and to plan how to move my little family back to Fargo.

Back in Fargo, I reestablished my contacts at WDAY and, with Ken Kennedy's help, talked to the Powers family, the owners of the Powers Hotel and Coffee Shop. There hadn't been live entertainment in Fargo, perhaps not anywhere in North Dakota, but there was a good organist named Lloyd Collins, who played up on a little riser in the Coffee Shop, and I was soon up there with him.

The Powers was considered *the* hotel in Fargo, and the Coffee Shop was the favored spot of the college students. We were soon jammed to the rafters, and I answered as many as ninety or one hundred requests during an evening, especially for "The Music Goes 'Round and 'Round" and "Deep in a Dream."

Lloyd Collins had boned up on the songs of the favorite composers I mentioned earlier, plus Johnny Mercer, who not only was a favorite lyricist ("I Thought About You") but later became my mentor when I began writing songs.

My salary was $15 a week for six days plus a Sunday matinee performance of semi-classical songs such as "Would God I Were a Tender Apple Blossom" and Tom Powers' favorite, "I'll Take You Home Again, Kathleen." I took her home quite a few times . . .

84

By this time I had found the Hogan Apartments, within walking distance of WDAY and just down the street from the Powers Coffee Shop. Oh happy day, when I sent for the family in Hillsboro! An inventive tribe, we were, and with paint and brush, needle and thread, polish and shine, we made the best of our apartment in a burned-out building. We walked very carefully over some planks that were laid across from one fire escape to another.

We had all sorts of guests: doctors, lawyers, day workers, college students, newspaper people, ice skaters. I used to keep a guest book until it got me in trouble with my boy-friends. We celebrated one birthday for three full days. I recall Bob Donahue, who worked at the Fargo Forum, kept getting back in line for a birthday kiss.

There was my friend Johnny Quam, who was *really* important in my life. Not just because I liked him, but also because he worked in a dry-cleaning shop and could keep my "other dress" clean. Seriously, I really did like Johnny, and, when he bought tickets for GONE WITH THE WIND, I thought we had both hit the big time. I planned what I was going to wear just as though I had a choice. We also celebrated our first Christmas together since the house burned down in Jamestown.

With my puny earnings, every once in a while I would fall behind in the rent and would go downstairs to see Mrs. Hogan and play a schottische for her on the piano. She was mad for schottisches and would extend the rent time.

Meanwhile, we were doing so well at the Powers that our competition, Le Chateau, had to import a singer from Minneapolis! Competition or not, she turned out to be one of the best friends I have ever had in life, and I'm happy that I could do her a good turn by introducing her to Leonard Feather, the noted jazz critic. They are still happily married.

I thought Jane Feather was the cat's pajamas. Still do.

85

## MISS PEGGY LEE

*  *  *

I met Janie the first time in Grand Forks at the Belmont Cafe. She was so pretty and had the biggest soft brown eyes. She was, she says now, sizing me up, and I was probably doing the same.

My fans—bless them—tended to make remarks like, "Well, she didn't have near the people you had" or "She's okay, but I like your singing better . . ." Secretly, I enjoyed that a little, but that's only human, isn't it?

I *loved* Janie's clothes. I was still operating on "that one" and "the other one." She knew I was working almost around the clock and that my wardrobe didn't exactly extend all the way around, so that lady just out and out said, "Would you like to borrow some of my clothes?" I had never even *heard* of such a thing, and I still feel the rush of gratitude about that moment.

Jane and I kept sending customers to each other, thereby greatly increasing the night life in Fargo—to the benefit of both Le Chateau and the Powers Coffee Shop.

It was so good to have a friend I could share my troubles with. Trying to support my family wasn't too easy. Marianne kept house and cooked the meals while Della read book after book. Clair couldn't seem to find employment. Once in a while he and his friend Murphy could find a bit of Sunnybrook and came home with fumes of whiskey trailing.

But fifteen dollars a week was not exactly adequate to feed six people—Della, Tyke, Clair, Marianne, Ossie Hovde and myself. Still, I was grateful for working, and I did enjoy singing, never mind the pay.

Sidelights: one night on a bet I chewed five packs of Beeman's Pepsin chewing gum (because, up to then, it was my favorite flavor) to win a carton of "tailor made" cigarettes for Della and Clair. My jaws ached for days and days . . . One of my favorite events was when we would all go on a picnic.

86

To fill the basket full of potato salad—homemade of course—dill pickles, bologna sandwiches, fried chicken, cookies or cake, watermelon and lemonade and go down by the river and spread out the picnic. Cucumbers and onions—oh yes, the smells of summer . . .

When Janie went back to Minneapolis, I really missed her, but we kept writing letters, and one day Ken Kennedy said, "I think I can get you a job with my cousin, Sev Olson, in Minneapolis. Would you like that?" *Would I like that?* Except for one thing, the notion of leaving my family behind. It had to be done sometime, I knew, but I cried for weeks. My family was pretty upset too, except Marianne, who always understood everything. She got herself a job working for a doctor, and I left for Minneapolis.

I auditioned for Sev Olson, singing "Body and Soul." I suspect he and Ken had it all set, but, anyway, first thing I knew, I was living in the Radison Hotel, which was merely heaven to me. When I'd plow around in those thick carpets, I'd just lose my appetite from being overcome by the grandeur.

I fell in love with Sev Olson. He was handsome and kind and funny; I just couldn't help it. There was no hope for it right from the start. He was married. I was practically dizzy just being around him, and he, unfortunately, shared my feelings. He would break into hives. I knew I was in deep water now and kept wondering what I would do to get away. Not that I wanted to . . . The fellows in the band were all so nice. Willy Peterson, Max, Nooky Norgaard—and all of them guessed what was happening, I'm sure, but they were as discreet as possible. They were all university students, as was Sev, but, hands down, he was my knight in shining armor.

I talked to Jane and to Jane's mother, Tody, about it. They were both fond of Sev and didn't quite know how to advise me, so I spent the next few months between pleasure and pain, until Will Osborne came to town with his orchestra.

And then I made my decision. It really hurt me to do it, but one night I couldn't stand it any longer and decided this was it. I had auditioned for Will, just in case, singing "I Can't Give You Anything But Love," and he said that I had the job.

So I told Sev.

He brought his wife Martie down to where we were playing, and we all wound up crying as they told me she was willing to give him up. But deep inside I still knew it was wrong to continue with the relationship, and so I stuck to my guns and managed to tell them I would be leaving in the morning. I didn't dare let any time lapse. He could so easily have talked me out of it. (I'm glad to know that they are still together.)

The next day I set out with a trombone player and his wife in their car, the back seat full of musical instruments, mostly his trombones, and there I was in the middle again, this time with a heater blowing up in my face.

As we drove along, I told them the story about the owner of the Marigold Ballroom and how he was always coming up to Sev on the bandstand and telling him to play something fast. One time Sev said, "We just played something fast," to which the owner replied, "well, that's not fast *enough*. You've got to remember, Sev, this is a big ballroom and by the time it gets to the other end it's too darn slow." A real genius, obviously.

Finally we got to St. Louis, and located the Fox Theatre, which was enormous and beautiful. Our booking there extended into the new year, and, on New Year's Eve just before they called "half hour," all the lights went out and the box office was robbed. We were calling to each other from floor to floor, "Do you have any candles? Do you have any extra candles?" We didn't have any electricity for the spotlights. We all tried to put our makeup on by the light of matches, flashlights and candles and then walked downstairs in the dark, trying to keep track of which floor we were on. For some reason none of us thought about any danger—an armed robbery or guns or anything of the sort—we just carried on, showbiz, you know, and the audience was wonderful, joining in to help us save the day.

So things were going along pretty well . . . until one morning I felt a lump in my throat and promptly went to a doctor and had the nerve to ask him if he could excise it then and there. Dr. Brown actually tried, but he finally gave up and told me to come back for proper surgery the next day.

I was trying to be so brave that I overdid it. It didn't strike me as odd then, but it does now. There I was alone in that operating room with the anesthesiologist and I asked, "Could I have gas instead of ether? Ether makes me so sick." (I was being so cool, so sophisticated.) He didn't answer. I tried it again. He was gathering his implements and seemed annoyed. This time he walked over to me and quite deliberately pushed me down on the table. I had been sitting there casually swinging my legs to show him I wasn't afraid. Now there was no more pretense. He fastened the straps, put the ether cone over my nose and mouth and began pouring, not dripping, the ether onto the gauze. I was fighting to stay conscious as I felt the ether dribbling down the side of my face.

"Where are they?" I screamed silently, "where is Doctor Brown?" I frantically wiggled my fingers to show them I was awake. I was hearing those weird flapping sounds again, coming from inside my head, and I continued to fight to stay awake. Finally, I heard them coming in the door . . .

Before I opened my eyes, I kept pulling at my mouth, and Max Schall, the band manager, was saying, "Don't pull those, Peggy, they're stitches . . . You've had a little accident . . ."

I certainly *had.* By the time the ether wore off, I was

asking for a mirror and not getting one. Finally, I remembered my purse was in the drawer next to me. The mirror revealed a scary sight: my nose was swollen, the front teeth had been broken off and gone through my lower lip, and somehow I had managed to cut my tongue. With a strange kind of speech caused by the stitches in my tongue and lip, I was calling out, "Oook what ey id to me . . ."

A nurse came in, thought I'd been in a car accident, and, after patting me, walked out the door.

Finally, Max came back and explained it all. It seemed that when they were moving me from the table to the cart, they dropped me on the hard floor—I think it was marble tile—and I landed on my face.

The nuns came to visit me and told me the hospital was built by charity, and I shouldn't punish the hospital for the actions of one man who obviously was not well. I was glad to be alive, so I signed away my rights although I wasn't of age. Actually, I'm glad I signed, although it's cost me a bundle since then, keeping up repairs.

After Dr. Brown arranged for a dentist to cap my teeth and I felt well enough, Max Schall, the band manager, Hank, the pianist, and I all took off for California by car, Will Osborne's band having broken up.


California.

We finally made it all the way after a frightening experience in the mountains just outside of Globe, New Mexico . . . There was a stretch of new road that, after a pouring rain, was a stretch of mud, and we were stuck in it with hundreds of other cars for hours until a tow truck managed to pull us out car-by-car.

Onward, the miles went by, until finally—beautiful California again!

Max helped me find an apartment on Whitley in Hollywood, which was much closer to the Jade than before, and I went back there, to be welcomed with open arms by Chuck Barclay, Irene, Bob the bartender and Paul the barboy, and, of course, Sue with her husband, Larry Potter.

A songwriter named Jack Brooks, who had written "Once Upon a Dream" and, much later, would write "Ole Buttermilk Sky" and "That's Amore," took a special interest in my singing and told me that he thought the Doll House in Palm Springs would be a wonderful place for me to perform.

The Doll House, not too surprisingly, was originally owned by some folks named Doll. It was their home, and they started serving dinners because Palm Springs didn't have many restaurants then, if any. Mr. Wrigley, of the Spearmint gum and Chicago Cubs Wrigleys, loved that sunny place, and the story goes that he would say, "Let's go to the Doll House for dinner," and the name stuck. Whatever, it became a very popular spot for world travelers and movie stars, and I recognized the likes of Franchot Tone, Peter Lorre, James Cagney, Jack Benny and Dennis Day. Of the lot, I actually exchanged words with only Franchot Tone and Peter Lorre. Normally, I was too shy to talk to anyone, but Peter and Franchot broke through my reserve. He played scary roles in movies, but Peter was a sweetheart.

The Guadalajara Trio was very popular there, and now and then I'd sing along with them . . . "Tonight will live forever." I can still hear them . . . and myself.

One night Freddie and Lois Mandel came to the Doll House. Freddie owned the Detroit Tigers and Mandel's Department Store in Chicago. They arranged an audition and brought along Frank Bering to hear me. Bering was a partner of Ernie Byfield, and together they owned the Ambassador East and West in Chicago.

It was closing time when they arrived, and the musicians had gone. "Well," I said, "there's a group down at Claridge's called The Four of Us. They'll play for me." Off we went, to find they'd already packed their instruments, but they took them out and played while I sang "The Man I Love."

It was at Bering's request that I went to Chicago. He said, "I'm hiring you more because of your enthusiasm than anything else." I wonder why *that* impressed me. It wasn't exactly a compliment.

The logistics of getting from point A to point B are interesting, at least to me: I believe it was Freddie and Lois who gave me a ticket to get to Chicago from Palm Springs. Some kind soul, probably a musician, gave me a ride to Los Angeles, and the point of departure was Union Station. Meanwhile, I had called Jane Leslie Larrabee (now Feather), told her of my good fortune, asked her to meet me in Chicago, and she agreed.

When I arrived at the Ambassador West, I found the lobby was even more luxurious than the Radison, and I felt self-consciousness flood my face.

"Will you please write your residence on the register," the clerk said.

"Oh, yes, of course," I stuttered, and then became confused because I really didn't have a home at the moment. "Well, I guess it's here," I said, and shrugged nonchalantly. (I wished he'd drop the subject.)

Finally, the clerk convinced me it could be my last home address, and I was then taken to a lovely suite, so lovely I stayed dressed up nearly all the time. Janie did the same when she arrived.

It was the Mandels who had arranged for the beautiful suite of rooms at the Ambassador, as well as half off on anything I wanted to buy in the hotel. Mlle. Oppenheimer, it turned out, would furnish my gowns and wardrobe. Each day a maid would come with a beautiful gown on a hanger and anything else I would want to wear. A fairy tale come true.

I also would get seventy-five dollars a week spending money, plus room service. But at first we were unaware of the room-service arrangement and nearly starved to death. Janie's mother, Tody, had sent some date-filled cookies that we ate right down to the last crumb. Other than that, we had a *very* small amount of money left between us for White Tower hamburgers. To the rescue came two hotel chambermaids, Iris and Tillie, who began bringing us coffee and rolls and whatever else they could find on the room service tables. I asked them both how they knew we were starving, and Tillie, in her sunny Irish way, said, "Well, we didn't see nothin' going in and we didn't see nothin' going out."

After that, I was treated like Eloise in the hotel, and the Mandels gave a party at their home to introduce me to Chicago society. When I tasted my first champagne, I *didn't* say, "It tickles my nose." I just got sick. But what a wonderful whirl! All those lovely gowns and the rest of it, sparkling forever in my memory.

Rather late at night after I sang, I would go to Rush Street and hear Laura Ricker and Baby Dodds—two of the truly old-time greats. Laura played the piano and sang, Baby sang and played the drums. Eventually, Laura would go blind; in fact, she was losing her sight then, but she taught me how to sing songs like "Let's Do It." Baby Dodds sang songs that he had composed. His brother, Johnny Dodds, was a famous jazz musician of the old school, and Baby had written a blues for him when he died. "Blues for you, Johnny, I hang my head and cry . . ." I don't remember any more of it, but it was a very moving song. They both had quite an effect on me, and, without reservation, I loved them very much.

It was a learning time, a wonderful time with uniquely American musicians.

*   *   *

Musicians. The word provides a perfect segue back to the great Benny Goodman, to the time in 1941 when he came into my life and I was swept up into a world of big-band singing and hit records. And, most important of all, to a year later, when a man named David, David Barbour, came into my life. David—my true love.

# Book Two
# IS THAT ALL THERE IS?

# Four

THE DAY Benny hired guitarist David Barbour, a new life was about to begin for me. We were in Detroit, and I had just come off stage after singing "These Foolish Things" and was slowly going back over to the iron steps that led upstairs to the dressing room. The notes the guitarist was playing circled around me as I placed one foot on the step, moved back down, turned around and went back to the wings to listen. And from then on, every time he would play I would listen.

David Barbour—almost from the start, the man of my life. I also watched his every move. It was his way not to seem to pay any attention, but when I saw him proudly showing pictures of his little girls to Dick Haymes, I thought I would die, until I learned from Dick they were his sister's children. My feelings for David grew and grew. When I noticed he didn't eat very much, I would fix up his meals at the coffee shop counter in the New Yorker—a little salt and pepper, a little butter, a little coaxing.

When we would go walking, I just thought he was eccentric when he would step off the curb and walk in the street. Of course, I would step off and walk with him. The problem of alcoholism never entered my mind. He was so precisely neat, his behavior impeccable, plus his wonderful wild sense of humor.

But one night he didn't arrive at the usual time, and my stomach was doing flips. I went to his room and found him anything but sober. I ran to the house doctor and asked if he could give me something to sober him up, and he mixed something in a bottle that I promptly ran back with for David. Benny was strict about being prompt and even more so about no liquor. The doctor's magic elixir seemed to pull David together, and we got through that one all right, but something . . . experience . . . told me it would only be a matter of time . . .


Wartime. In addition to the bond rallies, we were now playing in hospitals. There was a threat of a recording strike, so Benny recorded everything he had in the "bank": "How Deep Is the Ocean?" was one of the last ones. We did some sextette numbers—"Where or When" and "The Way You Look Tonight"—at the Liederkranz Hall. Benny wanted to use one microphone for the musicians as well as the singer, which called for more gymnastics. Lou McGarrity, playing trombone, would first crawl up in the air (on boxes), then we somehow managed to remain relatively silent and hold our breath in passing each other as I crawled *up* for my vocal and he crawled *down*. Those recordings may seem rather moody, and somehow they were, but it was also, after all, a little dangerous . . . either of us could have crashed to the floor. But if Benny said do it, we did it.


Oh, the glamorous life of a star. I would find a bench in the restroom and take a little catnap waiting through all the other recordings to my own "Why Don't You Do Right?"—which was the *very* last one.

Usually there was little time for sleeping. In New York, besides the Paramount Theatre, we were playing a set in the Terrace Room at the New Yorker Hotel. Popsie, the band boy, used to bring us sandwiches because they played only newsreels between shows, which didn't leave much time for casual dining, especially for a lady with makeup and hair and all. We worked seven days a week and after several weeks were like those little Swiss toys in a cuckoo clock . . .

One evening my body must have been at an all-time low. I went home to my apartment and fell into bed—makeup, pompadour and all. I could have slept on nails.

The phone rang. I stumbled to it. It was Sam, the door-man at the Paramount. My eyes like saucers, I picked up the receiver. "Hmmmm?" Sam said, "Fifteen minutes is in."

I almost said, "In where?" but couldn't speak. I turned around a couple of times, grabbed my favorite ensemble—gabardine suit and top coat. No time for stockings. Just shoes. Never mind the hair.

As I stepped into the elevator, people stared at me, and, as soon as I realized the pompadour was listing over one ear, I didn't blame them. I just hoped they didn't also notice I wasn't wearing stockings. It seemed like forever until we reached the ground floor . . . they never took their eyes off me. I made my escape to the street and caught a cab. "Paramount Theatre backstage," I growled, and the cabbie roared away to the theatre.

Sam was holding the door as I streaked through and jumped into the elevator. I thought I heard Benny announcing me, probably did. I slipped into an off-the-shoulder black "Yukon Lil" gown in about ten seconds, still didn't touch my hair. Ten seconds to slather my face with greasepaint. With hands shaking, I tried the mascara and stuck it in my eye. Then I couldn't see, so I stuck my finger in the pot of lipstick and deliberately drew two parallel lines for lips. Still hadn't combed my hair. I quickly chose a big pink French rose and pinned it inside the pompadour. Get the picture? A lady clown, right?

Now a dash for the stage. Blessed Sam was holding the elevator for me. I ran across stage as Benny was going into what I would learn was his third announcement. "And now ladies and gentlemen, our charming and lovely vocalist, Miss Peggy Lee," followed by the orchestral introduction.

I burst through the curtain—and the audience laughed. Benny's mouth dropped open, the orchestra snickered, and I thought desperately, "I'll sing so good they won't pay any attention." Oh, really?

Each morning I had to warm up to hit my first note, which was C above middle C. The song was "Don't Get Around Much Anymore." Well, the first note was terrible, echoing all the way up to the top balcony. The rest of the notes were similar, and the audience was falling apart, joined by the orchestra, which could no longer play. They were doubled over.

Somehow, we got through it and, as Benny stepped to the microphone to announce my second number, I gave him a shove and ran to my dressing room and locked the door.

Why Benny didn't fire me on the spot, I don't know, but I do know he wasn't too happy about seeing David and me so close together.

He gave David his notice.

(Some people have said that Benny Goodman had a crush on me. Years later, after Alice's [Lady Duckworth's] death, Benny and I would have dinner together. The fact is, we were always friends.)

It was 1943 now, and we all packed up and left New York for Los Angeles, where I was to do a film called THE POWERS GIRL. David, although sacked, was still with the band for a few weeks. Getting his notice seemed to make him realize he loved me enough not to want us to be separated—so he *finally* asked me to marry him. I was so excited I couldn't stop grinning, even while we got our blood tests and license. I bought a lovely dress and we went to City Hall with my sister Marianne and David's best man, Joe Rushton. David wasn't inclined to have big ceremonies. Ours was simple and conducted by Judge Lilly—a lady judge. We had dinner at Musso-Frank's, and I was so in love with David I don't even remember what we ate. (And by now you know how important food, or the lack thereof, had been in my life.)

Someone had found us a duplex apartment across the street from the Los Angeles City College, and I became so busy decorating and keeping house I wasn't even aware that "Why Don't You Do Right?" had become a monster hit all over the world. Not, that is, until the telephone began ringing with offers I never would have dreamed would come my way.

The telephone in our modest apartment was a stand-up with the receiver hanging on the side. It sat on top of a Chinese red lacquered drop-leaf table. When it rang, I would usually trip over the carpet or the cord and listen to the fabulous offers to play this theatre or that hall and hear myself say, "No thank you, I'm so happy being a housewife." David thought I was crazy and would often tell me so, but love is a powerful thing, isn't it?

When we would have company, I was forever making curried this or curried that because it sounded so exotic. Eventually, I curried myself right out. Our first guests were Jess Stacy, a jazz pianist who was going with singer Lee Wiley. They raved about my curry, and after that you couldn't even talk to me. I was the curry queen.

Then *it* happened. The doctor told me I was pregnant and we were overjoyed. David had a smile that lasted during the whole pregnancy. I knew I would cherish what David might say when I told him I was pregnant, but I didn't expect what I'd heard after I'd run all the way home.

"David, we're going to have a baby!"

A long pause, then, "Why, Peg, I hardly know you."

We named our little girl after grandfather Nicholas. I wanted to call her Nicole, but Nicki won out.

At the beginning I needed some special medical attention . . . it seemed I had two large tumors. When Nicki was born, I really found out how much David loved me, as if I didn't know before. She was an eight-month Caesarean, and I had pneumonia. David was so frightened, they told him my chances seemed slim, and I guess they were. They gave me a spinal, so I could hear everything he and they said, including the doctor running alongside the gurney and telling the nurses to "find my damn shoes, find them now!" and the nurse running with him and saying, "Where are the beads? Where are the beads?" I thought they were looking for a rosary instead of an identification bracelet.

David called my beloved Marianne, and cried and said, "I'll never do that to her again." (We both wanted more children, but it turned out to be impossible.) When they wheeled me back into my room, I kept looking at the picture of some pansies at the end of my bed and said to my nurse, "Don't they have dear little faces?" She thought I was delirious and was seeing babies. They promptly put up the bars on my bed and replaced the pansies with a picture of a smiling baby.

Nicki turned out to be beautiful and healthy, and very early on showed signs of high intelligence. David was, as you might guess, mad about her. She learned to laugh early and loved to rock her high chair until it started to tip. Seeing this at a distance, I would run and slide in, as though to first base, and she would fall on me, and laugh and laugh, and so would I.

When David and I married and left Benny and decided to settle down in L.A., David had to get a California union card.

He could earn only a pittance until he had played in L.A. a certain period of time, and he had to do things way beneath him to establish himself with the union. For the time, I had stopped working altogether, and Benny Goodman was getting all the royalties from my hits, but, still very much on cloud-nine as a newlywed, I couldn't concentrate on such mundane matters.

As a newlywed, I was, as they used to say, a caution. When the stove would catch fire, I would use a North Dakota remedy and pour on generous amounts of salt to kill the flames. This would usually happen when I was making toast in the oven. David would come out rubbing the sleep from his eyes and say something like, "I'm not going to eat that—salt or no salt."

My experience with the iceman was also something to shake David up. Our little apartment didn't have a refrigerator. Instead, there was an icebox—a very nice one, mind you, but an icebox. The iceman, who was not a teetotaler, would bring our big cakes of ice up the stairs, the ice resting on a thick rubber pad on his back with the water melting behind him.

David worked very late at night, playing at a joint on Skid Row called the Waldorf Cellar, and I would be up waiting for him, then we would sleep until late in the day. Well, it seems that during my pregnancy I walked in my sleep and, because of the pregnancy, could not lie comfortably with any night clothes. The iceman, on this occasion, evidently had taken a day off to get drunk, and as a result our rationed food spoiled. I resolved to find another iceman, which thought I evidently placed in my subconscious. The next day I was dreaming, literally, and went walking around the apartment in the nude as I wound the clock. I set it for two P.M.—why I picked that hour I don't know.

All of this, remember, while sound asleep. The dream continued, and suddenly the iceman appeared in front of me looking horrified and trying to back *down* the steps as he repeated rapidly, "Yesma'amyesma'amyesma'am . . ."

I said, "We won't be needing you anymore," and walked into the kitchen and placed the alarm clock on the icebox. End of dream. I slept on, until I heard the alarm and got up to find it in the kitchen on top of the icebox, set for two P.M. I thought I had gone bonkers.

The iceman never returned.

I told the obstetrician about it, and he prescribed tying one of my legs to the end of the bed. We did that, but, after the iceman, sometimes I would have an awful time trying to convince David I was awake.

Perhaps because of the jazz sound of "Why Don't You Do Right?", Dave Dexter saw the potential of a jazz singer in my voice. For whatever reason, he asked if I would come down and record a couple of songs for an album called "New American Jazz"—"Ain't Goin' No Place" and "That Old Feeling." Eddie Miller played a classic saxophone solo on "That Old Feeling." It was fun to sing again, but it didn't mean as much to me as staying home and keeping house.

The record was a success, and soon a lot of people thought I should go out again, including David, who may or may not have been influenced by the manager, Carlos Gastel. David's argument was by far the most interesting to me—use the talent given to me instead of resenting the fact that I hadn't down the road. I needed that . . . I really didn't have all that much self-esteem going for me—the scars of my childhood weren't yet healed.

The next step was my meeting Carlos, a formidable manager, who handled such stars as Stan Kenton, Woody Herman, June Christy, Mel Torme and Nat King Cole. A large, very pleasant fellow with a great sense of humor, he introduced me to one of the finest agents ever—Tom Rockwell, the founder of General Artists Corporation and discoverer of a list of star talents that included the Mills Brothers, Perry Como and Dinah Shore, and for him each talent was like a jewel for which he provided the setting.

There was another agent on the grand scale, Levis Green, who had plans for me to replace Lana Turner, who, I was told, wanted out of her studio, but, in the end, it was Ava Gardner who wore the crown. Actually, I turned it down, which, in looking back, may or may not have been imprudent. But all I really wanted to do was to stay home and be Mrs. David Barbour.

The songs on "New American Jazz" made a pleasant debut, and what a thrill to turn the radio on to D.J.'s Al Jarvis or Gene Norman and hear "That Old Feeling" and "Ain't Goin' No Place." Suddenly, I was also meeting people such as songwriter Buddy De Sylva, Glenn Wallichs and Johnny Mercer (who together founded Capitol Records). Sy Devore was the leading tailor of the day, and those fellows were conducting business upstairs over Sy's tailor shop on Vine, just below Sunset. (Sy's shop would be the beginning of the large round Capitol Building on Vine as it stands today.)

At one of these meetings over Sy Devore's tailor shop, it was decided that David and I would record for Capitol, which brought up the subject of material. Well, during the time I'd been pregnant with Nicki, I began to write down ideas for songs. For instance, on one particular time several things happened that delighted me . . . someone brought us a pheasant, another person brought over a bottle of fine wine, the telephone was full of nice messages—some of those offers I mentioned, and, finally, I said to no one in particular, "Well, it's a good day!" Which struck me as a good title. As I busied myself with housework, I began to sing a little "dummy" melody, and, as the words kept popping in, I put down the vacuum or whatever and wrote them down. When it was finished, I put Nicki in her baby buggy and practically ran down to my sister's apartment house, called up to her window and sang my song. I think she always took some pride in having been the first person to hear "It's a Good Day!" And I couldn't have been more pleased that she was the first to audition it.

When David came home, I couldn't wait to sing the song to him, and then he got some manuscripts and worked out the harmonies for what would be our first big hit.

"What More Can a Woman Do?" was also inspired by my feelings for David and our life. This time I was washing dishes, and just sang out my love for him . . . So, that's how these things happened, and it was Johnny Mercer who felt the songs had strong potential. He was right. When I was working on "I Don't Know Enough about You," he made some wonderfully constructive comments, including "tear it all apart and do it over again." Actually, it was fun reconstructing it, and no doubt it was a vast improvement. Probably one of my best instructions on construction—and by a master . . .

We were often invited to Carlos Gastel's home when he was married to Joan. (Carlos was managing both David and me now.) Joan had to be the soul of patience, because life was one big party, or one big martini, for Carlos.

He had a very nice boat that was called a "stinkpot" by the more refined sailors, who had only sails and small auxiliary motors for emergencies. Some of these sailors, although they couldn't help but like Carlos, would look down their noses at him because he drove his boat like a truck driver who had over-imbibed.

I'm sure he didn't have to pour it down his throat, but Carlos was really a bad influence on David. David's favorite was a boilermaker—bourbon and beer. The beer always looked so harmless by itself. (He even fed the goldfish bourbon!) I think one of the main reasons I would go boating with them was to maintain some sanity, although I suppose what happened on board wasn't exactly normal . . . David, for example, liked to play marlin; he would jump in the ocean and I would have to reel him in like a marlin.

We had all the usual domestic crises in our household but never any serious quarreling between David and myself. There was some playful pushing if he was drinking, but mostly he had a lovely, quiet disposition. I did too. I wish I had it now. The years of things being difficult finally hardened up the edges a bit, developing my already over-developed sense of responsibility. And I was exceedingly neurotic about Nicki. I said before how I didn't sleep much, listening and watching her all night long.

I was, no question, under a lot of pressure from all sides. Being a wife and mother, as I mentioned, was the only full-time career I wanted, but MGM was being persistent, and so was Capitol Records, and Dave was saying I had too much talent not to use it, I'd be sorry later, and so on. I was very confused, very unhappy, and, when Nicki cried, I would hold her and rock her, and I think I probably cried more than she did.

It was at this point that Ernest Holmes, founder of Science of Mind, came into my life. My early experiences with organized religion had not been exactly positive. My first minister, when I was a child in North Dakota, had been a Nazi, literally, a member of the Bund. It wasn't until I met Ernest Holmes that I would realize that we live in a universe that is primarily spiritual, and that it is possible to get everything we need, health, money, happiness, through the scientific application of prayer and meditation.

David and I had a neighbor named Honey Frambach. One day she knocked on my door, introduced herself, and I invited her in for a chat.

"I never see you go out," Honey said.

"We can't afford it, to tell you the truth." (It was true at the time, with me being a homebody, wife and mother, and David struggling.)

The subject of spiritual beliefs somehow came up, and she asked me if I'd heard of Ernest Holmes, then told me about some of his ideas.

"He sounds wonderful," I said. "I'd love to hear him."

She volunteered to take care of Nicki if I wanted to go hear Dr. Holmes speak, and a short time later I went to his institute at Sixth and Vernon in Los Angeles. I was the first one to arrive, and as I sat in the lecture hall I noticed a small brass plaque with a name on it on the chair in front of me. Curious, I circled around to see whose name was on the back of the chair I had selected—it read "Estelle Frambach." Listening to Dr. Holmes, I thought I had, indeed, found something I could seriously relate to in Science of Mind. I have never stopped in that conviction.

About this time I went back East to substitute for Jo Stafford on the "Chesterfield Supper Club" radio show. When I arrived in New York, I had such stomach flu I couldn't even drink water. Carlos had to sit in my suite, because I couldn't be alone. On the day of the show, I couldn't get out of bed. Carlos rang Dr. Palmer, who came over, took a look at me and said, "You can't make it, it would be unwise for you to even try."

I wasn't convinced. How could I fly all the way from California—it was a very big deal in the day of prop planes— and not do this show? I called Ernest Holmes in Los Angeles and explained my predicament.

"Just lie back down and rest for a minute," he said, then told me to affirm the omnipresence of God, and the omni- science of God, who knows what needs to be done. Affirm, too, His omnipotence, so nothing is impossible to God. Fi- nally, Ernest stressed the value of being grateful and of giving thanks.

It worked, I got well enough and went on for Jo Stafford and did the show. When I told Ernest Holmes about this, he said, "Please come and see me when you get back to L.A." I did, and it was the beginning of a lifelong friendship.

I was still worrying about my baby, crying nearly every time she did. Finally, Nicki became ill, and I went to Ernest Holmes and poured out my heart to him. "Peggy," he said, "you're going to make that child really sick by your constant worry. You must learn to trust, to have faith. You and I will do some work for her right now, and you'll see that she is all right." We did, and it was a healthy beginning to a healthy mother-daughter relationship. It wasn't magic . . . it was the discipline of faith. Nicki was so precious to me, and I knew she would be our only child, and understood I really had to overhaul my thinking. With Ernest Holmes' help, I did.

It was about that time that David's mother, Bessie, came out from the East to live with us. I nervously tried to make every-thing as perfect as I could for her, and then David sprung one on me. "Peg, I'm working at the studio when my mother gets here, so I'd like you to go down to Union Station and meet her."

Meet her? Find her! How about that? I have, and had, no sense of direction, but I was pretty good at streetcar tracks, so I finally figured out how I would take the red car down to Union Station and splurge and bring her home in a cab. Only when I think of it now is it funny . . . Miss Capable was a complete failure at finding places . . .

"David," I said, "I've never even met her. I want to welcome her *here.*"

"Oh, you can welcome her there."

I might have sensed that there was something strained in

109

their relationship, but I didn't then. Well, I got up in the middle of the night, checked the apartment, did the washing, made some food for lunch, got myself dressed after giving David his breakfast and met Honey Frambach, who was going to watch Nicki while I went to pick up Bessie. 'Cause "I'm a Woman, W-O-M-A-N!"

My sisters and I had been looking for a little apartment for Bessie that David and I could afford and that would be close to us and comfortable. Della and Marianne and I painted the place, put up curtains, some of David's and my prints for the walls, did everything we could to make it livable.

When we got back from the station, we rather proudly took her downstairs, and she promptly refused to stay alone on the ground floor. So my little dining room became her bedroom with a folding bed.

No wonder Dave took up his old hobby again. He had gotten off the stuff when we married, but now with Bessie on hand . . . she called him "Sonny"—David was definitely not a "Sonny." I learned only now that David had had a real problem with alcohol before we met, and, in hindsight, the little incidents when we were with Benny seemed to be part of that.

Meanwhile, I had been working outside of home as well as in, and the doctor sent me to Palm Springs. (The "season" was over, and it was *hot.*) I had a white count of 17,000—a high white count indicates quite an infection, and my condition was severe enough to require hospitalization. When he got my white count down a bit, he wanted me to go to Palm Springs and completely rest and soak up the sunshine. David asked Bessie if she would go down with Nicki and me, and she agreed to go—for a fee! This, at a time when we were supporting her.

Well, we went, but I might as well have been alone. After *that* I gave up my earlier fantasy of adopting her as a mother . . .

\*   \*   \*

Now the recordings began in earnest at Capitol, and, when the first came out, you could tell that either they were doing a great job of promoting or we had a lot of genuine hits. Well, both were true and offers really began flooding in.

And in the midst of it all, something happened that I never could have anticipated, although in hindsight maybe I should have. Benny had convinced David and me that I should go to the Golden Gate Theatre in San Francisco and play with him there for one week. I did, and while I was there, a young Navy fighter pilot, Dewey Martin, came to hear me, and decided he would marry me (and he *did*, briefly, years later). I seemed to have a strange attraction for pilots. But at the time David and I were a devoted couple, and the pilot was just a member of the audience, regardless of his own thoughts.

Tensions did, though, begin to gnaw at us—mostly from this personal-appearance business. And along with it were the sessions of David and Carlos at the bar, which, in a way, were understandable . . . I mean, they made each other laugh, they were buddies, and neither realized he had an alcoholic problem.

Mel Powell's memory picks up the story: "As time went on, Peg got stronger and stronger and better and better. One night we were playing a gig and she had a lot of fever. It was up to 101. She felt the show must go on. She was up against the piano, singing. She had refused the ingestion of medicine, she had refused doctors. She was busy with Science of Mind, whereas, you and I, certainly I, would have been to thirteen, fifteen specialists to find out why my nose was clogged. But with Peggy it was all a question of thinking pure. She began to faint and, as she was going out, she said, 'Oh, shit, I've killed myself,' as she gracefully fell to the floor . . ."

Well, at least I was graceful. And obviously my self-proclaimed death sentence was premature.

*   *   *

A lot of David's and my friends thought I was being a posses-
sive wife because at parties I was always urging that we go
home. But what it truly was—I could tell when David had
reached the danger point, and they couldn't really see it from
their casual viewpoint.

I remember one time when we were driving home, I saw
a police car ahead of us. "David," I said, "there's a police car
just ahead, be careful." "Yes? Okay, I'll catch him," said
David, and put his foot on the gas pedal! I don't know how
we missed that one, but we did manage to arrive home safely
without doing anyone any harm . . .

Except, of course, the drinking *was* doing harm, because
now he was showing signs of ulcers. I had him on a strict diet,
but it didn't help much with the bourbon chaser.

Building our first dream house on Blair Drive in the
Hollywood Hills did seem to make him happy, though. He
came home one day wearing a plaid lumber jacket and work
shoes and proudly announced, "Well, we broke ground
today!" I really cracked up because it was all so unlike the
impeccable man he seemed to be, starting with his clothes.

We made trips day after day and supervised every detail
of that house, and how we loved it! Each time, we would say
to Nicki, "We're going up to see Nicki's house." When we
were there, we would say, "This is Nicki's bedroom, this is
Nicki's bathroom . . ."

Well, the day arrived when the house was finished, although it had seemed it never would be. I was doing some
last-minute packing. After bathing and dressing Nicki, I put
her in her crib and pulled up the sides, all the while babbling
about taking Nicki to her brand-new home. When she kept
looking sad, I finally said, "What's the matter, honey, aren't
you happy that we're going to your new house?" She began
to cry. "Do I have to live there all alone?"

The startling insight of little children—you hear talk about it, but it jolts you when you are smack up against it from your own . . .

It's a fact that I used to spend as much time looking at David as I did looking at the house. What a magnificent face. I used to think he was a cross between Cary Grant, Abraham Lincoln and Jesus. (How does any man live up to that?) He was thin, and, as I said, usually impeccably dressed—tweed jackets and birdseye shirts with a rather thin black knit tie. Sometimes cashmere pullovers. And brown eyes, Italian eyes, kind of a shy smile. If he felt especially affectionate, he'd call me "Dolly" or "Normer." And, at his best, David had a wonderful dry sense of humor, great with a joke or funny line.

Our songs were Duke Ellington's "Perdido" and "Warm Valley." "Chelsea Bridge" wasn't bad either. One day I got so carried away listening to it that I poured salt instead of sugar into the apple pie I was making to surprise him.

When we moved in, we were just like any other perfect couple who had built their first dream house. The landscaping had been completed, and they left us just enough room to put in some bedding plants around the patio so we could play in our own soil.

By now I was singing with Bing Crosby on the "Kraft Music Hall" and Jimmy Durante on his Rexall program. Crosby and Durante—not one but two of the greatest entertainers who ever lived—and I had the pleasure of going to the NBC and CBS studios and working with them. I became a "regular," and every week there was a parade of stars—Judy Garland, Oscar Levant, Tallulah Bankhead, Claudette Colbert, Greer Garson, Margaret O'Brien, Zsa Zsa Gabor, Charles Boyer and George Sanders. Working two networks simultaneously, I guess I met just about everyone in radio in those days.

We had found a marvelous housekeeper and a nurse for Nicki (no, she wouldn't be all alone, as she'd feared). Martina Garberg was one of the most efficient, capable, loving persons one could ask for, and dear Alice Larson was the same. They would take turns traveling with us or taking care of Nicki. Our house was filled with music and laughter. All we needed to complete this picture of wedded bliss was a pet—a dog. She came up out of the Warner Brothers hills, dragging her poor hind legs, and had a film over her eyes so that she could barely see. David and I brought her inside and gave her a bit of nourishment before we took her to the veterinarian. He didn't hold too much hope for her, but we were determined to try. With special care and time, she got herself back together.

I don't know why, but David named her "Banjo." Maybe he wasn't sure she was a she; he never was much for animal husbandry. Finally, she was home again and what a lovely surprise to see the beautiful coat of fur growing, and the soulful eyes.

During this time *Life* did a photo layout on us with Banjo lying in the background of one of the pictures. Well, Frank Weatherwax, the world-famous trainer, saw the picture and recognized our dog as one of the offspring of his famous "Lassie." One day he came to drive by our house and saw Banjo cavorting in the front garden. He then set some wheels in motion that had a fairly profound effect on several people. For one, I was in Chicago headlining in the Chicago Theatre and evidently creating quite a stir, because the Chicago *Tribune,* or *Sun-Times,* had a big black headline: "PEGGY LEE STEALS DOG!" The phone rang off the hook with calls from the press asking me if it were true. Had I really stolen a dog? The story went on to say the dog was sired by "Lassie." They were suing for one million dollars for ruining the dog's education, and that was *before* inflation.

I indignantly made a statement: "If befriending a starving animal is a crime, I am guilty!" And how could they sue me? How could I know the animal had such an extraordinary education? I must admit, though, I felt rather important to have such a big headline.

I called home to assure the housekeeper, Alice Larson, that I wasn't a thief and the lawsuit would be taken care of, but I was in for another shock. I was told the former owner had not only found our home but had walked into our garden and told our gardener he was taking Banjo. I asked, "How did Banjo react? Was she glad to see him?" When my gardener assured me that she had shown dislike and fear, I decided to fight for her. By this time, David had returned, and we had our business managers, George Stuart and Dick Shipman, and our lawyers do some investigating.

We learned that the previous owner had worked for Frank Weatherwax as a trainer and somehow had been given Banjo (who had been named "Lady"), but the plot thickens . . . The owner had given the dog to this caretaker, who had been in jail on a morals charge. Banjo obviously didn't cotton to the man and had simply run away into the Warner Brothers hills. Ran to us, and stayed our beloved pet for many, many years.

As I said, I was appearing with Crosby and Durante, and once, when Jimmy was ill, I helped out by acting as a hostess. The marvelous Frank Morgan (the Wizard of Oz) was the star guest host. Jackie Burnett had written a successful, but fairly complicated, production number, "Any State in the 48 Is Great," especially for those not used to singing.

After dress rehearsal Frank decided to fortify himself with something from the bar across the street. I was getting nervous because the announcer was warming up the audience for the live show, which was to begin in minutes. At the last moment Mr. Morgan walked in with a big smile on his face.

Seeing my look of panic, he looked down at me and said, "Stick with me, kid. I'll get you in plenty of trouble."

Actually, it was a very funny show, including Victor Moore getting his foot caught in one of the tin cans that had been dropped by the sound effects man and clanking his way to the microphone to sing with Frank Morgan, Arthur Treacher and yours truly . . .

Those were the days, my friend.

I used to call Durante, Mr. Love. It seemed to me he *was* all love. He once said to me, "Someday you'll feel something come back to you from the audience and then you won't ever feel afraid again." He was right. Today I *feel* love from the audience in return for what I am giving.


Life was mostly so beautiful and happy that I began to be afraid it wouldn't last. And it didn't. It had been creeping up on us. David was having more and more pain in his stomach until, finally, there was nothing to do but get him to another doctor for a second opinion.

There was now no doubt about the bleeding duodenal ulcers. Diet hadn't worked, it became acute, and we rushed him to St. John's Hospital, where Dr. Arnold Stevens took him immediately to the operating room.

It seemed forever before I saw Dr. Stevens again, and when I ran to meet him he wasn't smiling. "I think he's going to make it, but it's about a fifty-fifty chance. We had to remove nearly three-fourths of his stomach and he's lost a lot of blood."

"But he *is* going to live . . . isn't he?"

"We've done all we can do. It's in God's hands."

For twelve days and nights I sat in the little waiting area near David's room, making frequent trips in to check on him. During those times we talked of our love for each other, and he promised to hang on. He asked me not to let his mother in the room because she made him nervous. That put me in a difficult position, but my vows were to him, so I kept them. At least until he was out of the danger zone.

Whenever I could be certain he would be all right for an hour or two, I would rush home for a shower and a change of clothes. Nicki, with Martina's help, would pick a camellia from the bushes in front of our house to take to her daddy as a reminder that he'd better get well and come home.

It was his humor that saw me through. One time they were wheeling him to the operating room for a second surgery, and I ran alongside the gurney trying to think of something to say, but all I could think of was, "I love you, David, I love you." He looked at me through the tubes and oxygen. "Stop nagging me," he said.

During this time I was in frequent touch with Ernest Holmes, and am convinced that without the power of affirmative prayer David would not have survived. In affirmative prayer you don't just say please give me something; you state the fact that as a child of God you are entitled to your birthright, your abundance. If we have a lot to learn, we have to stick around to learn it . . .

I also became close friends with the nuns and the priests at the hospital. They were faithful throughout and, incidentally, have remained so. (One of the young priests is now the head of a large Trappist monastery, and we have kept in touch.) Even the girls who washed the halls were thoughtful, putting cloths down on the wet floor so I could make my trips to see David without any interruption. I really believe everyone in that hospital had David on their minds and in their hearts. Everyone was so thoughtful and loving.

After a few more scares, our prayers were answered, and he came around. It was wonderful to see how friends gathered and lent their support. Then, about the ninth day, David said, "Honey, why don't you at least go out and have dinner? I'm much better today and you should do that. Will you, please? Just a little more, and I'll be fine." I agreed, reluctantly, and went to a nearby restaurant, edgy and more nervous than the situation seemed to call for. I just kept feeling that I *must* get back to the hospital, so back I went.

When I got in the elevator I met Doctor Davis, and, unlike his usual pleasant self, he didn't speak to me. I froze. It was obvious something was terribly wrong. The elevator door opened, there was a high-tension bustle going on, the sisters running this way and that, wheeling a resuscitator into David's room. I tried to get in, but they wouldn't allow me, Sister Ann Raymond trying to comfort me all the while.

I shall *never* forget this . . . As I was walking down the corridor crying out to God in silence, I suddenly saw a shaft of light coming from my *own* eyes down the length of the hall, and I *knew* David was alive and that he would live. I felt as though I had been lifted from the floor.

"I will set him on high, because he hath known my name" (Psalm 91:14).

I ran back to tell Sister Ann Raymond. At first she thought I was just hysterical or in shock, but as we stood there talking . . . "But you don't understand, Sister, I *know* he's all right!" . . . they came out of David's room saying it had been a miracle. He had been blind, now he could see. His heart had stopped, now it was beating normally. In fact, *all* his vital signs were perfect.

"Just a little more, and I'll be fine," he had said. Who had said? . . .

Three days later they discharged David from the hospital.

Praise the Lord!

I'll always remember our Jewish friend Mike Gould being very upset because the vigil light had gone out on the fourth floor. He kept pulling at me and each sister he saw to go and light it. We still say, "Keep it lit" when we meet.

Both Jimmy Durante and Bing Crosby were among the hundreds of friends who cared so much about David. Bing, in fact, used to call every morning at six o'clock to see how David was doing.

To celebrate David's recovery, we packed our luggage and ourselves into our convertible and drove to the Rosarita Beach Hotel, down between Tijuana and Ensenada.

It was the first time I had ever been across the border, and it was fascinating. After all the stress we had been under, it was also a perfect change. The totally relaxed attitude of the people was just what we needed after the tension in the hospital. True, we had to leave our little Nicki at home with Martina this time, but it was all for a good cause—to get David out of any association with that ulcer world. It was good for me, too. I was so impressed with the seemingly happy, relaxed spirit of the place that . . . you might have guessed it . . . it inspired me to write the song "Mañana." David got his guitar out, and we had so much fun putting it all together.

Of course, we had no idea it would be such a tremendous hit. I remember when we recorded it, how contagious the happiness was. And Carmen Miranda's "Brazilians," her musicians, added a lot with their effervescent samba rhythm. Carmen was often a guest with Durante, and she had called me about using her musicians. She also recommended classical guitarist Laurindo Almeida, who played with me for quite a while. What a dear lady Carmen was, and the Brazilians were perfect for "Mañana." When we recorded the song, we used what I believe was the first "board fade" . . . a gradual turning down of the volume on the studio recording equipment until the sound completely fades out. In this case, though, the Brazilians actually sambaed out of the studio and down the street, playing and singing "Mañana, mañana,

mañana is soon enough for me!" I suppose another way to do a board fade would be to have the audience get up and walk out. Just kidding.

We took the acetate home and played it over and over; it was almost like being a child on Christmas morning to wake up and dash out to the turntable and play it again and again—all the while doing the samba in my robe.

The record's sales jumped into the millions so fast you couldn't turn on the radio without hearing it—and then one day we were served with papers for a three-million-dollar lawsuit by a banjo player named Hats McKay. I don't know how many millions that would be today! It was, I was told, what's known as a nuisance suit, and I guess you could say a few million could be a nuisance.

We found an excellent attorney, Henry Gilbert, who was Irving Berlin's representative at the time, and there followed months and months of depositions and meetings, including some fairly colorful trivia: H. Edna Moon, a retired violinist and World War I acquaintance of Hats was to testify that he wrote the song in 1919. There was also Ginger Lee (no relation), who was the mistress of ceremonies at the Tropics Club in Imperial, California, in 1943. She said, "Hats sang his 'Laughing Song' there. He wore a hula skirt and tin plates for breasts." There was also a Nellie Brill . . .

As the trial date approached, Mr. Gilbert asked us to keep a large opening in our bookings and arrange to be in New York for the trial, so we went to New York and stayed at the Warwick Hotel.

The lawyer lined up some impressive experts to testify on our behalf—Deems Taylor, the president of ASCAP, Dr. Sigmund Spaeth, musical historian and tune-detective, Dr. Charles Kettering, head curator of the Edison Foundation, and Albert Osbourne, who was the handwriting expert at the Hauptmann-Lindbergh trial.

David disappeared. Days passed. It was impossible not to

worry. I wore paths in the carpet of our suite, called every musician's hang-out I could think of. No luck. If anyone had seen him, they weren't going to tell me. He came back, almost sober, the day before the trial. Who knew? . . .

When the trial began, Hats was on the stand constantly one-fingering "Mañana." It annoyed the judge. "Do you have to keep playing that thing?" he said.

I sat next to Deems Taylor, who, as I said, was president of ASCAP at the time. Once, during a less serious intermission, he related a story about himself . . . He was giving a eulogy at a memorial service for Jerome Kern, and, feeling the atmosphere was charged with serious gloom, he ventured to say something warm and less formal. He succeeded, all right. He said, "I've always been a great Fern can myself."

Meanwhile, the serious trial went on and on. Deems Taylor pointed out that it should be "painfully apparent" that when McKay performed the song he never repeated the melody the same way (even with one finger). Mr. Kettering, the head curator of the Edison Foundation, testified of many "public domain" resemblances for songs such as Vesta Victoria's "Now I Have To Call Him Father," "Jo Jo's Laughing Song" or "If You Had the Brains Your Mother Had." Albert Osbourne, the handwriting expert from the Hauptmann-Lindbergh trial, said that, after careful examination, it was his opinion the manuscript of Hats McKay's song was made with new ink on new paper.

About this time Judge Wasservogel motioned to me and said, "There's a phone call for you in my chambers."

I quickly tiptoed in and the voice on the phone said, "What did dey do to my goil?"

They must have raced down there, because, before we knew it, in came Jimmy Durante, followed by Eddie Jackson and Jack Roth, who were followed by an upright piano. There was a little bedlam in the courtroom while they placed the piano up near the judge, but he didn't seem to mind.

Jimmy began playing and singing his "Laughing Song," while explaining that every comedian had at least one. In their act they would play and sing the "Laughing Song," tell a joke and then vamp while the audience laughed. It was usually notated with the words "ha ha ha," which was exactly what Hats McKay had for the lyric to his version of "Mañana." Jimmy's testimony certainly bore out the public-domain argument, as well as gave us all a laugh and release of tension in the courtroom. I wished they could have stayed on, and I suspected the judge wouldn't have minded either.

When we took a recess, I tried to thank Jimmy, but he just shook his famous nose at me and said, "Dat's what friends are for." I wanted to cry as I watched them walk down the hallway and out the door.

The clincher in the trial came when Sigmund Spaeth opened the envelope from Hats McKay and found it very professionally and clearly labeled as a samba. Well, it happened the Brazilian samba was not in existence in 1919, when Hats claimed he wrote it. It proved our point beyond a doubt, and we won the case.

Deems Taylor took me to dinner at the Stork Club to celebrate (David didn't want to go, he'd been drinking). We went into the "leather bound" Cub Room, and he showed me a leather-bound wine list that intimidated me, to say the least. Unable to recognize one wine from another, I showed my exquisite sophistication by saying, "I believe I'll just have some Chianti."

Deems, a really nice man, couldn't resist: "And I suppose for dessert you'd like some cornstarch pudding?" Well . . .

During the tension of David's surgery and when we returned from Ensenada, Dr. Stevens became my hero for doing such fine work with David, and we all became friends . . . his wife, Jeanne, their daughters, Carol and Harley, and young Steve.

Next to the Stevens' house on Denslow there was a French Normandy house. They say houses reach out and claim you, and that one did just that. I asked Jeanne if she thought the house would ever be for sale and she said she didn't think the owners would ever sell, that they had built it, had chosen the hand-hewn beams, personally designed the three fireplaces, one round brick, another a black marble in the living room and still another handmade of ceramic tile in the master bedroom. I told her, "Well, just in case, if they ever do decide to sell, *please* let me know. And wouldn't it be nice to be neighbors?" Of course, I didn't really think it would be ours, but one never knows, and in a way it *did* seem to belong to us already . . .

Well, one day Jeanne called: "Did you put a spell on that house? It's for *sale.*"

We got right into the business of buying it and moving in as soon as possible. The morning the moving van came up to Blair Drive and started moving our sentimental things out of our first home, we got a little misty. David and I had built it and still loved it. We loved our neighbors, too. In fact, our friends, the Joviens, closed all their blinds all day so they wouldn't see the moving van go by.

Decorating was a massive job. This was a large house, and we started with a tremendous roll of hand-woven carpeting from China, the last shipment out before the closed-door policy that lasted for so many years. The paints and papers were all chosen; the fabrics for upholstery, the draperies, the curtains were all being sewn. I stuck my hand in and hand-painted all of the cupboards in the kitchen area. Someone told me later that the cupboard doors were sold separately. My pictures were all of Frenchmen with red berets, and the cupboards were labeled in French (still trying to speak French!) for whatever was in each cupboard. There was only one mistake on my part, *fleur* instead of *farine,* but it looked pretty, so we left it there.

Finally, everything was completed and we left to go on tour. Our first stop was Virginia Beach. It was one of their beautiful balmy evenings. The stage faced the ocean, and, even though the surf was gently pounding, it made enough sound to cover a soft musical note. (It seems I'm always listening for a note.) Ray Anthony was conducting his orchestra while David played. Gil Evans, one of the most gifted of all arrangers, was trying to cue me in to "Where or When." Twice the ocean breezes blew the note away.

What a setting. The moon, the darkening sky, the ocean, the music of Rodgers and Hart, Gil Evans and David playing. Finally I began to sing . . . and from out of all this loveliness came a bug as big as a hummingbird, drawn by the spotlight to circle around and around my head. "It seems we . . ." I sang, but the bug had everyone's attention. There wasn't a chance my eyes would stop rolling. I continued to sing, or tried to while keeping my mouth closed as much as possible. Try singing "Where or When" that way.

The audience was fascinated.

With all the chivalry he could muster, Ray picked up a giant stack of his music and hit me right on the head. WHAP. The bug was gone, and so was the music.

The musicians started laughing, and, as soon as I recovered from the blow, I started to laugh hysterically. The audience followed suit. We had to stop the performance. My makeup was washed away with tears. Finally, after a couple of unsuccessful attempts, we did manage to finish the program.

We took Nicki along on that trip and we had a wonderful time, but it wasn't enough to keep David on the straight and narrow. We came home to Denslow tired, and troubled.


By now my work with Bing and Durante was going full force, and my love for them both brightened my life. Years earlier

I had literally saved pennies to go see Bing's movies. Tears rolled down my cheeks if the leading lady didn't treat him right. In the film MISSISSIPPI I was emotionally spent when the brokenhearted Bing sang "Down by the River."

Through the several years I sang on Bing's program, I met the most fantastic stars, like Al Jolson, whom I also sang with, and Bing was always finding ways to help give me confidence. In fact, everyone connected with him was funny and nice and talented.

Bing and I were always the first to arrive for rehearsals—that was something that always impressed me, his promptness. And I always felt you could count on his honesty. Bing maintained a certain modesty, even diffidence, about himself, although he didn't wear it on his sleeve. I remember his saying, "I wish I could really make something of my life . . ." *That* amazed me, that he would feel so humble. I tried, in a stumbling sort of way, to tell him what the world thought of him, but I don't think I ever convinced him.

Sometimes when he'd find me at the piano, he liked to tease me . . . "Hello, Peg. Who are you today? Chopin or Stravinsky?"

"Oh, hello, Bing," as I quickly swept off the piano bench. I never wanted anyone to hear me play, or should I say, hear me *not* play.

The musicians would straggle in—some early, but very few were ever late. You see, the show was live for the East Coast and recorded for the West.

Well, one evening in San Francisco, Bing asked me to go to dinner with him, and, knowing how prompt he always was, I started very early washing my long blonde hair. It was a fairy tale situation, my idol actually asking me for a date!

Makeup and hair finished early, I eagerly awaited the sound of the doorbell. When it finally rang, I thought, I'll just put on a little of this hair spray to make sure . . . It was the wrong can, it was sweet-scented room deodorizer! Naturally

I turned all colors, and Bing thought it hilarious as I tried everything, and finally ended up washing my reeking hair.

For dinner he took me to one of San Francisco's great restaurants, during which I told him about my emotional experience with his movies, especially MISSISSIPPI when he sang "Down by the River." We then cruised all over that wonderful city until we found a pianist who could play the song in Bing's key, and he actually sang it to me at our table. Once again, all those years later, the tears rolled. A whole river of them . . .

Bing used to write funny little notes, which I would find in my mailbox on arrival at some city. It meant so much— especially out there on the road—to hear from someone like Bing. (Cary Grant used to do that, too.) Once Bing sent me a wire referring to a long-ago appearance of his at the Coconut Grove. It seems he had "hit the sauce" a little, and that was his last appearance there. His wire said, "Dear Peg, please pick up my laundry. I left there rather hurriedly in 1931. Love, Bing."

Bing also gave me the loveliest painting by Busquets, a modern primitive of Paris that inspired me to write this lyric, which Paul Horner set to music:

### Petit Chanson de Rêves

I long to go to France because I want to see
The things I've only read about of gay Paree
I want to hear where music came to Debussy
And that would touch the very heart
And soul of me
The Louvre museum, the gardens of the Tuilleries
La Rue Pigalle where painters paint
The things they see
And we may find a Renoir or a Claude Monet
A painting that would surely take my breath away
On top of old Montmartre the dome of Sacre Coeur
Where the view is endless and the air is pure

To see the palace of Versailles aglow with light
Then stroll beside the Seine upon a summer night
To fall in love with someone in a quaint cafe
To walk the city streets until the break of day
To fall so much in love that I might want to stay
To know my heart will break when I must go away
Little song of my dreams
Petit chanson de rêves

I've been as near as De Gaulle and Orly airports, but I've never been *in* Paris. I plan to go this year (1987), but that's what I said last year. Maybe I'll just sing the song.

Bing was also so protective of me. Once he found me standing rigid outside the studio at NBC and asked what he could do to help me. He was so sensitive to my early days of nerves and self-consciousness. This was just before air time on one of Bing's many Kraft programs. I managed to say something like: "When you introduce me, would you please not leave me out there on the stage alone? Would you stand where I can see your feet?" He agreed and always sort of casually leaned on a speaker or piano to give me the support and time I needed to learn about being at ease onstage.

You have to love a man like that. He offered everything— money, cars, his own blood, and even volunteered to personally babysit with our little daughter, Nicki, while David was so sick in the hospital.

The last time I saw Bing, we were both doing a benefit performance. It was beautiful, if brief. He called to me, "Hello, baby! So good to see you."

I was grateful I got to see him one more time.

Yes, once we walked along, Bing—down by the river . . .

Funny things happened.
Jimmy Van Heusen was doing some writing for a Crosby

show, and we were at the St. Francis Hotel in San Francisco. Somehow we got lost in the bowels of the building. We were bent over under the pipes and came to a sliding door. We had been rehearsing in a dining room and somehow took the wrong door. You could look right down into the kitchen. If we had taken a few more steps, we would have fallen into it. We finally did get out, and Jimmy and I sat on a curbstone and had a long conversation. You know how the houses are in San Francisco, right on the curb. If you opened the window in your house, you would be right out on the curb. We were talking away, and the people opened the window and said if we didn't stop that and get out of there they would have us arrested for loitering . . . Never mind, Jimmy is a wonderful man, worth getting yelled at for. Because David and I used to stay at his house a lot in Palm Springs, and he was always around the Crosby Show, I was able to hear many of his songs in their growing stages. Bing did many of his songs. His partner, Johnny Burke, was a great lyricist, as, of course, is Sammy Cahn.

Jimmy was on the tall side, and didn't have a lot of hair. Somewhere I've read that men who are bald are very virile— you've heard that. Jolly blue eyes and enormously attractive to women. Oh, yes, he had a lot of women crazy about him. For me, Jimmy was a very good friend.

So was Alec Wilder, creator of "Did You Ever Cross Over to Sneeden's?", "It's So Peaceful in the Country," "While We're Young," and "I'll Be Around." Alec was a lovable eccentric, and he and I would sit and talk about life for hours. Schmoozing, I think it's called. Which is talk with a lot of affection and closeness. Alec, of course, was also a gifted classical composer.

In 1948 I campaigned for President Truman's election on closed-circuit TV. The particular event was a fund-raiser, at which I sang—what else?—"I'm Just Wild about Harry." The President himself thanked me. Friends of mine owned the desk on which the Declaration of Independence had been signed, and it was being auctioned off as part of the fund-raiser. Journalists were flashing their bulbs at President Truman and me as we talked, and one of the photographers said, "Mr. Truman, do you want one with Peggy Lee?"

"I do," the President said, "but I don't know what she wants. I don't even know if she's Republican or Democratic. We have to get Miss Lee's permission."

I appreciated his good manners. He wasn't the kind of man to take advantage of his position. He was also perceptive . . . I'm nonpartisan—for the man, not the party. Though I occasionally campaign, as I did for Truman, I don't believe in confusing artistic ability with political savvy. I'm a singer, and that's what I want the public to support me for.

David and I had some radio programs for a while, sponsored by Rexall and Oldsmobile, and I did a lot of guest spots, all of which kept me *very* busy. And sometimes pretty exhausted. But sometimes we would bring the whole cast home for spaghetti or chili. I mean, David would invite them, I would cook, and then he would come and say, "Get rid of these people."

The pressure was obviously taking its toll. David, and, finally, Dr. Stevens and my manager, Carlos, told me, at the last minute, that David was not emotionally fit to go on tour, that I would have to go out by myself. David's drinking, they said, was out of hand, so I took off for St. Louis solo. (My health wasn't too strong either, and I would come home from this tour with pneumonia.)

Opening day, the orchestra leader, Griff Williams, came out to rehearse with, basically, tenor saxophones, while my arrangements were for a different instrumentation. Suddenly I realized nobody had made provisions for that—what I found in the music trunk were parts for trumpets, trombones, flutes, strings. No saxophones. I was learning the hard way. One call to our librarian from Carlos, or Dave, could have prevented this.

Griff himself was so drunk on opening night he introduced me as Susan Reed. No help there. I went to my own resources, and called Ernest Holmes. "You don't have time to feel sorry for yourself," he said. "Just put it together and do it. I'll work for you, too."

As if in answer, Mike Bryant, a fine jazz guitarist, called out of the blue. "How are you?" I said, "Come right down here and bring your guitar." He said, "I don't have one, I gave it away." I said, "Find one and bring a bass player, too."

I had brought Sid Hurwitz and Billy Exiner, who had played with Tony Bennett and Claude Thornhill. Bryant, the godsend, turned up with a bass player, a very good one. We then proceeded to pick out seventeen tunes, all standards—Gershwin, Porter, Arlen, Rodgers & Hart, Kern—tunes that have served me throughout my career.

But now came trouble from Kopler, the boss man. He thought that if you hired Peggy Lee you also got David Barbour, and he didn't want to let me go on. Said he would close the room. Wonderful. I had invited twelve blind children from a local school to enjoy the show. What was I going to tell them?

Enter the union people. They told Kopler, "If you're not going to honor your contract, we're going to close down your chain." That meant a *lot* of people would be out of work.

I called Carlos, who said, "Well, you're really in trouble." You notice—*he* wasn't, *I* was. I quietly went to my room as Kopler was saying, "No David Barbour, no engagement." And the union kept saying, "You don't let Peg sing, we close down your chain." I called Kopler and asked him to come to my suite. I also called the union men. Four of them arrived in dark coats and hats—tough.

Now, remember, there were entertainers who played the chain, and, as I said, they all would have been affected by the union's action. I told Kopler, "If you are not satisfied after one week, I will work for nothing. But if you are satisfied, there will be no need for you to close all the rooms." Which meant the several rooms in this one hotel and *all* the rooms in *all* the hotels in the chain.

Well, thank God, we were a big success. Sold out. I did encore after encore following the seventeen songs, and the children got to enjoy it all. Carlos flew in to take the bows. Kopler gave a big party for the union, the musicians and me. Great toasts were offered.

Afterwards, Carlos Gastel asked, "How did you do that?"
I said, "I did not do it."
Carlos said, "I've got a lot of money bet on a football game. Would you uh . . . pray for—"
"I don't pray for bets. If a football player had an injury, I'd pray for him. But not to win money."
Carlos, you see, always thought of me as being on cloud nine, but I'm as practical as anyone you'll ever meet. I know what it takes to make money. The actions more than the words. And if anyone makes fun of my beliefs, I clam up. I just want to leave a residue of hope. I've always been a non-sectarian. I've always known it was between God and me.


As some of you may remember, the two biggest shows on television in the fifties were Ed Sullivan's *Toast of the Town* and the *Jackie Gleason Show*. David and I had hired Jackie as a warm-up act while touring, and I had no idea he was such a big star. But he said yes when we asked him.

One night Jackie and I went to dinner between shows, and later the manager came to me. "You'd better talk to Gleason," he said. "He's very sick, I'm not sure he can go on."

Well, he certainly hadn't looked sick to me at dinner
. . . And then I realized he was only pretending to be sick as
a way of getting through to me. At dinner, I remembered he'd
offered to let me fly home in his airplane from Bridgeport,
Connecticut, where we were appearing.

Later, I told Jackie, "You'll be all right, I know you will."

"Okay," he said. "I'll go on, but you have to promise to
stay in the wings."

I agreed. And then, to my horror, he turned and played
his entire performance to me in the wings, totally ignoring
the audience. At the end he winked at me and said, "How was
that, Myrtle?"

After that he asked me if I would appear on his TV show
for DuPont. When I did, I was standing backstage before we
went on the air, shaking from fear. Art Carney came to the
rescue, introduced himself to me, wearing a raccoon coat,
and was . . . well, he was Art Carney. It did the trick and I was
okay after that. In a way Art and I were like two school kids,
Art always writing me funny notes. A lovely man.


New York—the Hampshire House. David and I were going to
have a big party for the press in the Cottage Room, so I called
Leonard Feather, hoping he would find me a good pianist to
provide some incidental music. Who he came up with was one
George Shearing, who had just come to the U.S. from England and wasn't yet known.

During the party I was talking to some reporters when I
heard this wonderful piano. I said, "Excuse me," and spent
most of my time after that standing at the piano, just listening. That night was the beginning of my friendship with
George Shearing. Later we would do an album together,
needing to start from scratch, as it were, because George is
blind and we couldn't use written music. We rendezvoused in

Florida to set the keys and figure out the arrangements. We were up seventy-two hours straight.

When I'd start buckling from exhaustion, I'd call Ernest Holmes, who would say, "Remember, you're not the one doing the work. It is not I, but the Father. He does the work."

I would think about that, and it did help to refuel my strength and energy so that George and I could go back to work. I was involved, I realized, in a collaboration of more than two.

Meanwhile, though, David's drinking got worse. He talked about insects, I suggested he close the screen. And I even got an exterminator. But when the man came, David wouldn't allow him to do his work. What David did was throw a book at me. (He never liked me to read.)

I realized . . . I could no longer deny it . . . that I was getting stronger and he was getting weaker. I hurt bad, but my love for David could stand a lot.

# Five

DAVID WENT to Cuba for a change, a vacation, and I came home from St. Louis and points east and west. Then one day, without any warning, Daddy appeared at Denslow, smiling, eyes twinkling, looking a little thin. "I just had to see you," he said.

I was so glad to see him I started to cry. "Here, let's go in and sit down, would you like something to drink?" I tried to compose myself. "How long can you stay? You will stay with us, won't you?"

"Yes, honey, I'll stay, for a little while anyway."

Never mind how long, I thought, it was just so good to have him near me. I had been working on an apartment over the garage—a practice room—as a surprise for David when he came back from Cuba, which was also perfect for a guest. I thought maybe Daddy would like the privacy of that room, but I wasn't sure when David would be coming home. Besides, I wanted Daddy close to me, so it was decided Nicki would sleep in her nurse Alice's room and her grandfather would stay in her room.

Nicki's room was all white-dotted Swiss with pale pink piping, the furniture white-trimmed with pastels. There was a canopy over the bed with yards and yards of organdy and more dotted Swiss, and the curtains were covered with miles of ruffles. It was about as feminine as a little girl's room could be—complete with a child-sized upholstered chair. As you might expect, Daddy looked slightly out of place with his six-foot-two rangy frame in the middle of all those ruffles—but he was happy, happy to be with us.

Alice and I got him settled, then we talked while we had coffee. We were both a bit reluctant, but he did finally tell me nothing had ever changed with Min. I hadn't thought it would. He also said Milford, my brother, and Emily, his wife, were awfully good to him. I knew they would be, they were always so good to me. That was very important, Daddy's life had seemed so unfulfilled, somehow. The fact that he finally had the nerve to make the trip out here—to defy Min and leave her behind—said a mountain of things to me.

But all the while we talked, I was aware of his cough. He told me he had long since stopped smoking, so it wasn't that. I took him to Doctor Cavanaugh, who, after examining him, said, "Peg, I wouldn't give you a plug nickel for his chances to survive over three months." I felt myself sink into the chair. "But, if you do exactly as I say, he could possibly last a year." Well, that pathetic promise and my own fierce faith at least gave me something to hang onto, and I gave the doctor my word . . . I would obey him to the letter—and I would pray to God.

I began to repeat these lines to myself: "Closer is He than breathing and nearer than hands or feet." It is remarkable how close those lines can bring you to God, if you believe them. You might close your eyes and try them yourself. *Closer than breathing.* That's *close!* God is, literally, in us, and when we are truly in touch with this great spirit, this universal energy, we get all we need. So often we are like a fish that swims all over the ocean looking for *water.* It's all around that poor fish, if only he knew it. We all exist in the context of God's love and happiness, but so often just don't see it.

God, I repeated to myself, was within me, working through me . . . no harm could happen to me when I let the love of God pour through me . . . If I expressed good, only good would return to me . . .

My father's illness was a challenge to my faith, a challenge that strengthened.

Daddy and I didn't *talk* about his condition, which was referred to as a respiratory problem. But I did stress the importance of doing exactly as the doctor ordered. It was the way he could get better.

He promised he would, but I'm not sure he believed me. I think he thought if he could stay with me, maybe it would be worth the fight, and how I wanted to keep him there. Down deep I was pretty sure he knew that constant cough was not a very good sign, even though he never admitted it.

We did whatever we could to make him stay happy. Daddy loved jokes, and I went about collecting them from any source I could. I called a lot of musicians. Musicians are always good for a laugh. We also took him to see the family when he felt up to it, and I'm sure he was tired some of those times. But he enjoyed the fact that I had a husband I loved, a wonderful daughter and a lovely home. He didn't know about David's problem; I didn't tell him. He was pleased with the lovely garden, the princess jacaranda trees, the fruit trees, my vegetable garden. He was glad to see that my life had apparently turned out so well.

And he was impressed with all the stars I'd met and worked with, especially Bing and Durante. He asked me all kinds of questions about what they were like. Nicki told him she liked Red Scallop and Jimmy Durandy. That made him laugh—and cough. He was so proud, absolutely astounded by my success.

The door to Nicki's room was always left open in the hallway so I could hear him. One night I heard him crying. I went in—I didn't turn on the light. For so many years I had lived in dread and fear of this time, and now here it was. Even when I was little, if Daddy would have a little palpitation or anything like it, I would react in terror, thinking he was going to leave me, leave me with Min.

"Daddy? What's the matter? Can I get you anything?"

"No, no, honey, I'm—I'm just—realizing—I haven't been much of a father to you." His crying made it hard for him to breathe.

"Oh, Daddy, don't cry. I love you. You must have done something to make me love you the way I do."

It was a while before he calmed down. Finally, he did fall asleep, and I went back to my room, wondering how long he had felt that way. He didn't know I had been listening. Thinking he was all alone, he had brought up from the depths what he must have been holding inside for years.

He seemed better the next day. Then Min called, and he told me, "Honey, I have to go back right away."

There was no convincing him otherwise, even though I pleaded. Knowing that Min's coming out would be unpleasant for us all, he was adamant about his going back, so I arranged for my brother-in-law to take him home on the train.

Until the last minute, we had stalled around, wishing he didn't have to go, until he realized we would now really have to hurry and rushed down to Union Station. Departure time was so close we put Daddy in a wheelchair and went running through the station down the platform to the train. Daddy, bless him, was laughing all the way.

I know it wasn't easy for him, but it did make it easier for

me. I think maybe I learned about laughing from Daddy.
I would see him only one more time.

There always seemed to be something going on at Denslow,
even if I thought I was taking a break between engagements.
Just before David came home from his Cuban vacation, and
just after Daddy left, my brother Leonard and his wife Olie
arrived without warning. I had to borrow the Stevens' pool
house next door so that David's new studio wouldn't be taken
up as guest quarters. I especially wanted to surprise David.

To top it all off, our second collie, Gay, had eleven pup-
pies—a mixture of collie and Labrador retriever. I never did
meet the Labrador, but David was a bit overcome when he
returned from Cuba and saw all the dogs.

The next year there was a gigantic statewide homecoming for
me in North Dakota. People came from all over the state,
including the governor and some *Look* photographers.

Not on the schedule was an unexpected blizzard. All
communications were down. Telephone poles were snapped
off for 100 miles around, leaving live wires exposed. My
brother Milford and I and Joe Cancelleri, who was working
for us as a road manager at the time, drove through the
dangerous area to see Daddy for what would be the last time.
The highway department gave Milford special permission to
drive in the area because he was a master electrician and
could avoid the live wires.

Never mind the cold of the blizzard . . . it was a wonderful, warm reception. I had just not realized that the people in
North Dakota cared so much about their home grown girl
singer. David was pretty funny with the governor, telling him
he hoped he was a better governor than he was a singer. He
was, by the way, and then some.

\* \* \*

Back in California, I tried somehow to manipulate David into Alcoholics Anonymous, but he knew what I was doing and wouldn't have any part of it. He would, however, go with me to entertain the members. Singing at AA meetings was one way I hoped to get him into the program, and I took along a trio to back me up. Ironically, I later learned that some of the members thought I was the alcoholic, which rumor was strengthened by the role I would play in the movie PETE KELLY'S BLUES.

Finally, because he loved Nicki and didn't want her to see him drunk, David begged me for a divorce. I could hold out just so long . . . and one day, brokenheartedly, agreed. But when it was time for the hearing, we were so friendly and obviously loved each other, the judge asked if this was a marriage or a divorce.

We did a final thing together with Bing Crosby and Gower Champion—the movie MR. MUSIC. "Let's Call It a Day" was recorded the night I gave David the divorce papers that I didn't want to give him. You can hear it in my voice. He took the strings off five guitars that night. Only once again did I get him to record with me.

It had been easy to remain close to David for Nicki's sake. (Much easier than divorcing him.) We loved her, and we loved each other. When I explained that to Nicki, she seemed to understand. Unfortunately, though, she first heard about it at Westlake School for Girls. I had wanted to tell her before, but David and Dr. Stevens, for some reason, wouldn't let me.

The escalation of my career, the move to Denslow, the endless personal appearances, recording, and promotional work all must have just been too much for him, and who should have understood that better than I? At least I had my gardening as a therapeutic hobby, there's something about the soil that can be very soothing, but David didn't have any hobbies, any release. He did try golf, and there's a typically David story that music publisher Mike Gould tells about that. He was making an attempt to play, and when he continued to miss the ball, he remarked dryly, "Golf is harder than oboe."

David and I stayed very close all the rest of his life, even though he remarried for a short while. Somehow I feel we were never apart, and he was a comfort to me on more than one occasion. We did have our tough times when he drank too much, but what I really remember is the love.


"Roger."

I was in Las Vegas when I met him. And when I first saw that face, I knew it meant trouble, but I also knew there was no choice. I don't think I've ever felt the same about any-one—except David.

He said, "Hello, I've been looking for you." And I swear I answered, "Where have you been?" I didn't and I don't say things like that to perfect strangers. But I did this time.

"Roger" had just come back from Air Force duty in Europe and was a member of a famous squadron. And so he was also a star. The gambling tables were jingling and the chips were falling. "I just caught your show," he said, "and I've got to tell you something. We had your V-discs overseas, and I thought you were black. Can you imagine what a sur-prise it was to see this blonde Scandinavian walk out when they announced you?"

I could see by his look that we both had a problem. I was still very much in love with David, and even though we were having big trouble with his drinking, in my book there was no room for cheating. He walked away then, and I really didn't think I would ever see him again.

But about a year later he came to see me at the Copa in New York City, and by now I was really on my own.

\*     \*     \*

I was living in New York now, using agent Tom Rockwell's duplex apartment on East Seventy-second while he and his wife Vivian were at their home in California. I had sold Denslow for a fraction of its real price because David, and then Nicki, who echoed what her Daddy said, told me they didn't like the house. I should have realized that was a pronouncement with more bourbon in it than common sense, but I was so shaken I just went ahead, wanting to make them happy. And that, too, was a sentiment freighted with more emotion than common sense. A good friend told me they had found David among boxes and barrels one night with a guitar and a bottle, playing and crying. That about did me in for a while. Many times since then Nicki has said to me, "Why did you listen to a child? Why did you *sell* it?"

In New York I was so lonesome for Nicki, and Alice too, for that matter. I'd been doing the Steve Allen show every early morning, singing and playing straight girl for Steve, and drinking coffee with Lemuel the Llama. Lemuel not only drank coffee; he loved the LifeSavers that I often gave him as a treat. Steve was so nice, it helped the ache in my heart. We did "Songs for Sale," and I had a program for Rexall, but even all that work couldn't keep me from missing Nicki. Maybe I was saving the "family farm," but I was also running myself into the ground.

At Christmas I sent for Nicki and Alice to come to New York so we could at least spend the holidays together. Down to Grand Central Station I went, eagerly awaiting their arrival. Everyone got off the train, but no Nicki and Alice. I panicked. Finally, with the help of the good old railroad detectives, I did manage to find them. You can't imagine the relief to see my little girl coming up the platform. Somehow, they had managed to make the wrong connection in

Chicago, but I had died a thousand deaths until I saw them.

Alec Wilder, that superb composer and friend—Mabel Mercer was now singing all his songs—pitched right into the Christmas spirit and came over dragging a huge tree into the apartment as though he had just cut it down in the forest. We had heard of making snow for the tree, but, unfortunately, had the wrong method. We whipped up boxes of Ivory Snow with the Mixmaster, and, as we covered the tree, its poor limbs bent lower and lower. Finally, though, we managed to finish it and turn on the lights!

Seeing Nicki again was worth everything, including staying up twenty-four hours a day, if necessary. I actually fell asleep in a chair in Hammacher Schlemmer, sitting straight up in the middle of the Christmas rush. They only woke me up in time for closing. Never mind. We did all the trimmings. Alice cooked a fantastically succulent goose. Alec joined us for Christmas eve and day. And Nicki loved the idea of *snow* for Christmas!

It really was a lovely Christmas.


The famous Copa . . . I played it many, many times. Jules Podell was the boss man of the Copacabana, a spectacular place in a spectacular era. Tough was the way he ran his business. Tough? They didn't come any tougher, but not very well known were the good things he did in secret.

Jules used to say in his gruff voice, "The mirrors are always clean at the Copa." In fact, the whole club and the kitchen were always clean. I can't say that for the dressing room in the Hotel Fourteen next door, but the Copa itself was kept in top-drawer condition. All of the men, maitre d's, captains and all, wore immaculate tuxedoes, shoes high-shined. And the world-famous Copa girls . . . they were known less for their dancing than for their beauty and how they would walk with their hands up and fingers extended as though they were drying fresh nail polish. It was Doug, the choreographer, who taught them to walk in this way. Three times an evening they dried their nail polish as they stalked around the floor show.

Jules was relatively short and strongly built. His neck was very short; in fact, he seemed almost all of one piece, one solid muscle. True, he drank a lot, but he always seemed to know exactly what he was doing. If Jules wanted attention, he would knock his big ring on the table and everyone would come running.

He was also very protective, if he liked you. One night I was taking my bows doing a little side step. The orchestra was playing "Well, All Right, OK, You Win" on stage, and a fan was feeling exuberant. She was a lady, or I shudder to think what might have happened to her. As I side-stepped by, she gave me a little whack on the thigh and said, "Atta girl, Peg." Well. Jules and the captains were there *so* fast. They escorted the lady and her party right out the door. I think they took the table as well, but as I came back, Jules was standing there with his warm, if infrequent, smile. "You okay, kid? All right!" And on went the show . . .

One day he called me and asked, "Will you do me a favor, Peg?"

"Of course, Julie, what is it?"

"I want you to sing for some nuns." Here was a man who only took one day off a year, Yom Kippur, and he spent the entire day in temple. Now he was asking me to sing for some young novitiates in a convent. He said, "I know the young nuns would like to hear you sing, and I know they would like to hear 'You'll Never Walk Alone.' That's one of their favorites."

"All right, Julie, what time?"

"I'll send a car for you at six o'clock. Then I can bring you back in time for the show."

I was curious, to say the least. The limo arrived, I was

taken to the convent, and the beautiful novitiates had nothing but good things to say about Jules Podell and how he almost singlehandedly supported the convent. When he came back, he said in his gruff voice, *"Anything* you ever want me to do, Peg, *anything,* you just ask me."

You can never tell about tough guys.

Mel Powell remembers more about Jules and the Copa:

"Once when Peggy was playing the Copa, she was having a big birthday party after the show for Jules Podell. It was a pretty elite mob, including Tony Bennett and Sammy Davis. They were all at a long table with Peg and friends of Martha and mine, including Nick, the Africanologist and his wife. It was the early morning hours and the joint was officially closed. We were having drinks, food, a lot of laughs and birthday greetings, and a band was playing off in an anteroom. Nick, the Africanologist, was absolutely bagged, and when he heard the band, he wanted to go into the anteroom. Nick, a big guy, knew his way around. Suddenly he was a little assertive, there was a commotion, and he came stomping back. Out of the woodwork stormed Jules' boys. This was a tough joint. It was like a George Raft movie, with all the boys in tuxedos. They encircled Nick. Nick was about to be undone when Peg spotted him.

"She got into that circle and identified him as a friend of hers, faster, more sober, more serious than anyone had ever seen. Saved the guy from probably a bad beating. After all, they were protecting Peg, but she said to back off. For Nick, the protocol against letting yourself be shoved was tough to overcome.

"Peg had called Jules, and when he came into the center of the guys, she said, 'The man doesn't know what he's doing, he's just drunk.'

"Peg was the one. I didn't see anyone else pay any attention. There she was; she's much more alert than she appears to be. And when action needs to be taken, that dame is going to take it."

Thanks, Mel. I think.


"Roger" was back. That man I met in Las Vegas about a year earlier had come back into my life. One night after the show at the Copa, he asked to take me home. If it hadn't been snowing, we probably would have been riding in a hansom cab or something that lovers in New York do, but it was snowing, and we didn't want to miss the beauty of the snow-flakes settling on our faces. We walked all the way home, not even aware of the cold. Certainly not *feeling* cold.

He took me to the lobby and, wisely, said goodnight there. The emotion between us was so strong it held us in that special, wonderful spell that can't bear to be broken. Finally, we managed to say goodnight . . .

In the morning I was still half-dreaming. He called me, and I knew it was no dream, what I felt and he felt was all true, and would remain that way. And it did, through months of pure joy and tears and laughter . . . and then through years of frozen memory. He wanted to be married. I wanted to be married. My divorce from David was final. Nicki came to New York with Alice and fell in love with him too at the age of seven.

The two of them had the most charming arrangement . . . Every Tuesday was *their* night out, and I was not allowed to go. They went to places like the Plaza or the Tavern on the Green. They rode in hansom cabs and would go dining and dancing and come home laughing and singing. He would carry her piggyback up and down the stairs.

The two of us went to the races and baseball games. We went to the opening nights of THE KING AND I and SOUTH PACIFIC and MY FAIR LADY. We dined at Danny's Hideaway almost every night, and the others we went to the Drake and listened to Cy Walter. Night after night we would finish our evening with a few sets at the Embers and listen to Joey Bushkin or Erroll Garner or Red Norvo. We drove to the country and found little out-of-the-way places, and we fed the ducks on the river at Westport.

We planned to be married in Greenwich, up in Connecticut. He bought me an antique wedding band—a hair ring in which he placed a lock of his hair and mine.

He was a Broadway star, and I'd meet him every night at the Henry Hudson Theatre. He had been separated for some time, and I had rationalized that it was all right. He went to California, where he had been a movie star and would be again, to ask for a divorce. I was so in love with him, nothing mattered.

But Roger didn't get the divorce. He offered to give up everything he had ever made, but she told him that wasn't enough. She must have loved him . . .

When we separated, I went into shock. I finally started dating again to try to pull my life together. We ran into each other at Danny's Hideaway, our place, and he was with her.

Roger couldn't bear to see me with another man. She saw his grief and left for California that night. He asked a mutual friend to ask if I would take him back. Of course, I would. In my heart we had never been separated. Then his wife became ill, and he reconciled with her . . .

Through the years he had several small romances, but every once in a while he would come to me and plead for us to find a way to be together. Each time I would send him back.

When Nicki was being married, Roger appeared and was almost like a second father of the bride. He helped me make two five-foot-long swans with chicken-wire frames, filled with thousands of chrysanthemums and bachelor buttons for eyes, that floated on the pool during the reception. He was a most welcome member of the wedding—even to David, the father of the bride.

Roger became a bigger and bigger star. While making his last movie, he called and we planned to see each other again. After all those years. We made a date, and then we broke it. He called once more and said, "I think I've hurt you enough, but you know I will always love you."

A month ago he died.


Sonny Burke called one day in the early 1950's and asked if I'd like to write a score with him for Walt Disney. Sonny was the Artists and Repertoire (A&R) man at Decca, where I was under contract.

Well, of course, a Disney credit was something that was to be devoutly sought after, and with this I didn't even have to seek it. I didn't mind surprises like that at all!

Sonny and I went out to the studios to meet the great man. Charming? Yes, he was. The first thing he said in reply to "Mr. Disney" was, "Walt, please. Everyone calls me by my first name."

Good heavens, how could I call this great man by his first name, but I did. First, he introduced us to the entire staff— the artists, the animators, the sound engineers—and showed us around with the enthusiasm of a young boy. Enthusiasm seems to be one of the keys to great achievement, and Walt Disney *had* it.

He also brought out the story boards, the preliminary drawings from which the animators would work. Walt began to tell the story as he moved along the board, and at the same time asked Sonny and me to be thinking of spots where songs would work.

Walt was encouraging about everything. I remember getting so involved in the songs that I wrote an extra eight bars to the lullaby "La La Lu" that "Darling" sings to the new baby in what was to become LADY AND THE TRAMP. "Lady" is at the bottom of the stairs—except, of course, there weren't any stairs. The magic of Walt Disney. First he heard the demo I sang to inspire the artists, then said, "Well, *this* must be added to the footage where Lady is feeling very insecure about the new baby," and so it was . . . "What is a Baby?"

This might seem like a small thing to do, but imagine how long it took to paint each picture of "Lady" with the four paws moving slowly up the stairs and singing the lyrics with different expressions on her face. Those artists were truly incredible.

In the original story, "Old Trusty," the bloodhound, was killed by the wagon. By this time every character was real to me, I couldn't stand it and actually started to cry.

Walt said, "What's the matter, Peg?" "That's too sad, Walt. *Please* let him live, please don't let him die . . ." "You need the drama," he said. "If everything goes along too evenly, you don't have a story." "Yes, but it's just *too* sad." "Well, I'll see what we can do, but the *rat stays.*"

And he did, the consummate villain. As usual, Walt was right.

One day he asked to speak to me privately. "You know, we have a delicate problem, and I wonder if you'd help us with the solution?" "Yes, Walt, what can I do?" "It isn't what you can do . . . it's really your permission I'd like." "My permission?" "Yes, you know the little dog Mamie from the dog and pony circus?" "Yes." "Well, Mrs. Eisenhower, our first lady's first name, as you know, is Mamie, and I wondered if you'd mind if we would name the little dog after you."

Mind? I was thrilled to have him name that dog "Peg." The animators had me lip-sync "He's a Tramp" and do a little undulating walk. I enjoyed being a dog so much I decided to try being two cats. Really, Walt chose me to be the Siamese cats and "Darling" the mother.

I especially enjoyed it when Walt turned me loose in the

sound-effects department to find the sounds that fitted the Siamese cats. Bells, cymbals, chimes, the works. I practiced singing one cat and then the other—a fifth away. Walt let me have all the freedom one could possibly have. No question, every person that worked on the film was touched by Mr. Disney's genius. An Italian award was given to LADY AND THE TRAMP that read: "In this troubled world, a visible island of poetry."

Well said.

Over the years LADY AND THE TRAMP was reissued again and again. In 1988—thirty-six years after we began the picture— the first week's box office receipts were 176 million dollars. It has outsold TOP GUN and CROCODILE DUNDEE in video cassettes (3.3 million cassettes at $29.95 and some as much as eighty dollars per cassette).

Sonny Burke and I worked for hire, which for me meant $250 a day, a total of $3500 over a period of three years. That's really not so much for originating four voices, but I was still relatively young and inexperienced. Every time I look, there's another bulletin on LADY AND THE TRAMP, the last being from Canada.

In November of 1987, I was contacted to do some more promotion work, only this time it had expanded to a satellite adventure. We were driven out to Disneyland in Anaheim and got up at 3:00 A.M. to be made up and ready for camera. I believe I talked to eighteen or twenty-two cities all over the United States and Canada, the interviews taking place with me sitting in front of the big Disney castle so familiar to us all. Besides the satellite interviews, I did others in my living room in Bel Air. They offered me an honorarium of $500! I've also promoted LADY AND THE TRAMP for over thirty-six years.

There was some public embarrassment from all this. I

was doing an interview one day on CBS radio in San Francisco and had just finished a long, detailed description of what it was like to be originating a duet with myself; one voice singing the first part and then overdubbing myself to get the effect of the Siamese cats singing as Siamese twins. "There are no finer cats than I am," to rhyme with "Siam." The engineer put the needle down on the record and two strange voices came out singing, "There are no finer cats than WE are," which of course does not rhyme with Siam or I AM. I was shocked. "I named these cats Si and Am and that wasn't even me, how could they do this?" At this point the show's host told the engineer to stop the record, and we briefly discussed the possibility that this was a bootleg record. It wasn't. It was number 1234, I believe, which is no longer released by Disney.

I received an apology, sort of, from the product manager at Disney.

On to more pleasant things. Such as Greg Bautzer, who was easily one of the most handsome men I'd ever laid eyes on. He was also the most eligible bachelor in Hollywood, and highly thought of—and no doubt desired—by every beautiful movie star around, including Lana Turner, Ava Gardner and Joan Crawford.

A really handsome lothario, Greg Bautzer. He used to send me the most magnificent flowers, jewels, other beautiful things. One was an ostrich made with a ruby eye and big black pearl with a diamond tail. But the nicest thing he ever did for me was to like my poetry enough to have a private printing of a little book called SOFTLY, WITH FEELING.

He often came to Ciro's. I sang there a lot when it was *the* most elegant place you could go. Ciro's and the Mocambo were *the best.* Herman Hover was the owner of Ciro's, and it was really a lovely place then. George Schlatter worked for

Herman, and we were always dreaming up some light-cue or other. It was frequented by a lot of Hollywood stars, including Merv Griffin and Judy Garland. Merv was so good looking.

When Greg and I would go out to dinner—it seemed to me it was every time—we would just arrive at the restaurant, and there would be a phone call from Howard Hughes. Greg would say, "I'm so sorry, I have to leave," and he would take me home and go off to meet Howard. After a while I guess I thought he was better off with Howard Hughes. So I changed the scenery for myself, and Howard Hughes gave Greg a brand new white Cadillac convertible that he drove straight up on my lawn. I wonder if that's what I got for telling Howard Hughes I didn't like his Constellation? This occurred when I was singing in Vegas and Howard Hughes and Jimmy Roosevelt flew in for dinner and to hear me sing. I was impressed—no one flew anywhere for dinner before the advent of the Jet Set. When they came to Vegas, Jimmy was trying to be helpful to me and whispered an aside: "You know, he likes airplanes," trying to give me tips for conversation with Howard. I promptly said, "I love flying. But there's only one plane I don't like—the Constellation."

Later Jimmy told me Howard built the Constellation, but I didn't understand when Howard gave me a grim look. That *mot* of mine ended our conversation, at least for that night. My problem with the Constellation had started one time when I was on a flight and looked out the window to see what appeared to be an engine on fire. The cowling was white hot. Burt Lancaster happened to be sitting next to me, on his way to Hollywood to make his first movie, THE KILLERS.

"What's wrong with that motor?" Burt said.

"I've watched it go from red hot to white hot," I said. "It must be burning inside."

Though we landed safely, the Constellation was grounded after that.

Howard Hughes stories are the stuff of legend. Once he crashed a plane into a house in Los Angeles and was taken to Hollywood Presbyterian Hospital. My thoracic specialist, Dr. John Jones, who was also Humphrey Bogart's doctor, told me that the first thing Howard had asked for in the hospital was his hat. He had to have that hat. When he left the hospital after a few days, he had a truck come and load his hospital bed and bring it home with him. He'd become attached.

Hughes would always send an emissary to make dates for him—in an old Chevrolet. He didn't like to be seen. When an emissary called on me, I said, "I'm happily married and I don't play around." Later, Howard hired David to do the film SECRET FURY with Claudette Colbert. David, loving a play on names, called it SECRET FURRIER.


And then there was Hal March.

One night after I finished my performance in the Venetian Room at the Fairmont Hotel in San Francisco, I had a date with Hal March. We went to a little place in Chinatown, and when we arrived, we were unhappy to see the place was closed. But the man who owned it recognized us and said, "Come in and have a drink. It's not against the law if I *give* you a drink."

So we went in. Hal, a very funny man, was quickly regaling us with his jokes. It was very dark in there, and at the far end of the bar I could see an Oriental friend who turned out to be Paul Wing of Toy and Wing, a vaudeville act I had worked with years ago. In fact, the characters in there were out of a story, including a retired army colonel behind the cappuccino machine. The darkness of the place added to the air of mystery. We weren't doing anything but laughing, and all of a sudden there was a banging on the door. "Get in the back, get in the back," the owner said. Ever notice when someone orders you to "duck" or whatever, you do it? Well,

A head shot from the 1950's.

Peggy Lee and
Nat King Cole.

The Peggy Lee poster
as Career Girl
of the Week.

Peggy Lee, Bing Crosby, and Sammy Cahn.

Peggy's

back

OPENING
Monday
APRIL 16th

BASIN
STREET East
137 EAST 48th ST.

Peggy's Back at
Basin Street East.

Performing at Basin Street.

With a poster of J.F.K.

NEW YORK'S *Birthday Salute* TO THE PRESIDENT
SAT. MAY 19TH 1962 · MADISON SQ. GARDEN

Performing at the Florida Disc Jockey Convention in Miami.

A front page photo
from the New York *Times*
of Peggy and
Jimmy Durante.

Lucille Armstrong,
Jim Lowe (WNEW),
Peter Dean and Peggy Lee.

Getting ready for a concert in Montreal. Twenty-five
thousand people showed up that night. That's Hugo Gravator,
Peggy's lighting director.

Christening a San Francisco cable car with Herb Caen.

A still from "Pete Kelly's Blues", 1955.

A costume for "The Jazz Singer", 1953.

With Danny Thomas in "The Jazz Singer".

With Danny Thomas
and Johnny Desmond.

Sonny Burke and Peggy Lee while writing the score
for "Lady and the Tramp".

Bing Crosby and Peggy Lee
taking a break on the set
of "Mr. Music".

Recording some scenes with Lee Millar
for "Lady and the Tramp".

Johnny Mercer, Peggy Lee and Glen Wallichs.

Peggy Lee and record producer Quincy Jones.

Peggy Lee and Andy Williams.

With Tony Bennett.

Going home to see Daddy
for the last time.

Danny Thomas and
Peggy clowning around.

*(Photo credit: Hollywood Pictorial Service)*

Frank Morgan, who played
the cowardly lion in
"The Wizard of Oz" with
Peggy Lee on the
Jimmy Durante Show.

Leonard Feather, noted jazz critic, and Peggy Lee.

we did too. Actually we ran to the back, tripping over a Harley-Davidson motorcycle that we proceeded to hide behind, the bike and ourselves sort of fitting into a little hole in the wall. It seemed a perfect place to hide. We crouched down, we heard voices, and sure enough, the police came right back there to where we were, playing their flashlights along the wall.

"Come out of there," said the police. We didn't move. For no good reason we felt as though we had done something wrong. Broken the law. Fugitives. Well, we did come out, nearly knocking over the Harley-Davidson, and explained what we *weren't* doing there. After the police satisfied themselves that we hadn't bought a drink, they left, but they also left us shaking.

"You'd make a lousy burglar, Peggy," the owner said. I asked why. "Because, honey, you left your beaded bag on the bar."

Well, they paid me to sing, not to be a heist person.

And speaking of singing, I was doing it again at Ciro's. Mike Curtiz came in to catch the show . . . perhaps Danny Thomas sent him in, I don't know. But at any rate he asked me if I wanted to do a film. Naturally, I was elated, but I think I suspected it was just another Hollywood conversation. Not so. The next morning I read it in a column, and the next thing I knew, Mike Curtiz was taking me out to meet Jack Warner to talk about making THE JAZZ SINGER.

I knew Danny Thomas slightly from seeing him perform or running into him at a benefit, but now we were thrown together going over the script, the music and the numberless details that go into the making of a movie.

They introduced Howard Shoup, and he began to pour out designs for the character of "Judy." I was fascinated with the lovely clothes, so beautifully made and fitting so perfectly.

Danny was a dream, and we established a friendship that

will last forever. We laughed and sang and had a marvelous time while we worked like there was no tomorrow.

Danny, interviewed on tape, said: "I have known Peggy for a long, long time. I was a fan and still am. We made the best version of THE JAZZ SINGER . . . the first one was Mr. Jolson, and it was very badly filmed, the first Vitagraph. Edward Franz played my father; Mildred Dunnock the mother; very *nice* Philadelphia people. And we had this beautiful synagogue. At the end of the picture they wanted to make Peggy Jewish; and they did, too. It was in the scene where she had come to visit for Passover. As her feet were leaving the screen, you heard her say, 'I haven't been to a seder since I was a little girl.' I fought with Steve Tillingham . . . 'Leave it alone, for God's sake. What's the matter with this guy being in love with a non-Jewish girl?'

"You knew Peg hadn't been an 'actress actress' any more than I was an 'actor actor.' We're both entertainers. And well, my God, she's Peggy Lee, an American treasure.

"That's why I get steamed up when I see a rerun of JAZZ SINGER on television, and they edit out her song 'Lover' in that nightclub. They also edited out all my songs. I don't mind that, but not to have *her?* They're crazy. They have so many commercials, they edit out anything they want to make room for more commercials. Cutting anything that Peggy Lee sings is to me a mortal sin. Oh God, she is so good. She's frighteningly good, awesomely good.

"Peggy's stage presence is so sweet, there's no cockiness about her. She's sure. There's a big difference between ego and assurance. Peggy has no ego, but she certainly has assurance. I mean, she takes the stage. And I think that's the hallmark of any good entertainer. Not to be nervous. Not to be scared of the people. To take over . . . take command of the people.

"She conducts an audience the way a conductor conducts a symphony orchestra. She gets anything she wants

154

from them. If she wants them to stand, she can make 'em do it. If she wants them to cry, they'll cry, and they'll laugh with her. She's a consummate entertainer. I had a great time with her on THE JAZZ SINGER.

"She is also quite a lady. Nature has dealt her a lot of blows, but she's gotten up and won every time. She's persevered. You know . . . the diabetes that she has . . . nature can be a bastard.

"One time she got in an argument with Michael Curtiz, the director. Michael was a Hungarian immigrant, and he wasn't too great with the English language. When he directed, he was great. He would sit down and talk to you, really get involved. He got very involved with Peggy. I mean, he got it out of her. In the early shootings he wasn't too happy with her *or* me. We weren't giving him exactly the emotions he wanted. Peggy said, 'I don't know, Michael. The way you talk and what you want . . . suddenly a door closes between us.'

" 'Now, Peggy,' he said, 'this time we are going to have a great scene, and we don't talk about no goddamn doors.' We all busted up laughing. She did too. But he got it out of her. He got it out of all of us. At the end of the scene he'd say, 'Excellent, we do it again.' And he'd cry every time if you really moved him.

"Peggy was delightful to work with. I got requests for more pictures with her, but she was busy and I was into *Make Room For Daddy* eleven straight years. But I adored working with her. Love her now.

"Peggy's style is *her*. There's nobody like her. She drops her head down, leans on the piano and just falls back to it as she's finishing. She's got moves, great moves. Her rhythm songs are great, and so are her ballads. She's complete, absolutely complete.

"And she's got a great sense of humor. She's a good lady. And if ever a phrase, 'an American treasure,' applied, it applies to her. Louis Armstrong was an American treasure, and

Ella Fitzgerald, who adores Peggy and her work. The real professionals appreciate her the most. I hope she lives a long, long time.

"She's given so much of herself . . . When this woman—this perfectionist—comes home after a performance, it's always bothered me that she couldn't come home to the arms of someone who really loved her. Many men thought an awful lot of that lady. But the one that she wanted . . . bizarre. Women are crazy, they're one-man people.

"She's got a tremendous inner spirit. Michael Curtiz saw it and wanted to bring it out. I don't believe that she knew how to bring out these things that were in her mind as an actress—the sadness, the inner sadness. Brilliant. Michael Curtiz saw that, wanted to get it from her, but I don't think she wanted to expose it. That's why she said to him, 'Michael, you just closed a door between us.'

"But he got it. The scene on the phone where she calls me and she was just a little high, 'I just thought that . . . Jerry, you'd do well if you came back to Broadway. Oh well, I just thought I'd call.' It was very sweet. There wasn't much dialogue but she had it in her face. And when she sang, forget it. The sun and the moon came out at the same time."

Danny could make a girl blush.

# Six

SOMEWHERE IN the whirl of my life, I met actor Brad
Dexter, one of the eligible bachelors that used to inhabit
Ciro's and the Mocambo. Brad was playing movie heavies at
this time. He was good looking for a heavy, with electric blue
eyes. What a big, sweet, lovable man he was. That's what it
was; he was so good to me, and I was in such a muddle trying
to do the proper thing. I was dating furiously; you might say
my dance card was filled. I was grieving for David, I was also
ill to the point of being hospitalized, and I hadn't forgotten
the Broadway star. David was actually a comfort to me at the
time. I pored over Ernest Holmes' textbook, *Science of Mind,*
and read everything else I could, trying to make some sense
of it all.

I wanted a home and a father for Nicki, and Brad was
good to her. He seemed genuinely to love her. I found myself
loving his kindness. He liked to work in the garden with me;
we liked going boating and dancing; we seemed to have a lot
in common.

Brad's career was just beginning to build, and Ernest Holmes said, "Are you going to get married?"

He caught me off guard. "Yes, I think so."

"When is all this going to happen?"

Well, Brad got on the phone with me, and the first thing you know, we had set a date and asked Ernest to perform the ceremony.

Greg Bautzer had been running first, but I put cold water on that when I laughed when he asked me to marry him. What a stupid fool I was! My low self-esteem came to the foreground again. But we did remain friends. (I tend to do that with the men in my life.)

For the big event, in the seven-eighths of an acre at Denslow, we tented and filled the entire garden with beautiful flowers. Ernest was there . . . I can still see his dear smiling face. My metaphysics teacher Anne Wright was my matron of honor, and she brought all the aristocracy of all the southern belles with her.

Meanwhile, I was upstairs trying to get into the gown Howard Grier had designed for me and having all the jitters a bride could have. Penny Bozocos did special things to my hair, weaving in flowers and magic. Then a new face appeared—one that would be with me for some forty years. Lillie Mae Hendrick. Well, she came over to me, took one look at me and suggested I take a little cognac for my "pale little face." I guess she became Mama Lillie Mae that evening. David was at the wedding rehearsal, playing his guitar and giving "fatherly advice," just like the father of the bride. He also had a long talk with Brad. (I wonder what they said.)

Lille Mae helped me finish dressing and took me to the staircase. I had the bouquet clutched in my hand. There were 400 people down there, including John Ireland and Dan Dailey, and the harps were playing like mad.

THE JAZZ SINGER came out in 1953, and the publicity department at Warner Brothers had gone all out, kicking things off with a premiere in New York. Brad and I proceeded across country on the Super Chief, and someone had told them which train, which car. When the train stopped en route, people would push themselves through those metal doors trying to shove a camera in, and then I heard it—they called Brad "Mister Lee." I think that's when I knew it wasn't going to work. I felt so bad and couldn't stop thinking about it.

New York, as always, was exciting. When the line "I haven't been to a seder since I left home" came out of the screen, a wave of "whatdidshesay, whatdidshesay?" went all over the Paramount Theatre. Danny Thomas was right.

Brad and I got along just great in many ways, it's hard to say exactly why it had to fail. As I said, I personally think the "Mister Lee" business didn't help his career and it kept gnawing at me. I was to come to the conclusion that I loved him, but I was not *in* love with him—that somehow I was living a lie. I tried to tell him, and asked him for a divorce. We had been married only nine months.

When he left Denslow, we were both crying. I hope he has found happiness. He deserves it.


So the fifties were years of romance and suffering. I traveled all over the United States and part of Canada and made plans to go to Europe. I had to work to keep myself from grieving about David. Part of the time I toured with Billy Eckstine, Mike Bryant and Sid Hurwitz, starting at the Chase Hotel in St. Louis and ending up in Vancouver, British Columbia.

Going from St. Louis to Vancouver, we experienced answered prayers. Flying up to Vancouver we hit some rough weather. It was scary. The stewardness was so nervous when she couldn't get the door open to the pilot's cabin, she took a coat hanger and began to beat on the door. The crew, busy trying to keep the plane from being jostled out of the sky, couldn't stop to answer her frantic banging. It made the other passengers afraid because it felt like something was terribly wrong and we were surely going down . . . We were mighty glad to land, I guarantee you.

We were playing in a place called the Palomar Supper Club. My dressing room had no door, so the musicians used to take turns standing guard. The clientele was mostly lumberjacks, all heavy drinkers. It was a "bottle club," that is, no liquor was served. You brought a bottle and were served ice and glasses. Having several bottles staring at you, I suppose there was a lot of "bottoms up" in the air. They also had to drink up the entire bottle. They came in as fairly quiet gentlemen, but after an hour or two, they were loud and boisterous. It was usually at that point that they would decide they were going to visit that blonde singer and see if maybe she wanted to dance. The fellows would guard me as best they could, and no one ever kidnapped me, but one night it all broke loose. There had been a radio contest before the show, and the winner, Shirley Someone, was seated ringside—that was the prize. A nice, quiet girl who had never been to a nightclub. The place was jammed, most of the folks were very drunk. I was singing "I Only Have Eyes for You" when suddenly one of the men cracked another over the head with a bottle.

"Are the stars out to-night? I don't know— 'CRA— A—CK . . . if it's cloudy . . ." The fight was on. I called to my secretary Donna, who was standing in the wings. "Where's Shirley? . . . or bright . . . Where's Shirley? Find Shirley . . . 'Cause I only have eyes . . . Donna, find Shirley! . . . for you, dear . . ."

The audience from stage-center all the way to stage-right were trying to ignore what was going on at stage-left. That, of course, was impossible. They had already called the police. Now the paddy wagon arrived and proceeded to pack the audience, screaming and yelling, into the wagons. That left me half an audience. I continued to sing. Donna raced out and grabbed Shirley. Now we lost a quiet one who broke out of the stage-right group and ran across the front of me, another followed and then another and another. We had only a handful left by the time the song was over.

To recover, I went deep-sea fishing in Horseshoe Bay on my day off. Vancouver I remember as a land of intensely colorful flowers—deeper and prettier than anywhere else. I didn't get paid for the engagement at the Palomar Supper Club. The owner had a big black car pick me up and bring me to dinner in his home, where he had a parakeet I rather liked. He said he'd get me some birds. What I got was the bird, all right . . . his check bounced and I had to pay my musicians.

I still wanted the birds, so I bought a dozen parakeets to bring home and was sure I would have to smuggle them across the border in my hatbox. (Someone told me it was illegal *after* I had purchased them.) My road manager Joe Cancelleri had charge of feeding them apples and seed. I would carry the noisy box under my mink coat. People stared, and I nearly fainted when the stewardess said, "May I take care of your birds for you, Miss Lee?" Turned out it was as legal as daylight to bring birds across the border . . .

Dear, patient Joe, he was always helping me out of some mess or other. Like the time we had chartered a plane and landed somewhere in Montana in freezing weather. David said to Joe, who was trying to stop a dog from lifting his leg on Dave's amplifier, "Joe, did you take care of that union thing?" "Union? Who cares about the union? If that dog ruins your amplifier, who's going to fix it in this Siberian waste?"

This was a time when I should have been home with Nicki more, but some of David's business mistakes were extremely hard on our finances. He was giving away money to people without telling me. He had an ally in my neighbor, also an alcoholic. David wasn't working; I was, and he stayed home. I had nothing to do with business at all and totally trusted him. One time, when he and Carlos were drinking, it was decided to give away the copyright to "Mañana" in return for two tickets to the Rose Bowl. When I realized they weren't kidding, I quickly agreed to do a benefit in order to procure the tickets for them.

Another business calamity involved a future President. David purchased some choice land in the Doheny Hills from Ronald Reagan and Jane Wyman. It was three acres with a view of forever, a most desirable property. The streets had been named after birds, so we named ours Oriole Way and planned to build a home there. After maintaining the taxes for ten years, David *sold* it at a loss. In the late fifties I learned from Sy Devore that a friend of his had made a killing on some real estate in the Doheny Hills. Sy didn't know we had owned the land. Sy's friend made a three-million-dollar profit on it.

And so it went.


Daddy died in April. I was coming into Los Angeles on the plane. Something told me very clearly that my Daddy was making the transition. Dear Daddy . . . I could see him everywhere. When we landed, Ed Kelly and David met me at the airport. That was unusual, so it reinforced my feeling that Daddy had gone. They were relieved that I seemed to know. I reminded myself of what Daddy had told me when we went back for the homecoming and Joe and Mel took me to see him for the last time. He and I had had an opportunity to be alone, and he asked me to read the 23rd Psalm. When I finished, he said, "I never understood that until now." The room was still, he went on, "I don't want you to come back when I go. You go on and do what you're doing. Maybe folks won't understand but *we* know, honey, and that's all that matters."

I kept to our pact and sent my sister and brother-in-law,

Jack Martin, back to represent us. A chapter in my life was forever closed.

The fifties, as you've already seen, were a very creative time for me. George Pal of Puppetoon fame hired me to do JACK AND THE BEANSTALK and JASPER'S IN A JAM, among others. I was the voice of a harp in one film. After that George asked me to write some songs for TOM THUMB.

It was a thrill, of course, to see and hear Russ Tamblyn sing and dance to my newly created songs: "Tom Thumb's Tune," "Are You a Dream," "One for You and One for Me," "Sleep in Peace and Wake in Joy." The orchestra played "Tom Thumb's Tune" as a waltz, a march, a fox trot, and Russ danced it. I believe it had one of the longest playing-times for any single piece in a movie.

I recorded "Johnny Guitar" for the movie of the same name . . . what an experience to write with Victor Young and then have your own song be the title song of a film. Vincent Gomez played the guitar, Victor Young conducted.

Spanish music generally interested me in those days. Laurindo Almeida and I wrote "The Gypsy with the Fire in His Shoe," and Dan Dailey tried to do a flamenco dance on the recording, but somehow it didn't quite work. Sammy Davis, Jr. came in, danced on a wooden platform, overdubbing, and this time it was perfect. Like he is.

I kept playing Ciro's, where so many stars came every night. And those chroniclers of the stars, Louella Parsons and Hedda Hopper, were almost always ringside, at separate tables, of course, taking note of, say, whom Alan Ladd was with, what Van Johnson was saying to Mickey Rooney or David O. Selznick to Darryl F. Zanuck. In those exciting days, Ciro's upheld the glamor-image of Hollywood. Business was booming. Judy Garland and her husband Sid Luft were regulars at Ciro's, as well as in my house on Denslow, where they proudly brought young Liza. (Judy Garland was not *always* in as much pain as is commonly thought. When she sang at the Coconut Grove, bandleader Freddy Martin told me that she never returned his handkerchiefs, nor did she cry quite as much as it appeared. In fact, she had a wonderful, wild sense of humor and laughed at least as much as she cried.)

About this time, Sonny Burke and I began working on LADY AND THE TRAMP, and writing was becoming very important to me. "Where Can I Go Without You?" with Victor was a mild hit. Las Vegas was roaring. I also played the Sands for Jack Entratter, while Kay Starr was wowing them at the Flamingo with her "Wheel of Fortune," Jane Morgan was "Fascination" itself at the Desert Inn, the Ames Brothers were at the Sahara, Danny Thomas was on the boards and Don Ameche was starring in SILK STOCKINGS. A wonderful, exciting time.

And a wonderful, unexpected happening for me was a baby white Pekingese that fell in the pool at the Sands and was rescued by one of the fellows who jumped in, tuxedo and all, to pull him out. I fell in love with that puppy while nursing him back to life, and got him a mate. I named them Little One and Little Two.

Nicki's school, the Westlake School for Girls, was quite grand. Occasionally, *I* poured tea with the hat and the obligatory "little white gloves," which also became a code between Nicki and me whenever the occasion called for especially good manners. "Nicki . . . little white gloves." "Yesss, mother."

They say that French is, or was, the language of diplomacy, but I was no diplomat when I was a little girl in North Dakota and took books from the library and tried to teach myself the language. North Dakota—with its heavy Nordic population—was not exactly the place *parlez français*. I dreamed about going to France, so I guess it wasn't too surprising that I wanted Nicki to learn to speak the language, but it was a constant battle for six years to keep her in the class. Oh, she was a good student and so Madame Egan put up with her, was firm with her, but Nicki had to be talked into continuing every year. Many parents will recognize *that* little tug of war.

I also promised Nicki a little sister . . . from France, and did adopt a little girl through a foster plan. I promised to take her to France and I did—but much later and only to the Riviera.


During the time I was still working on LADY AND THE TRAMP, Jack Webb called: "I have a wonderful script, I don't know if you'll be interested in the role, because we're not going to shoot you in the best light. It's not glamorous and we'll deliberately light you poorly and things like that for the character, but if you like this, I'll send the script over, and you call me as soon as you've read it."

It arrived by messenger. I read it and immediately called Jack. I told him I couldn't wait to play it.

The part was Rose, in PETE KELLY'S BLUES, basically a nice girl trying to succeed as a singer, but not getting the right breaks, who becomes the girlfriend of a gangster and, because of their relationship, gets a pretty low opinion of herself. She starts to drink and becomes an alcoholic . . . Edmund O'Brien was very convincing in the role of the gangster, who's in the protection racket. He's Rose's man, and he goes to Pete Kelly to get her a job singing in his band. He forces her onto Pete, who was played by Jack Webb of *Dragnet* fame.

In the drunk scenes I had to sing off-key and out of tune. At one point O'Brien gets angry at Rose, beats her up and knocks her down the stairs. She suffers a head injury and goes crazy, and from then on thinks she's five years old and has a scar on her face. There is a rather famous scene from the movie when Pete Kelly goes to visit her in the asylum. She remembers nothing. She has a rag doll, and she sings a song called "Sing a Rainbow." A glimmer of something gets through to her and she says, "Were we good friends?" Which is as close as she gets to reality.

When we shot the scene, I patterned it after a little girl I had known who was mentally ill, and when she'd talk, she'd stare blankly at me and say, "Were we good friends?" I'd sing little songs to her and that one little good turn gave me the perfect way to characterize Rose—and get the New York Film Critics Award for my performance. I also received the Laurel Award, the Audience Award and was nominated for the Oscar.

Rose was my first important movie role, and I learned everyone's lines, which amused Jack Webb. Jack was also directing, and he said to me, "I watched you sing and want you to do what comes naturally to you." As we filmed, not a word of Richard Green's script was changed. Jack Webb shot long master scenes as though we were doing legitimate theatre. The only problem was the noise on the Warner Brothers lot. We were in the path of the planes going over. Jack arranged to move us all over to the Disney Studio and use their sound stage. That made it possible for us to do Rose's big insane scene in two takes, and they used the *first* one, didn't cut it. This is a much more satisfying way to shoot a scene than the usual Hollywood method of letting an actor get out a word or two and then hearing the director say, "Cut." It let me really get into the emotional content of the scene.

Since PETE KELLY'S BLUES was shot for the wide screen, when it's shown on television today, you miss a lot. In the insane scene, for instance, neither Jack nor I are even on the screen. You can just make out somebody's nose. But at least the dialogue is still there, and the viewer has a sense of being there right in the scene.

They were wonderful actors in the film—Lee Marvin, Martin Milner, Edmund O'Brien and Janet Leigh. Little known is that Jayne Mansfield is the cigarette girl in the movie. She had red hair then, and she was beautiful.

Arthur Hamilton wrote the songs that Rose sings. I loved the new songs "He Needs Me" and "Sing a Rainbow," and I also sang standards like "Somebody Loves Me." It was difficult to put those words in sync after having purposefully sung them out of tune and time as Rose did in her drunken, confused state. Ella Fitzgerald was magnificent singing "Hard Hearted Hannah" and the theme for the picture, lyrics by Sammy Cahn, "Pete Kelly's Blues."

I finished my part in the picture the day we did the insane scene at the Disney Studios. Richard Green must have done a lot of research on the character of Rose; she seemed to be a composite of so many singers I've known along the way, and I hated to leave her there.

James Dean was making EAST OF EDEN during that time, and he used to come over and visit me in my trailer—or was he coming to visit Rose? He'd arrive like a friendly cat. We were two shy people in a little room being very comfortable with each other. Jimmy was forever speeding around in his car, and it worried me. He was to die in a crash in Paso Robles, California, before he completed his next film, GIANT. Jimmy was an unusual, quiet, intense person, and he wanted to be friends. He was one of those people you could not forget. You could feel things simmering and sizzling inside him, and his silence was very loud.

The picture completed, I moved out of Rose's trailer and said my farewells. There was to be a cast party, and I wanted to be there. At the same time there was also a personal appearance scheduled for me at the Lilac Festival in Seattle,

Washington. My manager Ed Kelly, my hairdresser Penny Bozocos and I drove up there together, Ed Kelly at the wheel. Penny and I fed him radishes and ice cubes and used a lot of Sea Breeze and witch hazel to help keep him awake while he drove all night. We plastered his face with Ocusol pads. But the only way to stay awake was to keep talking and singing and laughing. I don't think you can go to sleep when you're laughing, can you?

My manager Kelly kept looking at an old covered bridge waaay up ahead and saying, "Biggest goddamn truck I ever saw," which I guess is how it looked from a distance. We finally drove over it, and he was quite surprised. I think he expected to hear a crash.

Dawn came, and we were still driving; the radio was playing the current hit "Good Morning, Judge. Why Do You Look So Mean, Sir?" That revived us a little. Then, after having passed miles of beautiful greenery and trees and grass and picnic tables, we stopped in a peach grove that looked freshly plowed. We spread our linen tablecloth on clumps of dirt and had lunch.

Just before the trip I'd had some kind of heart episode; no real damage, but I was supposed to be careful. The doctor had told Kelly to be gentle, no big shocks. He held my arm when I walked, and he did this so constantly I thought we were at risk of being joined at the elbow.

We checked into the hotel, had a rest, I showered and washed my hair. Now it was time for makeup. About ten or fifteen minutes earlier Kelly had tried telling me that a bomb was set to go off at seven P.M., but he couldn't bear to say it because of my heart so he told me there was a "little fire" in the hotel. I kept telling him, "I can't smell any smoke, where are the fire engines?"

He pointed out that the windows were closed. "There *is* a fire, we *do* have to get out."

"Are you kidding me?"

"No," he said, and I could see he was serious. I was still putting on my makeup for the show, while down below the bullhorns were telling people to evacuate. Kelly made three trips to tell us to get out. He had already warned the musicians, and they were now gone. Penny was busy getting the jewelry. She had set my hair with beer (at that that time, beer was supposed to be the best thing to set your hair), and I had decided to use grease paint. I have no idea why . . . it *might* have been because Dan Dailey had told me I never wore enough makeup, so I let the pendulum swing the other way.

My suit had a large white ermine shawl collar, which I promptly managed to get grease paint all over. I also had a new heather mink that now was also covered with grease paint.

Kelly said evenly, "We have to get out, there-is-a-bomb-in-the-hotel."

"Oh . . . okay, okay . . ." I was locking the door, and Kelly, who was already running down the hall, shouted at me, "Don't lock the door, takes too much time." Obedient child, I ran back and *un*locked it. Kelly said, "Oh, my God, I don't *believe* her. She's going back *in* again." We now had about ten seconds left, according to the police.

With all the news cameras on hand, the police kindly put me in their squad car . . . after all, I was a mess, a blob of makeup and beer. Probably no one would have recognized me, although they were saying something about Peggy Lee being there for the Lilac Festival. Kelly had our car brought out and we raced to the theatre, late for the performance.

We were so tired, we were punchy. I dressed in some temporary shelter at the Festival, and the show went on. Immediately following, I washed off the grease paint, we got in the car and went spinning down the road. Kelly, a great driver, was determined to get back for the PETE KELLY cast party, but, as Quincy Jones and I used to say, "Even a mink has to lie down sometime." We just had to stop and rest.

So we drove to a motel and went to bed for about two hours, got up and filled the car with gas and ice cubes and took off again for L.A. At first there was *no* traffic, but, after looking, another car did finally show up and tailed us until we finally slowed down to let them pass. Do you know what we did? We three grown-up people? We stuck our tongues out at them, and Penny and I stuck our thumbs in our ears.

Have another radish, dear.

Well, we did make it back for the cast party and there was much excitement about the film and talk about my perform- ance as Rose. As Jack had predicted, it was a highly successful role for me. I could hardly believe it when I won the Motion Picture Exhibitors' and the New York Film Critics' Awards, not to mention the Oscar nomination. Jack said I would not win the Academy Award because I wasn't signed to a studio, but being nominated by my peers was more than enough for me.

On Oscar night Jack Lemmon and I were co-presenters, and, after some makeup person with all the best intentions in the world had thickened and blackened my eyebrows, I think Jack must have thought I was Groucho Marx. I thought so, too.

I didn't really expect to win, so I wasn't disappointed, but it's rather nice that after all these years, someone will say to me, "I still think you should have won."


Denslow was sold and I was looking for a home again. The real estate person said, "You'll love *this* house. It belongs to a writer and he's off in Europe someplace." I learned there had been many, many tenants and each one had left at least one layer of wallpaper on the dining room walls. "It's all right if you want to decorate it your way," the realtor said. "They all do." When I first saw the house, it seemed just right— tucked away in Coldwater Canyon with lots of trees and shrubs and ivy. Cozy and isolated, it had three bedrooms and a pool house.

Of course, no one told me it was *haunted,* and if they had, I wouldn't have believed them. Alice Larson, my housekeeper, wouldn't have either, she was too sensible. Maybe my sister, Della, or my brother-in-law Jack. Mama Lillie Mae would, though, because she knew the house. I just kind of smiled and thought, "She'll get over that."

My manager Ed Kelly and I were planning a big tour, but first I needed to redecorate. As soon as I'd pulled up the window shades I saw why they had been pulled down in the first place—a paint job was desperately needed. In broad daylight I could see that the place wasn't cozy so much as it was downright tacky. We began painting before we moved in, and it was someone's idea that *everybody* was going to paint a little. Family and friends, lots of friends—a regular paint party. We ordered *so* much paint the manager of the department came over to see what we were doing and, don't you know, *he* joined, too? It started being fun . . . Tom Sawyer stuff, remember?

Russell Birdwell was my press agent at the time, and since I didn't want any Russian wolfhounds—his suggestion for a publicity shot—he became quite frustrated with me and sent a regiment of waiters from Chasen's with all kinds of hummingbirds' wings and things under domed covers. The waiters were followed by photographers, whom we obliged by posing with our paint brushes. I guess that wasn't Mr. Birdwell's idea of glamor, because I never saw any of those pictures in the papers.

We painted not only the *inside* but the *outside* of the house. The dining room wallpaper had to be steamed off to remove it. It was so thick it could have been used for sound-proofing. Things would go along quite nicely until the cock-tail hour, and then whoever came over—merchants, doctors, lawyers, chiefs—would make a mess of something and it would have to be redone. That house was busy as a beehive. The walls were wheezing with music and laughter. Even if I'd agreed to pose with Russian wolfhounds, no one would have noticed.

The first night I slept there was uneventful enough. If there were any ghosts around, I slept through the floor show, but then I was so tired nothing could have disturbed me. The first odd thing I noticed was my daughter Nicki dancing with the weeping willow tree when she came home from school, but that seemed normal enough for a young girl. Then Alice giggled and told me she saw the kitchen stool *walk* across the floor. Alice was a very practical woman but she always giggled a bit when she got nervous. Like if she broke a vase, she would laugh as she said, "Heh heh heh, I just broke your vase, heh heh heh." Well, pretty soon everyone started mentioning they heard the empty coat hangers go dancing across the rods, and two of us heard a little popping sound that would go through the house, but only at night. I should have known something was awry because Lillie Mae had been making lovely big hampers of food for the crew, and finally when she came over with the last load she let out a "oh no, no, not *this* house." She had worked and lived there with a famous lady star who was living in the house with a very famous director. One night the star had been locked out in the nude when she went to get her barking dog. A tree fell on her.

Shortly after we moved in, the lights in the pool house started going on and off, and *no one* was down there. "That's grandma," Lillie Mae said. She explained that the director's grandmother had stayed in the pool house and added, "She passed away in that pool house and she's never settled down. Better leave her alone . . ."

Other strange things were happening. The lights by the front door started blowing out . . . we would hear footsteps and then my dogs would bare their teeth and growl as the hackles on their necks stood right up. They'd *never* done anything like that before . . . always had been serene, sweet dogs. Also, the dining room buzzer continued to buzz at intervals when no one was even sitting at the table. My sister Della walked across the living room, tripped on absolutely nothing and broke her leg. Off to the hospital she went. My brother-in-law became very ill. Off to the hospital *he* went. We all started calling the ghost "Grandma" after the director's grandmother. The others said Grandma liked me and that was why I wasn't bothered. Of course I wasn't . . . I'd had to survive with Min.

But then I got my comeuppance . . . I got sick, really sick. They called Dr. Cavanaugh and he said I absolutely *must* cancel the tour, and Ed Kelly had to find out where we had sent Stella Castellucci's harp and Milt Rhinehart's trombone. I think we'd sent them to Boston. Kelly kept comparing the scene at my house to YOU CAN'T TAKE IT WITH YOU, what with the dogs wandering around and the piano being played in between some jazz records.

Dr. Cavanaugh said, "Thank God you didn't come home in a box." Just before I left for a four-month rest in Palm Springs in the home of my friends Nat and Valerie Dumont, I was sitting on the couch watching Alice, my housekeeper, and Jack Martin, my brother-in-law, bring some things up from the cellar. Jack said, "Be careful, Alice, Grandma might be down there." Alice laughed. But suddenly the trap door picked itself up—it had been leaning in the *opposite* direction—and hit Alice on the head, knocking her down the stairs. She wasn't laughing anymore.

I left with a nurse for Palm Springs.

All tanned and rested, when I returned to L.A. I went back to work, singing at Ciro's. Bob Calhoun knew I was looking for a home and he told me about a wonderful house on Kimridge Road. I couldn't wait, so we got a giant flashlight and went up to Kimridge that very night. Bought it by flashlight then and there.

It was even better than he said. Brand new. A view from every room. It was next door to George Putnam, whom I had known back in the Middle West. He had two adorable daughters, who loved to talk to me through the fence. We added two new dogs, little pure white Pekingese with black eyes, to our menagerie. Life was great. This time I would have the pleasure of putting in a pool and landscaping. My sister Marianne said my trees "had wheels" the way I moved them around, but they thrived.

Nicki and I were very happy with our new home and got everything out of storage after "Grandma's" house. It was good to see our furniture again, and have it stay stationary, like with normal people.

About Marlene Dietrich. She was often at Ciro's listening to me. And over the years Marlene continued to come to see and hear me—concerts, benefits, theatres, and once in the Hollywood Bowl. I think she liked it that I tried to approach singing as theatre, complete with lighting, staging and acting.

I always adored Marlene Dietrich, so it was a triple thrill when she wrote about me in her book. One day she called and asked me about a musician, she was looking for a replacement for her guitarist. In that low throaty voice with the delightful accent, she said, "Hello, Pageeeee . . . ? Could you help me to find anozer guitarist? I have this fellow who plays only a plinka, a plinka, a plinka plink and now he wants more money, what shall I do? Shall I just pay him zis money or perhaps you know someone else?"

She was, indeed, paying him well, and he was a fine guitarist, but not quite so fine as to demand the salary he planned. I gave her a couple of names, and I don't know what came of it, but it strikes me that some people don't know how gigantic the demands made on a performer, especially a woman, can be on the road. It isn't easy. They add up, as the business manager says.

The pressures of being on the road make home that much more important. I loved my new home, and my friends often said Kimridge Road was always their favorite, that I always thought Kimridge was so romantic. Well, it was, on both counts. It was cozy and lovely. It was a low-slung house on top of a hill with an Oriental look and a view of seven mountain ranges. The bedrooms for the ladies were soft and pale. Nicki's room had a white marble floor, mostly covered with white fur. Her bed was gold-leafed wrought iron surrounded by clouds of yellow chiffon. The canopy was caught back with gold-leaf antique carved wooden cherubs. The white marble continued down the hall to my boudoir, which opened on a very private little garden with a trickling fountain. I've always loved the sound of water, the serenity it brings. I could meditate or take a sunbath, maybe write a poem or a lyric, or do a sketch to paint later.

Inside my bedroom the pale blue velvet king-size bed was up on a white carpeted platform. All across the back of the bed were white louvered shutters, and on each side my dear friend Eddie Tirella had painted some wonderful *trompe l'oeil*—blue sky with wispy white clouds and a white railing that held two graceful white urns. At the end of the bed were yards of sheer white curtains that I could open or close by pushing a button by my bed. Magic!

For another touch of glamor, there were crystal chandeliers hanging from the ceiling, with mirrors that reflected the chandeliers forever. Add a couple of pastel-and-greenish silk print French Louis XIV chairs and a chaise longue and you have quite a bedroom.

Eddie Tirella—"Eduardo" as I nicknamed him—made

life a joy for me. Time after time the doorbell would ring and there would be an enormous basket of flowers with Eduardo hiding around the corner so he could watch my face when I saw his gift. "Let's go the nursery," he'd call out, and I would come running to jump into his Morgan car. We'd come back several hours later with the Morgan filled and overflowing with plants and flowers for the Japanese garden we were planting. It looked like a planter—the Morgan, that is.

Workmen did an excavation for a large fish pond that was about thirty feet long and a good four feet deep. We stocked it with perch, goldfish, carp, and catfish, and planted it with a rock garden that nestled ferns and ivy, moss and every kind of plant that would feel at home there. My favorite was a very old wisteria vine that was thick enough and strong enough to weep over the pond.

One day I was dressed to the nines to go to a luncheon (which I seldom did or do), but I was ready for it with a beautiful Rex hat and a Jacques Fath suit. In those days we always, as I taught Nicki, wore "little white gloves." I stopped to speak to Eduardo and noticed one fern jutting out of the rock garden. So, with all the faith in the world, I tiptoed around on the rocks—and promptly slid into the pond among the lilies, the water hyacinths, and the mud. Well, at least I managed to save the hat.

We had big mounds on two sides in which we planted Rangoon lime trees, evergreen and all sorts of plants, bushes and trees that Eduardo had researched for a Japanese garden. We also built an authentic bridge over the pond from the front entrance over the garden to the pagoda on the other side. We painted it burnt orange and built a giant moon gate at the entrance. We hid a water pump among the plants so you could hear running water everywhere.

So many happy events would take place there over the years, like a seventeen-piece brass choir playing "The Lord's Prayer" on Easter Sunday, poetry readings, a classical guitar concert by Laurindo Almeida, and a Japanese costume party.

At the housewarming, I didn't dare try the saki because of our guest list, which included our neighbors Charles and Prudence Elam, Alana Edan (a visiting Israeli star), Mrs. Kuto, who played the koto or was it Mrs. Koto who played the kuto (no, it was Mrs. Kuto who played the koto), and then there was Prince Edam. I was in full Japanese makeup and costume. The prince grandly opened the moon gate for Jayne and Steve Allen, and Steve said, "May I please see our hostess?" He was looking *past* me at the gathering of guests. I think he thought I was a geisha girl. Duke Ellington very grandly escorted Mrs. Kuto (who played the koto) to the living room, where she assembled herself elegantly on the carpet and played the most beautiful music. Duke was a wonderful guest. The warmth he spread around could get you through a cold winter.

One day Duke Ellington brought me the tape with the theme music from the movie ANATOMY OF A MURDER, and I was impressed. He just said, "Here you are, your Highness—write this," and he left. (Duke nicknamed me "The Queen.") When I thought about writing a lyric about a murder, it seemed like a challenge, but for any one of you who write lyrics . . . I just got lucky when I found the poetic symbol. Jimmy Stewart played the detective who liked to go fishing to think about solving a case (as, by the way, did the author of the book of the same name, Judy Voelker, pseudonym "Robert Traver"). So he became the symbol of the fisherman. The trout is the man who committed the crime—the one who will be caught. I didn't have a symbol for Lee Remick, but her beauty was symbol enough. Still is. I finished the lyric and gave it to Duke Ellington. The Duke liked it all, and that was enough for me.

\*　　\*　　\*

Back at Kimridge Road, we had a very special wedding, a double wedding. My friend and bass player, Max Bennett, wanted to be married to a lovely girl named Judy Stone, and his beautiful sister Mary, who was my secretary at the time, wanted to be married to my drummer Mel Zelnick. Well, what more romantic spot than the Japanese garden? I spent a lot of time planning the floral arrangements. I wouldn't think of letting anyone else get into that act! People saw a good deal of this figure in white running around with a trowel and pruning shears, having a ball!

It was a triple-mixed marriage—Catholic, Protestant and Jewish—so I asked my friend Dr. George Bendall, an associate of Dr. Ernest Holmes, to perform the non-sectarian ceremony. I wound up having to be the surrogate mother of the bride for Judy, but there was no way I could make it fit Emily Post. Finally it was agreed that her stepfather would give her away, while I sat with her real father. Go figure it.

I ran out of the garden just barely ahead of the first guests, who came through the moon gate, frantically saying to myself, "If I can't see them, maybe they can't see me." Oh, and what a sight they saw! To the beautiful music of the harp being played by lovely Stella Castellucci, they looked over to their left and saw the curved bridge over the pond all wrapped in white satin and white carnations. The pagoda was covered with lilacs, carnations, lilies-of-the-valley and baby roses. The back of the pagoda was a solid mass of cymbidium orchids placed in a large fan shape. The water was quietly gurgling, the harp was—what else?—heavenly, and an occasional bird would fly and pause over the wisteria weeping on the pond.

The brides were excitedly getting dressed, and the "surrogate mother" was rushing into the shower, just in time to dress for the occasion. I donned a special sky-blue organza with a matching garden hat. The brides were radiant in their silks and satins.

Guests were wandering through the house getting ready for the ceremony. The staff was out in the kitchen area seeing that plenty of champagne was being iced. There was a happy, busy hum everywhere. Little One and Little Two, our tiny white Pekingese, were lolling in the Greek sheepskin carpet, amusing the guests, who were trying to guess which was white Greek sheep and which was white Pekingese. (The latter have big black eyes.) Meanwhile, the assembled friends were sending out rays of love to each other, an altogether perfect ambiance for a wedding.

There had been no time for a rehearsal with Dr. Bendall, so we went over the details verbally. Then the guests took their seats, and Dr. Bendall and the two grooms stood there in sartorial splendor waiting for their brides. Finally came the wedding march, and the radiant brides emerged from the house and walked over the flower-covered bridge to take their places next to their new partners. Dr. Bendall began the ceremony, reading some lines from Kahlil Gibran's *The Prophet.* We were all mesmerized by the physical and spiritual beauty of the occasion . . . when suddenly there was a quiet rustle through the guests. I suddenly realized that Dr. Bendall did not know the couples and, with the four rings and the double-ceremony, he was marrying Max to his sister Mary. They and the assembled guests were more or less in shock. I slipped to the side of the pagoda and whispered in Dr. Bendall's ear, "Stop the wedding, that's Max's sister."

Of course, we had to laugh and begin again. He then pronounced them men and wives. I don't remember who caught the wedding bouquets, but I know it wasn't *moi.* Everyone went smiling, laughing, kissing, and hugging into the champagne reception. Mr. and Mrs. and Mr. and Mrs.


In more tranquil moments, the clouds would float over the swimming pool and I would lie on the island looking up at the sky and listening to the music coming from the outside speakers. Maybe this really was heaven. We had nice neighbors, the Putnams, and I adopted a wonderful creature that was part bobcat and part just plain cat and named him "Rusticat."

I had recently returned from New York after the pneumonia episode and had to spend seven months in bed, but I used to sneak out into my private garden and paint there. Oh, I loved that place.

Clothes and the fifties . . . it was a big time for both. Edward Sebesta was making magnificent clothes for me then, using all kinds of beading, wonderful fabrics and feathers. Indeed, he had a feather man who was making a giant cape out of *coq* (rooster) feathers. Edward and I needed six hundred dozen feathers and we were about one hundred dozen short. (Did you know they have to bleach and then dye vulture feathers? They're really beautiful. The thing is to get the vulture to sit still for all that.)

One day the feather man was just fed up. It was a hot, humid day, and he was surrounded by feathers and orders for more. *Coq* feathers? Yeah. Ostrich feathers. Sure. Vulture feathers? Yup. He got very drunk and disappeared. And you know, I don't blame him . . .

One day I was doing a style show for a charity event. It was all Don Loper clothes and Somper Furs. Van Johnson, one of the stars present, noticed I had an ermine coat to model. He said, "Throw it on the floor, Peg, and drag it!" After my heart surgery, he sent me a wire: "Sing out, Louise!" (Louise as in GYPSY.) Van gives good advice.

Here are some interim notes on Kimridge, beginning with Harry, the butler, who had the highest recommendations . . . I was told he had worked at Scotland Yard and had even been a chauffeur at Buckingham Palace. Nicki and I were so impressed *we* dressed up and stayed that way for the first week. Harry was most distinguished and preferred sit-down dinners—all of the best silver, crystal and china were out for each meal.

One evening when Art Carney was a guest, Harry came around with a full battery of silver. Artie promptly dropped a serving spoon, which clanged to the floor, and said in his best Ed Norton manner, "I beg your pardon." Harry responded with his very quiet "Carry on" (pronounced "Ceddy on"). After Harry left the dining room, Artie, as Norton, pretended to be crestfallen. Or maybe he wasn't pretending . . .

The next evening Ernest Holmes came to dinner (not having previously met the handsome, proper Harry). As Harry opened the door to down-to-earth Ernest, he said in his archest British accent, "Good evening." Ernest stuck out his hand. "Hi, I'm Ernest." Harry wasn't prepared for that, because I had given him a profile of the brilliant and distinguished Dr. Holmes, but he rather quickly regained his composure. That night must have turned Harry around . . . one shock after another followed, the guests including Dr. Holmes; Jimmy Marino, a protege of Albert Einstein; two geologists with bandaged hands (from a Mexican plane crash) and, again, Mr. Arthur Carney. Jimmy and the geologists had just returned from a trip to a gold mine high in the mountains in Mexico with the Mayan Indians. Harry, stunned by all of this, nevertheless "ceddied on," as he himself would say.

In fact, he "ceddied on" so well he went on to become the manager of a fine hotel in the U.S. of A. . . .

Ernest Holmes loved Sunday night suppers, and by now we were such good friends they were often at my house. Ernest personally cooked, and I still think his baked beans were the best ever.

One such Sunday, turkey was on the menu—I met a

life-long friend-to-be, George Bendall, who, on his first visit, accepted the honor of carving the bird. A wonderful fellow, but carving was not his thing . . . the turkey sailed all over the kitchen, we brushed it off, put it in the broiler to sterilize it, and proceeded to have dinner. We still laugh about it.

Hardly a day goes by now that I don't talk with George. I would do that with Ernest, and when he left us, George sort of took over . . . I suspect Ernest told him to watch over us. Ernest and George were really like two guardian angels, and I remember once when I was very troubled about Dewey Martin, the very good-looking actor, Ernest said to me with typical New England candor, "Now, Peggy . . . you don't have to *marry* them all." Peggy heard but didn't always listen . . . I married Dewey, and, later, the only explicit advice Ernest ever gave me—he usually said pray for guidance—was to divorce Dewey . . . Dr. Barton said "either get a divorce or a crash helmet."

Jimmy Marino was not only close to Albert Einstein but to Robert Oppenheimer as well. I met this young man when I was singing at the Fairmont in San Francisco, he came right up and introduced himself as a fan, which was the beginning of a long and fascinating friendship. I was able to discuss my theory about color and sound waves with this brilliant young scientist. It had begun when I had been chosen by Bing Crosby Enterprises because of the song I introduced, "While We're Young," which I planned as a special feature with a screen full of color patterns for a future performance. They were produced by my sounds hitting the chemically treated screen. I told Jimmy that I saw a connection between this and the colors I'd seen in my mind during an accident, when I was hit on the head. After my injury it occurred to me that those color and sound waves might be used as a healing device. I still think so.

Jimmy was working on the H-bomb at Cal Tech, and he actually brought my idea to Einstein, who, I was told, thought it had merit. He was even scheduled to come to dinner and talk about it, but that was just before his death. He did give me an autographed book, which I will always cherish.

Jimmy Marino and I had an ongoing discussion about God (he claimed he didn't believe in God). He was short from having had polio, and he had a withered arm. Because he couldn't do physical things he would have liked to do, he poured everything into science. He often talked to me about the sorrow that Oppenheimer felt about the A-bomb.

Jimmy also invented a machine to refine uranium ore at the mine site, and was instructing people how to use his machine when he slipped and fell into the machine and cut off his good arm. They brought him to the Navy hospital in San Diego, and I hurried to see him, wondering what I could say to him. Before I could open my mouth, he held up his withered arm and demonstrated how he had learned to write with it! Given his professed disbelief in God, we never discussed what had made that miracle occur.

Jimmy came to live in my house to recuperate for nearly a year, during which time I had a steady stream of scientists coming to visit. One day Jimmy just seemed to disappear from the face of the earth, leaving behind his books, which I still have. He knew so much about the A- and H-bombs . . . I really suspect he was either kidnapped by some other country or done in by someone who thought he knew too much.

After my seven months' recuperation from pneumonia, Dr. John Jones sent me to St. John's Hospital and introduced me to "Charlie," the respirator. Charlie and I became constant companions for the next ten years. He nearly saved my life.

All during this time, I was doing a lot of writing and a lot of recording. It seems to me that songs I really had to fight for turned out to be successful (remember how I started this book with the story of my fight to do "Is That All There Is?"). "Lover" was another. It was both exciting and difficult. Richard Rogers was usually very strict about how his songs were interpreted. In fact, when we would receive his scores at Capitol, he would send instructions on how they were to be performed. All of us respected him so highly that we were happy to follow his orders. A bit later on, when I did "Lover," I apparently forgot that. My idea for this recording came about because of a French movie I'd seen. The star, Jean Gabin, was a very attractive man who had joined the French Foreign Legion because his girlfriend had really treated him badly. As they were riding out into the desert he waved a banner to change the gait of the horses. He signaled them once, then he did it again, and it struck me, as I was watching, that it could be a musical key change. In raising the key, it would also have the effect of seeming to go faster. Then the rest of the idea came: the gaits of the horses resembled Latin rhythms, and if you started combining them—2 and 4, ¾, ⁶/₈—with all of those rhythms, it got to be like the whole regiment was running off together at top speed. Then I thought, all I need is a song that goes with that rhythm, and, because of the star's love for the girl, I thought of "Lover."

I met with the rhythm section and said, "Will you play this and will you play that and let me sing 'Lover' about this tempo?" We started having a marvelous time. The bongos would be playing straight eights. The congas would be playing six-eight and other Latin rhythms, and the drums played a straight fast four. We tried this in clubs and concerts, and people went wild over it, including some pros.

I remember Hal March came into my dressing room one night and said, "I just ate my shoe!" Chino Pozo got down on the floor and pushed the bongos the whole length of the dance floor with his nose! I got letters from people like Pete Rugolo and other arrangers who said they appreciated having someone think of something different that could work in an exciting way. It did seem to open up a new world of ideas in music. David Barbour and I were also about the first people to use the echo chamber on, I believe, "It's a Good Day" and "Don't Smoke in Bed." These caught fire as well with audiences, and then the changing-keys technique began to be part of many other arrangements.

The board fade (a gradual fade out) was used when we couldn't think of an ending for a recording. Dave Cavanaugh used to say, "The alternative is that we could have the audience get up and walk out slowly." Dave Cavanaugh was my record producer *and* beloved friend. He died much too young—heart. "Lover" gave him the idea to do those Broadway albums *Latin à la Lee* and *Olé à la Lee.* I also contributed the design for the covers, and *Latin* became a Grammy winner. *Olé* featured my gentleman friend of the moment . . . I talked him into posing in the "suit of lights" for both albums. He didn't like that too much, and we broke up before it was nominated for a Grammy. He wanted to marry me, but I was in love with a jet pilot. They were both handsome devils, though.

When I asked Capitol if I could record "Lover," they said no because Les Paul and Mary Ford had a gigantic hit with their version and they didn't want to create competition. I said, "This is different," but I could see their point.

I was at the Copa at that time, and one night Sonny Burke came in with Milt Gabler of Decca Records, and when they heard me sing "Lover," they got excited. "We *must* have this." "Would you record it?" I asked. "Of course," they said. So I left Capitol for five years and went with Decca. Naturally, our first recording was "Lover." They got the unforgettable Gordon Jenkins to do the orchestration, and we recorded it at Liederkranz Hall in New York. They hired an enormous orchestra—over thirty musicians, including eight percussionists. I have always been fascinated with percussion. (When the University of North Dakota conferred an honorary doctorate on me, they made special mention of this.) For "Lover," Gordon Jenkins and I also had back-up singers. I was so impressed and so thrilled when I got up there and they started to play *that* arrangement. I thought I had died and gone to heaven. But there was just one problem—they couldn't pick me up on the vocal. It was impossible with eight percussionists, and the acoustics in Liederkranz Hall are, well, they're a bit "live."

We spent the whole session doing "Lover," and when we got to the end of the time, we hadn't even started the other pieces for the day. I started to cry and said something melodramatic like, "Well, it's just another dream gone wrong." I went home to bed, and somewhere in the night I had a call from Morty Palitz, who said, "Peg, I've been working with Charlie here, he's the chief sound engineer. We think we have the problem whipped, if you'll agree to go for another session." Well, of course, I jumped at it. I couldn't wait for morning to come.

They had built a sound booth (isolation booth). Maybe Morty Palitz and Charlie had a "first" there? Anyway, I had never heard of it before, and I don't think they had either; otherwise, they would have set the whole session up that way from the start. I was a pretty happy lady when I went home that day, and so, I think, was everyone else.

Sonny Burke said that, when he heard it, he pulled his car over to the side of the road and just sat there and listened to it. A lot of singers tried to do other songs that way, and a lot of them did succeed, but some didn't, because they didn't seem to understand that the lyric had to fit the *mood* of the rhythm as well.

"Lover" was ideal for the technique because it didn't have too many lyrics—and they said the right thing—so you could break up the time. Meanwhile, everything was sailing along under you. "Lover" hadn't originally been a fast tune;

as a matter of fact, when Richard Rodgers heard my recording, he said in *Time* magazine, "Oh, my little waltz, my little
waltz." But then he became so fascinated with it that he told
me when he lectured, he always discussed "Lover." He told
his audiences, "If you don't change the interpretation of
songs after a bit, they will die. They don't need to just stay
in their original interpretation all of the time." Hearing *that*
made me feel even better about "Lover."

A song does have a much better chance at longevity if it
can be performed in different ways. "Lover" became the cri-
terion for every drummer who worked for me.

Dwight Hemion and Gary Smith, brilliant producers,
asked me and Lena Horne and Vic Damone to do a television
special that would be a tribute to Richard Rodgers. It was
good to work with Vic and Lena. Actually, I'd known Vic since
he worked at the Paramount Theater, and I mean before he
was on the stage, and I've loved running into him on the road
over the years. We'd always see each other at airports and
crossing the lobbies of hotels. Vic and I would look at each
other and say, "We're ships that pass in the night, aren't we?
But this is ridiculous, we have to work together." But somehow it had never happened. I'd spent most of my time with
musicians, doctors, scientists and writers. But now, at last, on
the Rodgers tribute, Vic and I got to sing together.

And Lena. Once, we stood talking to each other in Vegas.
Lena was closing at the Sands and I was opening there. I
remember she had bows on her shoes, and as we talked Lena
looked down and said, "These bows are so *big.*" I knew what
she meant . . . she'd been looking at them for a couple of
weeks.

After the special, Richard Rodgers sent me a telegram.
"I'VE NEVER ENJOYED HEARING MY MUSIC PER-
FORMED MORE THAN I HAVE ON THIS OCCASION,"
he wired, and that, coming from him, was an honor. To top

that, he soon gave me carte blanche to do whatever I liked with his songs: "You interpret my songs any way you like," he said. "I trust your taste."

Another favorite composer of mine was Victor Young. Victor did all those movie scores for movies like GOLDEN EARRINGS and THE TEN COMMANDMENTS. Whenever a picture was in trouble, the producer would say, "Get Victor Young," and his score would bolster the film, making you think it was a lot better than it was. When Victor talked to you, he spoke as if he were measuring off bars of music. I suppose the whole world was music to him. He would move his hand from left to right, making little chops like gentle karate strokes, marking off measures as he talked. When he once asked me to write some lyrics for him, you can't imagine how thrilled I was. He was like God to musicians. In stature, Victor Young was a small man, but a giant, nonetheless. (By the time I met him in the early 50's, I guessed he was in his early fifties, too.) He used to say, "The bass line is the roadbed, Peg." He'd make speeches to my musicians, Jimmy Rowles, Larry Bunker, Joe Mondragon, Marty Paitch—all great jazz musicians. "You listen to Peg, she knows what she's doing." Jimmy Rowles and Marty Paitch did a lot of arranging for me—and Jimmy! He's a champ.

I was writing with Victor at the time he died, including a poem called "New York City Ghost" that Victor scored and that is about nine minutes long. It was for the Los Angeles Philharmonic. He also asked me to recite it in the Hollywood Bowl, which seats about eighteen thousand people. I told him, "I *couldn't* do that." He said, "If I thought enough of your poem to score it for the orchestra, you should think enough of it to do it."

On the night of the performance at the Hollywood Bowl, I had a temperature of 102 degrees. I was also quaking in my shoes. I did it, though, and was amazed at the great reception we got. (Right after the concert, I received an emergency call that my brother Clair had been in an accident and had gone through the windshield. I was driven to the hospital and sat with him all night. Thank God, he came through it.)

Once when I was confined to bed, Victor Young brought me a black lace nightie—and two themes from Schumann and Hayden. He brought them, he said, for me to write Christmas lyrics to. But he really brought them to cheer me up. I remember, when he handed them to me, he said, like a tough little kid, "Here—get better." The songs became part of my albums *Christmas Carousel* and *Happy Holidays.* Billy May did all of the wonderful arrangements, with the beauty and humor that are uniquely his.

If you came in with a Victor Young arrangement, everyone was impressed. Every now and then he'd drop an arrangement on my lap like a gift. "Love Letters," for example, had five guitars on the recording, and he would sometimes come in and conduct. He was always helping some musician or other. He gave Marty Paitch his first opportunity to write for the symphony orchestra while Marty was working with me.

Victor was doing AROUND THE WORLD IN EIGHTY DAYS, right after THE TEN COMMANDMENTS, when he died on November 11, 1956. He was so pressured. Incredibly, he hadn't won an award until AROUND THE WORLD. He had a whole bathroom full of nominations, however (that's where he kept them). Victor's posthumous Oscar was awarded in 1957 for Best Score for Dramatic or Comedy Picture for AROUND THE WORLD IN EIGHTY DAYS, also the title of one of the most beautiful and elegant of his songs.

# Book Three
# FEVER

# Seven

WHEN, IN 1958, I wrote the special lyrics to "Fever," the first two verses were from Little Willie John's smash hit. I had no idea my version would set off such a rash of fevers. My friend Pat Shelton, fashion editor for the Chicago *Sun-Times,* told me that, when she goes to Paris for the big fashion preview shows, they always play my recording of "Fever" for the models on the runway. When she tells me that, I get a thrill thinking I'm at least, in a small way, part of the fashion world.

Pat says that Sonia Rykiel plays "Why Don't You Do Right" and "Don't Smoke in Bed," as well as "Fever" and others, and this by way of telling new and old song writers how important it is to secure copyrights. Recently I saw the printed sheet music of "Fever" and there are all of my special lyrics printed, with no credit to me as a writer. That apparently means I'm not credited with ASCAP or BMI either. Not fair.

When my recording of "Fever" came out, I had a recurring fever and periodically had to go to bed for an extended time. I asked my doctor to give me a reason to tell the press and he said, "Tell them you have mononucleosis, no one will know what that is." Oh, yes? Well, I did just that and someone looked it up and found it was called the "kissing disease." So a feature wire story went out saying, "Peggy Lee has the 'kissing disease.' She has the 'fever' from too much kissing."

Incidentally, I also did the arrangement of "Fever." I well remember the day I demonstrated it to famous lyricist Sammy Cahn and told him I wanted to use bass, drums and finger snapping. (Jack Marshall, my conductor on the recording date, won a Grammy for that arrangement.) Somehow it all worked.

"Hurricane Hazel, a real blowhard, came to town." That's what the newscaster was saying.

My crew and I were at the Warwick Hotel in New York City. Tom Rockwell was listening intently to the news broadcast while we prepared to leave on a midwestern and southern tour. I wondered vaguely why Tom was so concerned, "Hurricane Hazel" didn't mean anything to me. I wandered into the bedroom, where Lille Mae and Stella Castellucci were busy packing the gowns and shoes and assorted things a woman needs on the road.

"What's this Hurricane Hazel?" I asked.

"I don't know," Stella said, "I think they're naming hurricanes after women now."

Well, Hazel was, it seemed, a particularly wild lady. I went back in to talk with Tom and Kelly. "Is there a hurricane coming?"

"No, there isn't, but there is one down where you're going." Tom looked a tad worried. Now it was my turn to be concerned. "Do you mean we're going to fly into a hurricane? Tom, I don't like the idea of that—"

"Well, maybe it will blow out to sea," he said, which sounded pretty good, but not good enough. So we changed our plane reservations and opted for a bus ride. Billy Eckstine, who was with the show, stayed with the plane and missed the whole thing. Pete Rugolo came along with us and his orchestra on two big tour buses. We took off for Cape Charles with George Kirby, the Rugolo Orchestra, the Drifters, Ed Kelly and my group. We ran smack into Hazel at Cape Charles. I've never heard a wind like that, she was wild all right! We missed the first ferry because Charlie Carpenter, the tour manager, was arguing about the fare, and I missed my rehearsal because Pete's orchestra went on ahead of us. We had actually planned to rehearse on the ferry boat! So after taking a small but precarious walk, four of us held hands and tried to walk a short distance, but anything less than four people would have taken off in the wind like paper dolls. Gene DiNovi, I recall, was holding my hand and, of course, laughing and laughing, as was his style. We were trying to find something to eat, but, before we could, the bus took off again. The driver, Mike, and Charlie thought that the weight of the bus would hold us down, but we learned that was not quite true. I remember seeing the neck muscles and tendons standing out on Mike's neck as he rode that bus like it was a bucking bronco. Chino Pozo was hanging on the overhead racks and saying in his thick Cuban accent, "I go anywhere with you, Peggy Mang!"

The bus was careening madly down the highway, and the wind at times lifted it, actually lifted it off the road. The wind picked up a great tree and threw it across the road in front of us. Several of our fellows organized a way to push the door open. There was a hydraulic door on the bus, but it was no match for the force of the wind. Big billboards flew through the air, and it really took some doing to move that tree. We were coming into Salisbury, Maryland, so we decided to stay and try to take shelter. Six people had been killed there that day!

We found a motel, and, believe it or not, at first the owner didn't want to give us all shelter because some of us were white and some of us were black. Finally, he relented and we crowded into the place. Stella and Lille Mae were understandably frightened. Well, we all were a bit unsettled, you might say.

The motel was shaped like a *U,* and from our cabin we could see the whole complex. We were wondering about the eerie stillness, when suddenly the roof flapped like a petticoat and then flipped up and tore off. The whole roof came off *except* where we were!

Pete and I were trying to be Boy Scout leaders. I remember seeing a sign just before we got to the motel—it advertised chicken and now we all piled into the bus and rode back there. The owner, in a state of shock, at least was friendly. His electricity was out but there was some gas. So Pete and I, chefs that we are, cooked everything we could find on the gas stove. Mike parked the bus so the lights would shine inside, and we dined by bus-light. We hadn't found any food since New York City, so we were ravenously hungry. Pete and I rattled those pots and pans and gave everyone a full plate. For dessert we had melted ice cream. By that time the hurricane had blown out to sea, and the relieved proprietor, when asked for the tab (there were seventeen out of the twenty-three people with us), said "That'll be seventeen dollars."

With very little sleep, we took off the next day for Raleigh, North Carolina, and the rest of the tour would be similar to the beginning, more *sturm* and *drang* than glamor. I think it was Raleigh where I lost my shoe. I was wearing a beautiful beaded lace by Don Loper and some fragile, dainty sandals by Mr. Sidney. The dainty little fragile strap broke, and, since I couldn't sing very well on one foot, I took the other shoe off. The gown was ballet-length and the audience seemed to love the improvisation. I called to Lille Mae to bring my spare pair, and she kept repeating, "That's just the trouble, that's just the trouble!" as she kept throwing things out of the trunks, looking for the other pair of shoes.

Meanwhile, the audience, getting into the act, rose to its feet and started bringing me *their* shoes, tossing them up on the stage. It was hilarious when people began to try to find their own pair, and it wound up being the finale for the performance. What sweet people.

In Des Moines our group was getting mighty sick of the bus, so we took a train for one night. When we arrived, the depot was deserted, except for a group loading a coffin onto the train. I saw the ambulance, ran up to the driver and asked him if he could take us to the auditorium. There weren't any cabs, after all. When he agreed, we loaded our luggage and drums and other instruments into the ambulance. Our happy group was at least an improvement over the driver's passenger coming to the train. When we told him we were in a hurry, he turned on the siren, and soon we were followed by a police car. Not as an escort . . . the officer tried to arrest us; apparently it was against the law to use the siren unless someone was sick or dying, or, I guess, dead. Anyway, the officer stormed to the door: "Who's sick in here?" I admitted I was the culprit and he let us go with a stern warning.

Now, though, it was time to dress and *Stella's* shoes were nowhere to be found. I loaned her a pair of mine, but they were twice too big for her dainty feet, and she looked like Minnie Mouse playing the harp. I couldn't look at her and keep a straight face.

A few more "greasy spoons" and we were on our way back to New York City and on to home and California.

My playing invalid to the police officer wasn't altogether an act. I knew before we came back home that I would be having surgery. I was told it was a probability when we left, but now it was a reality. (It would be only a small example, or sample, of what was to come. In fact, I would learn to think of the hospital as "the garage.")

After the operation there was Dr. Garbak, who kept an eye on me, as did Dr. Stevens, and they let me out a trifle early for the holidays. I quickly, and happily, found I was surrounded by men—Jimmy Marino, Dave Barbour, Dr. Garbak and Harry the butler. When I tried to stand and walk to my bed, I fainted dead away! When I came out of it, I thought I smelled vinegar, and I was right. David (of Italian descent) and Jimmy Marino (likewise) had, in their nervous state, poured first vinegar and, then olive oil on my head. They thought it was an old Italian remedy. I thought it was more like a salad.

So I spent a little time at home recuperating and gathering strength to go down to Palm Springs. It was so peaceful down there, I took my paints along and painted a picture of the beautiful mountains just outside the door.


Surgery notwithstanding, it was so good to be home. I was greeted by an unusual request from Countess Carpenetta. She was a charming lady, and she told me she wanted me to pose for a painting, and, although I was still tired from the surgery, I consented to pose. I also found myself agreeing to her bringing an Indian gentleman along with her. They arrived with her painting equipment and easel, and, as she set it up, chatting as she went along, she introduced me to the young man, wearing a beautifully wrapped turban. "You won't have to sit absolutely still, only once in a while," she said, "but I thought you might like to talk with my friend here, that is, if you wish, and I'll just paint away."

As I looked at the handsome young man with hypnotic eyes, my thoughts flashed back to an incident in San Francisco at the Fairmont Hotel. It was 1945. Nob Hill had resounded with the shriek of sirens heralding the coming of heads of government to the Fairmont, the Mark Hopkins and other hotels on the Hill. Molotov, the Soviet foreign minister, was one of the visitors there for the founding session of the United Nations. Police and security were everywhere. I happened to be singing at the Fairmont, and a group of fans were gathered in front of the hotel waiting for me to come out. Can you imagine, with all the heads of state and important people from all over the world, the police were shooing my small group of fans away, saying, "Molotov is gone, Molotov is not here . . ." They replied, "Who is Molotov? We're waiting for Peggy Lee." It was in the papers next day.

The San Francisco press had invited me to be a hostess for them at their Press Club. To this day I remember that with great pride. For being a hostess at their reception for the delegates to the United Nations meeting, I was given the "Black Cat," meaning that I could always speak "off the record" and it would be honored. (The Black Cat had its own story, which they told me. It seemed there was a feline survivor of the San Francisco earthquake, named "Stormy," found amid the ashes when the Press Club was destroyed by fire. Naturally, it was black from the soot, and was part of the legend of the club itself.)

During the meetings at the U.N. and the reception at the Press Club, it was apparent that anti-Americanism ran high from India's representatives. I met Krishnamurti's aide, and, as he extended his hand, he said, "You are the only American thing we have in our home."

Not too pleased by that, I said, "I hope that won't always be so." It set off a chain of events in my life that to this day amazes me. And the young Indian who came to visit me with Countess Carpenetta was another link in the chain. The countess continued to paint that day, seemingly ignoring us, and, as I looked back from my daydreaming at the young Indian and looked into his eyes, I had to ask him, "Why does India have such angry feelings about America?"

199

"Because we don't get the complete picture of America," he said. "We see only violence and things we don't approve. If an American finds a man down in a well, he would, from the political standpoint, dangle a rope a little way down while he is saying, 'If you live our way, I will drop this rope down to you.' All the while he is telling the man who is drowning, 'You should not be down there.' Well, along comes a Russian and he looks down at the situation and gets a rope and, without saying anything, he just drops the rope down. Now, which of these do you think the man down the well will choose?"

Right or wrong, it planted a seed in my mind. Ralph Carmichael and I wrote a song called "Meals for Millions" and recorded it at Capitol Records, the proceeds going to Meals for Millions. We were working with Eddie Albert and a lot of other good people, sending soybean flour—which tasted terrible, but not if you were starving in Southeast Asia—wherever we could to feed as many as we could.

About this same time, in the late fifties, I met a young doctor named Dr. Verne Chaney, a thorastic surgeon who gave up his profitable practice to help people. I hadn't forgotten the conversation with the man from India, and when I heard of the things Dr. Chaney was doing, I accepted the title Madame Chairman for the Thomas Dooley Foundation. We preceded the Peace Corps by a few years. Ahead of his time, Thomas Dooley had seen the Vietnam problem, but he was dying of cancer, so Verne Chaney took over the whole project. We sent food, medicine and Disney films to Laos, Cambodia and Vietnam.

One proud day for me, they christened a little hospital boat *The Peggy E. Lee* in Union Square in San Francisco. I believe I sprinkled Herb Caen with champagne when I hit the boat. One other time, I really got him wet hitting a cable car. I love Herb Caen. "My" boat was sent over to the Mekong River and traveled up and down before and throughout the entire Vietnam War . . .

It was a wonderful feeling to be present in San Francisco again when the late Eugene Burdick (co-author of *The Ugly American* and co-author of *Fail Safe*) presented the "Splendid American" award to Henry Cabot Lodge for his work in Southeast Asia. But it was chilling to hear him talk about the terror of the Viet Cong planting severed heads on poles in front of the houses the heads came from.

I could reflect back to the young man from India and realize that what was beginning here with this new United Nations was linked to his philosophy and sincerity. So many wonderful things happened as a result of that one conversation with a man I had never seen before, nor have I seen since . . .

Back in New York, Dr. Verne Chaney and Thubton Norbu, the brother of the Dalai Lama, came to my suite, and Thubton was carrying a little black-and-silver furry ball that turned out to be one of the dearest gifts in my whole life. It was Sungyi La (meaning The Honorable Lioness). They told me that the Dalai Lama was aware of the work being done by Meals for Millions and the Thomas Dooley Foundation, and they gave me the Dalai Lama's book, *My Land and My People*, a prayer scarf and an autographed photo that I will always cherish.


Still the late fifties, and enter Cary Grant. I was playing at the Flamingo in Las Vegas, and one night Cary Grant asked me to join him for supper after the show. As luck would have it, I wasn't feeling well but told him I would surely be feeling better. "Why don't I just meet you in the lounge when you're ready? I have a feeling we're going to be very good friends," he said. I tell you, there is no charm like the charm of Cary Grant.

By the second performance, I was weaker than ever, and, to make matters worse, I was wearing a fifty-pound beaded gown that Don Loper had created for me. (We called it "The

City of Glass.") As I did my final step off stage, with the heavy beaded gown propelling me along, it was apparent there was no way I would be able to see him that evening. I left a message for him that I was too ill and would he please call me? I didn't hear from him. Much later I learned the messenger had his own motive regarding me, and he didn't deliver the message. Mr. Grant must have thought I was terribly rude. Our paths, however, were destined to cross again . . .

Opening night at Basin Street East in 1959 was electrifying. The red carpet was rolled out for the people spilling from the limousines. Kleig lights shot up among the New York skyscrapers. Stars and lights and flowers. Everything shining. The orchestra was hand-picked. A lighting booth had been installed, and the lighting director had a myriad of light cues to play along with the music. The performance began and was lifted high by the enthusiasm and excitement of the audience. Standing ovations, bravos. The reviews were spectacular, and after opening night the lines formed four abreast around the block. They would continue to do so each time I played there. God bless New York!

Newsweek credited me with "single-handedly reviving the supper club business." I sang and sang and sang. They loved it all, and so did I. It was good to see my friend Phoebe Jacobs, who worked as an assistant to the owners and who had been with Basin Street from the beginning. She worked with Mitch Miller and Morty Palitz of Columbia Records. (Phoebe is currently historian of Louis Armstrong.) Speaking of my first Basin Street engagement, Phoebe says: "Miss Lee would require certain things. 'Don't forget I need a sweet potato for that number.' Mo, one of the proprietors, would say, 'Does she want it candied or . . . ?' "

I also wanted a white rope, so they got me one from the *Queen Mary*. It looked superb on stage. The owners were wonderful, they looked like Laurel and Hardy or Frick and Frack. Mr. Lewis loved to effect a tough-guy image, and Mr. Watkins had exquisite taste and a manner very much like Rex Harrison's. They had opened Basin Street in October 1958, in the grand ballroom of a hotel at Forty-eighth and Lexington, able to accommodate 450 customers, including the bar and lounge. "Basin Street started out to be a nightclub," Phoebe says, "but by the time Peggy got through with it, it was a concert hall."

This was a hectic time, because I was also doing a series of TV specials for Revlon with John Gielgud, Carol Channing, Alan King and Abe Burrows. Soon, according to Phoebe, people would call for reservations and say, "How much will you take for a seat?" There was such a crowd on Saturday nights that it provided a part-time job for her seventeen-year-old son, who would make seventy-five dollars for keeping people in line and forming them into an orderly file when it was time for them to come into the lounge area. Sidney Roth ("Big Broadway Sid") was the maitre d' at B.S.E. "He had worked the nightclub circuit most of his life," Phoebe says. "He had never seen the type of crowds that P.L. attracted. New York was Peg's."

The waiters lined up the tables bar mitzvah-style to get as many customers in as they could, and soon there were 610 people at every performance. "We had to hire only skinny waiters," Phoebe says. "After opening night, P.L. became the hottest ticket in New York." I could look out in the audience and see the likes of Judy Holliday, Quincy Jones, Ray Charles, Judy Garland, Tallulah Bankhead, Count Basie, Joan Crawford, Cary Grant, Ella Fitzgerald, Sophia Loren and Carlo Ponti, Marie and Jimmy Durante, Lena Horne and the faithful Marlene Dietrich. It was heady stuff.

"Peg would be introduced without fanfare," Phoebe recalls. "Just: 'Ladies and gentlemen, Miss Peggy Lee.' She wove a spell. Put a hush over the crowd."

I was doing two shows a night Monday through Thursday, three on Friday and Saturday. Dr. Martin Stone, president of the American Medical Association, made reservations for every show every night. Then New York had a big snowstorm, the mayor declared a state of emergency, and all moving vehicles were ordered off the streets. Mr. Watkins, the proprietor, wanted to put a padlock on the door. Phoebe said, "No. We have five hundred reservations, including Dr. Stone. And all the people in the hotels around the club want to see Miss Lee." The butcher and baker couldn't deliver, so there was no food. Phoebe went out and paid five dollars to school kids with sleds to go with her to grocery stores in the neighborhood and buy all the chickens they could find. The chef, who was oriental, created haute cuisine. That night of the big storm, the club was filled and Dr. Stone was at his usual table. He'd arrived at Basin Street East in a bobsled. TV crews showed up from every network that snowy winter's night. They couldn't believe all these people would go to a nightclub on a night like that.

Edgar Bronfman, chairman of the board of Seagram's Industries, frequently came to see me. Active in cancer fundraising, he asked me if I would chair a gala at $500 a plate. Basin Street rented china, sterling, and crystal for the fundraiser. We had programs and menus with all the dishes named after my songs. The proceeds went to the Runyon Cancer Fund, Meals for Millions and Girl's Town.

When I said I wanted to live at the Waldorf, Basin Street made inquiries for me. Henry Kaiser, who owned an apartment there, said he would love to have me live in his apartment while I was in town. Nicki, my hairdresser and I moved into real luxury—four bedrooms, four bathrooms, and a dining room the full length of the suite. Adlai Stevenson was my neighbor and, I'm proud to say, ardent fan. The Shah of Iran lived above me and another neighbor, Nathan Cummings, had a $6 million art collection in his apartment. Sammy Cahn arranged for me to see this extraordinary collection, and soon I was spending hours at Nathan Cummings' place in the Waldorf Towers looking at Rodins, Renoirs, and Miller sculptures. He told me that he had many more paintings at the Metropolitan Museum of Art. Around dinnertime I told him that art for me had to yield to the prosaic . . . that my cook had already started dinner.

"I wish I could have a home-cooked dinner some time," he said.

"You can," I said. "Just come downstairs."

Not a man to come to dinner empty-handed, he arrived at my door with a selection of frozen Stouffer's items and heads of lettuce. A man of parts, was Mr. Cummings . . .

During my second engagement at Basin Street, we had to turn a lot of people away, and so Phoebe Jacobs prevailed on Capitol to record at the club. I was hesitant. One night Cary Grant was in my dressing room and I was telling him about them wanting me to record at the club. The real problem was, I had a bad cold and didn't want to record at all until I got over it. But when Cary said it was a good idea, I was easily won over. If you listen to the record, *Basin Street East,* you sure can tell I have the cold. It turned out to be a hit, on *Billboard* for forty weeks and still sells today. Maybe I should always sing with a cold . . . a different sound . . .

Phoebe says that "at Basin Street East it was a love affair between Peggy and the busboys, waiters and captains. Every night was New Year's Eve for them. They went home with bundles of money. B.S.E. had the best food and wine brought in when Miss Lee was singing because of the clientele she attracted. The help would pool their money to buy P.L. a gift or flowers. There's a waiter at Gallagher's who used to be a busboy at B.S.E., and he was able to buy his house in Queens because of the tips he made when Peg was at Basin Street. Bob Kiernan, a lighting apprentice, learned so much from Peg about special gelatins, cues and colors that Frank Sinatra paid him handsomely to light for him at Radio City Music Hall.

"Miss Lee was the forerunner in recognizing Quincy Jones and Ray Charles. She inquired who arranged for Quincy Jones, and when I told her he did his own, she immediately spoke to him about conducting for her. Later Quincy wrote 'New York City Blues' and 'Grain Belt Blues' with Miss Lee. And she was the first popular artist to salute Ray Charles. He heard about it and came in to Basin Street East one night. Afterward he cried in my office and called her 'Sister Peggy.' Nicki and my daughter were ardent fans of Ray Charles."

After a performance I would need to unwind and so I'd take my friends to my apartment for breakfast. Martha Raye, Judy Garland, and Cary Grant would sit around the table while I prepared, among other things, frankfurters or onion sandwiches with champagne. Cary thought hot dogs and champagne were a funny idea but loved the end result. "A refreshing change from caviar," Cary said. Who else but Cary Grant could get away with *that* line? One night Ray Charles wanted pizza, so we all took off for pizza. People, all sorts of people, would come back to the Waldorf with me after a show: Benoit Dreyfus, jeweler; Bill Harbach, producer; Bill Mandel from Revlon; Fred Klein, the man of a thousand voices. We'd all march to the Waldorf, singing, and have a good old get-together. I'd take off my gown and get into a hostess outfit and make hotcakes for everyone. One night Charles Revson sent a washtub full of roses.

It really seemed like the whole world was coming to Basin Street East. Phoebe told me Tony Bennett had called from the Detroit airport at 1:30 A.M. asking the time of the last show, which was 2:15 A.M. "This is Tony Bennett," said he. "Will you hold a table for me? I'll be right there." He made it in time for the last show. One night I looked out over the crowd and saw Count Basie, Cy Coleman, Louis Armstrong and Lauren Bacall. Another night I saw Robert Merrill, Duke Ellington, Tony Quinn and Johnny Mercer, Jack Lemmon and Elizabeth Taylor and Richard Burton. Jackie Gleason and Art Carney would come in—Jackie would still call me Myrtle. I didn't know why, but I loved it.

Anthony Quinn had cabled me from Italy: "YOUR REC-ORDS KEEP MY SANITY." Worn-out after a day's shooting, Tony said he would get out a bottle of wine and put on one of my records. Later on Tony and I would do a TV special together. I really admire Tony.

I guess you could say the people of New York adopted me during the B.S.E. days. Vinnie Promuto, captain of the Washington Redskins, was always there to help me get through crowds. They had constructed a marquee and had my name up in lights, and the street in front of B.S.E. was chaotic. This was a residential area, and mounted police had to be there to handle the crowds. The writers were great to me—Murray Kempton, Albert Goldman, Tommy Thompson—all did big pieces on what was going on at Basin Street East.

One night I saw Nat King Cole and Ella Fitzgerald in the audience and just decided to do an impression of Billie Holiday for them. Phoebe Jacobs remembers it this way: "P.L. was singing 'God Bless the Child,' which Billie wrote. Ralph Watkins, one of the owners, had often booked Billie herself to sing at his previous club, Kelly's Stable. When Ralph heard Peg singing that night, he turned white as a sheet, it was so much like Billie, but of course Billie was already dead. Later Nat King Cole came into my office and cried, saying, 'That was Billie.' "

"Nicki and my daughter were very good friends," Phoebe Jacobs says. "My kid came home one time from stay-ing with Nicki and said, 'Miss Lee put oatmeal in her bath.' P.L. had lovely skin, so I decided to try it myself, except, not knowing how much oatmeal to use, I put a whole box of Quick Oats in the tub. Needless to say, we needed a plumber. It's actually Aveenol Colloidal Oatmeal Bath, which is powdered for the bath. Use it and at least you don't need a plumber . . ."

"Sometimes they would close rooms for her after hours at '21' and El Morocco so she could have little parties. If she wanted to go to a store, Douglas Whitney, who collected Rolls-Royces, would send one over. I used one of his cars to go to Bonwit's and buy Easter bonnets for everyone, and then he sent over three Rolls when she took a group to the Easter Parade on Fifth Avenue and then to Mass at St. Francis of Assisi Cathedral. Another time she wanted to see some friends off on the *Queen Mary* at eight in the morning." I filled up the whole front of the Rolls-Royce with lilacs, leaving just enough room for the driver. I put on a red wig and a hat to go onto the ship to see my friend off. As the Rolls pulled onto the pier filled with lilacs, all the stevedores yelled, "Hey Peg! What are you doing up so early?"

You think I was disappointed the disguise didn't work? I loved it.

Phoebe recalls, "At Basin Street, P.L. was wearing all the designer gowns long before they would come out from the designers, like Norell, Stavropoulos, Jean Louis and Galanos . . .

"Peg had perfect pitch. During the course of her engagement, she had one favorite piano tuner who came every day to tune the piano. One day he sent a substitute. Only Bill, the handyman, knew the regular tuner didn't come. Before the show Peg said, 'Who tuned the piano?' She knew it wasn't her favorite one. She once heard a screw in the piano. No one else heard it. But when they finally took it apart, they found the screw."

On February 3, 1961, it was one degree above zero at 2:30 A.M., when Jimmy Durante arrived for my show at Basin

Street with Rocky Marciano and Zsa Zsa Gabor. At the beginning of my performance, I called Jimmy "Mr. Love" and began to intersperse my songs with phrases of love for him. Then I sang "My Romance" from JUMBO, in which Jimmy had costarred with an elephant twenty-six years earlier. Finally Jimmy could restrain himself no longer. He hopped on stage, took over the piano and gave us all a preview of his show, which was going to be opening at the Copa nineteen hours later. "Miss Lee stood modestly aside," Arthur Gelb wrote in the New York *Times* the following day, "her back turned to the audience." Jimmy sang his classics, "Inka-Dinka-Doo" and "Won't You Come Home, Bill Bailey." When he was finished, everyone got to their feet and cheered. Me too.

Sometimes I would walk home from Basin Street East to the Waldorf. One night a fellow drove by in a big bread truck and yelled, "Hey, Peg, you want a ride?" I got in the truck and he said, "You want a loaf of bread?"

"Sure," I said. "What kind is it?"

"Fink's, the best rye bread in the world."

He was right about that. I walked right into the Waldorf carrying my loaf of Fink's rye . . .

Finally, it was time to say good-bye to Basin Street East. Princess Grace asked me to come to Monaco to do a gala, and Señor Wences would be on the program with me—I was a big fan of his. I accepted gladly.

Phoebe says, "she gave gifts to everyone who had anything to do with her show at B.S.E.—key rings, lighters and pocket watches engraved." Mere tokens . . . nothing to compare with my appreciation for these loyal, helpful people.

With Cary Grant, I went out on Forty-eighth Street to feed my pigeons one last time. They were waiting for me as usual, knowing that I would feed them peppermints from Cary's pocket.

*   *   *

So now it was 1961 and bon-voyage time. Edward Sebesta
made a whole wardrobe for my trip to London and Monaco.
These were happy, sad days. My business manager of fifteen
years, George Stuart, was suddenly taken ill while working on
my income tax (that's no joke). His partner, Richard Shipman, and I spent a great deal of time at St. John's Hospital,
where the neurologist told me, according to George's instructions, that he had found cancer of the brain and that it
was inoperable.

I was so fond of George, like he was a member of my
family. I tried my best to help Dick keep him as comfortable
as possible, and, of course, delayed my trip to Europe until
George passed.

I was so happy to be taking my sister Marianne with me
as well as my Nicki, who promised me she would speak French
for me. Oh, ho ho! Jim Mahoney was just starting in the
press-relations business, and while we were flying to New
York, I turned to him and said, "Jim, there's something I
forgot to mention." "Oh?" "I want you to go to London with
me." "Egad, I don't even have my passport in order, I don't
have any clothes—" "We'll take care of that in New York,"
said I very grandly. We did manage to get his passport cleared
and he got himself some shirts and things.

I'll always remember Nicki, Marianne and I standing at
the rail of the *S.S. United States* with all the confetti and
streamers filling the air and realizing we were leaving the
shores of America for the first time; the sonorous ho-o-nk
when we all burst into tears. "Oh, beautiful for spacious skies,
for amber waves of grain . . ." Understand, I was, and still am,
a girl from North Dakota, U.S. of A.

There were some lovely passengers aboard. Among
those we knew were Estée Lauder and her party and Jackie
Gleason and his party. Ann Spalding Hamilton became a new

friend. The great movie choreographer Hermes Pan, who guided Rita Hayworth through her musicals, was also on board. Meyer Davis was the ship's orchestra leader, and Jim Mahoney borrowed a tuxedo from him (a little on the large side). Our first night out Jim and I were doing the cha-cha and he all but lost his trousers.

Hermes Pan was delightful. A hurricane was raging one night, but that didn't stop us from dancing. When the big ship tilted, we slid from one end of the dance floor to the other and I said, "Oh, Hermes that was *special.*" (Must have been a trip for spills, because later in London Quincy Jones and I ended up on the floor while doing the twist.)

My hairdresser, Faith Schmerr, had a "wnnerful, wnnerful" time and the "morning after" she and I were both sitting on the bathroom floor, she clutching her head and I clutching the bathmat with the eagle holding the sheaves of golden grain in its claws. The crew was passing out motion-sickness pills while she tried to make me look glamorous.

Dinners at the captain's table and in our own private little dining room were delicious. All in all, it was a beautiful voyage. We landed in Southampton, where we caught the boat train for London.

Jim briefed me about the British press and the press conference we would have on arrival. It was a champagne brunch, and I was very glad he had warned me. I declined the champagne. I had a healthy respect for the British press by the time we finished. It was rapid-fire questioning, and the reporters certainly had done their homework. You had to be on your toes. They were, though, very kind to me, I thought.

We were chauffeured to the Dorchester and passed Buckingham Palace, where I did *not* see the changing of the guard. Meanwhile, Jim Mahoney had radioed his wife Patti to meet him. She was as excited as a new bride, and, of course, with a name like Mahoney, right away they made plans to take a trip to Ireland.

I had the Oliver Messel Suite at the Dorchester, really a luxurious penthouse. When we first entered it, Jim Mahoney pressed some buttons . . . "I wonder what these—?" Before he could finish his sentence, maids, butlers and valets popped in from various doors, some even, I swear, from behind the bookcase, saying, "Yes, sir, yes, mum." I murmured to Jim, "I wonder what you press to get them to go back in again." I couldn't believe we were headlines in the papers. "PEGGY IS PURRFECT," they said. I told you the British press was good to me.

Armloads of flowers were brought into the suite, and I had my first sight of rubrum lilies. Many celebrities had stayed there in this suite, most recently Elizabeth Taylor and Richard Burton. The suite had a terrace that stretched around three sides, with a view of London that was just unbeatable. There was one pigeon, one big old pigeon who used to waddle around the terrace all day waiting for the tea sandwiches—I think he had eaten so many he couldn't fly.

I ordered a chicken pot pie, and waiters promptly came up with a battery of silver. I told the captain we would like to serve ourselves, which wasn't really to his liking, but we wanted to feel as though we were at home. I picked up the lid of the big silver pot and there was a little squab lying there all dressed with its feet in the air holding a piece of parsley. Someone had put on an album of Ray Charles singing "Georgia on My Mind" and it made me cry as Ray sang "Georgia, Georgia, no peace I find."

Isn't it funny how we pick out a spot and say, "That's my spot"? The lovely chintzes, the down-filled couches, the wonderful style of English decor didn't even soothe our mood. It seems like you just want some of your own dirt. (Actually, someone sent me some dirt in an envelope, presumably from home, and it really affected me. Of course it could have been from anywhere, you could have fooled me.)

* * *

It was the early sixties, and London was getting ready to swing. One night Quincy Jones and I were in a club doing the new dance, the twist. Quincy, a composer of music scores, would one day mastermind Michael Jackson. But that was the night we were enjoying ourselves so much we ended up on the floor.

I performed at the Pigalle. It had been sold out for some time in advance. It was a heady experience to have Princess Margaret and others of the royal party come to the performance. They laid sheets on the kitchen floor so she could come in through the back entrance.

In addition to the performing at Pigalle, I was doing television shows in Teddington, one of which I wrote with Robert Farnum (the dean of British composer-conductors). We would get very little sleep, perhaps two hours a night, because we had to leave for Teddington early in the morning and return in time for the evening performances at Pigalle. When we got back into London, I would lie on the cement floor in the Pigalle dressing room and take a nap while people walked above me in Piccadilly Square. I must have picked up a bug because I soon had—no pun intended—walking pneumonia.

At Pigalle there was a creaking old door that opened into an old spiderwebby closet . . . an air-raid shelter from the war. Lord, how brave, how gutsy those people were to withstand all of those bombings!

We made lots of new friends in London, and I found the English to be warm and friendly. Each time I've gone back to find them the same. Dennis Chappell is one person I especially look forward to seeing. Ours is a quiet friendship. One friend who became sort of a camp-follower, a super fan, was young Lord Rudolph. I think he was seventeen at the time, sensitive and impressionable. At the end of our visit to London, we went on to Monaco, and Lord Rudolph followed us. When we landed in Nice, I realized I was at the center of an international incident. We were met by the paparazzi, who followed us everywhere, flashbulbs blazing away. "LORD RUDOLPH FOLLOWS PEGGY LEE TO FRANCE!" This was bigger than "PEGGY LEE STEALS DOG!" I was pleased to hear that the Duke of Bedford, when questioned, said, "She is a sensible, sane woman and will know how to handle this."

I had some help. In addition to Lord Rudolph, Moe Lewis and a writer from *Punch* magazine, the musicians from my quartet, my sister Marianne and Faith Schmerr had all flown over to the Riviera. We took a helicopter from Nice to Cannes, and this flight over the Mediterranean gave me one of the scares of my life. I was happily taking in everything I could see, and as I turned to look back at Nicki, *I noticed her door was open.* I thought I was going to faint, but, instead, I opted to yell at the pilot, who spoke only French, and to point back at Nicki. He didn't understand me and kept nodding his head, *"Oui, merveilleux."* I was so frightened I didn't know how we got that door shut, but obviously we did.

In Cannes the press was on hand in force, shouting questions, trying to be heard above the flapping sound of the helicopter. I quickly realized the bug was catching up with me, and when we checked into the Hotel de Paris, Nicki called the doctor, who told me to go to bed. When room service arrived—Nicki had called as soon as we got there—I tried to order some Pouilly-Fuisse, and the waiter tried to jump in bed with me. I must have said something wrong. Pardon my French, or blame it. I spent too much time in France in bed, alone. Nicki could order in flawless French, but when answered in machinegun-like French, she closed her mouth and I doubt she's spoken a word of French since. Farewell, Madame Egan.

Eventually, it came time to do the gala for Princess Grace

and the Red Cross, and I looked forward to seeing Señor Wences . . . "E-e-e-s difficult?" "No, e-e-e-s easy."

Lord Rudolph, the faithful, was constantly offering a Kent cigarette . . . I guess it had something to do with the Duke of Kent. As we traveled around the French countryside, me full of wonder at it, Lord Rudolph, or Rue, as he liked to be called, was bored and unhappy. Moe Lewis would get impatient with him, because Moe, too, was trying to get me alone to ask me to marry him.

I remember being fascinated by Aristotle Onassis, the Greek shipping magnate, who was later to marry Jackie Kennedy. He and his entourage seemed to wander around like hounds in search of *joie de vivre.* (I would later meet Jackie and was invited to the Compound. She looked to me like a frightened fawn, but, obviously, she wasn't. She was a woman of courage.)

Dancing under the stars on the Riviera was heady stuff, especially when you had two men taking turns asking you to marry them. I was intrigued that the orchestra was playing "Moanin' " and couldn't understand how they could play such progressive jazz and not speak English, let alone not be American. Picture me standing in front of the bandstand saying, "Will you play 'Moanin' ' again?" *"Non parle anglais. Parlez-vous français, mademoiselle?"* They at least smiled at me.

But Riviera days and nights had to come to an end, and we took off for London again, this time by boat train. The smell of French bread, the pungent smell of salami, and wine . . . it was a very earthy trip.

When we came on board the ship, leaving England, everyone began to get misty-eyed. The *Punch* writer decided he wanted to go to America with me, and so did Lord Rudolph. Then the writer discovered his passport had expired the day before! That was all right with me. Rue offered to try to help him, but, of course, that wouldn't do. Ann Hamilton Spalding came back on board, and Jackie Gleason and his party arrived with photographs and acetates of his film GIGOT. He told me he was going to arrange for me to hear the tapes and I couldn't wait.

As we settled in for the voyage, Moe Lewis sent a case of Dom Perignon to my stateroom with instructions to "get rid" of the case in one evening. With a little help from my fellow passengers, I managed.

When I went to Jackie's stateroom to hear the music, I found he had arranged with the engineer to fasten the turntable in the center of the ceiling with four grappling hooks extending from each corner of the room. All this was because a stiff wind had come up and turned into a hurricane. Jackie kept trying to make his method work, but the needle was sliding to the center of the record and back. It ruined his acetates. I gave him a bottle of Dom and went to dinner with my party, plus Ann Spalding. What a charming lady she is.

Very soon signs were up all over the ship warning us to wear topsiders, and ropes were strung so we wouldn't slide over the railing. We were all having a wonderful time and no one was too much upset by the hurricane.

Finally we landed and all in one piece. I was scheduled to sing at Basin Street East again, and this time I'd be working with Quincy Jones. Quincy and I had written a number of blues pieces for a Capitol album called *Blues Cross Country.* He was absolutely perfect to work with. Years later, on the famous *We Are the World* video, people saw what a fantastic talent he is.

There was only one problem about reopening at Basin Street. The bug had gotten bigger, and soon I was having severe pains in my chest. One night the pain was too much for me, I had a 103-degree fever and called Dr. Palmer. When he arrived, I wasn't even able to stand up for him to tape me, so he asked Faith to hand him the tape. She was so frightened,

Peggy and Ronald Reagan.

With Bob Hope.

**Rehearsals at Basin Street East—Max Bennet, Benny Carter and Peggy Lee.** *(Photo credit: Bob Gomel, Life Magazine)*

At home in the Tower Grove Drive residence.

A typical glamour shot.

Peggy Lee and Cy Coleman.

A dear friend, Paul McCartney.

Another dear friend, Robert Preston.

A pensive moment during
a recording session
in the '60's.

With two very different but equally charming men,
Cary Grant and Alan King.

At the Queen Mum's Birthday Gala with James Cagney
and the Queen Mum.

With Walter Matthau.

In front of the Sydney Opera House, one of the finest in the world.

(Photo credit: Bill Mark)

Earl Wilson, Lucille Armstrong and Peggy Lee.

With Edye Gorme.

Jonas Salk, Earl Wilson and Peggy.

With Ray Bolger.

With Mayor Daley of Chicago.

Singing "Fever".

*(Photo credit: Bob McKinley)*

With Frank Sinatra.

With Ronald Reagan at a State Dinner, 1988.

Dear Peggy — A heartfelt thank you and every good wish. Warmest Regard. Sincerely — Ronald Reagan

Today, with a friend.

she taped me to the doctor! I laughed about a quarter of an inch, and then fainted. Doctor Palmer said, "Well, this is one you're going to have to miss." With great effort I begged, "Please . . ." And Doctor Palmer said, "If you can stand after I tape you, I'll consider it." I could stand, but with all the tape on me, I couldn't sit down. I *walked,* very slowly, from the Waldorf to Basin Street East, with my car trailing along slowly, in case I fell down.

We were sold out, so I went on that night, leaning against a pressing board, and managed to do two performances. I did begin to faint during the second performance and was barely able to signal Quincy Jones that they should jump to the final song.

The ambulance men were so gentle . . . "Yeah, Peg— you're gonna be all right." It was double pneumonia in both lungs, plus pleurisy. They sent right away for Nicki.

I left this earthly plane for a few seconds but was given the choice of returning. Many people have asked me to describe my out-of-body experience, and, since it made me comfortable with my own self, I decided it would be all right to add it . . . At a critical point in the illness, Dr. Palmer called in Dr. Daniel Mulvihill, chief of staff at St. Vincent's Hospital in New York City. I don't really know what procedure was used. My body was distended to an unbelievable degree. There were six or seven doctors, perhaps some of them were interns or residents. Doctor Mulvihill put a wide strip of adhesive tape around me, and, as he looked into my eyes and quickly pulled on the tape, everything in front of me disappeared. From my position in the bed, I went up and straight ahead, then turned to look down at myself on the bed from that vantage. There was no body, only consciousness. The pain was gone and a deep sense of serenity followed. Suddenly, I could see everywhere at once. I saw all of the doctors from their back as well as their front. I saw to the right, to the left and to the back of me all at once. I saw me in pain, and somehow was given the opportunity of reentering my body. It was all light. I was made to understand that if I returned, the pain would return, but I could go on if I wished. All fear was gone.

It was, literally, an enlightening experience, for which I am very grateful. It gave me a great sense of peace that I never had before. I used to fear death. I would never fear it again.

Basin Street East closed for several days while I was on the critical list. Then followed seven months in bed.

I'd come back to years of pain, but with the wonderful help of Dr. John Jones, I more than survived. We travelled with two I.P.P. Bennett machines, which I nicknamed "Charlie," for ten years. I had to have from three to five treatments a day. All I cared about now was hanging on.

# Eight

I WENT back to California and Kimridge Road. Love thy neighbor, the Bible says, and it's easy—if your neighbor is Frank Sinatra. When I heard he was building a house near me, I was understandably delighted. First of all, I was his friend forever after the way he treated me at the Paramount Theatre.

There have been very few men in our business who have affected me so deeply that I can't adequately express myself about them, and Frank is one of them. Cary Grant is another, Bing Crosby another. Yet we have been very close friends for many years in each case.

One year, during the time Frank and I were actual neighbors, I had to spend several months in bed, and Frank did something wonderful every day on his way down the hill to see Nancy and the children: lovely flowers, especially lilacs and roses; a book he found interesting; an album I would enjoy; an Aztec wood carving; telephone calls to see how I was feeling when he was away. A crew arrived and installed extra air conditioning in my bedroom because he heard the heat was bothering me. A truck pulled up with barbecues and flares or torches to stick in the ground when he personally barbecued for Murray Wolf and me. I mean, there were many other guests, but he personally served Murray and me because we were the "invalids."

Frank invited me to his house many times for dinners or parties or movies in his theatre. The house is gated, and a sign on the gates reads: "If you ring this bell, you better have a damn good reason." He had a lovely Oriental-type house right on top of a hill. Frank was single at the time I'm writing about, and one evening I saw PAL JOEY, his film with Kim Novak. His theatre has a bar in it, and there are deep chairs. In the living room is a lovely big fireplace. The house is always sparkling. Whoever chose his accessories had beautiful taste. This Los Angeles home is very sophisticated compared to his house in the Palm Springs compound, which he has since sold.

Our many quiet talks were on the subjects of life and music. Once, we planned a whole album together. It was his idea. He produced it, and it was first released on Frank's Essex label, which was a subsidiary of Capitol Records, and later the album was released on Capitol. We were "the folk who live on the hill" (from the song of almost the same title). The album was called *The Man I Love,* and Frank thought of everything to the last detail, including putting menthol in my eyes so I'd have a misty look in the cover photograph. (I didn't feel at all misty about the man I was holding, however.) Frank is a producer who thinks of *everything*.

The album was totally Frank's concept. He brought me a long list of great songs to choose from, and Bill Miller came over and set all the keys with me. Then Frank hired Nelson Riddle to write those lovely arrangements and Frank conducted them. A marvelously sensitive conductor, as one might expect.

Frank Sinatra has always been somewhere near . . . just touching the elbow . . . holding the hand . . .


Time passed, and now I was in New York again, singing at Basin Street East and living at the Waldorf. One day the phone rang, and that voice said, "Hello, Peggy? Cary Grant."

"Oh, *hello.*" My hands were shaking. I managed to pull myself together and ask how he was. He was fine. I was fine. Would I get him in to Basin Street? Would I get him *in?* Yes! Any time, any time at all. *You* bet.

Well, he arrived, and naturally there was a to-do. He sat next to Ray Charles and Quincy Jones. He loved talking with musicians. By the way, did you know he played the piano? Yes, he played *my* piano and read music, too. He called the next day and asked if I had any influence on how to get *out* of Basin Street East. I told him I could understand that he would have trouble getting out. "Oh no, it wasn't that," he said. "There was just such a line of people waiting to get in for the *next* show." What a charmer. And what a friend.

After that, he would call me and, occasionally, he would come over; he lived very near me. I would tell him a joke, he'd laugh and say, "Thanks, I can dine out on that for several weeks," or "I needed some new material."

Once he was interviewed at some length by a writer for a magazine article. The writer finished the interview and left, then realized he hadn't asked all of the questions he'd planned to ask, specifically, Cary's age. So he sent a wire to Cary's secretary that read: "By the way, how old Cary Grant?" Cary's answer: "Old Cary Grant just fine. How you?" He *was* ageless. Anyone could tell you so. It was so special to know him.

He asked me to write two songs for him to record for a charity, something for Christmas and something for New Year's. I got Cy Coleman to write one with me and Dick

Hazard the other. Dick and I wrote "Here's to You," which Cary also recorded on Columbia Records. I wrote the Christmas lullaby with Cy Coleman. Cary recorded these two and one other called "I Wound It Up," which I wrote alone. He wanted to develop it further, so it wasn't released, and we never got back into the studio with it. He asked me to go to the studio and be with him when he recorded . . . he was uncomfortable about singing, not being a professional singer, and we would rehearse at my house.

When Cary asked me to write the music to the movie WALK, DON'T RUN (Cary's last movie), I asked for Quincy Jones to do the score. I wrote a couple of the lyrics for "Happy Feet" and "Stay with Me," but they didn't get into the film, because I was once again hospitalized. Quincy's score was excellent, though, and I was awfully glad for him.

In June of 1986, Cary generously agreed to do an interview for this book, and here is some of what he said:

"We met when I called Peggy backstage in Las Vegas. A very sensible move on my part. I had always admired her talent. A most remarkable singer. She knows what every musician is doing. How many singers stand up in front of an orchestra and don't know what's going on?

"A darling woman with all sorts of stuff going on in her head. Her mind is extraordinary. She'll break into a story in the midst of conversation. Lovely stories with some philosophic overtones.

"When you go to see Peggy, you know what you're going to see, and it's marvelous . . ."

When Cary called me after the interview, I said, "You know, after all these years, have you ever noticed I never can say your name?"

"Why? For whatever reason?"

"When you walk into the room, everything stops for me. After all these years, I don't address you by any name—never call you Cary."

He said, "Why Peggy! You know I've always loved you. Even my wife knows it."


And now it was the 1960's. A decade for me of shock and celebration.

When Ernest Holmes died in 1960, it shook me up so much I was going to leave New York and come out to Los Angeles for the funeral and cancel a Revlon show. I called Adela Rogers St. John, whom I'd met at Ernest's old house on Third and Lorraine in L.A. "Adela, what should I do?"

"You stay here," she said. "That's what Ernest would want you to do. Let's arrange a memorial service here." Adela got me to sing "The Lord's Prayer" at Ernest's memorial, which was held in New York's Town Hall.

Adela told me she often prayed for me. "Expect the best," she would say, "and it will come." I do believe it is true that we are capable of doing powerful "treatments" for each other.


(When Louis Armstrong died, his widow Lucille also asked me to sing "The Lord's Prayer," at Satchmo's funeral. I loved both Louis and Lucille very much and went over to Queens for the funeral. At the service I was a little nervous. It's hard to sing at a friend's funeral. There were newsreel cameras going. I just kept looking at Louis in his open casket. The man, his music, are eternal.)


And now a celebration.

It was President Kennedy's birthday. I suppose he was almost everybody's idol, and I was eager to accept the invitation to sing at his big birthday party at Madison Square Garden, though my doctor was not ready to give me permission.

He was worried enough that I had gone back to work so soon after my frightening illness, and doing three shows a night. In the end Dr. Palmer didn't exactly give me permission; he just gave up. He couldn't quite believe that I was still alive anyway, and finally just threw up his hands. "Well, if she goes, she goes."

So I went over to the Garden with my light man, Hugo Granata, and the musicians. It was a buzz of excitement, the place fairly crackling with electricity. Hugo did his usual wonderful lighting set-up. Dinah Shore and a couple of other luminous stars used him too, but I worked in New York so steadily, I liked to think of him as "my man." Anyway, Hugo always did a lot of back-lighting and would warn me to take proper precautions with my gowns; in other words, have the gowns lined or wear a slip.

During the rehearsal the producer of the event told Hugo that Marilyn Monroe was coming and that she would sing "Happy Birthday" to J.F.K. Would Hugo do her lights? He asked if I minded, and I said, "Of course not, go ahead." I was, though, not too happy with a security man who kept telling me my band was too loud, and I was defending them— while asking them to play softer. But they were like race-horses, just ready to burst out of the gate. They couldn't wait to play for the President. I don't think they minded Marilyn Monroe either.

Marilyn was on before me. She walked out onto the stage as the lights went up full. The whole audience gasped, and I thought it was just Marilyn's charisma. I turned to look and I gasped too. She had *nothing* on under a sheer gown, and no wonder the audience gasped, and I'm sure J.F.K. did too. She looked stark naked. Well, I guess she was, except for a little chiffon. There was a whole lot of shouting going on from the press and the photographers. It's a good thing "Happy Birthday" is such a short song.

I finally got to sing Frank Loesser's "I Believe in You"

and a couple of others, but somehow I don't think it mattered. Well, I had been told I was the President's favorite singer, but we had to rush back to B.S.E. for the next show and missed the invitation to the private reception.

Every night, as by now you've gathered, was like New Year's Eve at Basin Street East. This one was no exception.


Another celebration.

David and I had a wonderful wedding for Nicki and Dick Foster. People came from all over. Everyone was so fond of both David and Nicki, it seemed only right that we all be together for the event. Since it was a church wedding and the reception was at our home on Kimridge, I got my florist business going again. Nicki being my only child, and a daughter at that, this event was extra special. I made two swans out of chrysanthemums, each five feet long. My helpers were my sister Marianne and Robert Preston. I should have refrigerated the tent, because a lot of our artistic endeavors wilted. We also had a large champagne fountain at the center of the tent, with ropes of flowers coming down from the ceiling.

David had quite a time keeping from laughing at himself in tails . . . he had a silly grin on his face as though he were walking outside of himself and seeing this stranger (he was not the tails type.) Nevertheless, it all went very well and then . . . Oh, how true that empty-nest syndrome is.

> The room was pale yellow
> And frothy and white
> The room was pale yellow
> And full of light
> The bridal veil was tossed on the bed—
> The flowers were fading
> And I—looked ahead

My little girl has gone away
All grown up and she's gone away
Married and all with the ring and the rice
Everything's tidy—and proper—and nice

We did it all with the little white glove
Engraved invitations and champagne and love
Every detail was refined to the bone
The house is now empty
And I—I'm alone

My little girl has gone away
All grown up and she's gone away
Married and all with the ring and the rice
Everything tidy and proper . . .
And nice

The many parties we gave on Kimridge Road! Two, three hundred people at a time, and always the New Year's Eve party. Then, as I said, we sold Kimridge Road and moved to a penthouse in a brand-new apartment building. It looked like a movie set, but I was paranoid about living there because I used to walk in my sleep—up there on the thirteenth floor, open all around, alone after everyone had gone home for the day. I was afraid I'd walk out the window.

We gave a big party there, hoping, to be truthful, to break the lease. Cary Grant was the guest of honor. Cy Coleman had just finished scoring FATHER GOOSE. At some point we put on my new recording of "Pass Me By" from FATHER GOOSE and played it at full volume and marched down the hall into the elevator, continuing to march in place, outside into the lobby, around the lobby, back into the elevator and back upstairs to the penthouse.

Cary Grant was the drum major; I wore some Indian footbells; Cy was, at least, a couple of trombones. Not only didn't the landlord object, he loved the excitement.

Eventually, I moved out anyway and bought a home on

Tower Grove Drive, which is about when Cary began seeing Dyan Cannon. He couldn't wait to have a child. I remember when he used to come to Tower Grove, and he and his little Jennifer would play on the floor. Cary worshipped her.

As for me, it was a special thing just to go riding in his car—a Rolls—with him. I always had a feeling of unreality about Cary. I could look at him and become speechless, as if we were introduced for the first time, and every bit of shyness I've ever had came out. Yet we had been talking and joking over the phone for twenty-seven years!

At my circus party at Tower Grove for my fiftieth birthday, I gave Cary some helium from one of the balloons and then asked him to say, "Judy. Judy. Judy." He said it but then told me he had *never* said it in a movie. It was just one of those lines that *sounded* like he might have said it.

I once sang "Mr. Wonderful" to Cary over the balcony at the Waldorf-Astoria. He liked that. There he was, down on the dais. I had just left it to come up to the balcony of the grand ballroom of the Waldorf. It was *his* birthday, and, during rehearsal for the grand bash the Friars Club was giving him, I decided to sing down to him from the balcony.

It's so difficult to think of a world without Cary Grant, so I think I'll just remember the last time I actually saw him. He and Barbara came to the Westwood Playhouse with Gregory and Veronique Peck and Robert Wagner and Jill St. John. After the performance he stood and smiled at me for the *longest* time, with the most special look of affection I've ever seen. I had no idea it would be the last, for now at least.

After little David was born, Nicki and David came to live in my penthouse and, then, to Tower Grove Drive for little David's first birthday. It was 1965, and David and I were discussing the possibility of remarrying. He believed he could handle it . . . he had been sober for thirteen years.

Four days later David was dead. I won't try to describe the shock to me, and to all of his many friends. Does one recover? In a way, yes. Does one forget? Never.

Life goes on. Helen Glickstein, Dr. Jonas Salk's cousin, and I presented a gala to raise money for the Salk Institute at the Empire Room of the Waldorf-Astoria. Kathy Levy was my new hairdresser and longtime friend-to-be. Dave Garroway, the master of ceremonies for the evening, was, as usual, brilliant. He pointed out that polio had been so thoroughly put down by Dr. Salk's vaccine that Dave Garroway's son could say, "Who's Dr. Salk?" when Dave told him he was to be the master of ceremonies at the party. Of course, Dr. Salk has never stopped being in the news for his contributions, but young people whose lives were probably saved by the vaccine didn't remember him.

One of the door prizes at the gala was a little black poodle, named Stanley by my niece Merrilee. He had been left behind by a couple of guests who had had a little bit too much champagne and forgotten him. When I finally found them and told them I had gotten rather attached to the dog, they said, "Well, keep him." Dear Stanley was once springing around my bathroom and landed right in the toilet. Well, there was a limit to the number of dogs I could have, even in California, so I wound up giving the dog to restauranteur Bruce Vanderhoff . . .

There was an amusing incident involving Kathy Levy—at least, I hope she thought it was amusing. I had come off stage in the Empire Room, running because I had only seconds to powder my nose, drink some water (or, in this case, Coca-Cola) and touch up my lips. Along the way I knocked Kathy flat as I fell down the ramp. She was holding the glass of Coca-Cola and it spilled in my hair. When assured she was all right, I ran back on stage again as though nothing had happened. I suppose, though, the audience must have wondered:

Why did she run all the way off stage to get her eyelashes and hair wet? Fortunately, they dried quickly in the spotlight, although one eyelash had a rakish angle to it.

My business is singing, but I also paint. For some time I'd been commissioned by Sylvania Company to do four paintings in behalf of an ad campaign, the subject of which was "The Sights and Sounds of the 70's." Pollution was on everyone's mind then, just as it is now. Looking for a positive approach, I painted fields of flowers, fresh lemons in the sunshine, two oranges kissing each other, and a chicken. Each time the Sylvania men would come, I would offer them cocktails and dinner and try to sell them on the idea of the chicken. The egg, I thought, was the symbol of new life and hope. "Now, Miss Lee, we're serious," they said. "We need your paintings." Fine. So one evening I sat in my living room with five canvases and started furiously painting chicken feathers. The other paintings of the flowers and fruit were faring well, but the chicken was not. He just sat there and looked out of the side of his head. After I decided on red wattles, I thought he must be a rooster. How could he have possibly laid that egg on the table next to him? Finally, I took a nice wide brush and swept it across the canvas. Now the chicken was standing in a bowl, and his legs were sticking out the bottom, like a pedestal for the bowl. Don't you know they wanted to buy *that* painting? But I wouldn't let them. It hangs in my living room today behind a potted palm. It looks very purposeful, as if to say—I dare you to say anything about that egg. About 200,000 of the other prints were sold and reside elsewhere.

I went back to North Dakota to receive a doctorate from the University of North Dakota. It was a beautiful, sentimental trip and I saw so many old friends. Ken Kennedy was still alive. What a joy it was to spend time with him and his wife Jeanette, as well as Sev Olson and his wife.

After Ken's death some years later, Lloyd W. Sveen wrote in the *Sunday Forum Fargo-Moorehead:* "Memories of Ken inevitably are linked to Peggy Lee. I was one of the pre-war college crowd hopelessly in love with her, mooning over her radio programs and seeing her in person every possible chance at the Powers Hotel. The story of Ken's discovery of her and creating the name Peggy Lee is well known now. Peggy was in tears at receiving word of Ken's passing. Here is her tribute to him:

" 'I know I'm only one of so many people who feel the loss of this wonderful man. My whole life would be different and less fulfilled but for him. I am proud that this rare person was my friend. He was responsible for nurturing my career; for changing my name; teaching me; advising me; being my friend always. If ever I needed help—and there were many times—he was always there, he and his dear wife, Jeanette. I will always see his smile, hear his voice, his laugh, feel his understanding and compassion—for he is not gone, nor will he ever be. Part of me will always be a part of him. I'll see you, kiddo. You are surely in our Father's special care.' "


Back home at Tower Grove Drive, the huge trees were so beautiful, and there was a profusion of geraniums and wild strawberries, and some lovely rock gardens were strategically placed around the two pools—the larger pool washing over the rocks to the wading pool.

Ken, and too many others, were gone. So count your blessings. I took some deep breaths and smelled the fresh grass being cut by Hugo, our gardener, who spoke with a Spanish accent. "Miss Lee, Miss Lee, there's a crack over here on the side." I had always lived on top of granite, often decomposed granite, so I didn't pay any attention. "Oh really? Well, maybe you could just fill it in."

"I did that, but it came back. You'd better come and look." I did. Yes, it was a rather long crack, but the hillside was large, covered with pine trees and Algerian ivy.

"Well, Hugo, can't you just fill that up and plant something there?"

"Okay, but you'd better watch this all the time. I know a crack when I see one." Couldn't argue with that. He filled it, and it came back again and again. He filled it, and it came back. He showed me again and we began to eye each other warily. "This crack isn't kidding," said I sagely.

The fence on the side began pulling an inch or two away from the house. One day, Sungyi La was able to get through it. Big Sur, my standard poodle, couldn't make it, of course. Not yet, but soon.

Inexperienced as I was with landslides (never had one before), they had just been something I saw on the evening news or read in the paper, but, of course, it couldn't happen to me. Or to this beautiful new house surrounded by spectacular pine trees.

The crack was running all along the side of the house where Nicki and her family were living. Then began a couple of years of too many sleepless nights for me and Nicki, but we skirted any talk of the *crack*.

And then it began to rain. It was one of those times of extended rainfall that broke all records. It rained endlessly, sometimes just sprinkling, broken by an occasional cloudburst. I wasn't even paying attention to the flooding they kept talking about, but I *had* zeroed in on landslides and the endless soaking rain. All through the night I would imagine, or perhaps it wasn't my imagination, the cracking sounds in the house. I gave myself all kinds of rationalizations like, this is a pretty new house, it's just settling. I was right. It was settling, but not in the way I thought.

Hugo smelled gas, and we immediately called the gas company. We found newspapers stuffed in a gas pipe under the sidewalk right beneath Nicki's window.

One morning I went around the side of the house. Oh, my God! The hill had left the house and was mostly down on Tower Grove Drive!

Well, hill or no hill, I had to leave for Las Vegas. Rats had come into the house, they'd been living under the ivy on the hill, so I had to move Nicki and the children out of the house, fast. I rented a couple of bungalows at the Beverly Hills Hotel and told Nicki to move down there and get out of the house. There were rats in every room. They ate the corners off some of my books and stationery. That house had been so pristine pure and clean; to think that the rats had been in there, it was almost like a rape.

Each night, between my shows at Vegas, I'd get a report from Nicki about the rats. One night Johnny Mandel came over with some cyanide pellets. Bless him. By the time I got home, it was time for the big caterpillar graders to arrive. I had to get huge wooden containers and rent space at another site for the big pine trees, then let the caterpillars start hauling away the dirt, while the rain poured on.

I think my grandson Michael got his love of trucks and caterpillars then. He was just a baby and seemed to never tire watching them go up and down that hill.

Later—I sorted out what had happened. These people who had owned our house had gone through a landslide, and during it their pipe broke beneath the hill. They scooped it all up and planted Algerian ivy very close together. California law says you must tell the prospective buyers of any such landslide or fault, but the newspapers stuffed in the gas pipe was proof they intended to ignore it all. There was no doubt it was fraud, and so we had to sue. They countersued my attorney Ludwig Gerber and myself for harrassment with intent to commit murder! The very word "murder" makes me shiver. Who was murdering whom? What about the newspaper in the gas pipe?

By the time the hill was rebuilt with steel and reinforced concrete, it was a far stronger hill than it had ever been, and feelings were assuaged.

To get some new growth planted on the hill in a hurry, beside the trees, we shot marigold seeds into the hillside with a special gun, and soon the whole hillside was covered with orange blooms.

One day a tour bus stopped in its trip up the hill for the passengers to admire the marigolds. They picked quite a few, but what amused me was that two repair trucks were sent to move the tour bus, which had overheated, one truck on each end of the bus. Except they got their signals crossed and pulled the bus right in half! So they had to transport the passengers, all gaily carrying marigolds, down the hill. That hill had a life of its own.

We had swimming parties and barbeques and music rehearsals. Jack Lemmon, our neighbor across the canyon, told me he used to enjoy the music coming out of the hill.

One of these times the music was a rehearsal for a Julie Andrews special that involved a helicopter. A helicopter! What a wonderful way to go to work! Julie Andrews was my hostess for this unique adventure. At rehearsal for her award-winning show, she asked if I would like to ride to work with her in a helicopter. Since I lived very near her, I gladly accepted. I would have anyway. She has always been fascinating to me, as to millions of others.

I asked Julie if we could fly over Nicki's house in Cheviot Hills. I wanted to drop something on the roof for the children, and she agreed. So I lugged my giant six-foot plastic bag of rose petals I'd been saving up in the kitchen to see if they'd fit in the helicopter. You see, every week a silent lover sent me six dozen roses, so I had plenty of petals! I wonder what happened to him.

Just to walk into the entrance of Julie's beautiful home and on through to the really interesting kitchen was an experience. There was something elegantly homey about it, the smell of coffee and toast, and hearing her call up the grand staircase, "Blake, Blakie? Are you there?" That lovely English accent.

We chatted away as we drove to the Bank of America Building—a little about the show, a bit about Bill Harbach and Bill Davis, who were producing and directing, and what a marvelous crew we had. When we got there, she took me around a kind of secret route to the elevator that led up to the roof.

By George! Maybe she *was* Mary Poppins (I felt like Little Bo Peep). We crawled up into the copter and she proceeded to unwrap the map of the area. Nicki and I had arranged to have a bright red beach towel on the roof as a marker. Julie sat in front with the pilot. I sat in the back with my huge bag of rose petals. We took off from the roof. Over the roar and rattle of the helicopter I heard her "direct" the pilot: "Turn left, no turn right, hold it just a moment. Peggy, do we go this way?" pointing a finger.

"Please don't ask me, I get lost in my own driveway. Look for the red beach towel, they said they'd have it—"

"There! I see something red." And to the pilot, "Over there, please. See that red—? That's it, that's it." She called to me, "Now, open up now, toss them out! Now!" I wrestled with the bag and somehow pushed the petals out of the copter. They looked so beautiful . . . a shower of rose petals falling down, down, down.

On the wrong house. What else?

The show won an Emmy, and Julie and I, joined by Peter Ustinov, went on to do a Christmas special in England. I sang a jazz version of Tchaikovsky's *Nutcracker,* playing the Sugar Plum Fairy, dressed up like Mae West.

* * *

In 1970 I decided to keep my fiftieth birthday a secret but gave a big party and invited one hundred guests to come dressed as clowns. We had the whole back garden covered with a circus tent, and I rented all sorts of circus accessories, including peanut and popcorn wagons. We had calliope music as well as a loop-tape of Barnum and Bailey circus marches. It was a sight to see a bunch of clowns come tumbling out of all the grand limos, Rolls, Mercedes and the like.

Hermes Pan and Rita Hayworth, in disguise, won the prize for the most classic clowns. Rita was a frequent guest in my home. A charming woman. Her daughter Princess Yasmin is active in the Women's International Center, an organization working for peace, and later I would receive their Living Legacy Award, presented to me by Dr. Jonas Salk. A real thrill.

Much as I liked Rita Hayworth, I thought my sister should have won the prize at my clown party. Atop her rosy cheeks and putty nose, she had a miniature derby, with a daisy standing straight and tall in the air. I was a lion with ostrich plumes wrapping my head for the mane. The judge, who was a real-life judge, came dressed as the devil. Clay, now my road manager and lighting director, came dressed as the tin-man clown, courtesy of Paul Galbraith, who does those fantastic paper sculptures on television. Everyone danced and cavorted, laughed and sang. The cake, of course, was a circus. It was a super night. And I was the big five-o.

Speaking of clowns, I'm reminded of my clown piece in FUNNYMAN that ends with "What Kind of Fool Am I?" . . . At the party my son-in-law Dick Foster did a pantomime that reminded me of Jerry Lewis, who is a legitimate registered clown. Jerry sent me another washtub of roses.

*   *   *

They talk about accompanists that try to steal the show
. . . It was the afternoon of a large important gala, I'm talking
Texas large. The immense ballroom was filled with what
seemed to be hundreds of tables. There were clusters of
waiters busying themselves with laying the linens, and the
florists bringing in colorful flowers. From where I stood, it
looked like a very pale blue haze of linen with flashes of coral,
white, pink, yellow, green and blue flowers. They left a ring
in the center, perhaps, I thought, for some kind of candle
centerpiece. I turned my attention to the rehearsal. My conductor asked me a few technical questions, and then we were
about to begin.

Suddenly, way down at the end of the ballroom, the
doors burst open and a team of men came through carrying
pale blue bird cages, each with a matching pale blue bird
inside. A bird in a cage for each table. Strictly Texas. And the
cages—tall, slim, delicately wrought like Dufy cages.

The orchestra was tuning. It was time for me to sing. My
conductor nodded. About three or four notes into the first
song, the *birds* began. To sing, that is. Just a few—then more
and more of them. I stopped. They stopped. I began again.
They began again. I thought . . . well, it seems we have real
songbirds. The orchestra played the instrumental segment of
the song, and the birds just listened. I tried again—they followed me. My God! What am I going to do? They want to sing
with me. Half-a-dozen tries later, we were convinced that, left
to their own, they would, indeed, sing with me. At first I
thought it was a compliment, but after a while . . .

We had a conference with the florists and the management. As long as the birds didn't sing while the orchestra
played, they could sit in the center of the table. When my
performance began, they would be removed to an adjoining
ballroom, where they would stay while I sang.

236

We were backstage while the thousand or more guests were having a great evening. There was some chirping here and there, but it all blended with the laughing and conversation, the clinking of glasses, the clanking of silver.

After dinner, on cue, the florist removed all the birds from the tables and they were all closed up in the room next door. I heaved a sigh. The orchestra began the overture. All was well. They announced my name and I made my entrance.

I began to sing.

The birds, hearing me *through the wall,* began to sing along with me.

Those birds had great ears, but as "back-up" singers, . . .


Life, as you've seen, wasn't always a cabaret, but at Tower Grove Drive on New Year's Eve . . . well, the New Year's guest list read like this: Rudolf Nureyev, Margot Fonteyn, the Fifth Dimension, Bob and Dorothy Mitchum, Victoria and Ed McMahon, Cary Grant, Bobby Darin, Mia Farrow, Laurence Harvey, Margaret Whiting, Tony Bennett, Andy Williams, a passel of my doctor friends, Natalie Wood, Bob Wagner, Quincy Jones, Shirley MacLaine, and Helen Glickstein, Dr. Salk's cousin, came from New York to surprise me. Ed McMahon and Victoria were on their first date that night, one that would lead to their marriage. We put the sound system all through the house and we all sang "Auld Lang Syne" until the house fairly lifted off the hill.

Bobby Darin, a guest, needs a special word. Bobby, a victim of rheumatic heart disease, donated his heart to medical science. He had often come to visit me at my home and we became close. Some people thought he was a smarty. Well, he was smart, quite, but not a smarty. Bobby was very mature for his age. We sang together on television. One day he came by to see me, then he was leaving to go up to Big

237

Sur and live in a place near Pfeiffer Beach. He was wishing I would talk him out of it. He seemed to know he was going . . . but I had no idea.

Back to the New Year's party that night. Steve Allen and Jayne Meadows provided the entertainment in the Yellow Room. Afterward, guests began to drift into the other rooms, but Bob Mitchum, I noticed, stayed over in the corner, sober, serious, and quietly singing "America, the Beautiful"—and, no question, meaning every word of it. I'd met Bob at children's parties over the years and we also had struck up a friendship. We'd drink our lemonade together at those parties. It's a picture that doesn't go with his legend, but it goes with the person.

Another event revealing something of a famous person's character . . . Maggie and Jean Louis had introduced me to Rudolf Nureyev. One night he invited me to come to his performance at the Music Center as his guest and then to dinner. The others at our table were Robert F. Kennedy, Elizabeth Taylor, Richard Burton and Pierre Salinger. R.F.K. and I eyed each other like a cat and dog, and when the photographers rushed up to our table, R.F.K. elbowed me out of camera range. Nureyev corrected him on his manners. Later, Rudolf asked me to dance with him. I was so nervous I couldn't. I just couldn't get anything to work right and gave up.


In 1971 Adela Rogers St. John wrote me from the Madonna Inn in San Luis Obispo, in the midst of the same hills and valleys as the Hearst ranch a few miles to the north. Adela no longer wanted to run a home and was happy living at the inn. She wanted me to help her save the Catholic high school, which was connected with the beautiful old Mission San Luis Obispo. "The school will have to close next fall unless they can find some funds," she wrote. "I am always unhappy when a good parochial school goes. Mr. Madonna would have a lovely room here if you'd come and try to sell some tickets and get a basic fund going. This is a relatively small operation here and all the switchboard know of our friendship, so he's asked me if I thought you would come up and sing for us one night in May, on my birthday. It would be a lovely way for me to celebrate it. They want you to stay in the Austrian Room, which is a joy. Think of it and ask for guidance, as we always do."

At this time I was pretty involved doing Revlon shows—specials with Alan King and John Gielgud—but I went up to do the benefit, bringing my musicians to the Madonna Inn. Later Adela, the musicians, their wives and I toured the Hearst Castle. Dear Adela, we were friends so long, and when she passed recently, I sang "The Lord's Prayer" at her service.

I really don't know what tells me to sell a house—maybe I want to find another place to decorate—but, in any case, I found a little jewel box up on Blue Jay Way in the Doheney Hills. It was so tiny that my dog Genghis and I lived alone there for a while. It bothered me because you could see into the house from almost any place outside. Lloyd and James, Lillie Mae and Virginia had all worked for me up on Tower Grove Drive, but I couldn't bring them to live in because there was only room in a little guest house that I hadn't yet furnished. My dog Genghis was such a good guard dog that he would not go to sleep one night until I put on the security system. I've never figured out just how he could tell the difference between the red and green lights. I thought dogs were supposed to be color blind.

Some five years later, in 1976, I was off to Japan on a concert tour, and was also representing the U.S. at the Mitsukoshi

Department Store's celebration of our bicentennial. Mitsuko-shi made bronze busts of four of our Presidents, and they commissioned Max Factor to make the mannequins for the gowns worn by the Presidents' wives. These gowns, part of the Helen Larson collection, were all the actual gowns.

We took the bullet train to a magnificent manmade lake surrounded by castles that were copies of famous European castles. Pine trees stood all about. While we were at the lake, the symphony did *Swan Lake* at the beginning with the ballet and then presented the most fantastic fireworks display as they played the *1812 Overture* and "Stars and Stripes Forever." Part of the fireworks were actually under water. Imagine the beauty of a Japanese night, the giant pines witnessing it all, the ballet, the music, and then the orchestra playing "Stars and Stripes Forever." It's no wonder we all cried.

At my concerts the Japanese called for encores of "Johnny Guitar," "Fever," and "Is That All There Is?" They knew them so well that when the orchestra played the first chord of "Johnny Guitar" they immediately applauded in recognition. They're serious music fans, and at rehearsals the orchestra really whipped through the arrangements.

I began painting fabric designs for Mitsukoshi. Everything and everyone was so lovely, except for one ride in a 747, coming from Sapporo and Osaka to Tokyo in a typhoon. I had the first of many heart-spells just before we hit the typhoon. I was on the floor and the Japanese aboard were taking such conscientious care of me that I was soaking wet from damp cloths and ice cubes. When we reached Tokyo, I had to be taken out a side door.

I hated to leave those people.


The next year I decided to travel to London and do my show. My friend and banker Jon Hanson went along to attend the proceedings at the Royal Command Performance for the

Queen Mother on her birthday. At her request I sang "The Folks Who Live on the Hill," and, when I met her on the reception line, she had tears in her eyes. Later I was told that my version of this Jerome Kern song is one of Her Majesty's favorites. When you meet the "Queen Mum," even if you don't plan to curtsy, which I *had* planned, you might curtsy anyway, when your knees buckle. Some of the other performers at the Queen's birthday were Larry Hagman, Mary Martin, James Cagney, Pat O'Brien, Aretha Franklin, Victor Borge, Sammy Davis and Henry Mancini. Royals, all.

During these excitements I continued to have arythmias and fibrillations and more than once had to call Dr. McEachens and have him listen to my pacer-tracer. The heart has its own natural pacemaker; I'd recently taken a bad fall coming out of an elevator, and it had impaired the mechanism that controls the heartbeat. Dr. McEachens would hear from me from London, Japan, Australia, Canada—you name it.

From London I went to Amsterdam and the Amsterdam Hilton, where I had to call a doctor to help assemble "Charlie," my Bennett respirator.

I'll never forget the mustache on the doctor who attended me—I've never seen a bigger mustache in my life. It extended a good seven to eight inches from his nose on each side! Very successfully waxed, it flapped as he talked. Jerry Powell, my musician on keyboards, and I found it very difficult to keep from laughing, although this was quite a serious matter.

Sometime during the next couple of years, I gave up Charlie, who had been traveling with me for the past decade, including to London, and finally my lung was better. So I gratefully passed off the machines—I carried a couple of spares—to the American Lung Association. Doctor John Jones had said most people who had my condition didn't live very long. He must have scared me into getting well.

I was playing at the Vieux Carre in Amsterdam. It was a

magnificently appointed theatre, and Princess Marguerite and her husband Prince Phillip Von Volenhauven were in the audience. It was so cold in the dressing room I had to wear my mink to put on my makeup. I had been attacked by a seventy-year-old woman who had crawled up the ladder to my dressing room and tried to hang onto my legs! I'd been told that royalty would be in attendance, so, while shivering with the cold, I was also trying to practice a proper introduction. But every time I tried to say "Her Royal Highness Princess Marguerite and Prince Phillip Von Volenhauven," it came out "Your Royal Harness," and, wouldn't you know, I said that on stage as well. They were a charming couple, and generously good-natured about my difficulty, as was the audience.


I returned to the U.S. with my resistance down to sing with the symphony at Walnut Creek near San Francisco. And was hit with a 105-degree fever. I barely remember singing that evening and only babbled as we flew home. When we arrived, we called Dr. Jaime Paris, who told them to pack me in ice and bring me to the hospital. I was told that I had a heart condition, diabetes and Meniere's disease, a disorder of the inner ear. I went blind temporarily, and the doctors informed me I had to retire. I said, "Retire and wait for what?"

Being blind—the strange thing that strikes you is wandering around feeling walls and familiar furniture like you've never known them. The worst feeling was when I felt paralysis coming over one whole side of my face, like a claw had hold of it and was twisting it into a grimace. When the paralysis came, the sight went too. I could *feel* the terrible expression as my face twisted, and I avoided every mirror in the room when my sight returned. I would walk holding my I.V. stand, which I called Fred. One day I accidentally saw my paralyzed face. I was horrified and wouldn't move. My therapist Fran Owen worked daily on that for hours at a time, during which sessions the neighbors, I was told, could hear me screaming.

Still almost blind, I promptly booked myself into Australia, Orlando, Florida, and everywhere else I could. Fran Owen traveled with me; she pulled me back together. Saved me from falling off the stage in Australia—"Stop," she'd say, or "turn right," as I tried to make my way off the stage. In Orlando my friend Pat Shelton saw me walk straight into the lights. I was still partially paralyzed on the right side of my face and nearly blind. Dr. Richard Barton, Dr. Paris and Dr. McEachens all again concurred—I should retire. I guess they were right, but I was too stubborn. I had a little more work to do and a lot more wisdom to gather. The doctors kindly said, "All right, we'll try to help you as much as we can." And they have, they have.

The spectacular bird's-eye view from Blue Jay Way reminded me of the property David had sold, and I wondered how life would have been . . . Would we have built a home up there? No use crying over spilled love or money. But I was sort of restless there, so I went to Detroit with a Stephen Sondheim company. SIDE BY SIDE BY SONDHEIM was fun, and on our days off I cooked for the cast—mostly fried chicken and potato salad. I enjoyed getting to know what it would be like in real theatre. It was also in Detroit that I met Paul Horner, who later would write the score with me for PEG, my Broadway show.

Back in L.A., after making a few improvements to the house, I, of course, sold it, and to a very happy tenant. And then—what else?—I was out house hunting again with Genghis, my little black Lhasa Apso. As we rounded a corner on Bellagio Drive, I said, "*That* house." The realtor said, "No, that's not on the market." I had gone through more than a few houses in the Bel Air-Beverly Hills area, but none had attracted me as much as this place. The owner was an Iranian, and somehow I talked him into selling me the house.

Some of my friends thought I was foolish, but I could see the house all renovated and shining. My buddy Genghis gave me the straight-ahead signal when he christened every bush. When I opened the front door, I saw that the foyer was just as I had pictured it would be. Genghis was shivering with excitement—he had good taste. The house—I'm still there —is a stately French Regency with a two-story foyer. From the ceiling hangs a huge crystal chandelier made in the 1700's; in its original state it held candles, but it ended up in a Packard car showroom and acquired lightbulbs. Genghis had already chosen his place of honor from which to welcome the guests—directly under the historic chandelier.

The first thing I decided to do was repair the mansard roof and paint it different shades of peach, apricot and nude. The staffing, an elaborate architectural molding running around the ceiling, should remain white, I decided, as well as the office, the studio and kitchen—white lacquer. Even the big white wooden chandeliers would be white lacquer. In such a setting every piece of fruit or vegetable would be an accent-piece.

Driving away, my mind drifted with the windshield wipers as we sloshed through the rain. How had I come this far? My mother loved beautiful things and did lovely touches on our own home, and how she would have loved this place on Bellagio. My mind shifted to the funeral so long ago . . . and I saw Mama as she was, and realized I was passing another milestone in my life.

It was so much fun to decorate the house. Bruce Vanderhoff, who owns Le Restaurant, was a great help. He found a magnificent mirror that just fit on the mantle in the living room, wonderful marble and etched glass, and he rounded up an entire crew of craftsmen. My major domo Jose Prado and his family have had a great part in the refurbishing of this house and continue to keep everything fresh and beautiful. I think they must feel they have part of it, and they do. But when I came here, I only knew I felt at home. And that seems to be one of the things I've looked for all my life.

There's something about this place that is conducive to writing or painting. But I've admired my daughter's work so much that I decided to stop painting. Perhaps when she's established as the fine artist she is, I can try my hand at it again. Mothers and daughters shouldn't have too much competition with each other. Meanwhile, she is having her first big West Coast exhibition, and we're all excited about it.

I said my legitimate theatre experience in Detroit got me thinking more about the stage. One day in the theatre we had a little conversation during rehearsal, and Paul Horner, one of the accompanists, was over on stage left playing a beautiful melody. I called to him, "What is that, Paul?" "It's mine." I walked over to him. "Does that have lyrics?" "No, I was hoping you might want to write some."

So there it was, his dream and mine. I didn't want to let any time go by, so I just began writing immediately. I could hear the title in his music. "I Gave It Everything I Had." The cast came on stage again after the break and we played it for them right then and there. They were very encouraging and urged us to keep on writing.

There began a period of years writing PEG for Broadway. It was between engagements that we wrote thirty songs for the score, and when it was finished, we began having backers' dinners at my house, served by Le Restaurant. At first we were just more or less auditioning the songs for people and were pleased with their reception. The one night when Marge Cowan and I were giving a birthday party for Irv Cowan, they said, "Sing the score." I happily complied. It may be hard to believe, call me naïve, but I didn't have the show-backing in mind. Elizabeth Taylor was there with Zev Bufman, and the waiters could hardly keep their minds on the dinner. It was during the time she and Richard Burton were doing the play PRIVATE LIVES on Broadway. I'll always remember how Danny Thomas jumped up and said, "I'll give $250,000!" It snowballed from there with the Cowans, and Zev Bufman wanted to back the play for Broadway.

## PEG

Score by Paul Horner and Peggy Lee

| | |
|---|---|
| Creative Consultant: | Cy Coleman |
| Director: | Robert Drivas |
| Executive Assistant: | Victoria Lang |
| Costume Designer: | Florence Klotz |
| Costume Execution: | Barbara Matera |
| Set Design: | Tom H. John |
| Lighting: | Thomas Skelton |
| Musical Director: | Larry Fallon |
| The Rose: | Nicki Lee Foster |

Backup Singers

| | |
|---|---|
| First Soprano: | Mary Sue Barry |
| Second Soprano: | Doris Eugenio |
| Alto: | Rose Marie Jun |
| Tenor: | Brian Quinn |
| Tenor: | Steve Clayton |
| Strings: | Ellen McLain |
| | D. Michael Heath |

Arrangers

| | |
|---|---|
| Artie Butler | Bill Holman |
| Billy May | Gordon Jenkins |
| Johnny Mandel | Don Sebesky |
| Tore Zito | Larry Wilcox |
| Philip Lang | |
| Sound: | Scott |
| Sound Consultant: | Phil Ramon |
| Production Photographer: | Martha Swope |

Orchestra Members
The Quartet:
Piano:    Mike Renzi
Drums:    Grady Tate
Bass:    Jay Leonhart
Guitar:    Bucky Pizzarelli

Reeds
Ralph Olsen    Ed Salkin
Andy Drelies    Frank Perowsky
Joe Temperley

Trumpets    Trombones
John Frosk    Harry Divito
Brian O'Flaherty    Sy Berger
Frank Fighera    Tommy Mitchell

French Horns
Doug Norris
Fred Griffen

Guitar:    John Basie
Percussion:    Joe Passaro
Synthesizer:    Lou Forestieri

Strings
Lou Ann Montesi    Winterton Garvey
Amaura Giannini    Abe Appleman
Richard Henrickson    Bruce Berg
Stanley Hunte    Valerie Collymore

Celli
Avron Coleman    Zela Terry

It took a long time to get to the point of the *Playbill* lineup. For a year we worked with such people as Bill Luce, the playwright (THE BELLE OF AMHERST, which starred Julie Harris), Danya Krupska, choreographer, director Bob Kalfin. As happens sometimes, they were all changed, and finally we worked with Cy Coleman (SWEET CHARITY) and Bobby Drivas. Cy was a child prodigy who's never stopped being brilliant.

Bobby Drivas was an actor-director who chewed gum constantly, his handsome, clean jaw-line working away. One day I bought the cast and crew packages of gum and we were *all* chewing away when rehearsal resumed, imitating Bobby. He didn't even notice, he was so busy chewing. (Recently Bobby tragically died of AIDS.)

My granddaughter Holly, who has grown into a lovely young lady, is talented in many directions; and she's a wonderful companion, laughing and crying right along with you, whatever your mood. She made the move to New York with me when we leased Bellagio Road to some very nice tenants and, in exchange, leased a brand-new apartment in New York.

I had to buy furniture, because the New York apartment was unfurnished. After rambling around a big house in Bel Air, it was rather strange to move into such a small space. People would come over and say, "Oh, look what a big apartment you have," but I didn't realize that. I had a great view of the East River from five rooms. Phoebe Jacobs, my old friend from Basin Street East, went shopping for furniture with Holly and me, and very soon we had it looking good.

We started rehearsing PEG in New York at the Minskoff and then the Michael Bennett Studios. It was a whole brand-new world for me. I learned to respect and admire all those people who come in for so-called "cattle calls" to audition. I would see them day after day, with the sounds of counting-out tempos (1-2-3-4!); dancing and singing; feet coming in contact with the boards of the floor; passing by each other, carrying coffee or sandwiches. Everyone had a big bag (shoes, rehearsal clothes, books), and I had two of them with everything under the sun in there (scripts, Granola Bars, something for Genghis). At times I'd have Genghis with me, and he'd look so tiny in that huge rehearsal hall, but he'd communicate with me from one end of the room to the other (and he loved to share my Granola Bars). He rarely barked, letting me know his wishes (needs) by what I can only describe as telepathy.

I'd see Paul Horner, who wrote the score with me, and somehow we had lost the simplicity we had going in L.A., but not our friendship. Actually, by now, you could hardly recognize it as the same show. The Cowans and Zev Bufman had brought in two new partners, producers Georgia and Dominic Frontiere. One night Zev Bufman took me to see Cicely Tyson in THE CORN IS GREEN. I didn't know at the time that I would be asked to perform in that big theatre. PRIVATE LIVES with Elizabeth Taylor and Richard Burton had closed early at the Lunt-Fontanne. They planned to play for eight months, but played for six because Burton had to go back to England. That left Zev with thirteen to fourteen months to go on the two-year lease, and that's where and when we came in. I was told I had to play the Lunt-Fontanne Theatre. Never mind if the dressing room was floors up and they had to build a bathroom upstairs (I hope someone enjoys it). I couldn't handle the stairs, so they did install an elevator.

While all of this was going on, I repeatedly asked when we would open, so I could get some theater groups going. I asked David Powers, our press agent, when I could start promoting the show with disk jockeys. He had no answer. The Ash LeDonne ad agency had a beautiful poster that Nicki and I designed. By now THE CORN IS GREEN was closed, and we were in the theatre for rehearsals. I didn't see any marquee going up on the theatre (and it never did!).

On November 20, 1983, in the Sunday New York *Times,* there was a full-page ad listing the *wrong* telephone number (586-5555). If you called it you didn't even get an answer. The number should have been 575-9200. "Theatre Guide," a free listing in the Sunday *Times,* did not run a listing on the same day our big ad ran! Phoebe called Victoria Lang, Bufman's assistant, and she said it was the New York *Times'* fault. I'm *sure* if the *Times* made such a mistake, they would have corrected it, if asked. So there was really no proper advertising. The posters were never distributed—except that ever since our opening in New York, they have been leaking out of some warehouse as collectors' items, and I'm told they're for sale in some shops.

We began previews on December 1, to open on the 14th, which is probably as bad a time as one could find to open in New York City, especially with no advertising. After all, people are concentrating on Christmas shopping and holiday parties. The weather was bleak and slushy and cold. I kept hearing the phrase "tax loss" and wondered what it meant, but I sure didn't like the sound of it. The excitement was growing—at least for me—and, I think, for Paul Horner and the inner core of the faithful.

H.L. Wade, a fan for many years, flew in from San Francisco; Dr. Hutcherson and his wife Gail, my dentist Dr. Stone and his guest, and suddenly there it was, opening night, beautiful flowers everywhere.

When I walked out on the stage, I could feel something like cold steel pressing on me, a precognition that reviews would be bad. I was right. The drama critics weren't music critics, which I wish we'd had. Ours wasn't a musical comedy, complete with lots of songs and big orchestra and chorus. We had no dancers. Ours was a musical, but that's not so easy to classify. Three days after opening, Irv Cowan said, "Tomorrow is your last show." That was so shocking it didn't even get through to me. We determined to be brave and hoped for a miracle. I called Greg Bautzer to see if he could help me get some more money, if that was the problem. Greg was my lawyer, and a man with financial connections, and we were by now old, old friends. He said he would get right back to me. But then, when I called the Waldorf, the Cowans had already left for Florida. They weren't going to be there for the closing performance! Who would put up further backing under such circumstances?

I was very proud of my daughter and granddaughter. They almost held back the tears when the packed house, despite the reviews, was told, "This is our closing performance." Grady Tate made an unscheduled speech to the audience that was truly eloquent. Orchestra members Mike Renzi, Jay Leonhart, Bucky Pizzarelli and the others fought back the tears at the emotion-packed closing. A fan taped that performance, and on it you can hear the six to eight minute standing ovation. The producers never heard that. The final blow was when the company manager threatened to put me in jail for taking my own music home for safety reasons! Holly and Nicki and I were hugging each other and crying. We had a bleak Christmas. I thought my heart was broken, and maybe it was.


One of the stars on the team of arrangers for PEG was Johnny Mandel. Johnny once told me he "scored the scenery" in Big Sur when he wrote THE SANDPIPER. It's magnificent scenery and a beautiful score. I think I've worn out perhaps six tapes and several albums of it. I carry that and Delius' "On Hearing the First Cuckoo in Spring" whenever I travel. When Johnny wrote "The Shadow of Your Smile" for the movie THE SAND-PIPER, he sent me a pencil lead sheet (a sheet of music done sketch-like with pencil instead of ink—the very earliest version of a song). Mutual friend Eddie Tirella brought it along to me. Before I could even turn around, everyone had recorded it, and I was just one of the group. When I had explained my disillusionment to Eddie Tirella, Johnny called and told me the publisher had given it out, and he had a new song he wanted me to hear for a lyric. I was so glad to see him. I was really fond of Johnny. As soon as I played the melody, the lyric began to dance around in my mind. It was finished in less than an hour. Johnny looked at me in astonishment. "How did you do that?"

"Do what?"

"Write those lyrics so fast? Did you know you wrote what's in the film?"

"No . . . what film?"

"THE RUSSIANS ARE COMING, THE RUSSIANS ARE COMING."

"I did? I didn't know it was from a film. I just wrote what I heard in your music."

"Well, you must see this film. I'll take you down to the Directors Guild Theatre and you'll see."

So we went to the theatre, and I was amazed when I saw the love scene played out on the screen. It was "The Shining Sea" and that's what was up there on the screen. The shining sea, and the young Russian and the girl, and the seashells, and kissing the hollow of her hand and his leaving her—it was all there. Funny how these things happen.

We loved the Shining Sea
He gathered sea shells there for me
His hands, his strong, brown hands . . .

We'd sit there on the sand
He'd kiss the hollow of my hand
His kiss . . . I miss his kiss . . .

I hear the grey gulls cry
I see them dip their wings
I feel the pounding surf
And other things . . .

I can't believe he's gone
I think I'll go where he might be
I'll go . . . I need him so
I need our shining sea.

Johnny wrote some superb arrangements for my album *Mirrors,* especially "I Remember." "Say It" is like glass, and there are some beautiful deep dark colors in "Little White

Ship." One section with the bass clarinet is so beautiful—"To places dark and deep . . . where you can fall asleep . . . and *dream . . . Passage* to places." The songs are by Lieber and Stoller.

When you hear Johnny's music, it's like, not just a bed of strings, but an ocean of strings, mostly calm, and the moving progressions under the water show what an artist, what a craftsman he is. His music floats. It was not surprising that I wanted an arrangement from Johnny in PEG.


On the subject of great musical talent, it's hard to think of the music business without Gordon Jenkins. He could make such beautiful, broad brush strokes with his arrangements and such clear, strong, lovely compositions, but he left us in June of 1986, not long before we heard "Goodbye," played so often when Benny Goodman died . . . Gordon wrote "Goodbye" for Benny's closing theme.

I remember the first arrangements he did for me at Decca. It was spring and I was in love with actor Robert Mazurvy. I was all excited because after the date we were going to the Drake Hotel to hear Cy Walter's piano for the first of many times. We would drink Piper Heidseck champagne and watch the captain make Steak Diane and tiny, thin julienne French-fried zucchini, but when I saw Gordon and that enormous orchestra, I forgot all about that stuff and sang "I'm Glad There Is You" and "Forgive Me."

Gordon and I were to work together many times, and each time would be memorable. Remember how he orchestrated "Lover"?

The last time was when we were rehearsing PEG. Cy Coleman, Bobby Drivas and I decided to use as many of the top arrangers as we could think of to do the songs most suited to their particular style of writing. We chose Gordon to write "Mama."

253

I didn't know Gordon was ill, and when we called and spoke to Bev, his beloved wife, she said, "Well, Gordon can't speak, but he most certainly can write. You can talk to him and he'll write down the answer." I thought, "My God! what an example of courage!" We went through all of the details, and he enthusiastically wrote down all the answers we wanted to hear. Later Bev told me that Gordon couldn't get the song "Mama" out of his mind.

When the finished arrangement came into the rehearsal hall, we couldn't wait to see what he had written. Cy, Bobby, Mike Renzi, Grady Tate and Jay Leonhart, with all the tech crew, eagerly listened as Cy and Mike played lines from the arrangement on the piano. It wasn't surprising that we were all in tears before it was finished. You can imagine how we felt when we finally got to orchestra rehearsal! It was beautiful, so moving.

Every time I sang it, I had to steel my emotions. The thought of my Mama, coupled with Gordon Jenkins' inspired writing, was almost more than I could control. I had hoped so desperately that I could record it. When Gordon died, we all lost a major talent. But at least he was able to do *Trilogy* for Frank Sinatra. I lost two good friends then—Francis "Sonny" Burke, who produced *Trilogy,* and Gordon.


After PEG, I picked up the pieces. After all, I had my family, my sister Marianne was there. I couldn't know it would be the last year of Marianne's life, and I still had Genghis and my new friend Mario Buatta, tall, distinguished and *funny.* He's a brilliant interior designer—years later the government would call on Mario to restore Blair House. One night when I was singing at a supper club, Mario brought Zip, a chimpanzee, and sat down with him at a ringside table. I couldn't believe my eyes. Surely Mario wouldn't actually bring a monkey to my performance. I decided to treat Zip as a person and he behaved well, listening intently and applauding in all the right places. Then people started disrupting the show, taking pictures of Zip, and I had to say, "Mario, don't you think it's about his bedtime?" Later in my dressing room I sat down with Zip, but still wouldn't pose for photographers. Zip then leaned over and kissed me, forever winning my heart. I'm fairly easy.

If Genghis, my little Lhasa Apso, had had hips, he would have had his hands on them. He looked at me out of the corner of his eyes and slid his pupils along the lower lid until they got to me. Then he slid his eyes back to the oversized teddy bear, dressed in a mink coat. Mario Buatta had brought me the teddy and placed it on my bed as a surprise. Genghis was clearly jealous. He was seventeen years old, but he seemed like a healthy little clown, a puppy. He managed to scoot that teddy bear, three times his size, from my king-size bed to the floor and out of the room. He jumped back up on the bed, gave a snuffling snort, curled up and lay down. As I smoothed out his fur, I gently remembered how this whole trip to New York had started.

Back in Bel Air, I had thought Genghis needed to travel with me, at least once. Then we could return home and he would have his own new dog-run. I bought a carrying case— actually a black-and-white-striped Lancôme bag, and had grommets punched in it, so he would get plenty of air. Then we got into our daily routine. I would tell him I was taking him to New York, at which point he would lift his little shoulders to let me know he liked the idea. I'd tell him every detail of how he would get in the limo with me and ride to the airport, how we would go through security and into the plane to wait for takeoff. Somewhere in my travelogue lecture, I would slip him into the Lancôme bag and zip the zipper, carry him around the house, take him in the elevator, saying there would be one in New York, as well as a terrace where he could look out and survey the New York world.

Day after day we rehearsed until he could hardly wait for the limo. Finally the day came, and he jumped into the bag. We got into the limo, to the airport, and through security. I talked to him all the way. It all went off beautifully until we got on the plane and there was a delay, but it worked out all right because the stewardess gave me permission to take him out and put him on my lap. He wasn't much of a lap dog but he was following orders. They brought around *hors d'oeuvres,* and he ate mine, as well as those of several other passengers. The plane took off, and he stretched out on his back, still on my lap. It was a perfect blue-sky day with lots of cumulus nimbus clouds floating around. He lay there for so long, just looking up at the clouds. Kind of like Snoopy, I thought, only Genghis was all black with a few silver streaks.

When we arrived in New York, he jumped in the bag and stayed in it until the hotel; got out and ran through the lobby to the elevator; rode upstairs with Holly and me, and scooted to the terrace I had promised. He let us know in no uncertain terms how happy he was to be there.

He made friends. Foobar was a dog who lived at the River Tower on East Fifty-fourth, and Genghis loved Foobar. Also the doormen Louis and Luciano, the bellman Jamie, the concierge Trebor—everyone we met he adored, including my wardrobe woman, who at first said, "I don't walk any dem dog!" but later was pleased to say, "Genghis *likes* me." He was the major domo, running the house, and he truly turned out to be a New York dog.


So, back on the road again. Holly and I went to Japan with The Quintet—Mike, Grady, Jay, Mark, and John. We had another successful stay there, but my little blackouts were beginning to worry me. One night after we came back home,

I was at Mimi's Italian Restaurant and Tony Bennett introduced me to Elizabeth and Donald Kramer. It was kind of like meeting another sister to meet Elizabeth. And Donald has such a great sense of humor. We began trading jokes, and we've been fast friends ever since. They introduced me to Julian Wills, who is the head of Arts International, and, before I knew it, I was recording a video cassette for that company. We recorded it in Atlantic City at Resorts International. The video wasn't easy—I sang for fourteen hours straight—but it certainly was fun.

We went off to London for one of the most memorable tours I've made there. Most of the cities were motor trips in a grand Daimler, and we enjoyed our stay at the St. James Club.

One engagement was in Scotland, and our road manager said, "We'll take a Viscount." It was a prop plane, not even a jet. When we woke up that morning, the sky was full of rain, and as we rode to the airport, the road manager said, "There's no ramp to the plane, we could provide a forklift." "A forklift?" It sounded like Australia, when the photographers caught me being hoisted by a forklift.

My guitarist John Chiodini and I couldn't believe our ears when we were advised we'd be using an old prop plane. We began to examine the plane, and I said, "Do you think we can fly this thing?" John said, "We can keep it up there with our faith," and we laughed a strained laugh as we loaded. Several minutes out of Glasgow, I looked at John in amazement—it was leaking on his head! It took every bit of faith I had, because it was very clear the plane wasn't pressurized. I thought we were flying out in the Twilight Zone. But we made it, literally, on a wing and a prayer.

I saw my old English chum Dennis Chapell again. I guess it wouldn't be England without Dennis. We came back to the United States, and during those days I was having an occasional heart episode, followed by an occasional angiogram and an occasional cardio version or an angioplasty, and in between I was feeling fine, so I was open-minded about blazing new trails.

When agent Irwin Arthur spoke about the Ballroom in New York City, I couldn't quite picture what it was. Taken literally, it could have been a place to stop for a one-nighter with a band, or a huge room with a stage on one end and a whirling mirrored ball hanging from the ceiling. When Irwin said, "They have a tapas bar," I thought he said topless! We cleared that up right away. I looked up "tapas" and discovered it certainly doesn't mean topless. It's gourmet *hors d'oeuvres,* tables piled with cakes, pheasants, cheeses—a Spanish gourmet smorgasbord, like a rich painting of great cornucopias of food and game. I also learned that Felipe Rojas Lombardi, a world-class chef, was in charge of the gourmet delicacies served in the Ballroom, in a dining area adjacent to the cabaret, or theatre space. Now it all took on a very different feeling. When it came to the financial end of things they were certainly being *fair.*

As I mentioned, I had been working with these fantastic musicians—The Quintet. We had been playing in London and all over the United Kingdom, winding up with a triumphant turn at Heritage Hall. We had been to Japan for a successful appearance there, so we were ready to jump into New York City. John, Grady, Mike, and sometimes Emil, Mark and Jay were on hand and well prepared. In fact, we had sort of an unwritten pact that we would work together again after the heart-rending experience of PEG.

So it was with happy hearts that we opened at the Ballroom in New York to cheering crowds and glowing reviews. Rolls-Royces and limousines jammed the street and lines formed again. I surely loved what critic John Wilson of the New York *Times* wrote: "She looked like a hip angel and she sang like one."

The management at the Ballroom was so thoughtful that they had a bathroom installed right off the stage for me. I was glad that I was able to let *The Hollywood Reporter*'s Radie Harris use it, when she asked me for directions to the ladies' room one crowded Saturday night.

Naturally, we were exceedingly happy about the Ballroom success, and Greg Dawson, one of the owners, became a good friend, as well as Felipe, Scott, and all the waiters, especially one named Michael, who took great pains serving me Felipe's delicious salmon cooked on mesquite. Then we sadly said good-bye to all our new friends, including Mario Buatta and Jerry Zipkin, and took a short hiatus while I had more tests taken.

After that I went back to work, this time in New Orleans. New Orleans has always been a favored place for me, but I wouldn't have dreamed it would almost be my last appearance. We arrived at the Fairmont (which had been the old Roosevelt Hotel) and were greeted by my dear friend Marilyn Barnett (who exudes the charm of New Orleans) and Oliver, the maitre d' I remembered from the past. Marilyn works at the Hilton Hotel in New Orleans as public-relations director.

It felt so good to be back in New Orleans, and after rehearsals we opened to a generous audience. We were also excited about going to the White House at the close of the New Orleans engagement. We were to appear at a state dinner, but then an unplanned, unscheduled appearance at Touro Infirmary changed things.

It was a sunny October morning, a blue-sky day. But inside the New Orleans Fairmont in Suite 579, it was not so sunny, and I needed help. I called to Toni Chandler, my assistant. "Toni, Toni, please come in, I'm having trouble with my heart. Get the nitro." I dropped the phone. Toni came running from her room. "What can I get for you? Here's the nitro. The heart box?"

"Yes, call Dr. McEachen." Thank God, I could call him

like that. I put the pacer-tracer over my heart. There was something wrong all right. Dr. McEachen's number was ringing. "Hello, Peggy?" His quiet, comforting voice. "Let me hear it," he said. I turned it on. After seconds he said, "Yes, you're in fibrillation. You'd better call the paramedics right away." Tony called Marilyn Barnett on another line and Marilyn immediately got busy calling Dr. Tom Oelsener at the Touro Infirmary.

I had felt more than a little concern the night before, and, after conferring with Oliver, the maitre d' of the Blue Room, I decided to cancel the second show. That was something major for me; something I *never* did, but, because we were going to the White House to perform for President and Mrs. Reagan, the prime minister of the Republic of Singapore and Mrs. Lee and other dignitaries, I thought it best to pay attention to the pain and irregularity of my heart, get some rest. I'd be all right, of course.

After several angioplasties the previous year, I felt like an old vet—nothing was going to keep me from the White House. Rick Swig, son of Richard Swig, owner of Fairmont Hotels, had given me permission to miss an evening, and everything was all set, except my heart. When the attack came, the ambulance man arrived almost immediately. They quietly and efficiently put me on the stretcher, listened to my heart with a stethoscope, applied a blood-pressure cuff, conferred on the telephone, carried me out the door, down the hall and into the ambulance. We were off, the light whirling around on top, but no siren. Toni slid into the front seat with the driver. Somehow she'd managed to call my musicians and they came running. Toni said I was so calm, she didn't realize how serious it was.

Riding down the streets of New Orleans, looking out the back door of the ambulance in the bright morning light, I was wondering, wondering. It struck me how different this was than riding along on a float during Mardi Gras. I guess I was a little hazy by that time. When we arrived at the hospital, they bundled me around on gurneys. It seemed as though everyone was running in and out with bottles and needles and tapes and tubes.

My friend Marilyn arrived. She called the White House and told them that I was going into surgery.

As usual at such times, there was a lot of confusion. My daughter and my granddaughter, Nicki and Holly, flew down on the "red eye," arriving just about two hours before the surgery. By this time Dr. Luke Glancy had spoken with Dr. McEachen, and had done an angiogram, and by the minute it was looking more and more urgent that we get things under way.

I was just lying there like a rag doll, full of pain, and when Nicki and Holly came in, I guess the doctors had all conferred with California and decided there was no time to waste and no possibility of going to California. Dr. Charles Pearce, leading a group of doctors, had been in and said, "Don't worry, honey, we're going to take care of you."

At the time I didn't even wonder about the diabetes. But it's not the best thing to have when you're going into surgery. They had the I.V.'s going and I did wonder if they were giving me glucose. When things are that bad, I guess you kind of lie back and know that God is working through every one of those wonderful, dedicated people. At least, that's what I did, in my lucid moments.

Nicki came in and kissed me. "Hello, Mama. I love you, we're with you." Holly said, "I love you, Mama Peggy, we'll be praying." The nurse came to my bed to remove my nail polish and Holly had to chuckle at how I didn't want it removed. "Just take it from one finger," I said. "Leave it on, and please let me keep my eyelashes. You're not going to be operating on my eyes. My glasses! Where are my glasses?"

The nurse patiently talked me into the polish remover and out of the glasses, which Marilyn took with her to the waiting room.

"Well," I heard someone say, "I guess we're ready." After the attendants moved me from the bed and brought the I.V. stand, which, as usual, I named "Fred," the jokes suddenly stopped and everyone came running alongside the gurney, blowing kisses. Actually, I had no sense of fear, just fatigue . . . and love. The clock was running . . .

I don't remember being in intensive care, don't know how long. There was a blur here and there, but even those could have been dreams. I just barely awakened to see the flowers. The flowers!

"Peggy. Can you see these flowers? They're from President and Mrs. Reagan!" My eyes tried to focus. Why don't I remember? What? Oh . . . I must have made it to the White House and it must have been a success . . . Someone else said, "And here's a telegram from them," and they read me the message:

> Peggy:
> Nancy and I are very sorry about your hospitalization. Our prayers are with you and we hope to hear news of your progress soon. Everyone missed you at the State Dinner last night and all expressed their concern. Please take care and God Bless You.
> Ronald Reagan

I thought, "The President of the United States—and Nancy! Can you imagine that! How did I ever get to here from North Dakota?"

I floated around in my thoughts . . . then, "Peggy, Peggy, can you wake up just a bit and help us?"

"Hmmm? Oh, I, yes. Lil? Is that you?" Lil Samardzija, the head of nursing, had a wonderful manner. I went in and out again . . .

Michael worked in the Coronary Care Unit. Young, tall and handsome and a very caring human being, he was so sensitive he could almost read my mind, and before I could ask what he was doing in my room, he put me at ease. He was just a total professional. One day they moved me into another place and I missed him.

By this time, I kept hearing about the hurricane going on in New Orleans and how in Bures, Louisiana, a tidal wave had washed all the coffins up out of the cemetery. My mind wandered off to the heat and the cold we had back so many years ago in Wimbledon, and old Hank Schultz, the town's alcoholic drayman I used to drag from the depot platform into the warm waiting room so he wouldn't freeze, and we became friends, and I used to feel so sorry for him . . .

There was old Hank Schultz
Chewin' on a plug . . .
And in between, he'd take a swig
From his jug . . .
Tobacco juice ran down his beard . . .
What a sad old man—sad and weird.

It was five in the morning when I heard that shot
I was freezing pumping water . . .
Should I run or not?
I knew it was a gun
Knew that something was dead . . .
Hank stumbled in the door
And sobbing he said . . .
"Come with me, kid.
Something's terrible wrong"
So I ran home with him
He was cryin' all along
She was lying in the bed
With a shot through the heart
And old Hank Schultz just fell apart.
Gun fell from her hand
And landed in the drawer

She was staring straight up
And she wasn't anymore . . .
   People talked . . .
People said "He must have shot her"
But I knew better . . .
He'd have stopped her if he could
I knew he wouldn't let her . . .
   Kill herself . . .
   Poor old Schultz . . .


Sometimes life is sadder than death. Once, I remembered, Hank let me ride in the dray wagon. He wanted to get the horses fed and watered, so he took me to the barn. He unhitched the horses and took them into their stalls. The barn was warm and had a mixture of smells—hay mostly, and horse, and a bit of a manure smell, but it was clean. Old Hank kept it nice as you could ask for, and the horses, you could tell they loved him. They kind of nudged him and stood there easing off one foot and then another, as they watched him get the hay and the oats. I was fascinated by all of it, and when a fly lit on their rumps, they'd whisk it away with their tails . . . Hank always looked like his clothes were way too big for him. I guess he liked them loose like that, but it all added to his tramplike air. He showed a gentle authority with the horses, though, and kind of a wistful friendliness with me. He was lonely; no doubt about that. And now he was even more lonely because she was gone. Even if she'd been sick, he'd had somebody to care for besides his horses. And now the whole town turned away from him. They didn't like the way he shuffled around with the aroma of whiskey and chewing tobacco, I guess, but more than that, they all thought he killed her.

I'd swear on a stack of Bibles, I didn't believe that. How could he be so kind to those horses? After that, he probably just drank himself away.

They say the past is prologue to the present. Maybe so, but it's also *part* of the present. At least mine is.

On October 22nd, 1985, Dr. James Conway stood in my doorway. "Hello, Miss Lee." Dr. Conway was a specialist in infectious diseases. "I don't wish to see you today," I said to his indistinct form. "Well," he said, "I'd like to examine you." But he didn't know quite what to say when I said, "Why don't you come back tomorrow?" It was just that I felt so tired, and I didn't know who he was or much care at the moment.

"I believe I'd better see you today," he said, and kept walking toward me, no matter how charming I thought I was being.

"Only yesterday we had a birthday party for my friend Mario Buatta," I said irrelevantly. "He at least was dressed for the occasion . . . He was wearing a cap with a dog sitting on his head . . . We had dinner sent in from Commanders . . ."

Dr. Conway wasn't interested and proceeded to examine me. I know he didn't want to give the diagnosis he found. It was a staph infection, plus another name I'd never heard before or since. So, back in the operating room we went to reopen the wound. I had had double bypass surgery and was cut open from here to here. His orders now were to leave it open for six weeks, and there began some *really* intensive care. I was so wide open the doctor could see my vocal cords. Nurses Wanda Grimes, Joy and Ilene Shaw started working around the clock, and I mean *they worked.* More flowers came, messages poured in, and they all bolstered my spirits.

Meanwhile, Dr. Pearce went to a charity ball and broke his leg as he was trying to walk his new dog, courtesy SPCA, in the puddles left by the hurricane. The dog was so grateful to be adopted he immediately became Dr. Pearce's guard dog and wouldn't let anyone help him. I discovered Dr. Conway had a marvelous sense of humor, and as soon as we could, we laughed at all the bizarre events. That helped. Dr. Conway was in every day, and I'm sure his diligence must have saved me during this last crisis. I could hear the organs in my body doing what they do . . . the lungs sounded like wax paper.

Then I heard talk of *debridements.* If tissue begins to heal beside an open wound prematurely, they put you to sleep and they snip it off. I heard them talk about those several times, followed by trips to the operating room. But all of this gave me time to think of what a wonderful mechanism the human body really is. All those people in the hospital were there to ensure my recovery, and I know it wasn't easy for any of them.

Frank Sinatra called many, many times. Sometimes I was able to speak to him, and when I did, he gave me strength and kept urging me on to get well: "We've got to get you home, baby." We talked about doing a benefit together for cancer research and St. John's Hospital in Santa Barbara.

I've been down before, many times, even had the death-experience, but never so far down as the Touro Infirmary in New Orleans. The doctors all said, "You've been to hell and back," and I must admit it was an *extraordinary* experience, needing every bit of the love that poured into that hospital to pull me back over the edge. Every prayer that was said, every card or letter that was written, every telephone call or telegram or flower or thought, every bit of dedication by the doctors, nurses and technicians, every last soul—it all helped.

Then, finally, the day came to be released, and when I left Touro, everyone lined up along the route my wheelchair would take me. It was time to return to California and St. John's and my own cardiologist, Dr. James McEachen and Dr. Paris.

Frank Sinatra called again and arranged for a private plane to fly me, my nurse Wanda Grimes, my assistant Toni, and my daughter Nicki back to the West Coast.

Flying home. Next stop Santa Monica and St. John's. ETA: On time. Courtesy of my friend Frank Sinatra.

Well, life didn't end right there. In fact, it was more like this was the beginning of a new life.

I immediately let everyone know I was ready to go again and began booking tours. Barbara Voltaire and I planned wardrobe and she began making beautiful gowns, evening coats and suits. It was so much fun getting all the musicians back into rehearsing. John Chiodini and I started writing songs. I didn't return to the Ballroom just then because, like they say, you have to crawl before you can walk, and the Ballroom, way up in New York, was a little too much for me to handle that soon. I also had to have my doctors' approval, and they felt something on the West Coast would be more in line. So we opened in the Westwood Playhouse in Los Angeles and the audience gave me a beautiful reception. There were flowers and excitement and everyone seemed genuinely happy that I had made it through surgery.

Then sorrow came. My beloved sister, Marianne, had been ill for a long time, and finally she left us. Her children, Lee and Lynn, Merilee, Nicki and I were holding her hand as she slipped away. I've never known a finer human being. I thought of how she would have wanted me to carry on, how she would buoy me up with her gentle loving spirit. Her daughter, Merilee, has a lot of her mother's qualities.

To have a person who cares about what you're doing, who's truly interested . . . it makes you feel as though you're really accomplishing something, and gets the juices flowing. And Nicki, I'm happy to say, really knows I'm interested in what she's doing too. She's become a genuine artist. She says she's a late bloomer, but is she ever blooming! She's doing watercolors and pointillism, and her show at Dana Point was a great success.

So life is good and I'm thinking of going to a little bit of everywhere, including maybe China or Russia and certainly France, Germany, Italy and Spain. It would be great to go to Japan again. I'm just so grateful to be here, to be alive—still curious, still loving. Of course, I have moments of getting annoyed about stupid little things but I'm working on it. Meanwhile, I take my philosophical jaunts. Right now I'm reading *Letters of the Scattered Brotherhood.* Open it to nearly any page, and your need will be helped.


I've sung in some awfully exciting places and will continue to do so as long as life will let me. Gino Empry, Canada's public-relations guru, who arranges and books shows, still gets me up to Canada, and I love it. Recently I had a marvelous time entertaining the National Ballet of Canada here in my Bel Air home—the dancers, the members of the orchestra, some of whom have played for me in Canada, the entrepreneurs and members of the press. It was an honor to meet the charming consul general and his lovely wife. Makes me think I can't wait to get back to Toronto, where I seem to play every year, then to dip down to New York City and play the Ballroom for an interesting and exciting time. I've enjoyed Atlantic City a couple of times, and even played Caesars at Las Vegas and Atlantic City with the beloved George Burns.

Oh, it wasn't too great to slip on the steel plate on the stage at Caesars and fracture my pelvis, to say nothing of a bruised tailbone. It happened the last time I worked with George Burns there. Clay, in the lighting booth, thought I'd had a heart attack and died. The audience had hardly begun their evening, so I said, "Bring me a chair and put me out by the piano." George stood in the wings while I sang. Nobody could figure how I was sitting there with a broken pelvis. Neither, I assure you, could I. I did the whole show sitting on one hip. There was a ruffle in the audience as the stretcher-bearers came through, and the minute the curtain went down I was placed on it and an ambulance was waiting. As I went by, George took that cigar out of his mouth and said, "You're a brave girl, Peg." Thanks, George. I love you. I've known him since the time when Gracie was alive.

The episode at Caesars changed the balance of my walking, but it's become a game of goals to get back together on my feet. The wheelchair has been a necessary aid, and the walker was help too. I got so good at the walker, I bought a stationary bicycle and proceeded to reinjure myself. Then, trying to walk around the pool, I irritated my toes until they became infected and that sent me to the hospital more than once. All of this is not meant to be a downer. I've been learning discipline, gaining a little wisdom from books like *The Life and Teachings of the Masters of the Far East.* I've been reading those books for twenty-five years.

I had done a painting for the Franklin Mint through Dick Hodgsons and was delighted when he told me that the American Beauty Rose Society was going to name a rose after me. Some time after that I received forty-eight Peggy Lee rose bushes. They had giant root structures and had to be soaked in every bathtub in the house before planting. I put them out in the garden, where I already had quite a collection of rose bushes—Abe Lincoln, Helen Traubel, Bing Crosby, Peace, Mon Cherie, Sterling and Royal Highness. When the Peggy Lee bloomed, it was extraordinary—seven-by-eight inches in diameter, big cabbage roses they are. The buds are peach colored and have delicate violet veining running from the center of the rose. There are also shades of yellow in with the peach and pink. Gradually, as it opens, its delicate perfume is released in the air throughout the garden. It is the most beautiful rose I have ever seen.

I'm not sure I'll be performing standing anymore, but I know I'll be walking on and off stage. You can bet on it! I plan to do another turn or two at the Pasadena Playhouse or some other theatres, and if the body is a little bit reluctant, I *know* the spirit is willing. I plan to be *without* diabetes *and* my glasses, among some other things I don't need, but I *do* need you, and if you like this book I hope to write at least one more—and to sing with those fantastic musicians I love so much. Two or three albums will be coming out, and there're still lots of songs to write and sing. I've started the Peggy Lee Scholarship Fund through the Women's International Center (with Gloria Lane, the founder) for musicians and singers. I'm trying to give back as much as I can to dear life. I want to be more active in The Songwriters' Guild and ASCAP and the arts in general.

By the way, Frank Sinatra and I did do the cancer benefit we had talked about while I was in St. John's. Then I joined Frank and Sammy Davis Jr. at Radio City Music Hall for a stunning evening for Sloan-Kettering. And not to forget Rosemary and Danny Thomas' St. Jude.

It's a wonderful life. And, if you look, you'll find me working everywhere.

And, oh yes, I think I've found that string that unraveled when Mama died. Now I know where she is. I guess I've been like that fish that swam all over the ocean looking for water . . .

# Discography

Over seven hundred songs by Peggy Lee are, or have been, available in the various forms of recorded sound reproduction. Many of those were written by Miss Lee, who has over two hundred songwriting credits, usually as lyricist, almost all of which have been published. The following listing of her albums contain the majority of her musical work. The Peggy Lee discographer, Wayne Rankin, began this research compilation in 1977. Where possible, the release date is provided; however, Mr. Rankin determined early in his efforts for complete details that a number of recording companies did not maintain dating information during certain years of their operations.

**ARTISTIC RECORDS**

ART 005      *Easy Listening*—Peggy Lee with Woody Herman and Dave Barbour & his orchestra (radio, summer 1947) (cassette # CART 005)

**A & M RECORDS**

SP-4547      *Mirrors* (11/75) (cassette # CA-4547)

**ACE OF HEARTS RECORDS**

AH 5      *Black Coffee* (reissue of DL 8358-Decca)
AH 26      *Songs From Pete Kelly's Blues* (reissue of DL 8166-Decca)
AH 75      *Sea Shells* (reissue of DL 8591-Decca)

**ATLANTIC RECORDS**

SD-18108      *Let's Love* (10/74) (also P-8511A Japanese reissue/Atlantic) (cassette # CS-18108)

## MISS PEGGY LEE

**CAMAY RECORDS**

CA 3003     *Peggy Lee*
CA 3003     *Peggy Lee's Greatest* (reissue of above with three additional songs)

**CAPITOL RECORDS**

AD-62     *Collectors' Items* (78rpm) with Stan Kenton & other artists
CC-72     *Rendezvous With Peggy Lee* (78 rpm) (reissued as EBF-151, H-151, T-151) (1952)
CD-3     *New American Jazz* (78rpm) with Jack Teagarden, Billy May & others
CD-41     *Jerome Kern's Music* (78rpm) with Margaret Whiting & other artists
CD-49     78 rpm album; various artists
CD-162     *South Pacific* (78rpm) with Margaret Whiting & Gordon Mac-Rae
EBF-151     *Rendezvous With Peggy Lee* (45 rpm album-2 discs) (also released as H-151, T-151, CC-72)
EBF-210     *Music Of Jerome Kern* (45 rpm album) (also released as H-210)
H-151     *Rendezvous With Peggy Lee* (10" LP) (6/52) (also released as T-151, EBF-151)
H-162     *South Pacific* (10" LP) with Margaret Whiting & Gordon Mac-Rae CC-72)
H-204     *My Best To You* (10" LP) (5/50)
H-210     *Music Of Jerome Kern* (10" LP) (also released as EBF-210)
H-9101     *Today's Top Hits—Volume 1* (10" LP; various artists)
T-151     *Rendezvous With Peggy Lee* (reissue of H-151 with four additional songs, 4/55)
T-864     *The Man I Love* (7/57) (reissued as STBB-517: *The Folks Who Live on the Hill*)
T-979     *Jump For Joy* (3/59)
ST-1049     *Things Are Swingin'* (5/59)
ST-1131     *I Like Men!* (4/59)
ST-1219     *Beauty And The Beat!* (1959)
ST-1290     *Latin Ala Lee!* (1/60) (reissued as SM-1290; also reissued on EMI STARLINE as SRS 5080 with one song deleted; also as STBB-517)
ST-1366     *All Aglow Again!* (5/60)
ST-1401     *Pretty Eyes* (7/60)
ST-1423     *Christmas Carousel* (10/60)
ST-1475     *Olé Ala Lee!* (12/60)
ST-1520     *Basin Street East* (5/61) (reissued as SM-1520)
ST-1622     *Season's Greetings* (with various artists) (10/61)
ST-1630     *If You Go* (10/61)
ST-1671     *Blues Cross Country* (3/62)
T-1743     *Bewitching-Lee!* (7/62)
ST-1772     *Sugar 'N' Spice* (10/62)
ST-1850     *Mink Jazz* (6/63)

| | |
|---|---|
| ST-1857 | *I'm A Woman* (2/63) (reissued as SM-1857 in 9/75; and as STCL-576 in 9/70) |
| ST-1969 | *In Love Again!* (2/64) |
| ST-2096 | *In The Name Of Love* (8/64) (reissued as SY-4618) |
| ST-2320 | *Pass Me By* (4/65) |
| ST-2388 | *Then Was Then And Now Is Now!* (11/65) |
| ST-2390 | *Happy Holiday* (10/65) (reissue of ST-1423 with three additional songs) |
| ST-2469 | *Guitars Ala Lee* (10/66) |
| ST-2475 | *Big Spender* (4/66) (reissued as STCL-576 in 9/70) |
| ST-2732 | *Extra Special!* (4/67) |
| ST-2781 | *Somethin' Groovy!* (8/67) |
| ST-2887 | *Hits Of Peggy Lee* (4/68) |
| ST-105 | *Two Shows Nightly* (Live at the Copacabana, 1967), pressed in 1968. (Note: LP release was withdrawn by Miss Lee immediately after initial pressings, as the artist felt that sound reproduction was inconsistent with her usual high standards. Fewer than ten copies have been traced as in existence in private collections in the USA.) |
| ST-183 | *A Natural Woman* (5/69) (reissued as STCL-576 in 9/70) |
| DKAO-377 | *Peggy Lee's Greatest!* (10/69) |
| ST-386 | *Is That All There Is?* (11/69) (reissued as SM-386 in 3/75) |
| STBB-401 | *Super Oldies, Volume 6* (12/69) (with various artists) |
| ST-463 | *Bridge Over Troubled Water* (4/70) |
| STBB-517 | *The Folks Who Live On The Hill* two discs (7/70) (record # DF-518; a reissue of T-864) |
| | *Broadway a La Lee* (7/70) (record # SF-519; a reissue of ST-1290) (Each of the above discs has dropped two songs from the original recording.) |
| STCL-576 | *Peggy Lee:* three discs, boxed set, reissued recordings (9/70) |
| | —disc #1: reissue of ST-2475, one song deleted |
| | —disc #2: reissue of ST-183, one song deleted |
| | —disc #3: reissue of ST-1857, two songs deleted |
| ST-622 | *Make It With You* (11/70) |
| ST-810 | *Where Did They Go* (7/71) |
| ST-11077 | *Norma Deloris Egstrom From Jamestown, North Dakota* (6/72) |
| STBB-2979 | *The Best of Christmas* (with various artists) |
| SL-6694 | *The Sounds Of The Seventies* (limited edition LP produced for Sylvania) |
| SL-6723 | *Raindrops* (limited edition LP produced for Abbott Laboratories) |
| E-ST | *Capitol Records Presents Those Classic Years, 1948-1956* (one Lee vocal) |
| 5C054-85001 | *16 Greatest Hits* (from EMI-Bohemia, Holland), 1976 |
| CAPS 1006 | *Songs For My Man* (from EMI, Great Britain) |
| SN-11969 | *Miss Peggy Lee Sings The Songs Of Cy Coleman* (1979) (cassette # 4N-16140) |
| 1547731 | (PM 231—Pathe Marconi EMI, France) (reissue of T-151), 1984 |

# MISS PEGGY LEE

## COLUMBIA RECORDS

CL-6033    *Benny Goodman & Peggy Lee* (10″ LP) (also issued as 78 rpm set #C-170, and as 45 rpm Extended Play set # B-406)

B-1636    *Benny Goodman Presents Peggy Lee* (45 rpm Extended Play single)

CL-2534    *Hot Canaries* (10″ LP) (with various artists)

B-2556    *Benny Goodman With Peggy Lee* (45 rpm Extended Play single)

PG-31547    *Benny Goodman: All-Time Greatest Hits* (two discs, reissues, two Lee vocals)

PG-33405    *Benny Goodman: Solid Gold Instrumental Hits* (78 reissues, 2 LP's, 1 Lee vocal)

20 AP 1486    *A Portrait Of Peggy Lee,* (CBS/SONY) 1941-1942 (with Benny Goodman & Orchestra)

SOPJ-22/23    *Elmer's Tune* (CBS Records-Japan) (with Benny Goodman & Orchestra, 2 LP's)

## CORAL RECORDS

CP-964    *Black Coffee* (reissue of Decca DL 8166)

## DECCA RECORDS

A-926    *Selections From Road To Bali* (78 rpm album, 3 discs)

ED 533    *Black Coffee* (45 rpm Extended Play set, 2 discs) (also released as DL 5482 and DL 8358)

ED-684    *Songs In An Intimate Style* (45 rpm Extended Play set) (also released DL5539)

ED-720    *Songs From Lady And The Tramp* (45 rpm EP set) 2 discs (also as DL 5557 & DL 8462)

ED-758    *Songs From Pete Kelly's Blues* (45 rpm EP set) 2 discs (also released as DL 8166)

ED-819    *Selections From White Christmas* (45 rpm EP set) (also released as DL 8083)

9-375    *Selections From Road To Bali* (45 rpm box set 3 discs with Bing Crosby, Bob Hope:1953)

ED-2003    *The Jazz Singer* (45 rpm Extended Play single) (1953)

ED-2117    *Selections From Kismet* (45 rpm EP set with the Four Aces and Danny Kaye)

ED-2401    *The Feminine Touch* (45 rpm EP set; with various artists; also as DL 8316)

DL 4004    *Original Hit Performances* (Early 50's): (10″ LP; various artists)

DL 5421    *Top Tunes By Top Artists* (one Lee vocal)

DL 5444    *Selections From Road To Bali* (10″ LP) (also released as A-926 and 9-375)

DL 5482    *Black Coffee* (10″ LP) (also released as ED-533, reissued as DL 8358 & AH 5)

DL 5539    *Songs In An Intimate Style* (10″ LP) (also released as ED-684)

DL 5557    *Songs From Lady And The Tramp* (10″ LP) (also as ED-728 & DL 8462) (1955)

DL 8083    *Selections From White Christmas* (also as ED-819, A-956; reissued MCA-7151)-(1954)

DL 8166     *Songs From Pete Kelly's Blues* (also on ED-758; reissued AH 26) (1955)

DL 8316     *The Feminine Touch* (with various artists; two Lee vocals) (also on ED-2401)

DL 8358     *Black Coffee* (reissue of DL 5482 with four additional songs; & ED-533 & AH 5)

DL 8411     *Dream Street* (reissued Vocalion VL 73776 with 3 songs deleted & 1 song added)

DL 8462     *Songs From Lady And The Tramp* (reissue of DL 5557 & ED-720 with 4 songs added)

DL 8591     *Sea Shells* (reissued on Ace of Hearts label as AH 75)

DL 8816     *Miss Wonderful*

DL 9056     *Around The Christmas Tree* (with various artists)

DXSB 7164     *The Best Of Peggy Lee:* two discs-DL 74024 & DL 74025 (reissued MCA 2-4049) (monaural: DXB-164/DL4024,DL4025)

DL 74458     *Lover* (monaural: DL 4458)

DL 74461     *The Fabulous Peggy Lee* (monaural: DL 4461)

**DRG RECORDS**

SL 5190     *Close Enough For Love* (1979) (cassette # SLC-5190)

**EPIC RECORDS**

EE 22025     *Clarinet A La King* (reissue of 78 rpm recordings on Columbia and Okeh labels by Benny Goodman & Sextet/Orchestra, with five vocals by Peggy Lee)

**EMI STARLINE RECORDS**

SRS-5058     *Latin Ala Lee* (reissue of Capitol ST-1290 with one song deleted)

**EVEREST RECORDS**

FS 294     *Peggy Lee* (reissue of various Capitol recordings)

**GIANTS OF JAZZ RECORDS**

GOJ-1001     *Benny Goodman: More Of The Fabulous 50's* (3 Lee vocals)

GOJ-1005     *Swingin' Through The Years With Benny Goodman* (one Lee vocal), 1977

**GLENDALE RECORDS**

GL 6023     *You Can Depend On Me* (1981)

**HARBINGER RECORDS**

    *I had Love Once* (for release in Spring 1989.)

**HARMONY RECORDS**

HL 7005     *Peggy Lee Sings With Benny Goodman* (reissue of 78 rpm recordings)

H 30024     *Miss Peggy Lee* (reissue of 78 rpm recordings with Benny Goodman & Orchestra)

**HINDSIGHT RECORDS**

HSR-220     *The Uncollected Peggy Lee* with the David Barbour and Billy May Bands, 1948 (LP and cassette—1985)

# MISS PEGGY LEE

**JOYCE RECORDS**
LP-5012      *Earl Hines' Jubilee With Harry James* (1 Lee vocal)

**MCA RECORDS**
MCA 2-4049   *The Best of Peggy Lee* (reissue of Decca DXSB 7164)
MCA-7151     *Selections From White Christmas* (Japanese reissue of Decca DL 8083)
MC-1794      *Perfect-Lee* (1984)

**MUSICMASTERS RECORDS**
             *Miss Peggy Lee Sings The Blues*, 1988

**PAUSA RECORDS**
PR 9043      *Sugar 'N' Spice* (licensed reissue of Capitol ST-1772), 1985

**PICKWICK RECORDS**
SPC-3090     *Peggy Lee! I've Got The World On A String* (reissue of Capitol recordings)
SPC-3192     *Peggy Lee: Once More With Feeling* (reissue of Capitol recordings)
PTP-2028     *Peggy Lee: I've Got The World On A String* (2 LP's, set of the above two recordings)

**POLYDOR RECORDS**
Polydor Super
  2383 448   *Live In London* (originally planned for release as Mercury record # SRM-1-1172)
Polydor Super
  2383 458   *Peggy*

**SANDY HOOK RECORDS**
SH 2109      *Peggy Lee On Radio* (with Woody Herman and Dave Barbour & his orchestra), 1947 broadcast recordings (1987)

**SOUNDS RARE RECORDS**
SR-5008      *If I Could Be With You* (with Benny Goodman and Tommy Dorsey), 1986

**VOCALION RECORDS**
VL 73776     *So Blue* (reissue of Decca DL 8411, with one song added and three songs deleted)
VL 73903     *Crazy In The Heart* (reissue of 3 songs from Decca DL 8816 and 7 songs from Decca DL 8358)

**WARNER BROTHERS RECORDS**
BSK 3653     Soundtrack Music from "Sharkey's Machine" (one Lee vocal)

276

# Index

Albert, Eddie, 200
Allen, Gracie, 269
Allen, Steve, 141, 177, 238
Almeida, Laurindo, 119, 163, 177
Anderson, A. L., 26, 27, 50
Anderson, Oleana, 26–27
Anderson, Josephine Mathilde, 26
Andrews, Julie, 233–34
Appleman, Abe, 247
Arlen, Harold, 71, 130
Armstrong, Louis, 6, 12, 155, 202, 207, 223
Armstrong, Lucille, 12, 223
Arthur, Irwin, 258

Bacall, Lauren, 207
Bankhead, Tallulah, 113, 203
Barbour, Bessie, 109–10, 116–17
Barbour, David, 23–24, 94, 97–98, 100–124, 127–34,
  136, 138–41, 145, 147, 152, 157–59, 161–62, 185,
  198, 225–28, 243
Barbour, David, Jr., 227–28
Barbour, Nicki, 102, 105–10, 112–14, 115, 117, 119,
  124, 127, 134–37, 139, 141–42, 145–47, 157, 161, 164–
  65, 172, 174–76, 181, 204, 206, 207, 210, 214, 217,
  225, 227, 231–34, 245, 246, 249, 251, 261, 266–68
Barclay, Chuck, 77, 78, 80, 91
Barnett, Marilyn, 259–62
Basie, Count, 12, 203, 207
Basie, John, 247
Bautzer, Greg, 150–51, 158, 250
Bennett, Mary, 178–79
Bennett, Max, 178–79
Bennett, Tony, 130, 144, 206, 237, 257
Benny, Jack, 91
Berg, Bruce, 247
Berg, George, 20–21, 23
Berger, Sy, 247
Bering, Frank, 91–92
Berlin, Irving, 120
Birdwell, Russell, 171
Bogart, Humphrey, 152
Borge, Victor, 241
Bow, Clara, 66
Boyer, Charles, 113
Bozocos, Penny, 158, 168–70
Brill, Nellie, 120
Bronfman, Edgar, 204
Brooks, Jack, 91
Bryant, Mike, 130, 159
Buatta, Mario, 254–55, 259, 265
Bufman, Zev, 246, 249
Burdick, Eugene, 201
Burke, Johnny, 128
Burke, Sonny, 147, 149, 64, 185, 186, 254
Burnett, Jackie, 115
Burns, George, 268–69
Burrows, Abe, 203
Burton, Richard, 207, 212, 238, 246, 249
Butler, Artie, 246
Butterfield, Billy, 11

Caen, Herb, 200
Cagney, James, 91, 241

Cahn, Sammy, 128, 167, 194, 204–5
Calhoun, Bob, 173–74
Cancelleri, Joe, 138, 161, 162
Cannon, Dyan, 227
Carmichael, Ralph, 200
Carney, Art, 60, 132, 181, 207
Carpenetta, Countess, 198, 199
Castellucci, Stella, 173, 178, 194, 196, 197
Catlett, Big Sid, 11
Cavanaugh, Dave, 185
Chandler, Toni, 259–60
Channing, Carol, 203
Chappell, Dennis, 213, 257
Charles, Ray, 203, 206, 212, 221
Chiodini, John, 257, 267
Clark, Earl, 38
Clayton, Steve, 246
Colbert, Claudette, 113, 152
Cole, Nat King, 104, 207
Coleman, Avron, 247
Coleman, Cy, 207, 221–22, 226, 246, 247, 253, 254
Collins, Lloyd, 84
Collymore, Valerie, 247
Como, Perry, 105
Cooper, Gary, 11
Cornell, Katharine, 11
Cowan, Irv, 245–46, 249, 250
Cowan, Marge, 245–46, 249, 250
Crawford, Joan, 11, 150, 203
Crosby, Bing, 113, 115, 119, 124–28, 136, 139,
  219
Cummings, Nathan, 204–5
Curtiz, Mike, 153, 155, 156
Cutshall, Cutty, 11

Dailey, Dan, 158, 163, 169
Darin, Bobby, 237–38
Davis, Bill, 234
Davis, Meyer, 211
Davis, Sammy, Jr., 144, 163, 241, 270
Day, Dennis, 91
Day, Doris, 6
Dean, James, 167
Dean, Peter, 12
DeProng, Louis, 77, 78
De Sylva, Buddy, 105
Devore, Sy, 105, 162
Dexter, Brad, 157–59
Dietrich, Marlene, 174–75, 203
DiNovi, Gene, 195
Disney, Walt, 147–49
Divito, Harry, 247
Dodds, Baby, 93
Dodds, Johnny, 93
Dooley, Thomas, 200
Dorsey, Tommy, 6, 19, 77
Dreyfus, Benoit, 206
Drivas, Robert, 246–48, 253
Dumont, Nat, 173
Dumont, Valerie, 173
Durante, Jimmy, 113, 115, 116, 119, 121–22, 124,
  136–37, 203, 208–9
Durante, Marie, 203

# INDEX

Eckstine, Billy, 159, 195
Edan, Alana, 177
Edwards, Blake, 234
Egstrom, Clair, 27, 30, 32, 37, 38, 43–44, 82, 86, 189
Egstrom, Della, 26, 27, 29, 37, 42, 82, 83–84, 86, 110, 171, 173
Egstrom, Emily, 135
Egstrom, Jean, 27
Egstrom, Leonard, 27, 30, 138
Egstrom, Marianne, 27, 30, 35, 37, 82, 86, 87, 101, 102, 110, 174, 210, 214, 225, 254, 267
Egstrom, Marvin Olaf, 26–27, 29–31, 33–35, 37, 38, 42, 45, 52–56, 66–68, 72, 134–38, 162–63
Egstrom, Milford, 19, 27, 29–30, 135, 138
Egstrom, Min Schaumberg, 28–29, 30, 34, 35,.37–38, 39, 41–46, 48, 51–53, 64, 67, 135, 137, 173
Egstrom, Olie, 138
Egstrom, Paul, 29, 30, 37
Egstrom, Selma Emele Anderson, 26–28, 29, 46, 244, 270
Einstein, Albert, 181, 182–83
Eisenhower, Mamie, 148
Elam, Charles, 177
Elam, Prudence, 177
Ellington, Duke, 12, 113, 177, 207
Entratter, Jack, 164
Erickson, Bertha G., 25–26
Erickson, Edward, 26
Erickson, Eric Emil, 25–26
Erickson, John, 25–26
Erickson, Julius, 26
Eugenio, Doris, 246
Exiner, Billy, 130

Factor, Max, 240
Fallon, Larry, 246
Farrow, Mia, 237
Feather, Jane, 7, 16, 19, 85–86, 87, 92, 93
Feather, Leonard, 85, 132
Fighera, Frank, 247
Finkbinder, Jeanie, 30
Fitzgerald, Ella, 156, 167, 203, 207
Fletcher, Ella, 35–36
Fontanne, Lynn, 11
Fonteyn, Margot, 237
Ford, Mary, 185
Forestieri, Lou, 247
Forrest, Helen, 5–6, 9
Foster, Dick, 225, 235
Franklin, Aretha, 241
Frontiere, Dominic, 249
Frontiere, Georgia, 249
Frosk, John, 247

Gabin, Jean, 184
Gabler, Milt, 185
Gabor, Zsa Zsa, 113, 209
Garberg, Martina, 114, 117, 119
Gardner, Ava, 105, 150
Garland, Judy, 113, 151, 164, 203, 206
Garner, Erroll, 146
Garroway, Dave, 228
Garson, Greer, 113
Garvey, Winterton, 247
Gastel, Carlos, 104–8, 111, 129–31, 162
Gastel, Joan, 106
Gelb, Arthur, 209
Gerber, Ludwig, 232
Gershwin, George, 71, 130
Giannini, Amaura, 247

Gielgud, John, 203, 239
Gilbert, Henry, 120
Gleason, Jackie, 131–32, 207, 210, 215–16
Glickstein, Helen, 228, 237
Goldman, Albert, 207
Goodman, Alice, 5, 23, 100
Goodman, Benny, 5–12, 14–20, 23–24, 94, 97–100, 102, 103, 110, 111, 253
Goodman, Freddy, 14, 22
Gould, Mike, 118, 140
Grace, Princess, 209, 214–15
Granata, Hugo, 224
Grant, Barbara, 227
Grant, Cary, 126, 201–2, 203, 205, 206, 209, 219, 221–23, 226–27, 237
Grant, Jennifer, 227
Green, Levis, 105
Green, Lil, 9
Green, Richard, 166, 167
Grier, Howard, 158
Griffin, Merv, 151

Hagman, Larry, 241
Haines, Doc, 59–61, 66, 68
Hamilton, Arthur, 167
Hammond, John, 8
Hanson, Harry, 63
Hanson, Jon, 240–41
Harbach, Bill, 206, 234
Harbach, Otto, 71
Harris, Julie, 247
Harris, Radie, 259
Hart, Lorenz, 71, 124, 130
Haymes, Dick, 6, 18, 97
Hayworth, Rita, 211, 235
Hazard, Dick, 221–22
Heath, D. Michael, 246
Hemion, Dwight, 187
Hendrick, Lillie Mae, 158, 171, 172, 194, 196–97, 239
Henrickson, Richard, 247
Herman, Woody, 104
Holiday, Billie, 207
Holliday, Judy, 203
Holmes, Ernest, 107–9, 117, 130, 133, 157, 158, 178, 181–82, 223
Horne, Lena, 187, 203
Horner, Paul, 126–27, 243, 245, 246, 249, 250
Hovde, Ossie, 82, 86
Hover, Herman, 150–51
Hughes, Howard, 151, 152
Hunte, Stanley, 247
Hurwitz, Sid, 130, 159

Ireland, John, 158

Jackson, Eddie, 121
Jackson, Michael, 213
Jacobs, Phoebe, 202–9, 248, 249
James, Harry, 6
Jarvis, Al, 105
Jenkins, Bev, 254
Jenkins, Gordon, 185–86, 246, 253–54
John, Little Willie, 193
John, Tom H., 246
Johnson, Van, 163, 180
Jolson, Al, 40, 125, 154
Jones, Quincy, 169, 203, 206, 211, 213, 216–17, 221, 222, 237
Jordan, Everold, 39, 42–43, 46–48, 51

# INDEX

Kaiser, Henry, 204
Kalfin, Bob, 247
Kelly, Ed, 162, 168–71, 173, 194–95
Kempton, Murray, 207
Kennedy, Jackie, 215
Kennedy, Jeanette, 230
Kennedy, John F., 223–25
Kennedy, Ken, 69–71, 84, 87, 229–30
Kennedy, Robert F., 238
Kenton, Stan, 104
Kern, Jerome, 71, 121, 130, 241
Kiernan, Bob, 205–6
King, Alan, 203, 239
Kirby, George, 195
Klotz, Florence, 246
Kramer, Donald, 257
Kramer, Elizabeth, 257
Krupska, Danya, 247

Ladd, Alan, 163
LaGuardia, Fiorello, 11
Lancaster, Burt, 151
Lang, Philip, 246
Lang, Victoria, 246, 249
Larson, Alice, 114, 115, 135, 141–42, 145, 171–73
Larson, Helen, 240
Lauder, Estée, 210
Lee, Ginger, 120
Leiber, Jerry, 1–2
Leigh, Janet, 167
Lemmon, Jack, 170, 207, 233
Leonhart, Jay, 247, 251, 254, 256, 258
Levant, Oscar, 113
Levy, Kathy, 228–29
Lewis, Jerry, 235
Lewis, Moe, 214–16
Lodge, Henry Cabot, 201
Lombardi, Felipe Rojas, 258, 259
Loper, Don, 180, 201–2
Loren, Sophia, 203
Lorre, Peter, 91
Louis, Maggie, 238
Luce, Bill, 247
Lunt, Alfred, 11

McGarrity, Lou, 22, 98
McKay, Hats, 120–22
MacLaine, Shirley, 237
McMahon, Ed, 237
McMahon, Victoria, 237
Mahoney, Jim, 210–12
Mahoney, Patti, 211
Mancini, Henry, 241
Mandel, Bill, 206
Mandel, Freddie, 91–92, 93
Mandel, Johnny, 2, 232, 246, 251–53
Mandel, Lois, 91–92, 93
Mansfield, Jayne, 167
March, Hal, 77, 152–53, 184
Margaret, Princess, 213
Marguerite, Princess, 242
Marino, Jimmy, 181, 182–83, 198
Martin, Dewey, 111, 182
Martin, Freddy, 164
Martin, Jack, 163, 171, 173
Martin, Mary, 241
Matera, Barbara, 246
Marvin, Lee, 167
Maxwell, Jimmy, 11

May, Billy, 189, 246
Mazurvy, Robert, 253
Meadows, Jayne, 177, 238
Mercer, Johnny, 71, 84, 105, 106, 207
Mercer, Mabel, 142
Merrill, Robert, 207
Miller, Bill, 220
Miller, Eddie, 104
Miller, Glenn, 5
Miller, Mitch, 202
Milner, Martin, 167
Minnelli, Liza, 164
Miranda, Carmen, 119
Mitchell, Tommy, 247
Mitchum, Dorothy, 237
Mitchum, Robert, 237, 238
Mole, Miff, 11
Moller, Clyde, 40
Molotov, Vyacheslav, 199
Mondragon, Joe, 188
Monroe, Marilyn, 224
Montesi, Lou Ann, 247
Moon, H. Edna, 120
Moore, Phil, 77
Moore, Victor, 116
Morgan, Frank, 115–16
Morgan, Jane, 164

Newman, Randy, 2
Norbu, Thubton, 201
Norgaard, Nooky, 87
Norman, Mary, 78
Norris, Doug, 247
Norvo, Red, 146
Novak, Kim, 220
Nureyev, Rudolf, 237, 238

O'Brien, Edmund, 165–67
O'Brien, Margaret, 113
O'Brien, Pat, 241
O'Flaherty, Brian, 247
Olsen, Ralph, 247
Olson, Martie, 88
Olson, Ole, 10
Olson, Sev, 87–88, 230
Onassis, Aristotle, 215
Oppenheimer, Robert, 182, 183
Osborne, Will, 87–88, 90
Osbourne, Albert, 120, 121

Paitch, Marty, 188, 189
Palitz, Morty, 10, 186, 202
Pan, Hermes, 211, 235
Parsons, Louelle, 163
Passaro, Joe, 247
Paul, Les, 185
Peck, Gregory, 227
Peck, Veronique, 227
Perowsky, Frank, 247
Pizzarelli, Bucky, 247, 251
Podell, Jules, 142–44
Ponti, Carlo, 203
Porter, Cole, 11, 12, 71, 130
Potter, Larry, 78–79, 80, 91
Potter, Sue, 78, 80, 91
Powell, Jerry, 241
Powell, Martha, 144
Powell, Mel, 5–11, 15, 20–23, 111, 144–45, 162
Pozo, Chino, 184, 195

# INDEX

Presley, Elvis, 2
Preston, Robert, 225
Promuto, Vinnie, 207
Putnam, George, 174

Quam, Johnny, 85
Quinn, Anthony, 207
Quinn, Brian, 246

Ramon, Phil, 246
Randolph, Lillian, 77
Rasmussen, Gladys, 72–74, 81
Raye, Martha, 206
Reagan, Nancy, 260, 262
Reagan, Ronald, 162, 260, 262
Remick, Lee, 177
Renzi, Mike, 247, 251, 254, 256, 258
Revson, Charles, 206
Ricker, Laura, 93
Riddle, Nelson, 220
Rockwell, Tom, 104–5, 141, 194–95
Rockwell, Vivian, 141
Rodgers, Richard, 71, 124, 130, 184, 187–88
Rogers, Ginger, 40
Rooney, Mickey, 163
Roosevelt, Jimmy, 151
Roth, Jack, 121
Roth, Sidney, 203
Rowles, Jimmy, 188
Rudolph, Lord, 213–15
Rugolo, Pete, 184–85, 195, 196
Rushton, Joe, 17, 101

St. John, Adela Rogers, 223, 238–39
St. John, Jill, 227
Salinger, Pierre, 238
Salk, Jonas, 228, 235
Salkin, Ed, 247
Sanders, George, 113
Sauter, Eddie, 9
Sawyer, Bill, 69–70
Schall, Max, 87, 89–91
Schertzer, Hymie, 11
Schlatter, George, 150–51
Schmerr, Faith, 211, 214, 216–17
Sebesky, Don, 246
Sebesta, Edward, 180, 210
Selznick, David O., 163
Shaw, Artie, 6
Shearing, George, 132–33
Shelton, Pat, 193, 243
Shipman, Richard, 115, 210
Shore, Dinah, 105, 224
Shoup, Howard, 153
Simon, Carly, 12
Simon, George, 12
Sinatra, Frank, 6, 19–20, 205–6, 219–21, 254, 266–67,
    270
Sinatra, Nancy, 219
Skelton, Thomas, 246
Sondheim, Stephen, 243
Spaeth, Sigmund, 120, 122
Spalding, Ann Hamilton, 210–11, 215–16
Stafford, Jo, 108, 109
Stevens, Arnold, 116, 122, 129, 138, 139, 198
Stevens, Carol, 122
Stevens, Harley, 122

Stevens, Jeanne, 122–23, 138
Stevens, Steve, 122
Stevenson, Adlai, 204
Stewart, Jimmy, 177
Stoller, Mike, 1–2
Stone, Judy, 178–79
Stuart, George, 115, 210
Sullivan, Ed, 131
Sveen, Lloyd W., 230
Swig, Richard, 260
Swig, Rick, 260
Swope, Martha, 246

Tate, Grady, 247, 251, 254, 256, 258
Taylor, Deems, 120–22
Taylor, Elizabeth, 207, 212, 238, 246, 249
Temperley, Joe, 247
Thomas, Danny, 40, 153–56, 159, 164, 246, 270
Thomas, Rosemary, 270
Thompson, Tommy, 207
Thornhill, Claude, 6, 130
Tirella, Eddie, 175–76, 251
Tone, Franchot, 11, 91
Torme, Mel, 104
Treacher, Arthur, 116
Truman, Harry, 128–29
Turner, Lana, 105, 150
Tyson, Cicely, 249

Ustinov, Peter, 234

Vallee, Rudy, 58, 60
Vanderbilt, Commodore, 5
Vanderhoff, Bruce, 228, 244
Van Heusen, Jimmy, 127–28

Wade, H. L., 250
Wagner, Robert, 227, 237
Waller, Fats, 11–12
Wallichs, Glenn, 2, 105
Walter, Cy, 146, 253
Warner, Jack, 153
Watkins, Ralph, 203, 204, 207
Weatherwax, Frank, 114, 115
Webb, Jack, 165–67
Whiting, Margaret, 237
Whitney, Douglas, 208
Wilder, Alec, 14, 128, 142
Wiley, Lee, 101
Williams, Andy, 237
Williams, Cootie, 11
Williams, Griff, 129–30
Williams, William B., 12
Wills, Julian, 257
Wilson, John, 258
Wolf, Murray, 220
Wood, Natalie, 237
Wright, Anne, 158
Wyman, Jane, 162

Young, Snooky, 1
Young, Victor, 163, 164, 188–89

Zanuck, Darryl F., 163
Zelnick, Mel, 178–79
Zipkin, Jerry, 259
Zito, Tore, 246